BLIND DATE

BLIND

Frances Fyfield

DATE

Viking

To Audrey Murray. A smasher.
Nothing in fiction could do her justice.

VIKING
Published by the Penguin Group
Penguin Putnam Inc., 375 Hudson Street,
New York, New York 10014, U.S.A.
Penguin Books Ltd, 27 Wrights Lane, London W8 5TZ, England
Penguin Books Australia Ltd, Ringwood, Victoria, Australia
Penguin Books Canada Ltd, 10 Alcorn Avenue, Toronto, Ontario, Canada M4V 3B2
Penguin Books (N.Z.) Ltd, 182–190 Wairau Road, Auckland 10, New Zealand
Penguin India, 210 Chiranjiv Tower, 43 Nehru Place, New Delhi, 11009, India

Penguin Books Ltd, Registered Offices:
Harmondsworth, Middlesex, England

First American edition
Published in 1998 by Viking Penguin,
a member of Penguin Putnam Inc.

1   3   5   7   9   10   8   6   4   2

PUBLISHER'S NOTE
This is a work of fiction. Names, characters, places, and incidents
either are the product of the author's imagination or are used ficti-
tiously, and any resemblance to actual persons, living or dead,
events, or locales is entirely coincidental.

LIBRARY OF CONGRESS CATALOGING-IN-PUBLICATION DATA
Fyfield, Frances.
Blind date / Frances Fyfield.
p.   cm.
ISBN 0-670-87889-8
I. Title.
PR6056.Y47B58   1998
823'.914—dc21   98-21218

This book is printed on acid-free paper.

Printed in the United States of America
Set in Sabon
Designed by Kathryn Parise

ACKNOWLEDGMENTS

Thanks go to David Ralston, surgeon, Roger and Susan Hawkes, of Hawkes of Lymington Limited, and to Steven Lee for introducing me. Also to Geoffrey Hawkes (no relation) and Charles Saunders, both of CPS, for their help and their contacts and their enormous patience. And, at the other end of the process, last but never least, Ursula Mackenzie and Alison Tulett, inspirational editors *par excellence,* who made me think as well as revise.

Full fathom five thy father lies;
Of his bones are coral made;
Those are pearls that were his eyes;
Nothing of him that doth fade
But doth suffer a sea-change
Into something rich and strange.

SHAKESPEARE'S *The Tempest*

PROLOGUE

"Ten to four? I didn't realize the time! Do come in." That was what she would say, hoping to sound sincere, ready to watch whoever it was carry muddy autumn rain into her house.

A small boy was at her heels, a duster clutched in his fist. He did this whenever she was cleaning: following her, being useful and anxious to please. He was too old for such copycat behaviour: acting like a baby. This morning and this afternoon they were doing windows from the inside, paintwork and the kitchen. Wherever she drifted, and dusted, he did it again: then touched it, smeared it and often ruined the effect. She did not mind and he did not care. He was content, biddable as long as he had her to himself and she listened to him.

What a trap she had made for herself, with all this domestic coviviality. The business of keeping open house was sometimes arduous. She remembered some stupid invitation to tea, saw the face through the window. Tea, for God's sake; as if she was her mother. Instead of a bored housewife, decades younger. Then she felt an odd squirming in her stomach, panic, because nothing was going well today, nothing had gone well for quite some time. She was suddenly afraid to let anyone in, no matter who they were and muttered her resentment to the boy. In the same breath she yelled, "HANG ON A MINUTE," through the door. "Be with you in a SECOND: I can't find the key." As if she would ever lose it. She wanted time before she answered her door. Never mind the house, she could do with a lick of paint herself, but politeness and reputation dictated that she open the door. They were never strangers after all: they were always the groups and the invited singles of her wonderful friends; the antidote to a dutiful, frugal husband and a predictable life.

All the same, as soon as she recognized the face through the blur of the glass set eye level in their panelled door, she felt fear. Nonsense, she did not know what fear was and this could not be fear in the primal state: it was merely fear of boredom and embarrassment, surely. She checked her watch. Time for the boy's dose of rubbishy TV. She was tearing off the last of the rings she wore and placing them into his pyjama pocket. Eight years old and he still loved fiddling with her rings. He should not have been wearing pyjamas at this time of day and she was ashamed of that, too. As much ashamed of dismissing him as she was of his willingness to go. You must not bribe the boy with television, her mother said, but he was already bribed into obedience. He was on his safe and resigned way upstairs, but that was not why, as soon as she opened the door, she knew the same fear. It had nothing to do with him.

Eight. The boy was out of sight, out of mind, and she was smiling. "Sorry about the mess," she said, whizzing round, plumping up cushions, looking at her own bare arms, red hands, messy hair. She smiled a lot. It was second nature. She knew it enhanced a natural beauty.

"Tea? I'll make tea. That's what I was doing."

But there was no tea and only stale biscuits to eat. It could not have been more obvious that she had forgotten the invitation, and, in the crossness which infected her movements, it was equally apparent that she had, at that moment and the hour to follow, far better, more important things to do. She dropped a cup, wishing she had thrown it, furious with herself for being *nice*.

"Where are your lovely rings today, sweetheart?"

The playthings of her underdeveloped son. He buried them in sand to tease her; threaded them on wool as if he was a baby. The voice from the kitchen entrance managed to sound both wheedling and masculine. The volume from the radio in the lounge seemed to be louder.

"Rings? Ha, ha! No, they don't go with housework. I've sold them. I'm fed up with possessions. Moving house makes me want to live in a tent, with nothing."

Where was the damned tea, and how could she make the biscuits appear edible? To hell with it; offer wine instead, make it easier all round.

"Here, open that, could you? Thanks."

"Where's your lovely little boy, then?"

"Out."

And she knew, as soon as she said that, how the fear was entirely real, because there was absolutely no need for such a lie.

"You haven't given me a hug." A hand touched her shoulder. She could not help flinching and she turned, her long blond hair flicking a face, and her whole body a gesture of apology. It was too late.

"You hate me, don't you?" The voice was heavy with resignation.

"What! No, no, of course not, I love you to bits!"

"No, you don't."

"Let me get past. Don't be silly. Please." She ducked under an outstretched arm.

The first blow to the back of her neck hit the hand she had raised to smooth her hair, stunned her, sending her crashing forward. She scarcely felt the second blow at all. Then she was scratching, clawing, rolling away. She pulled and pushed and moaned and howled and fought; biting, trying to evade, getting weaker, gritting her teeth to stop herself screaming the boy's name as the blows broke her fingers. *I must not yell his name*: he is not here.

She shrieked instead for her mother and for Lizzie and her own husband, in that order, but she did not yell for her son and she did not scream for long. The black plastic bag came down round her throat; good, thick plastic, designed for the thorns of garden rubbish, hiding her face and her neck. And that was the point when she lost the will, as well as the means, to resist. She struggled for breath and could not find it.

Then the kicking: judging the distance, kick; changing the angle, kick; kick, kick and then stamp: deliberate, ritualistic. A pause for breath; listening to the unusual sound of solid, walking shoes on bone, sinew and flesh, until all twitching, all responses ceased.

It took some time, this relatively quiet death. There was the sound of the radio downstairs, a television upstairs. She always liked to be surrounded by sound, even though television was severely rationed. No boy of mine will be brought up that way.

Even with this, and the images on the screen, zapping each other in cartoon death, he knew something terrible was happening. Why didn't she call for him? The walls seemed to tremble and close in on him, paralysing him. It was too hot in his room. He squeezed his eyes tight shut, pressed the rings into the palm of his hand and turned his face into the pillow.

Someone came upstairs, opened the door, looked in and closed it again, softly. After that, he could not move at all. It was out of the question. So he held onto the rings, squeezing them so tight it almost hurt, and waited.

Chapter

ONE

". . . the weather forecast for today is sunny in the south-west. Maybe showers later . . ."

"Turn that off!" Elisabeth Kennedy shouted.

People die in summer, although this family prefers other seasons. But I am not dead like my sister, merely disabled. If only he had used a knife. Then, Mummy, I could have died and gone to heaven. And you could have had a lovely funeral. Mary would have worn a mournful hat to hide her lack of tears; you would be dressed in deep blue, crying all the time. And afterwards, you would have made of me a plaster saint, painted in beautiful colours, told the world I was the soul of virtue, a child of talent, sweetness and light. Well, I am not. Nor was I stabbed through the heart in a romantic crime of passion. He used caustic fluid, which is what you use for cleaning out ovens. And that says it all.

I can safely say that no-one has ever loved me with quite such intensity.

There is a view of the sea from this window, calm and clear today, the route towards the sea through Mummy's garden. Mrs. Diana Kennedy is out there, barbering a flowerbed. A gate goes from the other end of the garden onto the cliff path, and from there, I can hear the sound of a child squealing at the water: I hope the little wretch gets wet. There are cut flowers by my bed, heavy, green curtains round the window and a pleasant breeze. Last year, the street on the other side won the prize for the best kept seaside village in the south. They dead-head the roses as soon as one petal turns brown. The place stinks, and the church bell strikes, every hour, on the hour, one, two, three, four . . . nine.

The door to the bedroom opened a crack, revealing a head before a body and then Matthew, Elisabeth's nephew, preceded by the cat.

"Get that bloody creature out of here!"

Matt scooped the cat into his arms, dumped it outside and slammed the door without ceremony. Then he thumped down on the end of the bed and looked at her critically. He never could avoid staring; and she was always faintly relieved by his consistent failure to disguise his curiosity.

"Someone phoned for you," he said. "I told them it was too early for me to go and dig you up out of the garden."

"Who was it?"

He rolled his eyes. "I dunno. Just someone. What's the matter? I can't help it if you look like you've been buried."

"Who was it, Matt?"

"Nobody. I made it up. Gran sent me to play with you, so," he shrugged his shoulders, "here I am. It's a beautiful day," he added, longingly, "in case you noticed."

"And you want to be out?"

"Yup. But I mustn't. I have to sit with you."

"Tell her I'm still asleep. I'll pretend."

He leapt to his feet, punched the air, "Yeah!", and then he had the grace to blush.

"Wait a mo'. Are you going up to see Audrey and Donald later?"

He shuffled. "I might."

"All right, then."

I love that child, Elisabeth Kennedy told herself, listening to his heavy steps taking the stairs down, three by three. Love him. Love his precocity, his way with words and his grown-up behaviour, his polite remarks about the weather. He has the manners of a bereaved child who has grown up round adults rather than other children. No other child of ten would remark upon the beauty of the day. He is the energetic dreamer who has filled his own world with imaginary companions. I love him so much, he shouldn't be in the same room as me; he deserves better. Because I am *not* loveable and I can quite see why.

She got up, padded clumsily. Unlike the cat, which had used Matt's exit as an excuse to return, there was no delicate economy of movement in her steps. She wanted to raise her arms above her head and stretch; wanted to reach down her back and scratch where the puckered pink scar itched like crazy, but the simplest pleasures defied her. She looked towards the enticing blue of the sea and heard the chuck, chuck of her mother's trowel in the flowerbed below, the genteel voice softly scolding, "Oh, really, dear, what has made you flop sideways? I wish you wouldn't . . ." Elisabeth's loathing of the summer sun filled her head with a growl.

She thought of her London home, bare, empty of frills, full of dust and eccentricity. It was big enough to swing that cat by the tail and throw it against the wall, spacious enough to lose the dog which had begun to yap outside, yruff, ruff ruff ruff, trying to make the threatening sound of a Doberman, failing dismally, stupid little dog, a bottlebrush on short, stumpy legs, barking while Mother's voice warbled with the affection she reserved for plants. "Silly, *silly* things . . ." The sea, twinkling, teasing; the sun beckoning, mockingly. With her good hand, the rest of her trembling with rage, Elisabeth picked up a silverbacked hairbrush from the dressing table and tapped, awkwardly but hard, against the window pane, until it smashed.

You cannot love me because I am foul. I may as well make it worse.

Mrs. Diana Kennedy stood back from the scattered glass which had spread across the soil and onto the gravel path. The terrier retreated, his bark turning to a whimpering whine for attention. Diana bent towards it and cuffed it lightly on one rough ear. Ywow, ywow, ywow; a short-lived keening before he gave up the effort and buried his nose to the underside of his back leg. These dogs are amazing, Diana had once said in her penetrating, youthful grandmother voice; nothing distracts them for long. She looked upwards to the silent window. That pathetic shower of glass was not meant to harm. Or not in particular.

She moved out of range, without calling the dog. The trug she had carried was full of glass splinters, so was the gravel in the path. How could Elisabeth fail to know that Matthew went around barefoot? Elisabeth did know, and she did care, and she still smashed things, knowing some other person would tidy it up. She was a thirty-four-year-old child, born to be endured.

March steady. Behave as if nothing has happened; breathe deeply. Collect trug. Collect gloves. Collect dog, move towards kitchen; carry on as normal.

Her white hair was piled on her head. The way it lay, wave upon wave, would have been the envy of a bride. The style had never varied. She had one, unhurried way of walking, one way of dress. Loose, tailored trousers, tapering at the ankle, topped by a neat shirt in summer, or a high neck in winter, with plain-coloured woolen or cotton jackets, as weather demanded. Two combs and a hidden array of pins held up her mane in a controlled sweep back from the forehead, sometimes soft, sometimes severe and always rather ageless. She walked with a swagger: her hips swung as she strolled, limbs still loose from sea bathing almost every day in summer (a vigorous breaststroke, head above water). Her lined face was the colour of walnut.

Really, the child had quite put her off the task of tending to that section of flowerbed. She needed to buy more tree bark to deter the weeds, doubted she could afford that luxury and wished that the wretched dog did not spend quite so much time examining its private parts, as if nothing else mattered and they were something of which he was proud.

Diana moved through the kitchen and into the hall. She stood at the foot of the stairs, listening. The stairs were magnificent with banisters of decorated oak which began in a wide sweep and branched to the left and right, leading to the family quarters on one side, the guest domain on the other. There was no barrier between the one and the other, which she found regrettable sometimes, although the guests who stayed here tended to know their place, and Matthew had learned his. Mrs. Kennedy remembered the early days, when her brochure had stated "Dogs and children welcome," before two seasons of a particularly beautiful, disruptive and destructive little boy had made her change her mind. Her grandson, Matthew, at his worst was an angel by comparison. He borrowed things, but he did not steal.

From the dining room to the left of the stairs, she could hear a murmur of voices. The last of the breakfast eaters, lingering over coffee, while Mary, cook, cleaner, treasure, chatted to them. No other meals were provided. Guests were urged to leave for the day as soon as possible, although they could make their own tea in the dining room, and sit there for a drink in the latter part of the evening. Sometimes, for form's sake, Mrs. Kennedy would join them in the comforting knowledge that they found her perfectly charming, while she found them, within varying degrees, either tolerable or detestable. She could not face them in the morning.

But a collision with Mrs. Smythe, coming downstairs as Diana herself preceded regally across the hall to the front door, proved unavoidable, so she forced herself to stop, as if pleasantly surprised, put on her air of distant friendliness and fixed her smile while her heart sank. Dear Mrs. Caroline Smythe had been a regular for a fortnight almost every year since financial necessity had forced Diana to accept her and her kind.

"Caroline, how nice to see you!" Mrs. Kennedy murmured, taking an apparently impulsive step towards her and extending her hand. God forbid that the woman should kiss her. "I saw from the book that you'd arrived yesterday evening, I was out, I'm afraid. How *are* you? I was just coming to find you."

This display of pleasure, as befitted a pair of widows of a certain age and long, if intermittent acquaintance, may have been entirely false, but Mrs. Smythe beamed. She was wearing a variation of her usual, jaunty headscarf and her fringe was a different colour. She was dressed in cut-off trousers, socks, hiking shoes and a flannel shirt, as if she was making for the cliff path and all the miles beyond, although she had never been known to walk further than a hundred yards. It was quite a change from the frothy frocks of last year. The woman was a miracle of reinvention, doing well for her age, whatever that was. No-one would ever guess they had been close, once, by mistake. A friendship born of crisis, as inexplicable as it had been temporary.

"Oh, Diana, darling," Mrs. Smythe murmured. "Lovely to see you, too, but, my dear, I am so sorry to hear your news. The poor girl! And here, of all places! I am so sorry. As if you hadn't had enough . . ."

Diana darling detached her hand from the other's grasp and resisted the temptation to wipe it on her trouser leg. Caroline's hands were always sticky, as if she had overdone the moisturiser on fat fingers so soft they could no longer absorb it.

"Yes, well," she said briskly, regretting Mary's inevitable propensity to share family gossip with regular guests, and also realizing that this encounter could not be curtailed without adding something to the information already received. She lowered her voice to one of intimate confidentiality. "Terrible of course. Bizarre, isn't it, to have a daughter with a dangerous job in horrid old London—although she'd already given that up, thank heavens—come down here for a break, only to get mugged by a madman in the village. Still, she's getting better all the time."

"Did they catch him?"

"Oh yes. A weirdo from down the coast. Confessed. He'd been barred from the pub. Kept on throwing things at customers on the way home. Troubles never come singly, do they?"

She had a dim memory of Mrs. Smythe's son, sliding down these banisters, screaming colourful abuse. Mrs. Smythe's boy, who must have been born when Mummy was too old to control him and Daddy was halfway to desertion, the very child who had caused Diana to prohibit children and dogs apart from her own, and for that, she supposed she should feel grateful. She remembered not to ask about the son, just in case she should be told yet again how well he was doing now and what a fine young man he was, all to remind her of a faint feeling of guilt. She could not quite forget the memory of longer conversations with Caroline. Diana should never have confided in Caroline Smythe whatever the occasion: she had known it even at the time and had resisted a repetition, using any subterfuge which came to mind, in the same fortnight, every year.

"I suppose that makes a difference to her recovery?" Caroline said.

"One would imagine it would," she added kindly. "I mean, knowing the danger's removed, the culprit apprehended." There was a mere tinge of a London accent in her voice; the use of words of more than one syllable sounded unnatural, as if she employed the longer words to decorate her speech rather than to explain herself. "But she was always a tough little girl and I expect she's being very brave. Isn't she?"

"Oh yes," Diana agreed. "Very brave indeed."

Diana was not going to tell this smiling face, or any other, that her only surviving daughter was being a selfish swine.

"She has to go to the hospital this afternoon. She hates the hospital," Diana added, searching for something innocuous to say which might also sound confidential.

"Oh dear. More treatment?"

She wanted the gory details.

"No. A checkup. And a demonstration."

Caroline Smythe looked uncomprehendingly sympathetic. She clasped her hands in front of her waist and leant forward.

"Would it help if I were to chat . . . you know, keep her company?"

"No! No, it wouldn't. How very kind of you, but it wouldn't." This time, the recoil was obvious, albeit quickly disguised. There was subdued laughter from the dining room and the sound of clattering plates.

Perhaps it would be better if they had children, and dogs, Diana thought, excusing herself. She could hide in the crossfire: she might be able to pretend that she was not a woman pursued by a series of tragedies, or deny that she and Caroline Smythe were sisters under the skin of motherhood, as if that gave them anything at all in common.

Caroline Smythe stood in the hall, torn between the desire to waylay another guest in the interests of conversation and the need to go and change her clothes. It was ever thus. She would come on holiday to relax, to be alone, but faced with a day's solitude, she found it excruciating.

A small boy cannoned into the hall, skidded on the parquet, righted himself and made for the stairs. A lovely lad, manic as hers had been.

"Hallo," Caroline called after him, longingly, but he shied away, refusing any contact with her eyes, and pretended not to hear. No children, no dogs. All this family had ever done for her was offer hospitality, food and a pretence of friendship, laced with insults and rejection. She clenched her fists and, like Diana Kennedy, fixed her smile.

How do you make people love you?

Turning out of the front door, aware that the final, muttered, must dash excuse me, had lacked her usual refinement, vowing to make up for it later, Diana hesitated. Instead of walking towards the village shops, she turned right, and strolled towards the sea.

The village of Budley spread landward from a neat cleft between the cliffs which guarded the shoreline. The main street was an easy walk; the houses flanking it, viewed from the shore, were set in a series of ever rising terraces, smaller houses on the seafront itself, the more substantial further uphill. Standing on the promenade, a raised walkway with steps down to the beach, continuing at either end into pathways up the cliffs, Diana could turn slowly and see first the town, then the sea, then the cliffs bordering the bay. On a morning like this, the colours would blind her: cliffs topped with brilliant green, their raw sides russet red, the shingle of the beach a muted gold, the sea reflecting the blue of the vast and harmless sky. Then she would look at the town, the houses bedecked with flowers.

And her own house, of course. The most unusual, the biggest on this level and the only one with such a large, walled garden. Other houses, built further up the cliff path, had gardens too, but none so mature. And none with a door set into the wall, leading directly onto the lower reaches of the cliff path and the sea, so that it seemed even the sea was hers. When Diana walked back, she looked at her house covertly. Brilliant white walls, green shutters, grey, pantiled roof, flower boxes at every window and a peachy rose around the fine front door. Yes, it was enviable, solid, beautiful. She could only comfort herself with such thoughts; did so on a regular basis. Anyone seeing her stand in rapt, if secretive, contemplation of her own freehold, would imagine that she was looking at it in order to find flaws, such a perfectionist she was, but Diana was simply admiring what she had with fierce pride, imagining all she could improve if she had money, worrying about tiles and rot and still fortifying her private attitude that anyone who did not want to live, not only in her village, but more particularly in her house, must be stark, staring mad. She was quite sure she did not think this was simply because the polite and fulsome remarks of her discreet paying guests over the years had gone to her head: it was simply a fact.

She strolled uphill. A narrow stream flowed down on the right, with miniature bridges crossing to the front gates of the houses, the sound of the water a bubbling accompaniment to the civilized bustle of newly opened shops. It might have been the presence of this quaint addition which had made the village, high street and all, defy the presence, and accoutrements of the conventional summer tourist. There was no loud music here, no amusement arcade; no sellers of buckets, spades and windshields for the beach; no souvenirs or seaside rock. One shop selling ice cream and Devon fudge, three cafés and a fish and chip shop catered for all of that, disdainfully offering the visitors more than they deserved, while the rest remained essentially a place for the graceful enjoyment of those who lived in it, in a style befitting a population with an average age in excess of Diana's own fifty-seven years.

Costa Geriatrica, Elisabeth had jeered. Everyone here wanders round on sticks, discussing the state of their gardens and their health: no wonder it's so lovely. The only thing likely to cause a riot here would be a hosepipe ban. Well, perhaps by now Elisabeth had discovered there were some advantages to a place which made allowances for the less than fully mobile, despite the hills.

"Good morning, Mrs. Kennedy . . . Lovely day."

"Oh, yes, gorgeous. Aren't we lucky?"

"The lamb's good today. Saved you some. Delivery about lunchtime?"

One did not carry one's own heavy shopping in this town. One might carry back in triumph the dress you had bought from Molly's if you were thus inclined (Diana was not; too vulgar), but that was all. Transaction complete (on the account, please), she strolled through more of the same. Fruit, asparagus, furniture polish, paper goods, environmentally friendly cleaners, polite greetings given and reciprocated with a regularity and consistency which Diana regarded as quintessentially English and infinitely reassuring. Then on her way home, she was jarred by a sudden memory of Elisabeth lying in bed, reclining in state, announcing her own, alien opinions. "My God, Mumsy wumsy, if that man in the butcher's smiles any wider, he'll disappear up his own arse."

"You'd rather live in your crazy bell tower than *here?*"

"You bet. Soon as I can."

"What's wrong with people being pleasant?"

"Nothing, Mumsy. If only it weren't so fucking relentless."

Diana detoured home, excusing her self-imposed delay on the basis that young Matthew was keeping Elisabeth company, and thus making the mood of the patient sweeter. She herself felt suddenly helpless, furious that fate was undermining her yet again. Angry, that with all her hard won dignity, she still carried that contagion of pity which made people so sweetly careful of her, as if she were afflicted with some antisocial disease. Lately it had been less infectious because she was so obviously strong, but then the same unkind fate which ruled her life sent home to roost the daughter who was scarcely mentioned in the shops, because she had brought the trouble with her. No, not brought it, reinvented it. Disinterred it, unable to let it rest. With one daughter already in the graveyard, Diana Kennedy felt that these were challenges that she simply did not deserve. Only an iron will could resist them.

Steven Davey, son-in-law to Diana, watched her from the top window of the foremost house on the hill, owner lately deceased. A glimpse of her white hair lifted his spirits, assured him of the continuity of his life.

"The view's marvellous from here," the American said. "What's it like in winter, though?"

"What? The view?"

What did he mean? The view would be the same in winter; same sky, same stretch of sea, same outlook on the garden at the back, same view of the railings at the front. What did he think? Same view, different colours, less inviting in mid-December than July, obviously; did he want a guarantee of the weather? It was difficult to remain affable in the company of someone who was wasting his time, but the only way out of a downward route into ill manners was to act as if the man was the best friend he had ever had. He must resist the impulse to throttle him, pretend he was interesting and his questions intelligent, while acting at the same time as if he did not despise him for the simple crime of having limitless money. The village was rich, but this man, immeasurably richer. Rich and loud, the perfect North American cliché.

"Oh, of course, I see what you mean. The ambience in winter? Rather nice, actually. Usually mild, quite a lot going on, very friendly community coming into its own, if you get my drift. People remember that they know one another, need one another. Is there anything you'd like to see again?"

There was always this conflict: sell the house and gain the commission as well as the kudos and sense of achievement, or sabotage the whole issue, because he could not bear to have this idiot as a near neighbour. If in doubt, remain as charming as your mother-in-law throughout because you never knew if the customer might have nicer acquaintances he would recommend.

"You sure this is the finest house in town?"

Steven drew a deep breath. "Well I've lived here most of my life, so I'm bound to say that this is the finest village on the coast, aren't I? And I'm bound to say, that local opinion has this as the finest house. Because it has such a commanding position . . ."

"And because it's so expensive."

"Yes. And because it doesn't change hands very often."

"Pardon me?"

Steven did not hate Americans. He simply found them exasperating and uncomfortable because they did not speak his language any better than he could follow their laconic code. And they seemed to have the strange tradition that when they were buying a superfluous house with their ridiculous supplies of cash, it was the man who chose it, and houses chosen by men were always wrong for their women. Perhaps this creature who resembled a frog with the watchful eyes of a lizard would go home and insert a brick from the place down his wife's suspender, by way of a gift. Then they would visit once or twice over three years and sell it again because it was too far from an airport and she had not wanted it. He brightened at the prospect.

"This ain't the finest house," the American said. "Maybe the prettiest, but not the finest." He was standing by the window, jabbing his finger, pointing at the hill, to where the green shutters of Diana's house were distinctly visible in the sun. "Now that one there, that's the finest. By my standards, anyways."

"That one?" Steven asked, pretending not to understand. "Oh yes. Not for sale."

"Why, if the price is right . . ."

"Because it's spoken for. Anyway," he added, "it's got a curse on it. Now, are we finished here?"

Ever fastidious, he brushed the dust from the sleeve of his jacket, and fingered the knot of his tie. Such a smart young man, the American remarked to himself, disliking the vision of a well-dressed realtor so clean he almost shone with it. As if a suit, however casually cut, made any difference. Certainly not in this heat.

"That house got ghosts?" he asked.

"Some."

The American sighed and sat down heavily in the chair by the window, the only furniture in the room. "I just love ghosts," he said. "My wife, she always did love a house with ghosts. Tell me about *that* house."

It was less of an invitation than a command. Steven the servant shrugged. Why not? He could act as if there were a dozen calls on his time, but there were not, and he had given up pretending even to himself that the American was going to buy anything more than a portable antique in this town. Maybe a silver pepper pot from the messy antique and bric-a-brac shop opposite his office. There was also something about the man's superiority which he wanted to shock. Chicago would always condescend to naive little England, where everyone was nice and no-one died, as if they were all in a film.

"You're right. It is the finest house, even if it isn't the most beautiful. It's been in the same family for generations, passed down from father to son. The man who would be the current owner died after a sailing accident, oh, about thirteen years ago, leaving the present occupant, his widow, and two daughters, one she brought to the marriage, and he adopted, and then the one they produced. I married the youngest when we were both scarcely out of our teens."

The American chuckled. "Well, I never. You didn't let a good one get away. Do you inherit?"

"Someone seems to suffer untimely death in every generation of that family," Steven continued, as if talking to the wall. He was feeling bored and angry. "First her father, then my wife. We were living in London. She was murdered. In our house, culprit and motive unknown. He put a black bin liner over her head and kicked her to death. I brought her back here to be buried. We shouldn't have left. The finest house will belong to our son, when he's older, of course. So don't even think of it." He smiled, to forestall any suggestion of offence.

"Jesus."

There was nothing else to say. They creaked downstairs in silence, Steven closing the front door behind them, before they turned into the sunlight, blinded by it. Halfway down the hill, the American forgot to be tongue-tied. What did it matter if he offended this smart young widower? He was never going to see him again. Nor buy a house in a village which was clearly not as idyllic as it seemed, what with the weirdo summer visitors he'd heard about, throwing acid, for God's sake—who needed guns?—and now, this. He grabbed Steven's sleeve.

"That's some family history you have there. What about the other daughter? Can't you marry her and square it all up?" His laughter was artificial, embarrassed and loud, echoing into the walls. He was remembering the woman with the piled, white hair he had seen from the window.

"How very neat," Steven said with his widest, official smile. "My son would approve, but I doubt if she would. We both loved my wife. Goodbye, Mr. . . . what was your name? I do hope we shan't meet again."

Matt was on the beach. Twenty-five, twenty-six, twenty-seven stones he had thrown into the sea. His aim was to chuck one whole hundred; but the ambition had outweighed the interest. His skin was copper coloured with a clear demarcation zone where his shorts ended, his trainers began and the sleeves of his polo shirt flapped against his thin upper arms. The sheen on his uncovered flesh bore scant resemblance to the lily limbs which had begun to spread themselves on towels and chairs. A group of young women and men, day trippers from some-where else, laid out in rows to catch the rays, their English faces already pink. They had nothing else in common, except for a slight as yet faintly expressed, irritation with the boy throwing stones. As if one of the pebbles he skimmed on the flat water between the sluggish waves could rebound and hit some exposed flank of flesh.

He could hear his name being called from the door to Gran's garden— think of the pride of walking past them all, into his own door. Or maybe that was all in his mind, his name being called, like a constant echo, making him wander round with his fingers in his ears. Matthew! Come and help me. Or was it, Matthew, help? He sat heavily, listened, decided that twenty-eight stones were quite enough. He would try, once more, to make one of them bounce not twice but three times, in a minute. His feet scrunched slowly as he rose and walked down the line of swimsuit-clad bodies, stopping to stare. How strange it was that whether they knew one another or not, they arranged themselves with such symmetry, as if they were cars parked by an attendant in a car park.

He was looking for his mother. Long, slim, fair, beautiful, with a voice like music. She was not like Aunty Elisabeth; she was not like anyone, although Elisabeth came closest before she got so crumpled, and there was always the hope she could be here, even though he knew she would never be here, not a chance. Not a chance after what he struggled to forget.

He found himself examining a bare bosom. Two nipples; interesting. Someone told him to piss off. Stop staring, little boy, haven't you got a home?

"I'm looking for jewels," he told them under his breath. "There's treasure on this beach, did you know?"

He turned on his heel and faced Gran's house. Given the chance, they would send him away. Everyone was sent away, in time. Sent away or lost. He dreaded his turn for either eventuality and only knew he wanted to postpone it. He turned again, picked up a stone at random, watched for a space of seconds, and skimmed it across the shallows. Once, twice, thrice, it bounced. Someone who had watched him with sympathy rather than irritation, clapped.

It was indeed a place of enchantment.

Chapter

TWO

Yugh!
The familiar smell of the hospital corridor made Elisabeth sick.
With the taste of bile in her mouth, all she could remember was the
food and that miserable card, sent round with supper, asking what
she would want the evening after, which, when it arrived, was always
the wrong choice, a bland pulp, neither hot nor cold, never delicious.
The irony of it: to be hungry, with nothing good to eat; at leisure for
once to enjoy, while everything tasted of paper and all the time she
was outmanouevred by pain, pain, relentless, irritating pain. They
were all in it together, a team of torturers, led by a surgeon with
a smile as sharp as his scalpel and a bedside manner as plastic as
his art. A teeny-weeny man, a skin-deep bastard. (You are doing so
well, Elisabeth: we're all amazed: you must let us show you off . . .

a demonstration . . . let the others know how it's done . . .) And she, recalcitrant, but vulnerable enough to succumb to flattery, had agreed.

You should never agree to anything, skinny Lizzie. Never.

A porter was wheeling her into a lecture hall. Bright lights, a theatre full of people. She was one of the surgeon's triumphs.

Dream on, Liz. Waft your perfume, insist on a cigarette in a long, ivory holder: you've been selected for stardom, a celebrity at last. In a moment they would applaud, recognize the fact that she had come by this debilitating status and ugly hospital gown as a result of something brave. Not an injury from a boiling pan she had failed to notice, but a proper, full-frontal, national newspaper headline injury on a day when she was the only good news. Read all about it . . . BLONDE HEROINE RESCUES BOY FROM FIRE ON BURNING BOAT . . . *amazing courage . . .* BLONDE HEROINE HOISTS GRANNY TO SAFETY ACROSS RAVINE . . . SAS VENTURE LED BY . . . *near tragedy averted by stunning show of skill. Miss Kennedy clambers down the edge of a vat of hot oil to rescue a colleague stuck on ledge, overcome with the fumes. Hurray! She succeeds and bears her scars nobly. "It was in a good cause," she said, falteringly, from her bed of pain. "Of course I would do it again." The shy, brave darling, wincing slightly at the intensity of the camera flash, cornflower-blue eyes as bashful as a princess. We love you, Elisabeth.*

There was a man with a camera on the lecture room stage. She blinked at him, unable to detect personality; a photographer, she guessed, hidden by the glare, hired to record what the surgeon was about to describe. His purpose did not include communicating with the patient. She could not see his features, felt rather than saw a smile as he darted forward, knelt as if abject, raised his thumb, like that, and retreated into the shadows until summoned again. A tall man, with a pony-tail.

Celebrity. Heroine. Fool. You add insult to your own injury, letting yourself in for this, ticking the box, giving permission to be arranged so carefully on a trolley, paraded like a corpse at a state funeral. She was bidden to lie as still as if the couch was really a coffin. Reclining at the moment, with her back to the audience, spine exposed. Dream on, for a minute. Please, give me another minute.

... Miss Kennedy, resourceful ex-police officer, is currently indisposed after her outrageously courageous pursuit of an armed robber, who had terrorized the neighbourhood ... She floored him after a desperate pursuit, alone, unaided, unarmed, despite his knife ... then she dived into ice ... Our heroine on the mend ... We are proud of her.

Elisabeth interrupted her own daydream. Her mother would have liked this version, too.

The surgeon coughed, clearing his throat. "As to the cause of these injuries, ladies and gents, well, a sad tale. Elisabeth here was coming out of a pub, at the end of a birthday celebration. She took a short cut on her way home. Possibly not paying a great deal of attention, eh Elisabeth?" He patted her rump. "She tripped and fell. Unfortunately, there was at large at the time a madman who had taken to attacking young people of the district with various kinds of acidic fluids. In this case, caustic, which he either threw at or over Miss Kennedy. Her injuries are the more severe because she had fallen, because she was unconscious and therefore lay in this liquid for some time ..."

Don't say it, she pleaded silently. Don't say, she was *drunk*. As a skunk. Going home alone after an argument in a pub, tripping over ... going to sleep in acid, because she was stupid drunk. Unable to remember much after. Failure.

"She lay on her right arm and hip. Her chin also had contact with the caustic, but thankfully, movement of the head has minimized injuries here, while the elbow was burnt to the bone, with considerable inroads made into the flesh to the rear of the hip. Well, we couldn't mend that with skin grafts alone, could we now? So what we're talking about here is rebuilding that muscle with muscle of a similar type."

With loving care, he traced the long, puckered scar which led from the left of her mid-spine, into the left buttock.

"So we took it from here ... and here. The skin to cover it came from the inner thighs ... Here, and here."

She was sitting now, as guided, legs wide apart on the edge of the trolley, the gown bunched modestly, revealing no more than two expanses of purpled flesh. Healing: almost healed, but still as sore as if she had been dragged over gravel, and despite the modesty of the gown, the pose was faintly indecent. Then, again as instructed, she lay back, holding the right arm, temporarily freed from the sling and the bandage, across her chest, keeping her eyes to the ceiling, refusing to look at her own, reconstituted flesh. To think she had ever worried about her weight.

"The damage to the ribcage and the neck have been slow to heal and resistant, up until now, to any kind of graft. The skin of the inside upper arm can be ideal for the neck, and at last, we seem to have succeeded." He stood behind her, holding her head in both hands, turning her profile to the audience. The photographer took another picture, like a man fascinated by patchwork.

"There are always problems with mending the jaw and the neck, because it must remain mobile in order for the patient to eat, to communicate. The patient is always anxious to communicate, isn't she, Elisabeth?" He laughed. "Of course one wants a patient to eat and smile, but in this case, one didn't wish to encourage laughter, ha, ha."

Bastard.

One would have prefered it if the patient had at least wanted to smile. Rather than the screaming, the swearing, the corrosive, articulate anger, the tuneless singing and latterly, the constant flow of hot, furious tears. And the language, good God, her language. No fishwife was ever so fluent. The whole range of emotional responses was hers, excluding gratitude.

The photographer came back, slipped away again. Elisabeth adjusted herself to lie, fairly comfortably now, on her left side, with her head propped up in her left hand. In this pose, she surveyed the audience as the doctor continued, on and on and on in a fluent delivery which seemed to her a remarkably self-satisfied postscript to her humilation. Then she noticed it, a fresh, pink rose, placed close to her hand, so sweet smelling it made her want to cry. And then, laugh.

Staring out into the darkness, Elisabeth lowered one eyelid in a lascivious wink. She had tried the gesture in front of a mirror, making Matt giggle, aware of how absurd it looked from a face which seemed as if someone had taken a bite out of the neck, mended it with playdough and put it back crooked. The faces out in the black sea of the audience were doubtless perfect, but invisible, barred from her scrutiny. There was the sound of a high giggle, quickly suppressed. Mr. Ryman, a surgeon with a future and a paper to prepare, stood at the end of her couch; talking, gesturing, explaining a point, little glasses trembling on the end of his nose. With the clawed fingers of her right hand, Elisabeth pulled the material of the gown above her knees, winked again, extended one foot, wiggled her toes, bent her knee and extended her right foot until her big toe could stroke the cleft of his backside. It was a friendly, lascivious gesture which he did not notice until he jumped, with a ridiculous meow of alarm, the half-moon glasses clattering to the floor, the noise of that drowned in a storm of laughter. Elisabeth lay on her back and closed her eyes, aware of the camera again. She raised her good hand in a two-fingered salute, curled the other round the rose.

Deciding it was better to join in the laughter, the surgeon swept his glasses off the floor and put them back on his nose.

"As you will see, ladies and gents," he announced jovially, "the patient is making an excellent recovery. But it has been, and will be, a long process . . ."

Drunk again, Miss Kennedy. When will you ever learn?

If only that were all.

Are you intelligent? Do you hurt? Are you a failure?

Yes, yes, yes. And whose fault is it?

My own. I have never done a brave thing or a wise one.

Steven was waiting outside.

"What were they laughing at?" he asked.

"They're going to sell me at a discount," she said. "Put me up for auction. I should've painted my toenails."

"Car's outside. Can you manage the walk?"

He was deliberately brisk, because she seemed to be in danger of crying again, which he did not want. He was always slightly awkward with emotion, trying to hide it, as if she noticed.

"I don't see why you should pay and display if you're parking a car in order to carry a patient, be one, or visit one," she said distinctly as they crossed what felt like a mile of concrete, the urge to weep suppressed with every toddling step. Being drunk was never as bad. The urge to talk, more prevalent, was impossible to resist once she was settled into a seat and he began to manoeuvre the car, his own, nice, commodious piece of Eurowedge, out of the Exeter traffic. She longed to be able to drive herself, but none of that desire diminished the pleasure of being driven in a car where everything worked.

"I've got to go home, Steven. Got to, got to, got to. Soon."

"Yes, yes, I know, don't worry, we're on our way. Home soon." He missed the point.

She was scrunched up in the passenger seat, the whole of her throbbing with anger, holding the arm in the sling against herself, her feet braced against the dash, one foot tapping a rhythm. Her shoes were in the well of the car, somewhere. He disliked the sight of her thin, bare feet, raised to the level of her face as she sank down.

"Home?" she yelled, so loud he almost took the car straight across the roundabout. "Fucking home! No home of mine."

He was silent, smiling slightly, endlessly tolerant.

"I want, dirty, filthy, cold-blooded London," she continued. "I want muck in the street. Litter. Dead plants. Neighbours who do not give a shit. I want Patsy and all the rest who have better things to do. What an ambition. I want to be in a place where the natural behaviour of the people is rudeness and lack of curiosity."

"They won't look after you," he said.

"I should hope not. Why the hell should they?"

He drove.

"Do you remember Patsy?" she asked, her mind slipping into a different gear.

He had met her once or twice. In those far off days when Steve and her sister Emma and she all lived in London, inhabiting their different planets. Steve and Emma, the gilded couple with their baby son, living on the outskirts but upwardly mobile, Elisabeth in the middle, living in a series of flats before she found the belltower. She would entertain them from time to time with her own version of street wisdom, and even to Steven's untutored eyes, she seemed unlikely to make it as an officer of the law. He and Emma had talked about it, often. This is not what my sister should be doing, Emma had said, a policewoman, for God's sake; she only does it out of middle class rebellion. I worry for her. Emma worried for everyone: it was part of the sublime sweet nature which made her so phenomenal. Steven struggled, in a rush of conflicting memories, trying to find another face from the same era. Patsy.

"Yes. I think. Glamorous. Something in magazines."

"Well, she wrote to me the other day; it was like getting news from another world. She'll come and fetch me back, couple of weeks. I want to *hear* about people having good times; I want to be around people who do the things I want to do . . ."

"Listen to the good times?" he asked, feigning understanding.

"Patsy and Emma," she said dreamily. "Either of them. All I wanted to be."

He was inured to her insensitivity, and drove on, relieved that she had removed her bare feet from the dash and looked sleepy. The better profile was turned towards him, not as flawless as her dead sister, but the same perfect skin from this angle where the twist to the neck was not apparent. Those were the days, when he had driven them both home for weekends, his wife and her sister, as different as they could be in manners, and only, oddly similar in the quality of their skin. The children of different fathers, although both of them had only known the one.

"You didn't really want to be like Emma," he said.

Of course she had. Serene, undemanding, possessed of a handsome man who adored her. She straightened in her seat, ashamed. No-one would ever have wanted to be Emma if they could have predicted how short her life would be.

"Why do you have to go, Lizzie? We need you. You could stay on, get a job."

"It isn't my home, Steven. Matt thinks it is, but it isn't."

"Oh." He did not want to talk about that.

The car sped down the narrow hill which led to the outskirts of the village. Through the trees which dappled them in shadow, there was a glimpse of sea. The sky had dimmed to the deeper blue of early evening. He watched her watching the parade of shops as they passed. Mrs. Audrey Compton was watering the flowers outside her antique and bric-a-brac shop: he waved. She waved back with furious energy. Thank God she had taken in all the rubbish which littered the pavement by day. There it was, peace, tranquillity, order, and all Elisabeth Kennedy wanted was the dark comforts of metropolitan chaos. Plus shallow, clever, successful friends like Patsy.

"You can't go back yet," he said gently as they came to a stop. "You aren't really well enough. You won't be able to climb the steps. The place will be filthy."

"No it won't. Father Flynn keeps an eye out and Patsy said she'd look over the place."

His dim memory of Patsy did not accord with a comforting image of a woman at home with a duster.

Chapter

THREE

The din was terrific and the light varied from a ghastly blue through all the shades of the rainbow, obscuring faces into sharp angles devoid of distinction. The men kept their eyes on the girls, registering bodies long before faces. What they did with their bodies and their hair on the dance floor; the way they smelled with their sweat inside tight clothing and the sheen of it on their foreheads, raising the contours of less than perfect skin. Dancing close or the distance of embarrassment; whether they wriggled, pressed, writhed; small boned, big bosomed, big-headed: Rob could look at the bodies like a buyer in an auction ring, he and his mates fixing the prices. He failed to understand, as he jutted his own hips to the music, that the process of observation was equally brutal in his own direction. Even in this light, someone had noticed his white socks and over-shiny shoes. There were three girls who were prime among other girls for sticking together and making a noise, men drawn towards their circle, and there was a conspiracy percolating between them which he was slow to fathom. They were blocking him from the one he wanted. The one he wanted, probably wanted his friend, Mike, but Mike was being aloof, acting superior, as if he didn't care who liked him. Looking as he did, why should he worry? Mike was the enviable one. Regular features, melting eyes and amazing thick hair, nice build for an average height, although he always looked taller than he was. The hair added a charisma they all seemed to lack. Owl and Joe were shuffling about somewhere; Joe's damn pony-tail making a big man look like a wimp, and the Owl's huge specs the only feature which made his presence memorable. Neither of them was much competition, as far as Rob was concerned. They couldn't sell themselves, and if you can't do that, what can you do?

So bold Rob ended up buying drinks for all three girls, one round after another, taking some time to realize he was being outwitted because, after the third dance, the one he liked had pushed him away playfully, as if he had been getting too close, and he had followed her back to her gang where, by a process of nods, winks and patting of seats, they arranged themselves and neatly placed him as far away as possible from her. The sweet little blonde who was the one he had spoken to first, the one he wanted.

OK, suit yourself. The older one wasn't bad, he conceded, sulking, but the mutual indifference was palpable. Besides, the older one had cleared a space on that little dance floor, throwing herself round with lots of arms, trying too hard, so that after a while no-one asked her any more and she didn't seem to care one way or another, like Mike, as if she was there simply to drink and nod her head at the music, ignoring everything else. Mike sort of led their team: she led hers by showing off more.

They were all showing off, come to think of it: telling jokes and stories, every word bellowed, shrieking with laughter, waving arms, pushing back hair, moving their bodies, crossing and uncrossing their legs. Rob staggered to the Gents, slightly pissed, dizzy with drink and his own frustration. He looked longingly at the dance floor, searching for his three friends. They had broken the essential rule of cruising, which was stick together. Girls didn't make the same mistake.

And then when he came out, it was over. He must have been in there longer than he thought, resting his head against the mirror, not quite liking what he saw while hearing the rush of giggling footsteps past the door, the muted sounds of plotting in the adjacent Ladies' lav. His body ached, his head ached, and he wondered what he might have spent. Outside, a few bodies were dancing langorously now, all selections made, all rejections refined into this few, while those whose choices had been spoiled took the hint and left without parading their failure. Rob peered across at the girls' table. There was one woman remaining, the older one. Arranged in the dim light like a bunch of flowers, waiting for him. Anger swelled. This tribe of bitches had passed him from hand to hand, outflanked him and left him this. All that effort, to be left with the one he liked least.

"Look," he said, slumping next to her, "I wouldn't take you home if you were the last person alive." The words, once out of his mouth, were instantly regretted.

She was silent, her lips pursed, her hands clasped loosely over her knees. She had curly hair, smudged make-up, a plunging neckline and a short skirt over long legs which were, in this unkind light, faintly yellow. Her face was even older than he'd thought, almost motherly. She took one of his hands in both of hers and looked deep into his eyes. He felt paper scrunched into his palm as her lips moved nearer, mouthed a mocking kiss, then retreated. He felt something heavier land in his lap and, at the same time, recognized what was squeezed against his fingers. It was not her telephone number.

"Surprise, surprise," she murmured. "You ordered all that booze we didn't really want. And you dropped your wallet. Is your mother waiting up for you?"

He opened his palm, looked at the bill. The total swam before his eyes. He rubbed his sleeve against his face, smelling his own dried sweat.

"I can't pay this."

She got up, gracefully, brushing the skant material of her skirt, hauling a large handbag over her shoulder.

"Don't worry about it, sunshine. You just did. Only we went halves. Saves you two weeks worth of washing up. I hope you've got enough for your bus fare tomorrow."

He sat, paralysed with shame, looking first at the bill and then at her retreating back as she joined the remainder of her coven by the stairs. There was one, lonely fiver left in his wallet. By the time he reached the neon glare of the street beyond, he could see how she was the tallest, her arms round the shoulders of the others, all three of them helpless with laughter. From the darkness, Mike the Owl and big, untidy Joe emerged, waiting for him.

"Only a game," Joe said, looking at Rob's flushed face. Only a game. A laugh. A night out. The kind of night out which always ended up costing a bomb and made Rob feel at the end that he was paying in advance for romance which never arrived.

He was sick of it.

Another part of town; the same game. Patsy knew it was one she had been playing far too long. Looking for love. The hunt for the dream man, played by herself and Hazel and shy little Angela who had to be guarded as if she was blind. There's got to be a better way, Angela was thinking, remembering the features of the man in the bar, revolted by the memory of his closeness. Executive, he'd said: her mother would approve; she didn't, but could not manage to say so, either. The others had looked after her as usual, recognizing that she, the perfect, natural blonde, acted as a flame to draw the male moth which she did not know how to swat. She resented their protection as much as she hated her own innocence. She got silly with booze.

They paused in a doorway, helpless with nervous mirth, and for all that, it was still serious; another night's disappointment before they parted and went home, each one afraid that this was a pattern of life, repeated over and over like a tired joke told by someone who thought they were funny. They linked arms, walked to the taxi rank. The drizzle began. Angela's blonde hair, a beacon of gold in the indoor light, gleamed with moist drops and hung like damp wool.

"Bye girls." "Byeee." Only a game. Going home alone, again.

Inside her own flat, Patsy thought of Elisabeth and the thought of Lizzie frightened her a bit, until she remembered that Lizzie had a family at least and there was nothing to worry about for Lizzie, whatever else happened. Patsy did not have family, only money and success, but money made her careless, details made her lazy. She could have got those curtains fixed, for instance: they had cost so much and still never quite closed at the top. Summer rain on the lower rooftops opposite played strange tricks with the street lamps; bars of light extended across the white ceiling like half of a star sneaking into the room. The fingers of the star waved like the flames of a fire: she could almost have read small print in such light. The club where they had been might pay dearly for just such an effect. Elisabeth, come home: you always looked after me and I look after them. Tell me that life is fun, instead of this paranoid search.

It was not the transfiguration on the ceiling which woke her later, but cold, curling her knees to her chin. She had lain on top of the bed, still hot, unwilling to creep inside, dozed. Another cooler, August night, disturbed by dreams, and then, *that* sound had pushed a path right through the middle of her brain. *That* sound was the noise of a diesel engine, panting, three floors below. A taxi, like the one which had bought her home, that family of sound, not threatening in any way, but the more she came to concentrate, the more the sound persisted, became mixed with the hint of footsteps, then a door closing. She straightened stiff legs and contemplated getting off the bed and into it, postponing the effort which would make her colder for the minute, and still the diesel throb persisted until it was fearful.

Patsy shrugged into her dressing gown, heavy silk, pale lavender and instant warmth and padded to the living room for a better view. Opposite her attic-level apartment there was a block of purpose-built flats, snug enough dwellings with steps sweeping up to the front, unsuitable for some of the elderly residents who clutched the iron railing and took five minutes to get down. She had watched them. An ambulance stood with the doors open at the back, the interior of it glowing calmly, the engine throbbing warmth, the inside almost inviting, like a secret room. Moving up the steps from the basement area, two uniformed men carried a stretcher. The street light shone down on the hump filling it, hidden under a green blanket. Patsy could not see a head, only the form itself, aged into shapelessness, the prominent point either bosom or belly; a scrap of hair protruding from the cover.

The men were gentle and respectful, with a slight edge of carelessness, a nonchalance in their movements as the stretcher bumped against a lamppost. There was no urgency in the task; no rushing to close doors, present oxygen, scream away into the night. There was no fussing around the mound beneath the blanket, no real need to keep it warm. One of the men stood in the road and lit a cigarette.

A couple appeared, full of neighbourly concern. The woman signed a form and shook her head: then they all hung about in the street while the ambulanceman finished his smoke, their breath visible against the drizzle, talking without hurry, making the kind of chat which was simply the receiving and imparting of information, accompanied by nodding. Finally, the doors closed on the green blanket, to which Patsy's eyes had strayed, again and again. *That* diesel note changed from throb to roar. The neighbouring couple went back down the steps together, pulling their coats around themselves. Whom should they inform, what could wait until morning and what should they do with the cat?

I have no next of kin, Patsy told herself. I am entirely free to die like that.

She would die alone like that; in the middle of the city, like this, and wait for someone to find her, subject only to the kindness of neighbours. She could have diamonds, a girl's best friend, and still die like that.

She hugged herself.

I've gotta find myself a man.

Chapter

FOUR

Elisabeth had always loved the story of how her mother and father had come to meet. There he had been, standing in his own jeweller's shop, a shy man, although obstinate in his way, surveying all he owned and rearranging the display, when he had seen her outside with her nose pressed against the window. Not only Diana, with her long, blonde hair, but also the tiny child she was holding in her arms. She was pointing out the rings one by one to the baby who waved fat fingers and blew bubbles at the display of wealth.

Dorian Kennedy had been a romantic; not the type of romantic who was in tune with the chanting for peace and free love principles of the younger of his generation, but the introverted awkward kind, growing into a bachelor, preternaturally old in his thirties and wearing exactly the same clothes as his father. Until he saw outside his window two such pieces of perfection, they made his jewellery fade by comparison. So, he had invited them in, discovered a young mother, although older than she looked, alone in the world, steeling herself to sell the ring which was the only valuable souvenir she had left from the father of the child. It was a scenario so fitting Dorian's dream, he could not believe anything as heaven sent. The rest, as they say, was history.

Could that really happen? Elisabeth had asked. Could her mother's mother really have abandoned a beautiful daughter for the single crime of producing a bastard child? Yes, if she was old herself, sick with disappointment, and it was all in the dark ages of the nineteen-sixties, she could, she did.

Elisabeth had so often wished she had not been that child by the window. She wished she had been Emma, the one who had brought such unqualified delight, whereas she had not. But we wanted you, her father had said, you cannot imagine how much we wanted to love you: you are a pearl beyond price, a diamond. He stuttered when he spoke thus, always giving the impression he would take back his own, scrambled words as soon as they were out of his mouth. I waited a long time for you, he had said; and the subtext of this, to Elisabeth's mind, was, and look at what we got.

Not that Dad came to mind very often now, or at all. In fact he might barely have tripped across her daydreams, were it not for all these idle hours of recuperation when anything and everything flood-ed in to fill the gap and distract her from the more recent past. After all, he had been inconsiderate enough to die just before he could see her reach twenty-one. A middle-aged fool to take up sailing so late, desperate to get out of the house and remove his tired eyes from the contemplation of cheap engagement rings, watch batteries and all the things he was forced to sell. He was also a clumsy man when not han-dling a pair of tweezers or looking into a spectroscope. Inept with his borrowed dinghy, he came home one day, sick and shivery after he had capsized, took to his bed and never got up.

Perhaps he was like me, Elisabeth thought now. A person who wil-fully persisted at something he could not do and was then irreconcilable in defeat. All the same, it seemed an odd motive for dying.

Bronchial pneumonia in a small, thin man who had always resem-bled the runt of the litter, was a better excuse.

Something had reminded her of all this ancient history. Perhaps it was the voices downstairs, caught in the breeze from the far end of the garden where Steven and her mother sat on the bench, talking. She remembered Mother sitting there, first with the doctor and then, later, with Mrs. Smythe, all those years since. Or was that all in her imagination? And then there was that other memory of low-voiced, bitter rows, coming from another room making her feel as she did now, full of the longing to leave.

Her father had had so few passions in his life. Look at how they shine, he would say in wonder, never referring to the stars. Look at the fire, child; have you ever seen anything like that? He kept his heart locked inside a sapphire, adored all precious stones, but only revered the hardest: rubies, sapphires and diamonds. She was falling asleep, thinking how it was that lovely Emma had delighted in jewellery, whereas she had loved only the stones. She did not want to own them, or wonder what her father had done with them, but she loved and revered them, all the same. Those two outside, sitting with their coffee, talking about her, never looked at the stars either. Their feet were firmly planted on the ground.

"She's just like her father," Diana was saying to her son-in-law. "Mean, secretive and jealous. Also prone to excess. I'm sure she could have told us more about how the trial failed. She could have found out more than we were told. But she wouldn't." She paused. Irritation was exhausting. Positive comments were better for the soul. "At least this ghastly accident has stopped her drinking," she added.

"Without getting hooked on anything else, hmm? Look, Mother, you're hardly being fair. Secretive, yes. Difficult, yes, yes, yes. But mean? Never. Not Lizzie. We had our explanation, didn't we? It's not enough, but it's something."

Diana shifted on the bench, rearranging her jacket, noting the frayed cuff. Her white hair was almost luminous. Emma's hair would have been like that if she had ever lived so long.

"She was jealous of Emma. Terribly."

"I don't remember that stage. I remember the times when she was over-protective. She adored her."

"Oh yes, all right, she did. Not when Emma was a baby, though. She tried to throw her into the sea."

"Did she?"

"Twice. Once in the pram, once without."

Diana had begun to load the coffee cups on the tray, quietly preparing to move. It was becoming cold. A light from the dining-room window, where the curtains were half-drawn, illuminated the lavender in the flowerbed.

"I must go in," she said. "Caroline Smythe's leaving tomorrow, and I've mostly managed to avoid her, but she could come bounding out here anytime now, looking for company. She'd love to see you. Mull over old tragedies, oh God, she does love tragedy. She'll tell you about her son, I suppose. That terrible boy. You two were friends," she added accusingly.

He frowned, as if disliking the memory.

"Yes. For two weeks a year I became a bad boy, like him. Full of city habits. Stealing sweets and apples. Letting down tyres. Throwing stones at the cliff in the hope of a landslide. Wicked stuff. What was his name?"

"Surely you remember? Such a handsome pair you were," she said, rising. The dog at her feet growled. Diana shushed it and put a finger to her own lips. She whispered, "Caroline Smythe offered to keep Elisabeth company . . . can you imagine?" They both smiled, and began to sneak round the far edge of the lawn, avoiding the dining-room windows. Their feet were silent on the lawn, shoulders brushing the overhanging shrubs which were Diana's pride, the air thick with the scent of the stocks. They made casual but careful progress. It was ten-thirty at night, could have been the hour before dawn. Until a masked figure crashed out of the bushes, leapt into their path and stood before them, legs wide apart, the gun held in both hands to steady it, the voice low and threatening.

"Freeze!"

They froze. The tray carrying cups, transferred to Steven's hands, fell with a crash. He swore. Diana made an automatic gesture of putting up her hands. She had almost tripped over the trug with the weeds left over from this morning; she looked at the feet in front of her. Socks, but no shoes.

"You're not going to send her away!" the voice growled on as the hand holding the gun began to quiver. "You're not, you're not, you're NOT!" and on the final repetition the voice broke into a childish shriek. A light came on from upstairs, visitors' side, then another. Diana forced herself into a high, reassuring laugh, carried on at length. Apart from that, they stood in silence.

"Stop it, Matthew. Please," Steven said, calmly.

One by one, the lights went out. Mrs. Diana Kennedy's paying guests retired early. Restraining themselves from the company of children and dogs, even if their gracious landlady did not.

And in bed, more than half asleep against the sound of the sea, Elisabeth heard only the laughter and found herself dreaming of jewels. Bright gemstones, turning into traffic lights below her window rather than stars above.

She imagined getting up once the laughter ceased. Packing her bag, going away now, instead of waiting another week for her elusive strength to come back. Thinking of whom she might have betrayed.

One by one, the lights went out. Two men sat by the window, watching the monolithic London tower block three hundred yards away as family after family went to bed. Those who did go to bed. A dull light hung over the near distant city, the glow of a million lives.

"So you won't help, then? You set me up for this, even got me as far as Devon, and you won't help me?"

"I didn't say that. I didn't say wouldn't, I said couldn't. Not the same thing." Jenkins raised a slightly shaking hand. "Fingers burned, you see. To the stumps. I've still got a job. Want to keep it, such as it is. Wife gone, bairns gone . . . What I've got is this. Not much, but mine to use and abuse."

"I'm not going to fiddle with that, you know I'm not, as if I could or would. I just want to know more about Elisabeth Kennedy. You set me up. You sent me down to keep an eye on her." Joe emphasized, copying the older man's speech.

"She got the wrong man," the elder said, after a pause. The shaking of the hand was not drink, more the result of the coffee, consumed by the pint in dainty thimbles which looked as if they had been stolen from a Chinese restaurant. Everything else in this single man's abode looked borrowed, begged or donated from someone who would not miss it.

"But did she get the wrong man?" the younger asked.

"Yes, she may have done. He knew who was murdered, how it was done, with details, but that was all."

"You led her to him. You set them up, too. It's what you do, Jenks. Use people."

"All right then, it was *me* got the wrong man. And then set the wrong woman to find him."

"I don't understand. How did you find the man?"

Every time, he had to act as if he did not know. It was a routine they went through, so that each conversation would reveal more. The older man waved his arm, vaguely. DI Jenkins. He looked more like a stage policeman, grizzled by booze and life, a caricature of what he actually was. Joe could not imagine he was a great advertisement for the joys of an alcohol-free life. He would sit at the back of an AA meeting like a portent of doom.

"Oh, suspicion. A man who was lonely and violent, fitted the bill. Don't tease, you bastard. You remember, you fucker. *You* found him. You made the fucking connection."

Joe nodded, apologetically.

"*You*, Mr. Fucking photographer. You were the one came in and told us that you'd taken a picture for a woman who was making a claim to criminal injuries. Who looked a lot like poor, dead Emma Davey, whose pretty picture you had seen in the *Evening Standard*. You told us that your little, photogenic victim had told you about meeting this guy through a lonely hearts column. He went berserk on her. Tried to chop off a finger with a ring on it. With his teeth. We showed you all our pretty pictures, didn't we, Joe? Because we'd used you before as a freelance. Because you knew about injuries and I trusted you."

There was an explosion of coughing. The man was no advertisement for cigarettes either.

"So, we got his box number from the lonely hearts and set young Elisabeth on him . . ."

"I always thought you had more than that. And more than me. Hoped you did."

The coughing sounded like a wood saw, mixed with the sound of an axe.

"Oh yes, I did. You just don't want the responsibility. I had the man you'd found, a man with a propensity to violence. Not only a horrible little man with a penchant for blondes, but also a friend of the fucking family! Friend of Emma's, anyway: quite a regular visitor. One of the waifs and strays she seemed to collect. Oh, she did love 'em. The plainer the better, and God, Jack was certainly plain. He even lived in the fucking area. Go for it, I said. Had to be him. Fucking go for it."

"Straightaway? Just like that? Get Elisabeth to snare him, answer his next advertisement, make him confess?"

Jenkins heaved his large, shrivelled frame further up his chair, impatient.

"No-one mentioned seduction, not as such, flattery, perhaps. It was a police investigation. Nor was she *ordered*. She was an insistent volunteer. The last I would have chosen, not only because the murdered woman was her sister, but because Elisabeth Kennedy was never a very good policewoman. How *was* Devon, by the way? I hope you appreciated the countryside. How is she?"

Joe clasped his hands together, to keep them still. "I'd have thought she would be good for police work. Stubborn. That's how she is now. Sick and stubborn."

Jenkins nodded, as if he knew that already.

"Oh, she was reckless and brave, and terrified at the same time, never an ideal candidate. You don't want individualists, starting too old. God alone knows how she got picked for a uniform in the first place. But there she was, and she had this stunning resemblance."

"Not identical, surely? A stronger face."

Jenkins grinned. All his smiles seemed to have a touch of malice. "Lizzie didn't think they were identical. She thought we selected her because she was good. Didn't do her any favours to realize, after it was over that she was picked for the way she looked. Namely, enough like her kid sister to fulfil his fantasy, but not as pretty."

"I can't remember quite what the kid sister looked like," Joe said. "Not directly."

"Fucking liar. I showed you all the pictures, after she was dead. You were in love with that image. Emma Davey was beautiful. Not, I gather, as Miss Kennedy is now."

Joe was suddenly defensive. Remembered that bold, hurt face on the gurney, caught in the flash.

"Oh, I don't know about that. It would take more than a few scars to mar that face. Neck's twisted to the left, though."

"Serve her right. She was always turning round to see what was behind, always frightened, but she never learned to cover her back."

The man laughed without real mirth, the hand still shaking as he raised the cup. The habits of the alcoholic still led him to excess. He had little use for sleep. The ceiling above where he sat was yellow with nicotine.

"Poor cow. Thin Lizzie. All her efforts came to nothing. Bloody Jack gave enough hints of guilt, all right, not quite a confession, almost, but the judge wasn't having any. End of case, end of career. The last in a long line of Elisabeth's wee failures. She resigns, goes home to her mother and gets mugged in a Devon village, I ask you. How's that for irony? Silly bitch, useless as ever. Still beautiful, you say? Do I sense a tenderness for the lady? Not that she was ever a lady. Discreet, yes, never told her family a single bloody thing, but never a lady. Do you fancy her?"

"Lord, no. I'm just curious. I went all the way down there because you asked me to go. You get in touch after all this time . . . ask the impossible . . ."

The man stirred, looked Joe in the eye. One of his own, pale eyes, watered. There was a crust of yellow round the lid.

"Well, why not? You're half to blame. And you're sneaky. You could check on her without being obvious, hiding behind your camera. You wouldn't even have to bang on the door. And you know what? You're a kind of pervert yourself. I might have fingered you for a killer, except you like things already dead. Or half dead. You won't take pretty pictures of living things, not you. Not even kittens or puppies. You like things which can't move. Pervert."

Joe shifted beneath the watery gaze. The room was warm.

"I don't understand," he said, realizing he was sounding plaintive and naive, "how her family never knew about her involvement. They knew about a man being charged and rapidly acquitted. They knew about a supposed confession. They never seemed to know how Elisabeth was involved."

The old man looked at him, pityingly. "You don't think Lizzie travelled under her own name, do you? Prat. I suppose the family would have got to know if the trial had gone the distance, but it didn't. Lizzie was anonymous from the start. She was at the finish."

He put a finger to his lips in a parody of discretion. Shhh. Then he got up and stretched, without enthusiasm.

"She shouldn't have gone so far," he murmured. "That's what did for the judge. Activities beyond the call of duty, poor old fart. Couldn't see the truth in pillow talk. Goes back to Adam and Eve and the snake. Curiosity, you said? Killed the cat, my boy. Killed it. Now, fuck off."

"Do I continue? Find out what I can?"

"That's up to you. Suit your fucking self." Then he added, so faintly Joe could scarcely hear, "Please."

Down, down, down. Joe walked down more steps than he could count. One day, he would count the steps. For now he wondered how it was that a wheezy man, who looked so much older than his years, ever managed to climb so far, but this was only his third visit and it would not be his last, so he did not count today. Tonight, on the verge of midnight, he had another place to go; people to meet. Then he would go home. Somebody else's home, but still home. Jenkins had not quite specified trespass as part of the task, but he had supplied Elisabeth's address. Drunk on caffeine, Joe's head was still reeling from the cricket on the television which had stood in the corner of the room, silent, while both eyes went towards it, constantly. Someone in white, dressed in the garments of a lab assistant, ran languidly over a stretch of green. Joe had never understood the mysteries of cricket. He did not want to take pictures of people in movement: he knew his limitations. He loved portraits. Eyes in statues and paintings and patients, skin. They made him a living. Made him hungry for the faces which were still alive. And that was why he so liked hers. Alive, full of despair and never as pretty as her sister.

Then there was light and there they were, the lads, sitting in splendour. Mike, looking suave, Rob looking cocky in his shiny shoes but in that state of drunkeness which was no longer light-hearted, John Jones, all specs and similar, so shy he would run from his own shadow. It was funny how Joe could assume a different persona when meeting the lads. He presumed they all did. They had nothing in common apart from being single, and the fact that they had all worked in the same building, on the edge of the city somewhere, a greenhouse enclave, the executive and peculiarly male end of a big company which Joe had long since left. But while he was there they had crossed the barrier into a kind of friendship, each finally admitting to difficulties with girls. At least, pony-tail Joe had never actually had difficulties with girls, only difficulties with life. He suspected that Rob, a divorcee with attitudes to women which might have come out of the ark, had always had difficulties with girls; likewise John, otherwise known as Owl because of his specs. Such wits they were. Rob and the Owl, late twenties, the one boasting of wide experience, the other of virtually none. But he could never quite fathom why Mike, just on the right side of thirty, was still in the game. They joined together to go out cruising and drinking, because that was what they did. All of them seemed to need a team for moral support. Or maybe this companionship was one of those accidental things, formed on the spur of the moment and somehow self-perpetuating, because two of them wanted to continue it, Rob, in particular, always planning the next meeting, the others falling in, not wishing to renege on promises and, besides, what was the harm?

It was a long bar in the Critics Club, the last resort of late-night drinkers. Above the bar was a mirror, into which Rob glanced, constantly, tweaking his hair, squinting at himself, as if the key to good fortune lay in the foppish brown lock which flopped across his forehead. New man he was not.

"Where the hell have you been?" Rob shouted as Joe came in. Then he looked Joe up and down, critically, grinned, slapped him on the back and almost fell from the uncomfortable bar stool.

"Nowhere special, I bet. You wouldn't, would you? Not dressed like that. Jesus, Joe, where do you get your clothes? Oxfam?"

Rob and John always dressed as if they were selling something. Rob, because he was a salesman and knew no other uniform than a suit, although he abandoned the tie, John Jones because he copied Rob. If you take such a man as your role model, Joe had often thought, you are bound to fail, but Owl was a sweet guy, earnest, full of good intentions. Mike had mastered the art of casual dress, but then he was a boss, high on the company payroll for the best distributor of camera equipment. He wasn't quite Armani, Joe thought, but almost. They all earned far more money than he did. He was slightly their mascot. They all thought of him as a bit of a loser. No car, no expense account: a roving photographer, taker of snaps, mechanic if necessary, odd job man, with a pony-tail but without a mortage. Weird.

"You've not missed anything here," Rob added, signalling for drinks, nodding at the others, who nodded back, apart from Mike, who shook his head. "Nothing going on here at all. In fact we were going to pack it in and go home. But then we thought we'd wait for you, you bastard. Maybe have a council of war. 'Cos I'm sick of wasting money."

"Oh, I don't know, Rob, honestly. I'm not sure about this . . . There's got to be a better way than that . . ." The Owl looked owlish.

"Better way than what?" Joe asked.

"Better way than what he's thinking . . ."

"Who?"

"Michael. He suggested it." Suddenly he was Michael, an authority. They all turned expectantly on Mike, who stood more than usually aloof.

"Suggested what?" Joe asked, exasperated. This time they all stared at Michael, fixedly.

There was one thing about Mike which always impressed Joe, one of those features he suspected women noticed sooner than men. His voice, which was unfailingly pleasant, with a depth to it; an accentless voice which a girl on the other end of a phone might find sexy and a man, faced with a sales pitch, would find himself heeding without quite knowing why he was being hypnotized. You had to listen to Michael, not simply because he was good to look at, but because of that voice. Mike spread his hands, shrugged elegantly.

"I was simply suggesting that rather than spend our time, and rather large quantities of money in the pursuit of women, we should let them come to us. I mean, arrange for them to come to us."

"They'll flock, won't they?" Joe said. "Just like always." He found his heart was beating strangely.

"Well Mike suggested the lonely hearts columns a few weeks back," Rob said crossly. "This is only one stage worse. Or better. Cheaper in the long run. Less wearing."

"What is?" Joe asked.

"Going to an introduction agency," the Owl said. "It's the fact of thing Jack would have done."

"SHUT UP," Rob bellowed. "Just SHUT UP! Don't bring Jack into this. Don't even mention Jack."

Owl opened his mouth and closed it again. There was a full minute of silence.

"The most successful men I've ever met," Michael was saying smoothly, "have their social lives, love lives even, organized by someone else. Usually a woman. We don't meet women through work. We don't live close to brothers and sisters etc., we've all of us moved here, not born here. So we go round the bars looking for women, like sailors coming into a port and what do we get? Divorced women, married girls out for a good time, girls who don't want to be picked up, girls in groups, which defeats the whole object."

"Which is?" Joe asked quietly.

He thought about that. "To find someone who listens. Who wants to know you. Needs you," he said. "Loves you, I suppose," he added.

Blimey. That was a long speech for Mike, even if it was spoken in clichés, Joe noticed; as if Mike had a script.

Rob snorted. "Love? I don't want that. I just want—"

"Shut up," the Owl commanded. "We all bloody know what you bloody want . . ."

"It's an admission of failure, that's what it is," Rob continued, perversely. "It's puerile, it's awful . . . Go to an agency. Pay someone to find you a shag . . . God if anyone knew . . ."

"I think it's quite a good idea," Joe volunteered. Again that unaccountable thumping of his heart. He put his arm round the Owl. "Come on, John, it'll be a laugh." Then he turned to Michael.

"Do you have anywhere in mind?" he asked. "I mean, I wouldn't know where to start."

"I've been looking into it," Michael said. "And yes I do. Recommended by an old girlfriend of mine. She's married now, of course. She said the only problem with this agency is that they had too many women on the books, not enough men."

Rob looked more interested. "We'd be in a minority, eh?"

"Exactly."

Rob looked round the circular bar. Another dozen or so men. A pair of overdressed women sat at a table, not looking left or right, engrossed in their own conversation.

"They'll come running, will they?" he said. "That'll make a change."

■

When Patsy walked across the bridge at seven in the morning, the mist lying on the river was beginning to disperse into nothing with the magic of a spell. The sun struggled for ascendancy in a pink and grey sky, stiking gold on the distant palace of Westminster where the clock stood to attention like a soldier, in a shroud of scaffolding. The river's high tide, running fast and deep, covered the banks. There was nothing as calming as that savage water seen from the high safety of the bridge. The river was the sea drawn close. Patsy loved the sea.

Benign sunlight, the splendour of the view and the hum of a city yawning awake, created a frisson of happiness. Halfway across, she leaned over the parapet, and with the efficiency of an organized woman, scolding herself briefly for her lack of gratitude, told herself she was all right really and congratulated herself on a new crop of resolutions. To be able to see water was both luck and luxury. To be alive and well on a morning such as this in a big fat metropolis heaving with beauty, dirt, grace, energy, idleness and a rampant lack of shame made her own existence comfortably small and her problems smaller still. She could take that ugly black dog of depression for a walk over another bridge and hurl the beast into the foam.

Onwards and upwards to the seventeenth floor. The rise of the lift reminded her of her own achievements, but she had lost in the process. Nonsense: she had lost nothing in the climb to the almost top of her world. She had gained plenty, including privileges like this, of walking down a wide corridor full of women. This range of magazines, consumed by girl teenagers on the one hand, cookery freaks on the other, was owned by men, created, and marketed by women. At any given time, half of those whom Patsy would meet en route to her own room would be pregnant. How other women, undoubtedly with mixed ambitions, found men and turned them into fathers with such apparent ease was one of life's great mysteries. Somewhere in her life, she had lost a decade.

"Right," she said, after Angela and Hazel had closed the door behind them and the coffee machine grumbled. "Have you been thinking about this?"

They nodded, like obedient schoolchildren. They knew what *this* was, and it had nothing to do with work; although it did, at one remove, have plenty to do with the cut-throat but cosy, all-female atmosphere in which they lived by day and often well into the night. Even though Hazel, with her square frame and careless clothes, was an expert on articles about how to please your man in bed with an insight far from theoretical, while Angela, with that halo of hair, wore pastel pinks and a look of innocence which was all too real.

"So, what news on the research, Ange?"

She was flushed. "Well I'm still not sure this is all a good idea . . . I don't know . . ."

"Of course you know," Hazel interrupted. "We had this argument a week ago, after the last disastrous night out, and you agreed then, and what with you in advertising and all, well you'd know best, so come on, give." She did not add, you silly little virgin: the words merely hung unsaid, although tinged with an irritation which was also affectionate. Hazel had seen Angela's silly little house: she had also met Angie's mum: she understood how Ange lived in cotton wool.

"Well," Ange began in that small, hesitant voice which so charmed people on the other end of the phone and made them so reluctant to be nasty to her. "Most introduction agencies don't last long. Plenty of people think it's a good idea, and then go out of business, 'cos it's harder than they think. Apart from the very, very expensive marriage places. Somehow they last. I suppose it's like charging a dowry. We don't want one of those, do we?"

"Shit, no . . . Marriage? Jesus! I don't want that, I just want—"

"We know what you want, Hazel," Patsy said frostily.

"But there's one which has been going for years and years. Even if it does run on a shoestring. Perhaps that's why. I backtracked on her ads, from ten years or more. A woman runs it. Prides herself on personal judgement, no computer rubbish. I mean, if she's gone on that long, she must be successful, right?"

Hazel grinned. Patsy expected her to lick her lips. She crossed her arms.

"When do we start then? Appointments?"

"Next week? I've made them for you. If you want."

Angela was such a reliable little gem. She stood up and placed the particulars on Patsy's desk, determined now. They had nothing in common apart from the place they worked. They were the remainders of a larger gang, that was all, formed around flats and offices. They were an accident.

"I thought we might wait until your friend Elisabeth gets back," Angela said hesitantly. "She might want to join in."

"No," said Hazel. "We're fetching her back tomorrow. She's a bit of a cripple."

"Only I'm not quite ready for this yet," Angela said flatly. "You two can try it first."

There were times when she was hopelessly stubborn and beyond persuasion. Moments when obstinacy seemed her only strength.

"Fine," said Patsy.

"What if we get the same man?" Hazel demanded.

"It's all done on personal histories, profiles and an in-depth interview," Angela supplied as if reading from a bulletin. "Taking into account personal preferences. So you won't ever get the same man, will you?"

They watched her leave. Miss Pretty Froth. Over-protective dad. Not hungry enough yet. Silly, even after all they'd done.

Angela tapped down the corridor, looking busy. She could have died and gone to heaven, watching their faces! Little Angela, telling them what to do and where to go, when all along she had already done it. You've spent the last year dragging me round places, she wanted to say; no, be honest, I went willing. Only I was shocked, I tell you, shocked to bits. I can't help being shy; I can't help being frightened of my mother, even though she approves of me being friends with both of you, and I love you both, I really do, but it was time I did something on my own, so I got in there first, I did, I did.

Slowing down, sidling into the corner of the open-plan offices from which she had not made the crucial phone call, Angela felt a sense of enormous triumph. They'd be giving her an Oscar next. There, there girls, she would say; it wasn't so bad was it, admitting that your social life lacks a certain *je ne sais quoi*, such as men? She made herself forget the courage it had taken to get so far; how dreadful she had felt. Got there first, got there first, she found herself chanting. She was sick of being patronized.

She had nearly turned back twice. Sitting in the café, she had watched the higher windows of the agency on the other side of the road and found them unimpressive, despite a West End address blocked on a piece of paper so thick she could have eaten it. She wanted to chew it out of sheer anxiety, but Angela was thin, untempted by pastries, let alone paper. Up the stairs she had gone, pretending to drift like a blossom, closing her eyes to the scruffiness. And there was a lady, behind an unimposing desk in a small room, heavy with the scent of flowers. Now, tell me about yourself, the woman had said. Tell me about yourself and what you are looking for, and Angela had told her everything. About the bullying from her father and her school. About her over-protective mother and how she had been fat as a child. About the triumph of her independence at twenty-five and how it did not stop her blushing. About her little house, less than a mile from mother, secured with grilles at every window, her fear of bugs, germs and stray dogs. Her whole heart's yearning, not simply for a man, but for an ultra-conventional large, protective man in a suit, who would look after her and want her to wear white at the wedding.

Everything.

And the woman had said, trust me. I know exactly what you mean.

Chapter

FIVE

"Gemstones," her father told her, "are only at their most interesting when pure."

Elisabeth, smoking her endless cigarettes, stood by the kitchen window which looked onto the most prosaic part of the garden, divided from the rest by a wooden fence covered with clematis. She could not tolerate the sight of the sea. It had the challenging brightness of a brilliant, cut zircon. Instead, she was watching the washing line, where a tiny, spring-reared Blue Tit played. He swung from one peg to the next, examined each; let the momentum of his weight and the grasp on the peg tilt him upside down so fast she felt she could hear him laugh. Her mouth was open to laugh, but she could not; as if, like he, she had either lost the knack of making a sudden noise, or never learned it. There was a healthy, sweet smell of pure garden rubbish burning next door. You will not get that at home, her mother would say. You'll get dampness and darkness up that tower.

Now it was so near, she was afraid of going home. She was better, stronger, by degrees, and still afraid of the opinion of the world.

Hazel approved of Patsy's car because it was loud. Red, noisy, fast, sleek and eminently noticeable. A short, low-fronted dress rode far up on her thighs as she sat in the passenger seat, arm resting on the open window, black glasses over her eyes. Her hair was coloured auburn; it shone like metal in the sun.

They had skirted Exeter, disliked Exmouth; they had stopped for coffee and cursed the caravans which littered the roads like lumbering beetles. The roads were narrow, the luxury of speed forgotten. Here and there, Patsy pulled aside to allow for something bigger, although she usually assumed the right of way was hers. Drivers waved, nodded, smiled; they failed to blow horns, even when she was in the wrong. Road rage was a feature of another planet.

"Why are they so polite?" Hazel asked.

"Because they are. Look! There's the sea! Isn't it wonderful?"

"I can't swim," Hazel said.

They roared down the narrow street, too fast amid Friday lunchtime stares. Patsy wore white shorts and a cropped red top which matched her car, her hair a mass of curls messed into volume by the wind. She was awed by the prettiness of it all, yet still felt superior.

"Angela would love this," she announced.

"Your Elisabeth doesn't."

"Lizzie doesn't know how to be happy."

The words were out of her mouth, carried in a slipstream of resentment. A friend of hers, and Lizzie had been a good friend once, was not quite supposed to be a friend in need. Hazel would never be that and Hazel was along for the ride. Purpose; rescue Lizzie from her mother, who would not or could not take her all that distance, selfish cow, whereas Elisabeth herself must not take the train unaided, so here they were. Something like that. Patsy did not want to see Lizzie, first met in a shared flat another lifetime ago, in any other state than the one she remembered best, namely drunk, rudely cheerful and sportingly healthy. The way she had been before her sister had . . . died, for want of a better word. And now, this . . . clumsiness, turning her into a loser. Quite what it was about Mrs. Kennedy which put Hazel on the defensive immediately was something she could not pinpoint afterwards: perhaps it was the rigid dignity and lack of warmth, so alien to Hazel's own style, but her response was to act the clown. She found herself gaping at the staircase and coming over like a gorblimey Cockney released from school to view the interior of a celebrity house featured in *Hello* magazine. "Oooh, what a lovely pitcher! Innit big in 'ere! S'nice, innit, Pat?" But Patsy would not meet her eye. Instead she steadfastly smiled, behaving like a visiting politician until a small dog sniffed wetly round her ankles, then grabbed her calf with two, surprisingly strong paws and began to hump at her leg until she kicked it away roughly. It scuttled and slid into a corner where it barked with loud indignation. Two light grazes appeared on Patsy's waxed calf.

"You'll stay to lunch, of course?" Diana Kennedy murmured.

No cannibal would have wished to roast Elisabeth herself. She had the kind of extreme slenderness which Patsy could only associate with anorexic models, her skin like translucent china, her body like a jangle of wires, moving stiffly, all her athletic grace gone. Walking them round the garden like a tour guide, delighted to see them, grateful, attempting to be natural, she infected them all with itchy awkwardness. They were brown and she was pale, like a plant which had grown long and thin in the dark. The twisted neck reminded Patsy of a cockerel. She found herself speaking loudly, laughing a lot, out of her depth. Lunch amounted to cold ham, limp salad, and a bottle of warm-looking wine plonked in the middle of the dining table, defying anyone to take out the cork. Hazel hinted that a beer would be ever so nice: lager was produced, another following when she downed the first in one. The horrible dog examined toes under the table, and a small boy sat on Elisabeth's left, very close to her, casting venomous looks in the direction of the strangers. As the plates were cleared, appetite depleted rather than satisfied, the boy ceased to lean against Elisabeth, arranged himself bolt upright in his fine chair, clutching the arms of it and weeping. He made no sound in this process; no-one commented, he simply wept. Elisabeth's left hand grasped his and held it until the weeping ceased, as if she was holding him to some agreement, some mutual resolve forged long in advance. The room was cool, but Patsy sweated profusely. Diana Kennedy, dressed in her loose trousers and top, remained irritatingly serene.

Elisabeth's luggage was small enough to fill half the tiny boot of the car, until the boy, no longer weeping, brought her a bag of stones, double-wrapped inside pitted polythene bags which looked as if they had been used a thousand times. He placed the bag alongside hers, carefully, while his grandmother went indoors to fetch a cardigan for Elisabeth. "You might be cold," she murmured when she came back, and then Elisabeth looked as if she might weep, too, oh Christ. The boy was steaming off into the house once his gift was delivered, possibly to hide the resurgence of tears, while the dog barked.

"Get us out of here," Hazel murmured.

She had that slight, lunchtime indigestion, the result of a passable quantity of lager which was not quite enough to ensure either sleep or wakefulness. She got inside the car, her churlishness worsening by the second, aware that both she and Patsy had worn all the wrong things and behaved in the wrong way and this friend, who was Patsy's rather than hers, might, just possibly, be ashamed of them. Lizzie was clasping Mummy, gingerly. The frozen old bitch wasn't crying: she was patting her daughter's back like someone trying to bring up wind in a baby while keeping some distance from any mess which might come out of its mouth.

They set off into the green distance, Elisabeth waving frantically to a couple of indiscriminately old people outside a shop. All three of them were obscurely irritated in an understated way, two of them for having to feel sympathetic in the face of Elisabeth's obvious frailty, the third for having to accept it. They dared not ask her questions. In the backseat by request, Elisabeth turned and looked at the sea until it disappeared from sight.

"So, Lizzie," Hazel asked, uninhibited by the closer ties of friendship, "how are you going to manage in that weird place of yours? All them steps." She hadn't seen the place, only heard it described in unflattering detail. A signpost to the M5 invitation to civilization, cheered her enormously.

"Oh, I'll manage. The exercise will do me good."

"Do you think this is wise?" Patsy asked, too late. "Are you sure your mother wanted you to go?"

"Oh yes, she wanted me to go, she just didn't think she should want it. I wanted to go. I don't want Matthew to miss me too much." She did not expand and they did not persist.

As they drew nearer London, Patsy began to consider the enormity of what they had done. They had taken a sick young woman, albeit at her own request, to deposit her back in her own rented home, a place so eccentric it defied belief. Patsy toyed with the idea of responsibility, irritated by it. This was not the Lizzie she had known: this one was vulnerable. As if reading her mind, Lizzie leant forward, tapped her shoulder.

"I *shall* be all right, you know. Don't worry, I've worked it out, really I have. Don't be so maudlin. You've haven't kidnapped me, you've been very kind. If it all gets too much, I can go back. But I'm sick to death of myself. Tell me news. How's the love life?"

That was better. Elisabeth hungry for gossip, wanting other people to be happy, the way she always had, curious, never jealous Lizzie. Patsy and Hazel exchanged a meaningful look.

"The state of the love life is abysmal," Patsy stated cheerfully. "As it was before you left the scene, only worse. Not that you were coming out to play much, were you?"

"No."

"So Hazel and I and Angela, we've decided to take positive action. We're all enrolling with a dating agency. At least, two of us are, tomorrow . . . Angela's being a bit wet about it. It may not sound momentous to you, but it is. What do you think?"

Looking in the rear-view mirror, all she could see was a pale face, transfixed by horror, the twist of the neck accentuated.

"I'm not sure that's a clever idea. You're joking, aren't you?"

Patsy was suddenly angry. Stuck in her own car with a friend who wasn't even pretending to be fun.

"We've thought about it for weeks, and that's all you can say? Is it wise?" she mimicked. "Wiser than living alone or living with Mummy and getting yourself mugged, isn't it?"

Twenty miles of silence later, and then there was an apologetic laugh from the back.

"You're right, of course you are. Just keep me posted, will you? You don't have to nursemaid me, but I do want to know. Send me signals from the outside world, won't you? Until I can join it."

They called it her ivory tower. This was where Elisabeth lived, without the blessing of belief, in a church. Not, as Patsy might have approved, a glossy conversion no longer inhabited by the ghost of a previous congregation. This was a disused, slightly abused church, set back off the street with a passage down each side where weeds grew out of old gravel. It was disused only in the sense it no longer had parishioners. It was available for use: a soup kitchen at Christmas; meetings twice a week; band practices; exhibitions. The Reverend Flynn liked the exhibitions best. Even when they contained sculptures he did not understand, photographs he could not comprehend, items made of wire which he shuddered to examine and an audience who failed to notice the other surroundings, it was still a time when the glorious space came into its own for another kind of worship. He thought that was the proper, long-term future for a place which had been through so many incarnations since its early Victorian optimism. Victorian planning had erred. The tower looked as if it was simply glued onto the church, an afterthought, with no direct access from one to the other and, without working bells, no particular use.

Letting a helpful policewoman live in the tower bad seemed a good idea once upon a time, subject, like everything else in his worried mind, to second and third thoughts.

Reverend Flynn was here now, all fuss and anxious smiles, dwarfed by a posse of women, standing well back from them, uncertain of the odds and taken by surprise. He was not an old man; he simply looked as if forty years of constant movement had extended themselves into baldness and a twitch.

"Ah! Here you are! Well, what a surprise! Dear, dear me! Are you well, my dear? Yes, you are. No, you're not."

He wore an expression of acute anxiety, as if he had trodden on a nail and was trying to define the pain. Many moons since Elisabeth had helped him out with the vandals, yes. She had noticed the accommodation, yes. She had suggested herself as caretaker, yes, yes, and she paid rent, yes, but there was always a mute suspicion of anyone who wanted to live in the belfry. Although the general lack of fuss, the presence of a person about the place and a whole number of other, positive factors which whizzed in and out of mind like the parish accounts, made him pleased, all things considered, if only there were time to consider them.

"Hallo, vicar," Elisabeth said. "When will you ever stop putting your foot in your mouth? How's things?"

"Terrible. I didn't think you'd ever come back. I've prayed for you."

"Thanks," Elisabeth said, grinning in a way which reassured, despite the twist in her neck. "I'm sure that's made all the difference. Can you help me upstairs?"

He turned towards the others. Their look gave them away; he had seen it before. They wanted to go: they had done enough for one day. Patsy looked up at the front of the church and shivered. The church establishment, once a wonderful joke now spooked her: she could not stand the steps or the remnants of times past. And even if eccentricity in a friend was admirable, this was too much. She handed Revd Flynn a bag of groceries: Hazel put the bag of stones by the side door, equally unwilling to go further. They kissed goodbye airy kisses, not devoid of emotion. Promises to call hung on the air.

"Welcome home," said Flynn.

There was only one way in and one way out: a thick wooden side door. A tall person would bend to go through it and then onwards and slowly upwards, through the foot of the tower via steep spiralling steps, to the next door. About thirty feet of cold, uneven steps, then another door, entering into a huge absurdly high-ceilinged room which had once been the bell ringers' chamber. No-one had rung the bells for more than a decade. The ropes were still looped against the wall. There were elements about the place of a child's playground. Father Flynn dropped the bag he had manouevred up the steps before him and sat with a plumph! on a futon sofa. Then he patted a cushion and looked at it curiously.

"Do you know," he said, "every time I come here, I remember it's not so bad. Your lovely friend keeps it so clean: *so* useful. However did you get this up these steps? I always meant to ask."

"You don't get anything up those steps, Father. Except your own body with a small burden. Everything has to be of the kind which comes apart into small pieces. Probably makes this place highly appropriate for me, now." There was a sheen of perspiration on her forehead; it worried him. The temperature inside was cool, even though the early evening sun slanted through the enormous leaded window of plain glass. The place had missed her, although it looked welcoming. Her friend, lovely man, had seen to that. She would surely be gone by winter, Flynn thought. She *would* have to be, and he should really tell her now what the surveyor had said about the bells. His heart sank unaccountably then rose again as his eye took in the creature comforts she had provided for herself in here. Rugs on the wooden floor. A kitchenette, consisting of two electric rings, a microwave and a tiny fridge. The rudimentary bathroom in the alcove had been there since the Church had begun to convert the place to give it potential for a dwelling, and then given up.

"It *is* nice, you know," he ventured, as if to reassure himself as much as her. "And you don't have to go upstairs to sleep, do you? Not for the time being." The ghost of another smile lit her features again. She was in the corner, making tea. He felt he ought to help and knew she would refuse.

"Yes," she said. "It is. And once the diocese can make up its mind what it wants to do with the place, you'll probably be able to sell it for a small fortune. Until then, it's mine." It was a gentle reminder that she had already lived here for five years, according herself the rights of an occupant. Lived here and suffered here: he knew that. He nursed the tea, then swallowed it in a gulp, burning his mouth. The urge to look at his watch irritated him. He did it all the time, yet punctuality continued to elude him. There was always somewhere to go; some other person in greater need than the one he had seen last: he knew he spread himself too thinly, but could not stop it.

He could fair scamper down those steps, Elisabeth thought, shouting goodbye. He was like an alarmed mouse, scurrying not towards a corner, but to the next crisis. He was saying something as he went. About a cleaner and a key: she missed it. Thought of it when he was gone.

She waited for the slam of the door, a hollow, echoey sound which was a reminder of how solid it was, almost as solid as the door to this room, and the doors to the chambers above. I love living here, Elisabeth thought. Perhaps having a passion for the place one inhabits means that my mother and I are not so dissimilar, after all. Slowly, she mounted the steps to another closed door, and beyond, to the room which housed the clock and her bed. Father Flynn was right of course: she should ignore these levels of her domain, but not until she had proved she could climb to the top. Upwards again, the stairs steeper, the cobwebs gathering. The door of the belfry opened on oiled hinges. And there, dusty in the glorious light, were the bells which no-one used. Eight bells, provided by a benefactor. Seven treble, one tenor. Inscribed on the one side with the words "Robert Cross made me, 1895" and on the other with a dedication. Elisabeth moved around the awkward space and read each. "To God the Father, God the Son, and God the Spirit, Three in One, Be honour Praise, And Glory Given, By all on Earth, And all in Heaven." In the centre of these was the bell for the clock. Elisabeth moved and touched each bell, noting the rotting wood which held them aloft. There were steeply recessed, unglassed windows in the tower: the heat rose up here to a smooth and dusty dryness. On the top step, listening to the breeze which always moaned through the slats covering the narrow openings, Elisabeth Kennedy sat and wept.

She wept for her mother and the things left unsaid. She wept for the sister who had died. She wept for her own ignominious failure to trap the man who had killed her. She wept for herself and the failure which was her life. And she wept for the bells which were not used, like her own heart, rotting away.

Pray for me, Robert Cross.

Pray for me. John Jones, known as Owl, had found himself crossing himself as he passed the church on the way back to the office. Stupid. You prayed for the dead, and then only if you were another generation. Or you prayed for something important, like promotion, in the superstitious belief it might help. That was it. You did not pray for success with girls. You were not supposed to take love seriously: it was simply supposed to happen. You were not supposed to live as your parents had lived, with placid devotion; you were supposed to kick over the traces, regard companionship as an optional extra, like bread on the menu. OK, he had beaten the others to it. The thought of a dating agency had dogged his mind as soon as it was mentioned, but he had cleared the hurdle, done it. He felt himself shriven. The Owl adjusted his specs, went back inside the office. He was pleased that Michael was busy and Rob preoccupied. Big shots. They talked about it; he had gone and done it. He had confessed the need. The girl he would meet through the agency would be blonde; she would be shy; she would be beautiful.

Pray for me, Angela said in the afternoon, thinking of an icon she had once seen, wearing beautiful robes. Her office space was only a desk, with half a screen providing privacy. Inside it, watched by the huge eye of her computer screen, the girl whom Patsy and Hazel treated as a child sat surrounded by carrier bags. So agonized was she about what to wear for this meeting after work, she had carted the lot over the bridge with her in the morning. There would be no prying eyes today: no Patsy and Hazel to ask questions since they were bound for Devon, no insistence that she share the secret of the whole enterprise and ruin it, like exposing a film. There was a teddy bear in the corner with hair the same colour of corn as Angela's own, both of them similarly glassy eyed, as if both were prizes waiting to be won at a fairground. That was what Hazel would say, but Angela was in control, really, she was. She picked up the thick piece of paper, read it once more and stuffed it in her handbag. Then she took it out again, ripped it up and let it fall into the bin, so that no-one else would ever see what she had already memorized.

"Profile: John Jones is thirty years old. He describes himself as loyal, trustworthy and homeloving. He works for a successful company and keeps a cat . . ."

Hardly a mover and shaker, then, Hazel would jeer. Angela shuddered at the thought of scrutiny. A mere three lines and she was trying to convince herself that this might not be love at first sight. What, then? Practice? An adventure? An exercise in hope? The nerves were appalling. She glanced at all the other literature, containing advice. Meet in a public place! Don't invite him home until you know him! Don't forget precautions when meeting a stranger! Forget? They were emblazoned in her memory. The afternoon passed, each hour longer than the last. The clothes were finally planned down to the last detail, although she knew she might still change her mind. Would he like the way she looked? What would an executive want? She would take enormous care with make-up: too much was offputting, too little the sign of a lack of effort, or was it the other way round? First impressions were so important. Meet on the Embankment, six o'clock. He had a nice voice. She could get an hour in at the basement gym, tone everything, appear with the spring in her step and her hair shining, utterly in control.

Late Friday afternoon, the gym was almost empty. One disgruntled girl with wobbly thighs was leaving as Angela arrived.

"Don't know why you bother," the girl grumbled, "figure like yours."

Which had nothing to do with anything, of course. Angela sweated here in order to make herself worthy. She was never comforted by remarks like that, because no-one could see what she saw: a body unduly white and soft, refusing to respond to the kind of punishment which would make it like a ballerina's. All this effort was a way of earning undefined, future rewards, and also of clearing the mind of some of the debris, because as soon as she was on the treadmill, she could think only of her brief sense of superiority for doing it at all. Then she remembered she had not bought shoes to go with the dress in the carrier bag in the locker room; saw as her hands raised in desperation, the vision of herself in the mirror, small, tense, white and shiny with perspiration and her mouth open, a sight so ugly to her own eyes that her legs stopped even as she pressed the button to go faster. The machine went on: Angela catapulted forward, her head cracking against the mirror, the rough surface of the tread moving on, grazing her knees with its inexorable progress, the whirring sound drowning her yells and the one other person in there, laughing loudly before going to help.

The blood washed off in the shower: she was OK, really, yes, fine, but couldn't cancel any more than she could be late, because she only had his office number, not his home, and she couldn't, not at gunpoint, fail to turn up at all, because she knew how that would feel if it was the other way round. She longed for Hazel and Patsy and their teasing; instead there was only the cleaner on the sixth floor. She was shivering in the evening. Fine, totally in control with a bruise and skinned knees, rivetted by the impression she would make. Meet outside Charing Cross on the side of the river. Always meet the man in a public place, dear: we do what we can to safeguard everyone, but we do suggest a busy place for a drink on first acquaintance. *We* screen people for you, but you must take care all the same. She could hear the motherly voice, going on and on.

Angela leant over the wall of the river, ignoring the builders, the meeters and greeters; sick, but suddenly carefree. What did it matter after all? Her hair was yellow tangles, thick and untidy for the lack of time to treat it better. Nor had she managed to cover the bruise beginning to flower level with her hairline along with the small laceration beneath, or to deal with the grazed knees and the two fingers on her right hand where the knuckles were swollen. She looked at these with alarm. There was nowhere in her set of introduction agency instruction which mentioned the kissing of fingers. Men no longer greeted in that fashion.

"I'm sorry I'm late . . . It is, isn't it?" He stood there, appealingly awkward. Smaller than she had imagined, but dark-haired, impressively handsome.

"Angela, Yes. Angela," she breathed.

A breeze rose on the river. The sluggish tide, so deceptive in its power, turned as the warm air idled round her face, wafting the hair into a halo. The eyes which examined each detail were warm and curious, genuinely concerned. She found herself extending her hand, but when he grasped it, squeezing it as he bowed in mock gallantry and moved to kiss those swollen knuckles, she let out a cry of pain. He desisted in the kiss, squeezed again for reassurance. The pressure, gentle though it was, brought tears to her eyes. He rested her hand on the broader palm of his own, examined it carefully. She was wearing her best ring: a small sapphire glinted, briefly.

"You're hurt," he said, gravely. "What did you do?"

"Fell over, running," she muttered.

He laughed. Not like one of the girls would have laughed, but kindly, her hand still resting in his. She could feel his eyes travel to the red raw knees protruding from the tailored skirt which had been the final choice. No tights and no chance to buy some: she felt a fool.

"Running to, or running from?" he asked.

"I don't know," she answered, and her eyes filled with tears.

"I think it's best if I just take you home, don't you?"

She nodded, supremely grateful.

Taxis stormed down the middle lane, hell bent on a dozen destinations. A dwindling number of pedestrians tried to attract them, few paused to watch a wilting blonde being helped into a black cab by a solicitous man.

Pray for me.

The clock in the tower no longer worked. It had a blue face and two hands stuck permanently at ten to three. Elisabeth obeyed Revd Flynn's orders and slept on the downstairs futon, the dial on her watch telling her what time it was. She had looked at the bells, done her weeping, and that was that. Now, two minutes before midnight, and up above her there was the sound of scrabbling rats. Rats in boots, scrabbling at the edge of her dreams.

There were no rats. There was only the blessed silence she had wanted, until the sounds, teasing first, then insistent. Somebody was there. She sat upright with such an abrupt movement that she felt as if a bone in her twisted neck was broken. There was one way in and one way out, she remembered. This was the safest place on earth, her refuge.

And yet, someone was there.

Chapter

SIX

There were many reasons, past and present, why she loved the bell tower. At first, it was the quirkiness of it, as well as the pathos. The tower had stood above her, demanding occupation, dying to be rescued. And then, once it was inhabited, she could boast about it as a feature of her life, it gave her claim to distinction. No ordinary person would choose to live with spiders and Elisabeth had always been at war with the dual desire to merge with the crowd and also remain dramatically different. She knew no-one else who could dwell thus without fear of ghosts: it was the living she feared.

Then there was the ongoing, agnostic love not only of churches, but also of the bells, which always reminded her of the sea, and although these bells would remain silent, she revered their presence. Latterly, she loved the tower because it made her feel safe, preserving her from the demons outside, although she could do nothing about those within. Like Rapunzel, she could choose for whom to let down her hair, and if her tower were assailed, she could hurl missiles over those dangerous steps and cripple intruders. She could retreat to the pinnacle, with the silent bells, and remain inside the barricade for days. A healing place.

There had always been visitors: the man who had stayed for a while, the people who came to call, including the brave and neutered Reverend Flynn with his pockets full of keys. But no-one arrived without invitation. The tower, with its solid doors which enabled her to lock herself into each room, had become perfect for her needs. A gob of fear, feeling like gristle, surfaced in her throat, tasting of bitter disappointment. She longed for that treacherous moment of peace which had preceded such deep, deep, sleep.

Somebody was there and she knew she could not fight: she was weak. The scar on her back itched still: if touched, she would crack, like porcelain. Perhaps it was a new breed of rats, descendants of those who had eaten the rugs before she had driven them out, seduced them into the main body of the church and then into the scrubby garden behind. Regretfully, she had dealt with the mice, miniature survivors who informed their kin and never came back. There was a big, fat cat, feral, but sleek, prowling the perimeters by night, sitting in a shaft of sunlight inside the church by day, but even the cat could not come up the steps unless someone had opened the door and the sounds above her head were more ominous than that.

It was useless to pretend that the sounds she had heard were merely those of the church, breathing out the heat absorbed by day in a series of sighs, creaks and sharp cracks as stone and wood sighed and cooled. Someone had bypassed the door to her living room, gone on and up to the clock chamber and the bed. Even through that high ceiling, the noise of human life was clearly defined. A shuffling. Slurred steps from serious footwear. Now he was coming down.

The steps themselves, dipping slightly in the middle where the greater number of feet had worn away the granite, were soundless; the well of the tower impervious to echo. The heaviest tread of feet became relatively silent; there was none of the clatter the same feet would make moving across wooden floors. She stood behind the door. It swung open with the sound of a dog yawning. Louder than the beating of her pulse.

The room, with its vast window, was never dark. She could have read large print by the light of the moon and she could see him now, stooped to get through, hesitating on the threshold, an animal scenting humanity. He turned, not towards her, but towards the window. She aimed for the back of his neck with the broom. The stave hit his shoulder. Pain shot through her arms, she screamed, the broom clattered to the floor. She jerked, convulsively.

They regarded each other, his body perfectly still, hers in spasms. She could not control the violence of her shivering, the impotence of fear, even as she noticed the sheer size of him. He could pick her up and snap her in half. Would she mind? Would it matter if she were dead? She had so often craved a similar kind of oblivion.

The big man moved away from the blow, lazily, turning his back, unafraid of what she might do and the contempt implicit in his carelessness provoked a reaction. She bent to feel for the boom, fumbled for it and by the time her fingers closed on the handle, he was back with the coverlet from the bed. He draped it round her shoulders, crossed her arms across her chest, then wrapped the material tightly, knotting it behind. Elisabeth was swathed, like an Egyptian mummy. He lifted her, carried her across the room and laid her on the futon with the ritualistic reverence of a priest towards a sacrifice. Then he turned on the light and looked at her, sighed theatrically and wagged a finger.

"Listen, Miss Kennedy, there's something you've got to learn," he said. "If you want to pummel a bloke much bigger and stronger than you, you don't go full-frontal. You could have asked me in nicely, made me a cup of tea and then poured boiling water on me. You could have fucking dialled nine-nine-nine. Why didn't you?"

Her throat was sore.

"Why not?" he repeated.

"They wouldn't be able to get in."

"Ah yes," he said, squatting down beside her, keeping a distance. "The old problem of security. You lock the door behind yourself so firmly no-one can get in unless you get out. Didn't you get my messages?"

He was bulky; his hands large, his chest broad and his clothing was ludicrous. A striped flannel nightshirt, open over his chest, extending below his knees, giving a glimpse of a hairy leg and a skinny calf leading into a pair of unlaced boots. His hair tumbled to his shoulders; a copper bangle on his wrist. Thick eyebrows, unghostly brown eyes, dimples.

"What messages?" Her voice quavered.

"I left messages with a small boy in Devon. In fact, I had long conversations with him. I'm Father Flynn's new cleaner . . . the other one didn't like the ghosts. Anyway, the reverend said, doubtfully, I'll admit, that it was probably OK for me to squat here while you were away, provided you gave me permission. I told him you had; he gave me a key. I lied to him, I'm afraid."

"You're lying now."

He seemed to consider the accusation carefully, like someone struggling to understand a joke.

"No," he said. "I'm not a talented liar at the best of times. Certainly not at the moment." He was looking at her quizzically. She could not return his gaze, although she did examine him. The twist in her neck made her feel as if she was cowering, but the sharpness of the fear was gone.

"Listen," he said. "It's raining."

They both listened. Putter, putter, a sweet sound like a whisper against the huge window. She listened and hated him for her own weakness, loathed him for his calmness, detested his insolence and was afraid of him. Until she noticed again the detail of the nightshirt and the boots. His was a towering presence, and yet the frolicking of her heartbeat had slowed; still she could not move her arms. As if he sensed it, he raised her body with one enormous hand supporting her shoulders, the other loosening her swaddling clothes and plumping the pillow. The duvet was tucked around her, leaving the arms outside. The pores of her skin opened; sweat poured into her eyes: her hair was damp, her face ruddy and she closed her eyes, flushed with heat. There were movements around her. She could feel a damp tissue wiping her forehead and the hollows beneath her eyes, moving to the bones of her neck where perspiration gathered. The duvet was raised from her feet. In the months of nursing, in all her squirming resentment of that enforced touching, the hideous intimacy inflicted on the helpless by the healthy, she had never known such instinctive gentleness.

"Sorry," he said formally. "My name's Joe. I've no credentials. I'll go in the morning, but you really can't chuck me out in this." The rain had reached a crescendo of feather drums, hissing at the window without real force. She was warm now.

Chuck him out? The deference in his voice, the very ideal that anything of the kind was remotely possible, or that she might be in any position to insist—as if she could leap up with her china body and throw his hand downstairs, let alone his arm—made her want to giggle, although the sound which emerged was a helpless grunt and then she was suddenly monstrously tired all over again. Like her own life and death, what did it matter what he did? It was pain she feared. As long as pain was not imminent, she did not care. She was only dimly aware of her silence becoming the same thing as compliance or of him pressing a mug of lukewarm milk into her hands and sitting on the end of the bed, eating an apple.

"I'm mending the clock," he said, chattily. "What do you think? Don't mind the noise in the morning."

"You won't be here in the morning," she murmured. "I'll have chucked you out. Piece by piece. I'll lift you over my head."

He watched her. She was unable to fight that drift back into sleep: helpless against it.

Then he went back upstairs in his nightshirt and his boots. There was ample room for the other, large futon in the room which held the clock. He lay down on it, still in the nightshirt, hands crossed behind his head, and looking down at his boots, listening to the rain. It was slightly damp in here and smelled of oil. He had alarmed her, which was the last of his intentions, and he felt sorry for it. Jenkins would not be impressed. He had given Joe this crazy address in the hope that Joe would look out for his other protegé, not scare the woman to death.

Poor old Joe, he thought to himself. So quick to take the hint, but so impetuous around human beings, especially of the female kind. Better with the inanimate: better at photographs of objects and the dead. Better at most things than this. Quite happy to sleep with a pile of defunct machinery, and the clock was very definitely deceased.

Outside, according to the blue face of it, time stood still and nothing changed. What a sensitive soul you are, Joe, he told himself, trapped in a bulldog's body, big eyes, all snout and muscle, no bark or bite.

What the hell do you think you're doing?

At least, Jones told himself, he did not wear pyjamas. He looked at his own reflection, sadly. No wonder they called him the Owl. He could remember a note left on his desk at school, to be read in front of witnesses. Dear Jones, I would swim the deepest ocean for you, cross the driest desert for you, scale the highest mountain for you . . . PS, I'll be round tomorrow night if it's not raining. Love, Cleo: the secret light of his life at the time. How they had laughed and how he had played into their hands with his look of blank incomprehension. Nothing had changed much, except his head had grown to match the size of his ears. Mr. Charisma, squinting into the glass and trying to tell himself that the girl had simply failed to turn up because her mum was ill. Not a question of her seeing him first and running for cover; nor was it a question of him failing to see her because he was taking his specs on and off, wondering which way to present himself, clear-sighted, or comfortingly studious. Owl had never got on with contact lenses, always lost them. So much for stealing a march on the others and getting to the introduction agency first. All he had to his credit for this foolhardy piece of enterprise was a new line in rejection. It was certainly a coup to be dismissed by a girl before he had even met her. He wondered if he would have the courage to go back and try again. He looked round his neat suburban nest which somehow lacked a woman's touch and wondered, for the umpteenth time, why it was that the total bastards of his acquaintance always had success with the opposite sex, even though they offered nothing and he offered so much. He gave his heart on a plate, only to be asked if it could be eaten cold inside a sandwich. The girl, the one love of his life, she could do whatever she wanted; it would not occur to him to question or curtail. Owl wouldn't mind at all if she wanted to change the kitchen: in fact he would be grateful. He would not care if she said his choice in everything was lousy, including his clothes, although, come to think of it, he might be a bit sensitive about that. Dad called him bourgeois and Mum called him lovely. He wasn't fat. He had no undesirable habits. True, he wasn't charming like Michael, but he wasn't a pig like Rob or weird like Joe; he had a good job and money in the bank. He was offering fidelity, consistency, adoration and the continuation of the species. What was wrong with him?

Nothing. That was the problem. Until now he had never thought that he could ever be described as frightening but perhaps she had been repelled by the power of him she had seen from a distance. The thought bucked him up considerably. He bared his teeth. Perfect, white and even. Nice skin. If only that last phone call which had made him five minutes late, had never happened.

"Faint heart," he told the mirror, "never won Fair Lady."

Saturday morning the sun shone brightly, deceptive in its brilliance. In the shadows cast by the buildings across the narrow street where they sat, it was chilly.

"I see you dressed for the occasion," Patsy remarked. "More than you did yesterday."

"Oh shut up."

"You look like Miss Angela. Not exactly a woman of the world. Pretty, though." Angela was always mentioned, a benchmark to their bolder selves.

Hazel did not favour girly clothes and yet today, she had worn them: a dress of printed cotton, demure in the extreme, a trifle creased here and there and bit droopy round the hem, but attempting an image of femininity. Patsy had never seen Hazel in a skirt before, let alone a dress. Hazel had plump, short legs which were not her best feature. To Patsy's mind, the dress improved the overripe raw material.

"At least it ain't power dressing," Hazel snapped. "The way you look, this old hag will get you a New Man in a pinny with a permanent limp. A male chambermaid."

"It's only a suit," Patsy protested.

"Yeah. Only. You nervous or what? No, course not. You just haven't got nothing which isn't suit, or party. Am I right or am I right?"

She finished her coffee, stood up and hoisted a duffel bag which went ill with the dulcid frock. It looked as if it should contain the kit of a plumber or a selection of lethal weapons. Patsy imagined the IRA carrying around bags like that. Looking as furtive and determined as Hazel did now.

"Right. Your turn first. I'm going shopping. See you later. *Don't* tell me about it."

So it was Patsy who examined the descriptions at street level, next to the men's outfitters, Patsy who ascended the stairs in ever increasing darkness and knocked at the door. She made herself feel like the working woman she was (words like career woman were hopelessly out of date: any woman worth her salt had a career), remembering her poise, but all the same she was uncomfortably aware that this was no ordinary mission and nothing in her life to date had prepared her for what she should be and what she should say. Patsy had revised her image many times, from punk to shirtwaister to designer dress, from wildly ruffled to well groomed, from sporty to elegant and the other way round, but none of these changes had ever created the image of what she felt now. A thirty-something spinster with money in one pocket and a begging bowl in the other. The door to "Select Friends" was open. There was music in the background, Handel on a harpsichord, tinkling away at a reassuring level. There was a small outer room on this floor with a pretty desk, on which papers and leaflets were stacked against an enormous turquoise vase, containing a display of flowers so large it seemed to fill the room. Tall lilies stood resplendent among yellow and blue gladioli, surrounded by a cloud of fern, a wedding bouquet to dwarf the tallest bride. The smell was overpowering, as if the flowers had stood guard all night with the windows closed. Patsy touched the tallest lily. The bloom was waxen, and a tiny shower of bright orange pollen fell onto the back of her hand. If I filled my house with flowers, she thought, I would have to spend a fortune, and this indication of Select Friends prosperity cheered her. The desk was an antique replica, polished to a shine, without a trace of pollen or dust. The chair beside it was empty. Patsy stood uncertainly, wondering if she should shout hello towards the half-closed door which led from this vestibule. As she paused a voice echoed back at her, "Helloeeee! Do come in dear. Patsy isn't it? Sorry, we're a bit behind this morning."

Before her stood a smart lady of late middle age, with fashionable glasses and a summer suit of royal blue. The light from a window was behind her, blurring her features as she sat at a second desk, this one far more official than the decorative item beyond. There was a chair facing her, towards which she waved a ringed hand, and more flowers on a wooden filing cabinet to her left and the same smell, overlayed with perfume. The room was like an official bower, reminding Patsy of the waiting room of an expensive private dentist she had once used. Comfort.

"Kettle's on," said Mrs. Smythe, placidly, before launching into words. "Now dear, I know it takes a bit of courage to come to a place like this, but in case you were wondering, it might just be the best thing you've ever done. It's a jungle out there, isn't it? Beautiful girl like you must have a queue of men waiting in the wings, but that isn't the point, is it? It's finding the right kind of man to complement all the things you are. Emancipation hasn't done us all the favours we might have wished, don't I know it! I'm willing to bet that the sort of men you meet are either frightened of you or see you as a strong rock to which they can cling like limpets."

It was an accurate enough analysis, although Patsy was confused by the speed of delivery. She thought of Ben the impoverished, David the liar and John who had been decent and dull.

"Normally, you see, you'll meet a small range of men, all at a different stage in their lives to the one you've reached," Mrs. Smythe continued. "Either they're partnered, married, or still sowing wild oats. It takes them such a long time to realize the importance of stability, poor darlings, and it goes against the grain with any of them to admit it. Not manly, you see. They like saying they're islands, capable of standing alone. But the men who come to this agency are not like that. They've realized they've got stuck in the wrong groove. Playing the field has lost its allure. And they're all solvent, dear, as well as interesting. I wouldn't have them otherwise. I don't suppose you take sugar, do you?"

Patsy was so mesmerized she had not noticed the swift mechanics of tea making until a delicate cup and saucer appeared on the desk in front of her. The aroma of Earl Grey cut across the scent of the flowers. She could have been in the presence of Gypsy Rose Lee. Mrs. Smythe's smooth recitative could have been speaking her own mind. She felt rather emotional.

"There's a large form to fill out, dear," Mrs. Smythe was murmuring. "Because I need to know everything about you so that I can do my best, my very best. I hope you won't find it intrusive. Would you like me to leave you alone to do it by yourself, sorry the light isn't so good in here, or shall I help you?"

"Help me," said Patsy and meant it, looking at the form which had appeared as miraculously as the tea. It was a room which seemed to be in a constant state of evening, dim without being cheerless, womb-like, comforting without being cloying and, the woman on the other side of the desk, with her soft hypnotic voice, was like a fond but strict mother of the kind she had never had. All Patsy's ideas of how to behave went in flux: she was used to control and now she was pre-pared to relinquish it entirely. She had come prepared to fend off per-sonal questions, be economical with truth in the interest of image: now she was desperate to confide. Together they went through the form. Name, date and place of birth was the most innocuous infor-mation she was going to provide. It was what she said in between, the bits she forgot, later which took the time.

How did she decorate her flat? Did she like antiques? Not quite right, modern furniture was more her style now, along with designer clothes. How had she got on with her parents? Badly, a fact bitterly regretted since both were dead. No point of reference, you know? She found herself on the verge of tears. And why did she think she found it difficult to allow a man to get close? Did she react to criticism? What colour did she like best? How does one cope with loneliness? What were her worst fears? *How did you make people love you?* And that, in between what it was she wanted from a man.

Faith, hope, loyalty, love, friendship. "Is that all?" the woman laughed. Patsy, by nature deeply suspicious, laughed too. She came out of the agency feeling exhausted and inspired; a person who had con-fessed inside a cosy confessional and been granted not only forgiveness but the promise of a new life. Two hours had passed. The shadows had moved from one side of the street to the other. Hazel was waiting, the sun in her eyes.

"So what's she like?" she demanded. "This Mrs. Smythe, what's she like?"

Patsy felt dazed. Her hesitation was infuriating.

"She's nice," she said lamely. "Nice."

Hazel with the droopy hem and the jaunty step crossed the road and went up the steps. Patsy sat where she was, nursing a coffee, wondering without any self-criticism, how it was she had come to say so much, and drink, with such enjoyment, a kind of tea she had never liked.

When Hazel descended much later, far less aggressively than she had embarked, she met a man at the outer door. He stepped back with a slight bow and a smile to let her pass. She blinked at him and the outside world, stepped in front of him with murmured thanks and a wider smile, turned back to look as he bounded up the stairs. Not quite her taste, she conceded, as his immaculate brogues and the cuffs of his cords disappeared from sight: not tall enough and far too conventional, but if that were an example of the calibre of male who paid their money and took their chance at this agency, things were looking up. She wondered if Mrs. Smythe could drag as much information out of a man as she could from any woman. She did not doubt it for more than a minute.

He took the penultimate flight of steps two at a time and then on the last flight, slowed down and proceeded quietly, so that when he arrived at the open door, she had not heard him. Mrs. Smythe was wrapping up the flowers from the outer desk: there was a loud crinkling of stiff polythene and she was struggling to fasten an elastic band round the awkward stems, the better to carry them home. Her business for the day was done and she did not approve of waste. The task was absorbing; she was swearing under her breath as the slippy stalks evaded her grasp. Around her head, there was a halo of smoke from her cigarette which hung precariously from the corner of her pale mouth, giving her the look of an old-fashioned barmaid. To his eyes, the hair complimented that image. A dark golden crop today, as if she designed herself to match the flowers. He pulled at the cord which secured the spectacles hanging across her bosom: she dropped the flowers and let out a shriek. He picked up the flowers for her and began to rearrange them.

"Don't do that, darling. You creep everywhere, creep, creep, creep. You're nothing but a big creep."

He looked cross and crestfallen: he pouted. She could never look at him without a flush of pride which was more than maternal. It was a kind of wonder that she could ever, in her last, late flowering, have produced a creature who was quite so perfect. When Mrs. Smythe had visited the Adriatic, she had stared at depictions of Adonis with scorn: they were nothing like this. A picture of a Madonna and child in Italy had her making comparisons and finding the baby depicted such a poor specimen alongside hers. Photos of blithe young military heros with perfect hair and teeth provoked a similar reaction: so did portraits of divine aristocrats in the National Portrait Gallery. How could anyone parade their child as perfect when her son existed? He only ever pulled a face to annoy her: it worked every time.

"Don't do that, darling. Ruins your looks. I can't tell you, sweetheart, what a morning I've had. Late again, hid the computer, one must, of course," she pointed at the laptop standing by the door. "And then, the girls . . . Well I shall have some fun with them. Two friends, couldn't be more different from one another. Life's rich pattern, eh?" He pouted again: she wished he would stop it. He was managing to nod and pout at the same time, like a child doing a party trick.

"They're all so fucking pretty," Mrs. Smythe stormed. "So sodding perfect, so well paid, so absolutely pathetic in their little ambitions. Darling, thanks for that little man with specs, but where are the others? I need fifteen. I thought speccy four-eyes was so dull I could put him with last week's blonde, just to kick her off. With a bit of luck they'd bore one another to death inside an hour. Besides, he was the only man in the right age group. I know he was one of yours. Why can't I ever get enough men?"

"You could advertise, like before."

"Oh yes. Such a lot of trouble. Needs must. How are you, darling? So nice to see you unexpectedly. Even if you do creep. Oh my God, what's the matter?"

He was taller than she. In order to hug her and bury his head in her chest, he had sat on the outer office chair, embracing her round the waist. She could feel the dampness of his tears against her blouse. Her bosom was ample: she felt sticky in the hollow between her breasts; the place where he had so often rested his head. He was born with the most marvellous head of hair, and while most baby hair of that quality gave way to something worse, his improved. Thick hair, well styled: she cut it herself and knew, as her fingers touched it, how it felt almost as if it could be carved. She pressed his head into her breast, and then, with a savage yank, pulled it away, with her fingers twisted into the roots of his dark locks, staring into his eyes.

"Mummy," he said. "Mummy, Mummy, Mummy—"

"Has Mickey been a bad boy?" she cooed, releasing his hair. She rescued the cigarette end, plucked it out of her mouth, wincing as it stuck to her lip. She dunked the end into the turquoise flower vase and listened to the faint hiss which she wanted to emulate, only louder. She clasped him and resumed her stroking, unhinged and infuriated as she always was by his crying. The sound of his weeping, screaming, yelling for the few seconds when she had ever left him in his babyhood, would haunt her for the rest of her life. If he cried now, it meant that yet again, she had failed him, or, that he, yet again, had failed her.

"What is it, petlamb, sshhh, what is it?" He sobbed. If she detected something a little too forced about his grief, as though this display of emotion was as much for effect as genuine sorrow, she threw the thought aside as disloyal. Her roving eye caught the laptop standing ready for removal.

"You haven't been inside my machine again, have you?"

He nodded, insofar as he could. "Mummy," he repeated. The voice was muffled. "Mummy, Mummy, Mummy."

"And what did you find?"

"Nothing."

She yanked back his head again, extending his neck. Such an edible thing, a baby's neck. She noticed faint scratches on his face. Pressed his head back into her bosom rather than take a second look.

"Oh God," she said, reaching for another cigarette. "Oh bloody God."

The only time she had ever seen anything as perfect as her son had been the face of Christ on a crucifix in church. That too, would always haunt her. His face, wearing a crown of thorns. Wearily, she pulled off her wig. Let him see her own crown. The pink, shiny, bald patch down one side. Remind him of what he owed her. "What have you done," she wailed. "What have you done this time?"

Chapter

SEVEN

Diana Kennedy was sitting on the sea shore, watching the sun descend, exhausted by her own efforts to play with her grandson. Please leave me alone, he had said: you can watch if you want. She was ashamed because she was only making the attempt in the hope he would tell her secrets. If he would only love her in a proper childish manner, sharing his dreams with her, instead of in this dutiful, more or less obedient but distant way, she might be able to love him back. Let her hair down and become a shrieking, playful granny.

The only time he talked openly was when they swam and immediately afterwards. He could swim well, but he was afraid of the water and liked someone to go with him. Then he would shriek at the waves and say silly things.

The Persians, he told her, think that the world stands on a whopping great big sapphire, and that's what makes the sky blue, see? Like a mirror! The Persians cannot have lived here in winter, she had said, but this was a day in which Diana could believe in any myth, if only nature had allowed her to be a believer. She looked at the boy. He needed someone to make something of his rough stone; a kind of lapidary, perhaps. She was echoing the analogies of her dead husband. He had never stopped making these kind of allusions, spoken with reference to Elisabeth. They irritated her and yet stuck in her mind. He would have said that Matthew needed someone to study him, find the direction of the grain, examine the flaws, mark the place, cut and create the facets which would show the quality. As it was, he was more moonshine than moonstone.

Matthew lived between two houses; the small one owned by his father up the hill, and Diana's, where he spent his days when the weather was fine and his father at work, flitting in and out of the kitchen for meals and more or less obeying the stricture not to go too far away. When he was not on the beach or the garden he was in Audrey and Donald Compton's bric-a-brac shop, a venue of which Diana did not entirely approve, but at least he was safe and they swore he was not a nuisance. He collected stones and polished them in a tumbler in the bedroom he often used overnight, washing them with a greater enthusiasm that he ever had for washing himself and always in a way which filthied the bathroom. He seemed self-sufficient in his entertainments, or at least absorbed, although Diana had overheard his long conversations with imaginary companions. She had also heard the rumour that he was backward, and could not bear the thought that anyone would say anything derogatory about him. She yawned. He had the same colouring as his mother, but try as she might, Diana could not see him as compensation or a substitute for Emma, because he did not need her, and if he asked one more time when Elisabeth was coming back, Diana would . . . She did not know what she would do; speak to him sharply, perhaps.

No, he was not a gem stone suitable for a brilliant cut. He was a stone more suitable for carving. Jade, turqouise, lapus lazuli, like the colour the sky would become over the cliffs in an hour. Throw him amongst other children and he landed like a pebble.

It is our fault, she told herself. We make our children what they are, without the faintest idea of what we are doing.

"I'm hungry," he said, sitting by her deckchair in a way which showed he was poised for flight. Diana rummaged in her bag and handed him a pear which he took with thanks even though she knew he would have preferred something else. A polite little boy.

"When's Elisabeth coming back?" he asked. "She said she would show me the bells."

"Do you think it's time to go in?" she asked.

"No." He was very definite, open to neither bullying nor persuasion. Had he been born like that, or made?

Take the way they had treated him after his mother's death. He had been in the house. He was found hiding in his room. Diana knew how unreasonable it was to despise him for that; he was too small for his intervention to have made any difference, but it still seemed unmanly, even in a child. Make him relive it, some counsellor had said. He must talk through it, otherwise the experience will traumatize him for life, as if it would not, otherwise. So they had tried, the professionals and the amateurs, battered him gently with questions, cross-examined him with kid gloves so the bruises never showed, while Elisabeth howled her protest. And a fat lot of good it did them all. Matthew failed to communicate: they were none the wiser and he became as silent as his mother's grave. I was sleeping, he had lisped with his thumb in his mouth; very sleeping. He looked so innocent when he was asleep and Diana did not believe it.

"They said Matthew was wearing his mother's rings when they found him," Audrey Compton said to Donald as they sat enthroned at the back of the antique shop, one hundred yards away from the beach and comfortably situated at the top of the street. There was another shop, dealing in serious furniture, delicious porcelain and ancient lamps further down and better placed. Tasteful stuff, Audrey remarked cheerfully, not like us. Bric-a-brac stood outside on the pavement to lure in the customers and also because there was no room inside. There had been protests about this disfiguring litter on a public thoroughfare, until Audrey, never one to resist battle, had pointed out that it stood in the recess of their window, on their own property, and it came inside at night, and if the population didn't like it, they could lump it. Just because they didn't want three-legged chairs, 1960s table lamps and the sort of stock most of them would throw away, other people did, so there, and if they did not *shut up,* she would publish a list of all those well-to-do locals who came in to the shop to *sell.* Audrey had resisted what she called barrack-room language in this particular debate with the chief signatory of the petition. Otherwise, she could swear like a trooper or talk like the better kind of duchess. So Donald said.

"Poor little sod," he remarked now. "Who says he was wearing his mum's rings, and why not anyway? He's nothing but a mite now, he was only eight then. I buried my mum's wedding ring in the garden at that age, couldn't remember where I'd put it. Christ, there was a fuss."

"Someone told me that it was *assumed,*" Audrey stressed the word, accentuating her appetite for gossip and also her unwillingness to accept reportage as correct, "that the boy had let in the man who murdered her mother. Matt's fingerprints were on the inside of the door, none others so clearly detectable. Not his mum's, not the murderer's. Mum must have cleaned awfully thoroughly. What the hell kind of household is it where people clean door handles?"

"Such persons are not sane," Donald said.

"But they were selling their house, so they might have been keeping it sparkling. The way one does."

"The way one doesn't." They both laughed, his a deep belly rumble, hers a body-crumpling, tears-to-the-eyes cackle which erupted a minimum of ten times a day. She was a beauty, he thought, a beauty.

"But if they were selling the house, mightn't the murderer have been someone coming to look at it? Oh, they'd know if it was someone coming from the agents, the cops could find that out, but what if it was someone coming off the street. Looking at a 'for sale' sign and thinking, I fancy that. Or I fancy what's inside that."

Audrey and Donald had a deep and bitter mistrust of estate agents. Their shop stood opposite one: the proximity hurt, on a daily basis. They couldn't get over the idea of anyone being paid to sell something without risk or promise. Still, the fellows and the lady over there were at least well mannered, and if Steven did not work so near, they would never have had Matthew standing at the door and saying, "Can I please come in?"

Audrey was comfortably large, with a figure far more Victorian than most of her artefacts. She was rounded at every angle, a waist, a bosom, the calves of her legs and her forearms muscular, while her

ankles and feet were particularly small. The laughter had shaken the
crumbs which decorated Donald's sweater, onto his lap. When he
stood up, they would join the others round the legs of his chair. "Want
any help?" he bellowed, peering round the alterpiece which stood on
the table in front of them, sheilding them from view. Audrey was partially deaf: he partially blind: between them they could scent a customer from a hundred yards. Audrey continued mending the catch on
a gold chain, while the customer stood bemused, reading a plethora of
handwritten notices, attached to objects. PLEASE handle with care.
SIT on this at your peril! NO credit cards! If you drop this it's
YOURS!

There was a huge armchair standing by the front door, occupied
solely by an equally large box which held the skeleton of a chandelier.

Junk, from floor to ceiling, or that was what it looked liked. Nice
things happened to jostle with not so nice. They did not care. Audrey
officiated at local antique fairs with a few, selected items and behind
the table and the alterpiece, stuck inside a Tesco bag, or hanging round
her neck, was the serious side of the business. One had to have knowledge, or recommendation from an existing customer before one asked
either to buy or to sell. Only Matthew was allowed to play with the
emeralds.

"A boy who feels that way about stones has got to be a good boy,"
was Audrey's verdict. Matthew had crept closer when she had been
mending a broach, whenever that was, Easter time, in the holidays.
She had ignored him and let him hover until he stood looking over her
shoulder, breathing deeply. At one point he had sniffed and she had
handed him her hankie without a word. The next day he was back,
and the day after that he appeared again, this time with a topaz ring
which he said he had borrowed from his granny.

"And you'll take it right back in a minute," Audrey said carefully,
"before she notices." His big eyes, met her gaze and held the challenge. He was either truthful, an actor, or utterly stupid. She did not
say she had seen the topaz ring before. Diana Kennedy had been disappointed in the valuation.

"I want to know what it is, first. Why does she like it?"

"It's a nice stone, topaz," she told him. "Quite hard, nothing like a
diamond, and it can be broken easily down a line. You might be able
to scratch your name on glass with it, but you could still do it a lot of

damage with an accidental knock. This one was pink, which made it rarer than other forms. It could range in colour from no colour, to golden brown or blue." Did he know that when it was found, it could look like any old pebble, rounded by water? And that you measured its weight in carats, after the carob seed? And that such a thing could have great value or none at all? No, he did not know, but he liked pebbles. His aunt had bought him a tumbler for polishing. Audrey showed him a small diamond, made him look at it, then showed him a fire opal which made him gasp. "There are flames inside there," he said. After that, he came often, on the way home from school in term time. He had deft fingers where hers had grown less so. She taught him how to bite a pearl to test it and how to rethread a string making tiny knots in between each bead, and as a reward, gave him a lump of rose quartz to take home. "Put it on the window ledge and look at it in the light," she told him. "There's another kind of fire in there."

"Have you got any old dinky toys?" the customer asked now.

"Nope."

"Railway memorabilia?"

"Nope."

"Dolls?"

"Somewhere."

Donald turned to his wife. "How on earth can we be expected to know what we've got?" he said in an injured whisper.

"Rumour has it," Audrey continued, immovable from the subject of Matthew because she had not seen him today and whenever he was absent for long, she worried, "that Mattie's grandad left a cache of jewels somewhere. He was always disappointed that his wife never took the faintest interest in what was his passion and by the time he died, he pretty well loathed her anyway. His shop wasn't doing well . . . do you remember it? He put his capital in raw stones and hid them somewhere, so that she wouldn't find them and she'd have to work for a living. Hid them in such a way that the next generation might find them," she added dramatically.

"Rotten old miser."

Donald unwrapped a boiled sweet of the kind no-one else liked any more and pushed it to one corner of his mouth. A sudden, unworthy suspicion assailed him.

"Audrey, my dearest darling, you aren't by any remote chance encouraging this little chap in the hope he'll lead you to buried treasure, are you? We don't even know what *we've* got."

She slapped his knuckle, lightly. He was right: the thought was unworthy. What would they do with treasure, even apart from what they had? Furniture, objets d'art, chandeliers even; all acquired from those suffering temporary financial embarrassments over the years. It was both diplomatic and natural to forget who had sold them what.

"No, of course not. I don't believe a word of it anyway. Although I did know Dorian Kennedy all those years ago and he was a very strange, bitter man indeed. Done it!"

She slipped the mended chain into a box and stuffed it into the Tesco bag. He marvelled at her eyesight.

"No, I like Matthew hanging round because he's an extra pair of eyes and because he's . . . he's . . ."

"A gem," Donald finished. "Like his mother was?"

Audrey considered and shook her head. "Nope. That one was a softer stone. A nice piece of amber. Never fully formed."

The day resumed.

If the church below and to the left of Joe's feet was still in use, and this was the sabbath, then the congregation would be gathering. On balance, and although he regretted it, Joe was pleased that the clock did not work. Imagine, sleeping here to the sound of a massive ticking: it would induce madness, a kind of tinnitus, hearing life marching forward in seconds. He could see all his movements being made in tune to a giant metronome, everything done to a set speed. In the clock chamber, the high windows were on his left and right and the bed faced the backside of the clock. From his pillow, Joe could see two double doors, one at floor level which opened on to the pendulum, the second set several feet above the first and approached by a rickety set of wooden steps leading to a platform. Open these doors and one could step into an aperture behind the clock, where a man could stand to adjust it or to wind it, as someone had, once a week. Joe had tried, just for fun, but although the key turned, the machinery was fractured, the pendulum lay detached inside its own shelter, like an anchor without a purpose, and the hands of the clock would always remain at ten to three. He had tried to work out what it needed: he used the clock as a plaything and it had often occurred to him, in the weeks before Elisabeth returned from Devon, to move the hands of the clock forward from ten to three, just by five minutes, to see if anyone outside noticed. Since he did not particularly wish to draw attention, he had desisted. Instead, he toyed with the idea of dispensing with a pendulum and running the clock off a large battery, making it into a sort of huge wristwatch. The thought of a digital face peering out of the tower amused him too. Typical, this endless absorption with ephemera. There is no sense of priorities in your life, Joe, he told himself. You are always allowing yourself to be distracted by things which have no real importance. But the clock, and above all the workings of the clock, had proved a marvellous distraction while he waited, an uninvited guest in Elisabeth's empty tower, and made him feel less guilty about insinuating himself into the Reverend Flynn's favour with all those lies. At least he was doing something. The clock was beautiful, even though it might never function again, or the bell above it ring, and that was the whole point.

Joe went downstairs, squaring his shoulders. Stop messing about. Elisabeth was dressed and the bed tidy. Her hair was caught behind in a slide and he wondered if that had been difficult to do, because as he knew from his own, it took two hands to create a pony-tail and one of hers had only recently come out of a sling. But for God's sake, she was a convalescent, not a patient and, standing in the doorway, he reminded himself not to let slip the fact that he already knew even that much about her. She was a stranger, right? They were strangers to one another. He was relieved, but slightly miffed by her failure to recognize him. He was just a man who had taken her photograph and given her a rose and made no impact whatever. Typical.

Elisabeth was trying to open a tin. Beans, he noticed. Heinz baked beans, the stuff of student flautulence and good health. There were periods of his life when he had lived on little else. She was swearing.

"Good morning," he said.

"What's good about it?" she asked. "I've got a trespasser in my own home and I can't open a tin of beans. That's good?" There was a smell of burnt toast.

"Let me." He took the tin and opener from her hands, removed the blackened stumps of bread from the very old, no longer regulatable, toaster and began again. The surface of the table was spotless; the kitchenette area shone: she had been busy. They sat without a further word and consumed beans on toast. A knife and fork presented her with no problem, he noticed; nor would most tasks demanding less specific strength than an ancient tin opener which required the user to lean on it with full body weight. Of which she had so little. Joe coughed and stood up to make coffee.

"Milk? Sugar? You could do with a new tin opener. In fact the kitchen stuff could do with an update. I gather from this little lot that cooking has never been much of a priority."

"You wouldn't have to be a detective. When are you leaving? I could call you a taxi." Smoke curled from her cigarette. The light in here was blinding: it struck him as odd to be inside a room so light and yet so enclosed. You would have to stand on a chair in order to look out and even then the view through leadened panes and wavy glass would be imperfect. Perhaps that was what she wanted; height above the world and no view of it. A tower not of ivory, but of cold stone.

"It's all right," he said. "I've got a car, of sorts. Hidden wealth, you see. But no friends in high places."

"Plenty in low places, I imagine," she said, sharply. "Don't mess with me, Joe-without-credentials. I may be disabled, mentally and physically, but I used to be a police officer. More people apart with my teeth. Friends and enemies in high places, see?"

"And I used to be a medical student," Joe responded. "Only, I turned out to be more interested in anatomy than health. So that if you wished to tear me apart, I could tell you exactly how to do it with the greatest economy of energy. Or keep up a helpful running commentary while you performed. Like a butcher with a trainee."

She shuddered, a trembling of disgust.

He had not wanted to frighten her, but this total absence of fear unnerved him even more. Last night, a tremulous terror; this morning an icy and articulate distance clad in an almost friendly veneer. He could placate fear; he was accustomed to his large size creating a kind of reverence and respect, and found himself a little piqued that she did not seem to see in daylight the contrast between his size and her frailty. Such is vanity, but what could he do to re-establish the authority his bulk demanded, even among men? Roar?

"What are you going to do?" she asked. "Roar?"

Another spiral of cigarette smoke rose towards the distance of the ceiling. He watched it, doggedly, wondering what happened to smoke when it disappeared.

"I phoned Father Flynn," Elisabeth went on in her flat monotone. "He gets up early, which is more than can be said for some. Established you are what you say you are, cleaner of the parish. He says you turned up for some exhibition, said you were a friend and asked for a job. Medical student to cleaner, eh? I'm glad your career path is upwardly mobile."

She did not add that Flynn's breathless reference had been glowing. Or that it had sounded so wistful. "Lovely big man," Flynn had said, "came in with some others having an exhibition, as I remember, and never left: so kind of you to let him stay. An old friend, is he?" Nor did Elisabeth mention how her own fury at this outrageous intrusion was tempered by a sense of the ridiculous. Five in the morning, with the first sign of light, had seen her creeping up the stone steps to the clock chamber, clutching the key to that door, which she found in the cutlery drawer. Five past five, if only the clock had kept a record, had seen her leaving. She could not, even in her parlous state, feel fear for a creature so blithely dead to the world, clad in boots and nightshirt, with arms crossed behind head. So she had locked him in as a precaution until she could speak to Reverend Flynn, after which she was not inclined to let him out, but had still relented and crept back up again before he woke, and turned the key the other way. He was not so clever after all: he was arrogant. And the knowledge that she could so effectively have immobilized him turned the tables, whatever those were. She had won a battle for power without the other protagonist even knowing he had been engaged in it. The stupid man slept like a log.

He had none of the wariness of a thief, she had thought, although she mistrusted her judgement on that, as she did on everything, and there was something familiar about him, not the face but the voice, which had also diminished the fear into something smaller. I could have stabbed you, handcuffed you, at least locked you up, she told him, silently. And I detest long hair on a man, even hair as clean and shiny as yours. I don't like men unless they resemble little boys like

Matthew, which they only do in sleep. Otherwise, a man was a snake. Or a slug, leaving a trail of slime which clung to the clothes and transferred itself to the skin.

"Could you give me a day or two to remove my gear?" he was asking. "I can move myself pronto, but property takes longer."

"What property?"

"Oh . . . a coupla cameras. Things like that."

She nodded, oddly enjoying herself.

"Cameras? The typical equipment of a cleaner. What are you, a spy?"

"Wouldn't mind, if only it paid. A little industrial espionage wouldn't come amiss, if anyone would have me. Freelance photography of shop fronts and parish cleaning keeps a small wolf from the door, but not the larger variety."

He looked like a wolf, she decided. The hirsute kind who should have eaten Little Red Riding Hood and choked on the cloak.

"No wolves at my front door," Elisabeth said.

"Flynn would not approve of unChristian conduct on any day before Sunday," Joe said.

Flynn wanted him to stay. Flynn had been told a pack of lies and was halfway in love, she decided. She wanted him to go. Do not take on a large man full-frontal, he had said. She moved to her tidy bed, still puffing on the cigarette, and fumbled under the pillow. Then she held aloft a camera in her left arm, the strong arm which could conduct an orchestra. All he could see in the big, light room with the sun coming through the windows, was his Leica, held above her head.

"Don't know anything about cameras," she said, with a note of something slightly apologetic in her voice. "Except that they break."

"I can open tins," Joe said, desperately. It was not the best camera, only his favourite.

"Go," she said, flatly.

"Tomorrow?" He was half on his feet, ready to lunge, but she was far, far away.

"Now."

He did not move. She let the camera drop and it fell with a sickening sound. Not crunch, but thump. The sort of sound which could make someone pick it up, shake it and hope it was well, knowing it was not. He went.

—

Patsy came round on the Sunday evening. There was a man, weeding the ground round the side. About time, she thought, wondering how Lizzie could ever live here, wanting to keep the visit short and even shorter when Lizzie toyed with the wine instead of drinking it.

"Are you worried about something, Liz?" What a stupid question. This sullen friend was still seriously injured, looked half-starved, was unemployed and for the time being unemployable.

"Worry? I'm never quite sure what worry is. I looked it up, once. The dictionary says it is a troubled state of mind, arising from the frets and cares of life. Or, alternatively, the act of biting and shaking an animal so as to injure and kill it. No, I'm rejecting worry as being pointless, but I have, in the secondary meaning, been worried." Oh God; she still did that. Took refuge in words, went off at tangents, anything to avoid speaking clearly.

"Why did you leave the police, Liz? You never really explained." She never really explained anything, Patsy remembered in a fresh wave of irritation. She wanted a breakdown of some sort: she wanted Lizzie in tears, but Elisabeth remained so calm, and Patsy left, still in daylight without any explanations. "Don't come down," she said, "I'll be careful to close the door behind me." Coming out into the dusk and walking up the side of the church which she did not like to leave at night, Patsy felt faintly treacherous, again. It seemed wrong to leave Elisabeth alone, although that was clearly what she wanted. Yes, she had a phone, with answer machine, the only sound which really pentrated up and down in that tower; yes, she could get to a local shop; yes she had enough to entertain her; but it still seemed wrong. Then, coming towards her from the direction of her own car in the road, Patsy saw a man, his face obscured by a huge bunch of flowers.

She turned and watched him place them by the door of the tower, and then rather than stare, she started her car and left. She did not wait to see him go in.

Ahha. That was why Lizzie had left her family. That was why she was less than rapturous in her welcomes. It was a case of *cherchez l'homme,* just like that time when she had been incommunicado for six months, when she had been so bloody mysterious. That would have been a man, too. Elisabeth was not alone after all.

Patsy herself was the only one alone.

No-one had bought her flowers in a long time. They thought she could buy her own.

How did you make someone love you?

Darkness. It was odd that Elisabeth should find herself pacing the floor, talking to herself as she might have talked to the stranger. Imagining there was that large, strange man, listening intently.

Well you see, I've made yet another mistake with Patsy. I love her dearly in the full knowledge of what she is. But as soon as I saw her, I knew I wasn't ready to face her, even though I asked for the chance. And all because at that one point in my life, when nothing else mattered but catching that bastard killer I pretended to be her. I took her name and her background, turning myself into another person, bolder and more attractive, the sort who can seduce men. Make them love her. I lied. Took her name in vain, and lied. She went to the bookshelf and dragged a manuscript from the back. There was a suspicious lack of dust about the shelves. She read from the pages.

"There can be no doubt that the accused was the subject of deliberate and sustained entrapment by this anonymous policewoman, and that thereafter his responses, including the expression of his fantasies, were the subject of subtle manipulation designed to extract a confession. Behaviour which betrays not merely excessive zeal, but a substantial attempt to incriminate a suspect by positive and deceptive conduct of the grossest kind."

She put down the manuscript, feeling that all too familiar shame. There was nothing of which to be proud, no leeway in the words. The only saving grace in the whole debacle was the fact that her family had never known: they had applauded the efforts of an anonymous woman and never needed to know who that was. The judge's only kindness was to agree to that.

Entrapment of the *grossest kind*. She nodded. So that was what she had done. Assumed another persona, a gross one. She had hardly done justice to Patsy as a role model. She had stalked a man. In one way, killed him. So it was only fair that life and the real Patsy would exact a revenge.

Chapter

EIGHT

Elisabeth saw the flowers when she emerged, early on Monday morning. There were pale yellow roses among foliage, the stalks wrapped into a waterfilled polythene bag, as if whoever had placed them there was taking precautions against their neglect. They would last for days in the shade, like that, but they were looking sad. There was a note attached which said "Sorry," but it was the flowers themselves which startled her and made her heart pound. She had been more or less indoors since the Friday evening and this was the start of a new chapter. Sod the flowers. Today she was going to make herself merge with the crowds and not feel afraid. She was going to find her brave identity.

She had beaten the rush hour, but still the crowds pressed, giving her the sensation of standing beneath a wall which was about to fall. The escalator down into the Underground surrounded her with breathless warmth; she wanted to put her hands in front of her face and clear it away like cobwebs. She stood on the platform with the cleaners and early risers from a dozen industries and tried to look normal while longing for the colder days when a scarf would hide her wasted neck. The angle of her head gave her such a perverted view of everything. Looking at a poster, she could only see the snarling face of the villain in the new movie, never the blue eyes of the heroine. She read the advertisements from the bottom to the top, finding in each that they ended with a lie and began with a half-truth. On the train, she looked down like everyone else, then looked up, impressed at how easily everyone managed to avoid each other's eyes. She had what she wanted after all. Anonymity. They were all ugly people; she could ride along with them and no-one would notice. She got off the train at Charing Cross, walked up and through the main concourse of the railway station. What was it her father had said? *You have lost your eye for beauty . . . lose that you lose everything.*

The first surge of the commuter crowd was beginning. They loped through the barrier like a pack of dogs as she sidestepped her way into daylight and walked down a street to the river.

The street was dirty, and outside the shops, litter awaited collection. It was one of those streets which had moved from sleazy to scruffy. This too, was what she had wanted. A street where people plodded without pausing, always en route to somewhere else. And then there was the river.

Elisabeth walked by the water, then leaned over the parapet and looked at it. Water was always poetic, but this, at full tide, brown and boiling, was angrier than the sea. It could carry a body for miles and it was poisonous. It lured the unwary by the promise of pleasure: it would be the star of the millennium. In November there would be fireworks reflected in the water, as there was the first time she had met Jack here. Lured him.

From the middle parapet, at a later date, the fool had jumped.

Hazel did not notice the river as she crossed it at Blackfriars. She regarded all that water beneath the bridge, heaving away, with indifference. Londoners were a filthy lot, chucking rubbish in the water for about three hundred years, and on a warm grey day like this, it showed. A churning river making its way to God knows where from the devil knows what, behaving as if Monday was the worst day of the week, which it was not, as far as she was concerned. She saw most mornings through a haze, but today, she had a different attitude. Marginally different, anyway.

On Saturday night she had gone to bed with a nice-looking builder youth who had been doing up the flats where she lived. She couldn't help herself, and he had got aggressive when she told him to go on Sunday morning. The idiot thought he had found a billet, but men like that were only for fun. Cliché though it was to recite, the real thing needed brain as well as brawn, or business acumen at least. Inside her handbag, Hazel had this letter. Buttermilk paper: soft to the touch, so thick and fat she could have soaked and eaten it. The woman from the agency worked fast, although Hazel flattered herself that she was an easier candidate to match than most: plainer, simpler, less romantic, perhaps. A pragmatic woman. She stopped halfway across the bridge and read the letter again.

"Profile: Robert Bircham is thirty-ish, extremely fit, six feet tall. He is divorced, without children and he runs his own business. His hobbies are motorsports, fine food, theatre, books and music and he lives in his own house in Greater London . . ."

Right, Hazel had thought on second reading, and thought again on the third, I know what this character could be. A berk, who likes messing around with car engines and writes down the sort of gormless interests a civilized man is supposed to have when he fills in his curriculum vitae. Quotes that he likes books to prove he can read, likes music of course, as one does, but may mean all the usual fucking waltzes. His "own company" might be run, downhill, from his garage and he could be contemplating the sale of his ten-year-old Ford Escort to pay the next instalment of a massive mortage on a disgusting semi. Or, he might not. Might be . . . She shivered. Might be a self-made man to her self-made woman, who would recognize a rising star when he saw one, despite a lack of polish. She had been specific with the woman in the agency about what she had wanted and the woman did not think her requirements odd. He could be any old age, any old shape, but he must have his own house. Everyone else had a house, or at least, a flat of their own, as she had had, once. She had bought on a tide of enthusiasm when property had seemed a more solid investment than gold only to have it repossessed two years later after prices had fallen and the income, about which she had lied, failed to make ends meet. She had shrugged it away at the time, paid the debts, painfully, but ever since, she had suffered a sickness for that elusive sense of security. She wanted her name on a set of deeds, somewhere. She would sell her soul for that, let alone the body. Hazel put the letter back into the envelope and down into the depths of her pocket. It could wait for a while, kept secret. She glanced at the river, and then looked at the back of a man who overtook her with a bouncy stride, a nice, firm bum, displayed in tight jeans.

No, she had to find men in suits: and not any old house would do. Perhaps a house resembling Angela's, without all Angela's frills. Even dimwit Angela had a house. On account of the kind of parents who had never spent money but saved it all to give to her, so that she would be tied to them forever, poor cow.

So where was Angela? They were not unduly worried by her non-appearance at work that morning. Especially after a spy told them that she had been in a high old state of nerves on Friday afternoon, like the timid girl she was, going out later on some red-hot date. Secretive little minx, Hazel had said to Patsy. She's done a runner with some man. She's met someone behind our backs; no wonder she didn't want to go to the agency. She's languishing at home with a bloke she met on the bus. It was possible, but she'd never missed a day's work in two years.

A faint worry then, but only faint. Until the mother phoned in the late afternoon and accused them of kidnapping her daughter, because her darling had failed to pitch up for Sunday lunch. Hazel giggled; it was about time little Angela learned to play truant from that kind of chore. She wanted to tell the old bat to go round and check herself, but Patsy was shaking her head. If it was a case of Angela holed up with a man, the last thing she would want was a visit from mother. That would be the kiss of death, that would.

"We'll go," she said. "We'll go, after work."

Summer London, lazy and crowded out of doors, and there they were again on some errand of mercy. Hazel was annoyed by it, but they'd have a drink or two after. And she still had the letter in her pocket. She could think of nothing else.

Angela's tiny house was in a modern cul-de-sac, sheltering from the big, bad world of suburbia. This was not the sort of place Hazel wanted her house, because it took a train and a bus to reach, and there didn't seem to be a neighbour under the age of eighty. There were grilles at the windows, every piece of glass proofed against burglary. Peering through the kitchen window with the light in her eyes, all Hazel could see was the chintz of the curtains and her own reflection, then a narrow vision of a room with more grilles at the back. This was a miniature cage. She wanted an open house.

"Pretty, isn't it?" Patsy ventured, unable to think of anything else to say. They knocked and shuffled their feet, aware of their own conspicuousness. Such a quiet cul-de-sac. No children playing, no dogs sniffing, as if everyone had forgotten how to go outdoors or lived their lives in the little gardens at the back, each the size of a handkerchief. How bloody boring, Hazel thought, to want to be as private as this, as locked away as this. What was the point of having a house if you had to spend ten minutes getting in and out? To say nothing of the grilles. When she had her house again, the windows would be large and public, so that envious eyes could stare straight through and look at the goodies within, without squinting and peering as she did now, ready to say to Patsy, she's gone; leave it alone, it's up to her when she comes back. There seemed to be a buzzing in her ear, faint and from a far distance, like listening to a swarm of bees. She could only imagine the sound of a swarm, but her eyes were focusing on a bluebottle crawling up the other side of the window. In this house? Angela would have murdered a spider, let alone a fly, which invaded her space: the sight of an insect made Angela her most aggressive. Which was not saying a lot.

Hazel had a dim memory of going away for a couple of days, leaving the remnants of a nice fatty piece of lamb out in her hot kitchen with the window open. Coming back on a stuffy evening to find it covered in angry, blue-hazed flies, vying for space on a shrunken fragment of carcase. Silly Angela, to do something similar. Leave the windows so streaked. As if a hand had clawed them, drawn patterns in steam, before she closed the grilles for the night. Patsy was peering through the door. Counting the flies at the far end of the room, where against all odds, the grille over the glazed doors appeared to be crooked.

"Let's go," said Hazel, full of distaste.

"No."

The old man next door took some rousing from his TV. He accompanied them back with some suspicion, watched Patsy fiddle with the key he kept, standing back in disapproval at all this dramatic nonsense. He insisted on going in first. Then he barged past them and out again so suddenly they were bemused.

The flies buzzed at the small amounts of blood, widely spread. As if she had moved erratically, waving a sprinkler in some strange and savage rite, before someone had stopped her. Brown blood pooled on the blue carpet, stained with a pattern of white beneath her hands, again, not so much blood, as if she had little to spare. Angela lay in a foetal curl, her back resting against the security grilles installed for her own protection. White metal, wrought into a pattern to diminish its predominance, a failed gesture towards design. The grille looked like a set of prison bars: the figure looked as if she had flown towards them, a moth fluttering madly beating blindly at a source of light, and then died with broken wings. The blood was dry. She seemed to have hidden her own head inside a large bath sheet of olive green for shame, as if she wanted no-one to see her, beating her skull against the grille which she gripped with one, curled fist. Her feet were bare. There were white marks on the floor. The place stank of dead meat and terror. The weekend had been hot.

Patsy remembered, irrelevantly, a page from the practical tips section of a magazine. "Bloodstains: Soak as soon as possible in cold, salty water . . . keep changing the water . . . if the stain is old, sponge it with a solution of ammonia . . . leave for two to three minutes . . ." That was surely all they had to do. Throw water at her; soak her, then tell her to get up. They retreated to the door, hands over mouths. The old man was keening.

While they waited for the police, Hazel went back inside. Gagging, she made herself go upstairs. Everything spotless. Only the walk through living room, with two used glasses on a mantelpiece, an empty wine bottle on the floor among the carnage of the chase, and that naked, ringless, hand.

This time Joe counted the stairs up to Jenkins' flat, but by the time he was halfway, he had forgotten the count and told himself it would keep for yet another time. Same entrance, same low-key welcome which did not indicate whether he was expected or not, as if the occupant cared; same mild sensation of rot. Joe could not tell exactly what malaise afflicted Jenkins, but something did. When Joe had known him three years before and had been the butt of his teasing, Jenkins had been a different man. Awkward and belligerent, yes, but never small-minded or indecisive. Joe had considered bringing him flowers. The thought had occurred when he passed a park and seen roses in full bloom, looking overtired on their stems, drooping with heat, but it would have been a pale version of his anarchic self to stoop to the theft of flowers. In the old days, he might have called it liberation of captive assets, but those days were gone, with all their innocence. He had abandoned the stray idea of flowers of any kind and brought instead a pack of cigarettes and a carton of beers. It would make it easier if the man smoked and drank, instead of simply smoking. Joe could drink the whole pack and still count the stairs down, if he was allowed to stay that long, but even while they murmured hellos, he knew he had done the wrong thing and the pack of beer should go straight over the balcony, no matter whom it hit. DI Jenkins could not take his eyes off it, even as Joe sat. He might as well have been staring at a gun. Joe went back, opened the door and slung the pack into the landing. Either he would collect it on the way out, or some other bastard would be lucky. He would have been better to liberate the flowers.

"Water or coffee? That's the choice."

"Coffee. Yes. No. Maybe later." Not on an empty stomach, not this man's brew which was real enough to set the nerves dancing and, yet, inside Jenkins shrivelled fatness seemed to sit like liquid cement, never adding or subtracting from the slight but constant tremor.

"I want whisky so I drink coffee and smoke cigarettes, boy. Does that make sense?"

"Life over death, that's all."

Life was a still life in this room. Joe wished he was here to add to this life, instead of both of them examining one, small episode inside an encyclopedia of experience, getting the man to inspect one of the fattest goldfish in his bowl of memories. It would be cruel to inflict this on someone old, but this man was not quite enough to be his father, though he seemed older, and, like his father, the distance between them had nothing to do with age. Joe did not quite know what to do with a fifty-six-year-old who had foresworn drink, any more than he had known what to do with the exhortations of his mother and father to get a proper job darling; get a wife or a life, preferably both. It seemed to Joe that middle-aged people had always been in authority over him, holding out on him, expecting the impossible of him, exasperated by him, and he was not quite sure how to treat them as equals. When they reached his grandfather's age, they stopped being condescending about youth. He must stop making comparisons and take this man for what he was. He would like to take a photo of this face and touch it up with the mischief it had once had, now replaced by a grim, jeering humour.

"Can I bring my camera another time?"

"What for? You working for some glossy magazine?"

"Yup. We need male models." There was a rumble of laughter. The man waved, gesturing the room in general.

"A picture of elegant ruin against the backdrop of my fine decor. You could call it *fin de siècle*. The millennium beckons." He sipped the coffee. "What do you want? Is she well?"

"Elisabeth's fine, but I'm not. I need to know about the man who murdered Emma."

"How could I tell you that? We don't know."

"I want to go over it again. How you found him."

"I've told you, how many times? You found him, even if you didn't know who you'd found. It was all your fault."

"No, it wasn't."

"Oh, all right then. You merely made the observation that there was a resemblance between Emma and another, surviving victim. A casual mention of the rings and the hair. You formed the link. We did the rest. Found your little friend Jack."

"But there was something else, wasn't there? Something which made you sure?"

"Oh yes. Jack had the opportunity." Jenkins was talkative now. "He was devastated by her death: she had been so kind to him, I quote. We saw him in the first neighbourhood roundup. I couldn't bring him in for further questioning: it would blow sky high the only pretence of a lead we had. No way. I didn't even want to get a search warrant, so, as it happens, he was burgled. Such a coincidence. Some person took his videos and his porn movies, had a good look at his love letters, none sent, of course. Poor Jack. Quite an essayist, he was. Fantasies of sexual violence. Odd, he never reported the burglary, but we left his money alone, of course. Had a good look at his documents. He was a regular lonely hearts advertiser. And he had particulars of an introduction agency."

Joe laughed, awkwardly and a little too loud. "Plenty of people have those. It's difficult to meet people these days."

The man scoffed. "Oh is it, *these days?*" he mimicked. "Not in mine, it wasn't. You picked her up on a street corner, threw her in the back of the car and bought her a drink. No-one yelled rape either. What was I saying?"

"The agency. Named?"

"Something poncey. Select Friends." He drank water.

"The woman who ran the place clinched it for me. She said, yes, our man had come along to enrol. She'd fixed him up with one date who had complained. Not only was he undersized and sweaty, his talk was filthy. She called him in, read him the riot act, gave him back his money and showed him the door. He threatened to bash her head in." He shook his head. "Small men, so aggressive, aren't they?"

As if big men were not. That was what Joe had in common with the man he faced: he was aware it was his passport to the confidences he was given, even though the process of getting him to come across with unadorned truth had so far been akin to pulling teeth. Even slumped in his chair, the man knew all about being big and clumsy and the phenomenon of smaller men either running away, regarding him as a challenge or wanting to use him as a battering ram. Jenkins, now relegated to the fifth division of administration to see out his time, would never have trusted a small man. Diminished stature would have made him untrustworthy, like a lad with eyes too close together.

It was like an elaborate dance, with Jenkins, both of them circling one another: Jenkins wanting a partner for his own, obscure purposes and yet resenting him at the same time.

"Why don't you ask Elisabeth all this stuff, instead of asking me?"

"She wouldn't tell me. She's thrown me out."

Jenkins grunted. "You did well to get so far. Try flowers, boy, works every time, try flowers. It makes 'em love you."

"What really happened to Jack?" Joe asked. "What did you do to him?"

"Get stuffed, Joe. You know how it was, boy. You know perfectly well. He fell in love."

"I mean what happened to his murder charge? I was never entirely clear."

"Oh, that? Why do you so love to make an old man go over old ground? The murder charge failed for two reasons. Lizzie got him bang to rights on tape with all the right kind of fantasies. Had him telling her how he wanted to off a woman in exactly the same way Emma had been offed, only smothering her and buggering her at the same time. He even mentioned a plastic sack, although he preferred the idea of a blanket, more refined. Softer, you see, kinder."

"Emma Davey wasn't buggered."

"No, he hadn't got around to that."

"Well . . ." Joe looked around, uncomfortable. He wondered what Jenkins ate.

"Lizzie also got out of him a fairly accurate description of what the body would look like." Jenkins was shouting. "Got him guessing how many kicks it would take to shatter a skull. How hard you have to grind your heel into the neck to crush the thorax. The position in which she would lie when it was finished. Oh, he'd thought about it a lot." He seemed to realize he was shouting, lowered his voice.

"Two reasons why it failed, like I said. The judge took the view at the pretrial that Lizzie had trapped him. Lured him, seduced him, blow-jobbed him senseless, played havoc with his feeling and his prick, so that he would have said anything she suggested . . . anything. So nothing he did say was reliable. It was gross entrapment, he said. Darling soul. He was probably thinking of what he would do if he got his own balls tickled."

Another cigarette: another pause. Joe waited.

"And you know the rest, don't you? It *might* have been a purely legal decision, but it wasn't, quite. After Jack was charged, he went to his brief with a photograph. One of our best. An onsite police photo in glorious technicolour of poor Emma in her final, foetal curl." Jenkins described a curled question mark with his cigarette. "How the hell he got hold of it, God only knows . . . we're supposed to guard them like gold dust, but it raised the fatal question. Did Jack know what she looked like because he'd seen the damage he'd done to her himself, which was *our* case, or did he know because he'd seen a happy snap of the same occasion? The photo clinched it. That was the end, but not before Lizzie was branded. And even though no-one could work out *when* the little shit had got hold of the picture. Was it *before* he told Lizzie how he imagined Emma had looked, or after?"

"You showed *me* the photos," Joe murmured.

"So I did, boy. But you were an expert of sorts and you were on our side. My unofficial helper." He sank further into the chair. "Or at least you were, before either of us knew Jack's name."

"You made me love you . . ." The words of the song rang through Elisabeth's head like distant bells. How had she made the suspect love her? With a man like this creature—lonely, immature, unattractive and insecure, prone to bouts of sentiment and anger because he did not understand anything except hope—it had been easy. Because it was so false. "Look," she had said to him as they strolled along the Embankment, "I like you, but we have to get to know one another. I can't bear anything rushed: it always goes wrong and I can't bear to have my heart broken all over again. We have to be friends first. We have to know how the little black heart of the other one beats, what the mind thinks . . . what we both want. When we have no secrets, we can be intimate; not before." It sounded then, as she spoke it, against the background of the river and the traffic, the most specious, adolescent rubbish and she was almost ashamed to hear it coming out of her mouth, but Jack seemed to listen like a breathless little pupil in school, addressed by teacher for the first time and on the brink of discovery. On that November night he had clasped her cold hand between his two warm ones, stared and nodded agreement.

"I have fantasies," he murmured. "Terrible dreams of sex with faceless persons, dreams of what I would do if they wanted."

"So do I," she had promised, "the same, the very same." I want to know that the man who loves me is powerful enough to kill. Could you do that, lover? Could you? Tell Patsy. C'mon. Tell. He wanted to be led: he begged for leadership and guidance. "All this time," he said, "he had needed someone older and wiser, a woman rather than a girl," and Elisabeth had stood there with his breath warming her face, letting him touch her, leaning into him while the tape recorder worked to perfection. She hated him, hated his wide brown eyes, weak chin and soft, soft hands. "Goodnight, my friend," she had told him and kissed him on the cheek. She would always volunteer affection; it was easier if she touched him first, it gave her more control.

He would boast of what he had done, Jenkins had promised. If he was proud of it, he would boast, or, if he were ashamed, he would seek to justify it, but he would not, in an atmosphere of trust, keep it to himself.

The breeze from the river was becoming cold. Elisabeth had walked and sat through one whole cycle of the tide, telling herself it was over. All over and done and dead and forgotten, and now the evening crowd was coming out to play, their eager faces lit with predatory anticipation. She could see no innocent pleasure in the faces as she watched a couple meet and embrace. So easy to lie.

You have lost your eye for beauty, child. You can only see ugliness.

When she reached her own door in the shade of the tower, she felt for the heavy key she wore tucked into her belt and then noticed how the grounds to the side looked so much tidier with the grass out. The flowers which she had left to their fate this morning were gone.

She had not wanted them this morning: she was sickened by flowers, but this evening, she did. And she wanted to know who had sent them. She could put them on Jack's grave; making amends for something.

Jenkins had run out of cigarettes. Joe had cigarettes, so he was tolerable for longer. Jenkins could sound drunk, even when sober like this, talking almost aimlessly.

"Look, why was she so upset? No, when did she get upset? She was a police officer, not an avenging angel. The suspect, greasy little man, tells her things. Fantasies about subduing a woman, hiding her face. Fucking a body without a head. A woman as compliant as a corpse but not dead, yet. Then he tells her about how he *imagined* the body of his dead friend Emma would have looked . . . beautiful and blurred in death. 'A crushed gem', in his words . . . a shattered pearl. Can you shatter a pearl? Uncannily accurate. He must have known. Or had a psychic imagination. It was all on the very tail end of the tapes. We arrested him."

The cigarette worked as booze would have worked on Joe. The answers, half murmurs, halting and incomplete, lasted as long as the cigarette was half done, anxiety setting in towards the end, so Joe left the open packet on the table.

"*When* was she upset? Oh, when they confronted one another. Want to see? I've got the video. No, not that one, the one on the left. Stick it in, go on."

Joe inserted the video, watched the lighting of another cigarette. A blurring of the screen, a blush of images, a clear picture.

Man in plastic seat in featureless room. Door opens. Enter handsome woman: man leaps up, is restrained. The sound was low, muttered words. They hold him gently, Jenkins and another, smaller man, meaty hands and thin hands pinning down each of his shoulders, this little squire with a pudgy face and thinning hair. If the pressure of their palms caused pain, he did not show it. Inside a second, the restraint was necessary to hold him not down, but upright as he slumped forward. Weeping inconsolably, stretching one hand towards her, pleading. Elisabeth Kennedy, straight as a piece of pipe, hands clasped behind her back, implacable and calm. Joe could have hated anyone as immovable as this, felt himself flinch.

Jenkins laughed softly.

"But she wasn't really like that. Oh yes, God alone knows what she had done to him. She'd begun and ended by hating him, which meant there was nothing she wouldn't, or couldn't do. She could be ruthless." He pointed a piece of bamboo cane at his telly sceen. Joe could see him using it, to thrash.

"Revenge was her motive. She probably slept with him when the tape was off, though he never said so. 'I love you,' he kept on saying, 'you made me love you.' And then she lost it a bit, although that didn't show either. She adored that sister of hers, but dear old Lizzie, revenge weren't her dish. He was only a sad, sick little man, she told me, off the fucking record: and I said you're all cunt and shout, Lizzie. You're supposed to be the hard one, try. All that fucking while, she was soft as butter. If it were all about forgiveness, she would have forgiven him. We went on with it, but the judge, he doesn't forgive Lizzie. He's right. Could have been wrong. Easy."

Coffee, water, a biscuit. Two minutes between cigarettes, the voice rich and tired.

"He called it deception of the grossest kind. Not just a trap, but the grossest. He wasn't a total fool, that judge. He got it clear that our naive little pervert was gobsmacked by Lizzie. Would have done anything. Said anything.

"How *did* he know how the body looked? How did he really know? Was it the photo, or had he always known?"

Jenkins laughter was loud. It reverberated round the room. "Who knows? I fucking don't."

He nodded, as if Joe was management in need of convincing. "We weren't careful enough with those photos."

"Who gave it to him?"

"Someone with a chance. Anyone."

"But did he do it? Jack, our suspect, did he he do it?"

"You do go on. He might have done. After the judge ruled and he was as good as acquitted, the silly little fucker chucked himself in the river. Never listen to judges. Lizzie's never been the same."

He coughed his ghastly cough. "So who showed him the photo, fucked our case? Fucked up Lizzie's life? Thank God I could blame it all on that."

He was restless. Pointed the index finger of the heavy hand Joe had seen on the screen.

"There were dozens of photos, boy. Dozens of people to put one in a pocket. Even you. I let you see them. Could have been you, boy. Could have been you. You boys and we men, we stick together. It could have been you. You'd fingered your friend Jack without knowing it. Felt guilty, didn't you? It could have been you. Go home, Joe. Go home, wherever that is."

Midnight saw Patsy and Hazel huddled together in Patsy's flat. Hours of shocked waiting around, the notation of statements, the trip back to the office to search Angela's desk space, which had been as neat and tidy as a thoroughbred's kennel. Bit obsessive, was she? No, only well trained, a person who kept her life in control and secretly wished it was otherwise. Not a dreamer, not in particular, no. She was pleasant: that was what she was; sweet and biddable and anxious to please and frustrating, because somewhere inside an alternative person was waiting to get out, you know? What kind of person? Oh, I don't quite know, but someone who might realize that she was enviable, powerful even, with her efficient brain, and because she was so pretty; so very, very pretty.

Did you try and influence her? Yes: that was our fault; no, it wasn't. She was our discovery; we made her over for a magazine article. You know the sort of thing, turning a pigeon into a swan, we usually do it in-house. No, it wasn't our responsibility; she liked it. She wanted to turn into a swan.

Once home, reluctant to part, they amazed themselves by the inefficiency of the processes they had witnessed. Jesus, what clods, apart from the woman, all of them running around, trying to make out they were busy, when all the time, nothing seemed to happen. But it was empty rage. Rage and guilt, trying to tell themselves that they were not, at any remove, to blame. Or that they could have altered anything by being there sooner, perhaps on the Friday or Saturday, long before the insects. Miserable, furious, stunned, they were straight into the booze, voraciously hungry but not able to eat, in need of drunkeness, but not quite able to achieve it.

Then Hazel fell into sleep with a suddeness which was insulting, lying on the sofa like a plump puppy waiting to be stroked. The shaking had worn her out. Patsy covered her and then found herself padding around, smoking although it was not her habit but Hazel's, a stranger in her own home, looking for things to do to make herself exhausted enough to follow Hazel's example, and still not wanting to sleep for fear of waking up with the same, awful truth in front of her face.

There was a diesel engine outside. Throbbing. She could not look. Clean the kitchen. Already clean. Make coffee, no; eat, drink some more, Christ. Check the post.

The gas bill, the electric, the service charge, three postal offers full of cheats and lies and a buttermilk envelope. She opened it at the narrow end, as if trying to preserve it: the paper was welcoming to the touch; it seemed to stick to her fingers. It was the one element of hope in a day of destruction.

"Profile: Michael Jacobi is not the the kind of man who has difficulties with women. He is highly presentable, with a good career record. He says he is looking for a woman who is serious about partnership, because those he has met so far never are. He believes that two people should know one another well before they even embark on a relationship. They should be friends first, lovers later. He wants to hold and protect."

There was more. Patsy bit into the corner of the envelope and let her teeth sink into the paper, yumm, disregarding how it tasted foul, like a mouthful of glue. This was it. Out of all this carnage, promise with a capital P. Get a life. She was quite out of control, weepy and sleepy, the alcohol and shock working its own delayed response as she stumbled to bed and made her last resolution before sleep hit her.

I must, must, must, phone him tomorrow.

Chapter

NINE

"Look," said the Owl, muttering into the phone, "I don't want to complain, but—"

"That's what I'm here for, my dear. To listen."

"That girl, last Friday. She never turned up."

There was a long silence.

"Can you come and see me?"

He knew he looked furtive. It was five o'clock now and still hot: a muggy heat which made food decay and milk turn sour in the carton. Desks were emptying in all directions; no-one would miss him. And yes, he was angry enough, having thought about it, to take a taxi from his premises to hers and go all the way up those stairs. He'd been miserable at the weekend and yesterday, thinking about it and only calling today, late, sick of the seesaw of emotions which interrupted his life. Why shouldn't he complain? It cost enough.

Girls littered the route, lining the streets, not one of them blonde. The dim stairwell of Select Friends' premises, seemed crowded. All four floors below were in the act of emptying their workaday occupants, minor officials, computer kids, strange creatures emerging from small rooms in a headlong rush home. Owl kept his head down and his feet plodding upward.

Once inside the sanctum, the heavy scent of flowers seemed familiar, as if he had been a visitor a dozen times instead of once, and he was calmer, immediately. From the half-open door to her office, there came the murmur of a voice on a phone. In the tiny foyer, a desk apparently occupied by a receptionist stood empty with a jacket over a chair, as it had before. He waited.

She was smiling, like a waiter, formal rather than sincere.

"Sorry to keep you waiting out there. My assistant's gone home, you see." She shut the door behind them and sat heavily in her swivel chair. Owl had not noticed the furniture before; he also noticed now that she was older than he had first imagined. All the indignation he had planned faded as he watched her take off her spectacles and rub her eyes, like his favourite aunt. A copy of the late edition of the *Evening Standard* lay on her desk, open at the second page. He felt the way he did in the dentist, reluctant to describe his own symptoms, while she looked as if she might cry, which unnerved him more.

"Look, my dear, we might be in trouble."

"Pardon?"

"You heard me," she said wearily.

He felt chastened. His lack of confidence always made him react with a spasm of guilt at the merest hint of accusation, however obscure; he was always expecting something to be his fault, although the reference to "we" in this context, where he was the paying customer, puzzled him.

"Yes, I heard, but I don't understand what you're talking about. I only phoned to say that my date didn't turn up on Friday night and I wondered if you'd heard from her, because if this is what I've got to expect from any girl you introduce, it all seems a bit of a waste of time." The anger returned in force.

She pushed the open copy of the London paper towards him. In the corner, Owl saw the blurred snapshot of a smiling face half obscured by hair which the camera had rendered a shocking white. "Young woman murdered at home . . . Angela Collier, advertising executive, battered to death."

"Your date," Mrs. Smythe said, briskly.

The print blurred in front of his eyes. He had not seen the newspaper. Photographs were deliberately excluded from the agency's arrangements. (Can't have people being prejudiced by looks, dear, can we?) There had only been Angela's pleasing, hesitant voice on the phone and the profile he had carried in his pocket and the curiosity which had filled his waking dreams. He believed, all the same, that this was his Angela. The page dropped from his fingers.

"I told you, I didn't meet her," he whispered. "She didn't turn up. I was five minutes late. She wasn't there."

Mrs. Smythe nodded. "I knew it must be something like that. Don't worry, dear, I believe you. Even if others might not."

One hand moved to the pearls round her neck, while the other dabbed at her eyes. She opened a drawer in her desk and took out a bottle of sherry and two glasses, poured liberally, suddenly more businesslike. He hated sherry, but the gesture of solidarity appealled.

"I believe you," she continued in a normal, if slightly hostile tone from which any sadness had disappeared, "because she phoned me in the afternoon, a bit nervous, you know, seemed to be a bit hazy about the place and the time. I do like to be on hand for the nervous ones." She pushed the sherry glass towards him, an ornate thing with a red-coloured stem and the association of redness and blood made him shudder.

"And I also believe you because of the newspaper," she added, talking by now as if the conversation was entirely normal, stabbing one ringed finger towards the printed words on the floor on his side of the desk.

"It said," she continued, speaking of the Standard as if it were the oracle, "that a security guard taking the air outside Charing Cross saw her waiting. Then she met someone she seemed to know and got in a taxi with him. 'A good-looking man with thick hair,' he said, and that, dear, is hardly a description which could be applied to you."

Alarmed as he was, Owl registered the insult.

"And I believe you most of all," Mrs. Smythe finished, "because no one, I mean, no man who belongs to this agency could do any such thing! Harm a hair on any girl's head, for that matter! The idea! So it can't have been you. I simply don't deal with people like that."

Part of him wanted to laugh since her fervent announcement seemed to refer to persons who spat on carpets or swore, rather than murdered, but her belief was reassuringly absolute. Aunty would not tolerate a homicidal maniac, handsome though he may be. For the first time in his life, he felt his own lack of height and looks might be an advantage.

"So what do we do?" he asked. The sherry spilled over his fingers: he imagined the horror of explaining to the police, large men all, how he had hung around the Embankment like a fool, how he had gone to an introduction agency in the first place. Explaining at work that he was wanted for questioning, laughing off the presence of his picture in the paper and people saying, no smoke without fire when a man helps with enquiries, especially a little, bouncy man with specs and tears in his eyes, one who feared the revulsion and suspicion of women. For one silent and treacherous moment, he felt nothing but anger against Angela Collier and nothing but terrible fear for himself.

"Can't do anything for poor Angela," Mrs. Smythe announced after a pause. "But she and the *Evening Standard* could ruin this agency. So we do nothing."

Again, the "we." This time he did not notice.

"Nothing?"

"Absolutely nothing. I'm not suggesting lies, only silence."

"Won't the police come and see you?" he asked stupidly. Mrs. Smythe sighed, her sherry glass empty. She spoke to him as she might have done to a slow-learning child.

"Why? They won't, unless Angela left your profile and our prospectus lying around waiting to be found by prying eyes, and I did advise her against doing that, like I did you, don't you remember? Always tear up what you might not want other people to see. It's no-one else's business, is it?"

He remembered. It had been part of that confidentiality he had craved and she had created so well. Keep your private life secret, dear, I would; no point exposing yourself to be misunderstood.

"People do tease so," she murmured now. "They tease about the most important, hurtful things, don't they? I don't think ridicule gets any easier, does it? It isn't fair."

Yes, they did tease.

"You and I have so much to lose, dear. Can't have all those other, lovely girls on my books running for cover before you've met them, can we?"

He emerged, blinking into the daylight, with another profile in his hand, conscious that he had been given it as a kind of reward. He read it, going down the road, into the heat of the traffic, from which, post rush hour, all the girls had disappeared, except for those hooked on the arms of other men, happy, talking. He noticed no generation except his own.

"Hazel is thirty. She has a good job with a major company and never seems to meet men, because all her contemporaries at work are women. She says of herself that she is neither fashionable nor trendy, but she's in good nick, sense of humour in fine order. She wants to be loved, cared for and fascinated in return for same. Excellent homemaker . . ."

The Owl thought of his friends, and out of them all, he wanted to talk to Joe.

Joe was in the courtyard. He had just been stung by a wasp: he was holding a bunch of flowers and throwing stones at the window because the ever eccentric bell wouldn't work. He heard a stone land. The phone bleeped. He danced round it. Shut up! Shut UP!

There he was, a giant dancer, with clumsy, uncoordinated steps. The cat observed him from the shadows, both of them a little demented.

"Who is it?"

"Joe?" The Owl's voice sounded close to tears. "Joe, I've got to talk to someone . . ."

"You OK, mate?"

"Not really . . . I dunno . . ." The Owl was a man of few words.

"Look," said Joe. "Don't get upset by anything. Life's too short. Can it wait a day?"

There was a pause and a sigh. "I suppose so." Reception was bad as Joe moved closer to the door.

"Phone again tomorrow, then?"

"What?"

"Tomorrow!" Joe bellowed.

"What are you doing now?" Owl asked. "Why do you sound so funny?"

Joe had the distinct sensation that he was missing something important, but then he was trying to do something important. Anything else would wait.

"What do you think I'm doing? I'm trying to get a female to answer her door."

The feral cat was sliding round his legs. He was the only human being she ever approached. Why me? Why the hell *me?*

The sound of laughter disturbed him. The door had opened while he hissed into the telephone and gently kicked away the cat; the phone had become confused with the flowers and he almost dropped them both.

"I thought it might be you," Elisabeth said. "What do you want?"

"I want to come in. I'm sick of standing outside. I want to come in."

She smiled her crooked smile. The light was fading. She had not had this instinct to laugh at the antics of a fellow human being in a long time. Apart from a small boy who gathered pebbles, and that was not the same.

"Well, you'd better do that," she said. "And stop shouting."

They were all shouting at her without ever opening their mouths. Caroline Smythe survived her journey home with ill grace. She had perfected the knack of everyone on the crowded Underground, and then on the crowded train from Victoria to Clapham Junction, although she gave up smiling on the bus. There was no point, because they all seemed little and old like herself. On the tube, she had found that if she fixed one of the youngish ones with a smile, straight into the eyes, and looked them up and down, or if she simply wore a vacant, tremulous grin, she made them nervous enough to give up a seat. Then she could watch. Sometimes she slipped one of the agency cards into a coat pocket, but only in winter.

The journey was easier in summer, warmer and smellier certainly, but less encumbered by clothes. Her cotton heads showing a fringe in front and curls behind, itched. She could scan the faces and the bodies and work out which of the girls would suit her son, rejecting them within seconds of choosing. She would search ungloved hands for rings, necks and ears for nice pieces of jewellery, let her critical eye judge the state of their hair and their skin, then shake her head and move on to the next. It was crazy to make this journey in the rush hours when she could adjust her hours to suit herself, but she did, often. On days when she was tired, like today, they all came to look so similar.

On the bus, they all looked the same anyway, small or larger humps of people clutching supermarket bags, as if glamour was banned. It was the same when she trudged up her street, near, but oh so far from the trendier regions. It could have been anywhere, and every time she entered the house it seemed smaller.

When an estate agent had introduced it as a "cottage" to her new husband and herself, it had seemed large. Now, it was a claustrophobic little house, split into two flats, hers and his downstairs. She was perfectly well aware of why she endured the rush hour with such patience. There was always the chance Michael would be home. As usual, he was not, so she conducted a conversation with herself, scolding objects for being out of place, padding round on the worn carpet, examining each corner of her shabby abode, walking end to end in a matter of seconds. The lap top and the screen were the only new things. She wondered, not for the first time, if she should change the locks on her portion of the house, so that Michael could only get in if she let him, but the thought was unbearable. He would be hurt, even if he did ignore her as consistently these days as she merely pretended to ignore him. There was a silence about the place which told her he would not be home today, even though, God knows, he owed her. He owed her far more than attention and she was not going to let him forget it.

First, tea; gin in a minute. She adopted the kind of solace her mother had done, talking to the lap top for company, taking stock. Finally she decided, yes, OK, they were out of the woods for the present.

There was a small box room, big enough only for a small bed or desk. It had been his room about the time the bastard husband had abandoned them for the blonde, some time after what Caroline described as her "little accident." She went in. She liked being in a small room with the door shut. The room was always cooler, even on a day like this, for lack of sunlight on this side. Every inch of wallspace was covered in wedding photos, many of them removed from the office. Clients no longer wanted evidence of courtships culminating in white lace and public nuptials. They had never questioned this fictitious evidence, but these days they were keener on more informal success, they wanted partners, so she had bought the photos home.

As Caroline Smythe dived into the drawers of the desk, she spared a thought for Angela Collier, then peered at the photos. Every third one was of herself. Had she really looked like that, and if so, surely she could not have changed so much? No: despite her wonderful hair, she had never been half as pretty as that Angela and never pretty enough to warrant the husband who towered above her. Stupid little Angela, to want such a poisoned chalice as marriage and all for a single day of being admired. The little bitch deserved her fate; she should be glad to have her sweet memory preserved without tarnish from the future. This way, she would never find out what hideous damage a child could do to her, or how a husband would react to the resulting ugliness.

"That Hazel's got better ideas," Caroline muttered. She would find someone for Hazel. Some absolute bastard, with a house. Some poisonous, lecherous wretch, with a house.

"You should think of these, darling," Caroline muttered again, opening the top drawer of the desk. "Better than bricks and mortar." Even without benefit of sunlight, the contents gleamed. An art-nouveau ring, which was a strip of emerald surrounded by diamonds, extending in a wide band two thirds the way round, uncomfortable to wear, but impressive. A two-carat diamond ring, plainly beautiful, with a simple setting. There was an amber broach, nestling in cotton wool, which she did not like as much. Softer than window glass: it needed to be preserved from the others. There were two sets of amethyst earrings, rather elaborate, she thought and besides, the colour was pale, not nearly as interesting as the green tourmaline pendant which always seemed to wink at her. There were three large zircons, two in differing degrees of golden colour, one heat-treated blue, all set in silver. The things people chose, really.

"Poppets," she murmured. "Darlings. What have I done to deserve you? Loved too much, that's what."

They were undisturbed since the last time she had looked, at least three days ago. She rationed out the pleasure of her routine examinations and polishings, in case it should stale. They could all be altered. There was a man who could alter anything.

Then it caught her eye, the latest addition, so glaringly obvious in the centre of them all, she was amazed she had not seen it before. A pink stone with an old fashioned, round rose cut. She held it to the light and examined the tiny pearls which surrounded it. Could be a ruby. She had always wanted a ruby. It was an old ring, with an old setting: one of the little pearls was missing, how annoying. A gorgeous ring which looked as if it might have been bequeathed by a grandmother who had once been flash, in her day. If it was a ruby, she would forgive him. She would forgive him even if it was not.

Caroline tried to remember the first time Michael had stolen a ring for her. When he was little more than a toddler, making his first attempt to compensate for the accident. That ring had been nicked from the thrift shop, but he had the right idea, even then. There was no disgrace in the second-hand.

She leant over the drawer, picked up the ring with steady fingers. Then she spat on it and rubbed it against the cloth of her sleeve. Sherry rich saliva, even after the hour getting home, a tiny trail of spittle, carefully measured, absorbed by the cotton as she slipped it on her finger, turned the ring so the stone faced inside and rubbed it again, lovingly, against her blouse.

Then she found a gold chain from somewhere else, threaded it through the ring and hung the whole round her neck. It nestled into the sweaty warm cleavage of her chest. To be worn in secret, until it knew where it belonged.

Some old lady had told her that. Said it was the safest way to carry 'em. She splashed gin into a glass, felt a moment of sheer happiness. She may have a ruby: she wanted a topaz. She wanted, she wanted, she wanted . . .

A little bit of fucking respect. People bowing when she went out. A bit of class and prestige. She thought of what the cache in the drawer was worth on a good day, snorted. Not enough to retire with pride.

Not the stuff of a generous pension plan. Not enough to make up for what she might have been.

A gracious lady in a large house, surrounded by affection, respect and beautiful daughters. She had always wanted a little girl.

She could have been someone with fine, thick hair instead of her own, uneven stubble with the scarred patches. She had been able to cover them by pulling it all back when she was younger and her hair was thicker. That trick no longer worked.

That's what a son might have done to *you*, Angela, dear. Pulled the chip pan from the stove while you knelt by the oven. Left you screaming and your head a piece of patchwork. That's what happens after weddings.

"I've parcelled up your stuff," Elisabeth said.

It seemed such an old-fashioned way to describe the evidence of a lifestyle. A parcel. Somehow it conjured up an image of several bulky objects wrapped in brown paper, tied with string. What she really meant was two polythene sacks with his belongings jumbled up inside. One dead camera sitting near the kitchen sink, the rest piled alongside a sleeping bag upstairs, a set of tools and the other pair of boots.

"Can I sit down?"

"Yes of course. No hurry." She was like a gracious hostess, with a note of irony. "I'm sorry about your camera. I wanted to make a point, I suppose. I can buy you another. I'm rich."

"You don't look rich." She did not, either. She looked drab, but the smile, even grudgingly given, was a revelation.

"Criminal injuries compensation," she said briefly. "As well as a pay off from my previous employers. I don't need to work for a while. And I'm alive. That's rich. How about you?"

"Me?" The curiosity surprised him. "I told you. There's always enough work out there to make a living. Provided I don't become addicted to luxuries or get a mortgage."

"Dangerous things," she agreed, soberly, not taking her eyes from his face, "but I bet you have one, somewhere. The place where you live. You don't live here. You've only been camping. Why did you bring flowers?"

"To apologise for invading your space," he said smartly, proffering the blooms. She took them from him with a nod. No polythene, she noticed; no ribbon or any clutter. They looked as if they had come straight from a garden. She put them in a blue-speckled jug, arranged them deftly, stood back and admired as if judging a contest.

"Not as grand as the others," she said. "Nicer."

"Which others?" he asked.

"The others. Yesterday."

"Not me. I saw them. I didn't bring them. Promise."

The hand around the flowers was shaking slightly. It reminded him of Jenkins' tremor. She lit a cigarette. They would bond, Jenkins and she, beauty and the beast, over the nicotine. He could suddenly see them as vicious conspirators, infuriating everyone else with their reticence, locked into mutual mistrust, but still united against the world.

"If you didn't leave flowers yesterday morning, who did?"

"How should I know?"

"You know something."

She went to the fridge and pulled out a bottle of wine, handed it to him along with a corkscrew. The foil was ripped from the top of the bottle; an attempt had been made to open it. The corkscrew, like the tin opener, was the ancient kind which required coordination, curses and brute strength. He obliged, remembering not to smile, feeling her eyes shy away from him in irritation. She looked like a girl who needed a drink. According to Jenkins, she had been a girl who liked a drink rather too much, another thing which might have made them allies.

Elisabeth was trying to work out why she did not want to hit Joe, stick a pin in him and make him deflate. It was Matthew. She had told him about Joe on last night's call, only to hear him confess to several conversations with Joe. "I would've explained if you'd have listened," Matt had said, "I did try." The wee swine. Also, she had the dawning realization that whatever his reasons, it was Joe who had kept this place clean. Not Patsy, not any friend of long standing; no-one who had promised. There was a satisfying "popi," the sound of wine glugging into a glass. She took hers, greedily, then held it to the light, wiped the rim and sipped. Taking it for granted that he was invited to share, Joe still felt like a man standing motionless, waiting for a fierce little dog to stop sniffing his fingers and decide he was harmless.

"If you'd let me stay, I wouldn't make a sound. I could open all the bottles as well as the tins. And I could teach you how to defend yourself."

"Against what?"

"The man who brings flowers. The other man who brings flowers. Bloody awful flowers, I might add, but he brought them most days for a fortnight before you got back. As long as he sees a light in the window, he brings flowers. Flynn took the first lot; thought they might be for him. Then we left them. Someone comes and takes them away if you leave them. Carnations, ferns, hothouse stuff, suitable for a funeral on a freezing day. Why does he bother? Is it love?" She was shaking visibly now. The wine glass seemed to clatter against her fine, white teeth.

"Only problem is, he left a gift with the first lot that Flynn took, hanging on a stem. Flynn's too honest to put it into Church funds. Thought it was valuable, or something. He asked me to keep it, since I was a friend of yours."

He proffered, out of his back pocket, a single earring. It was moonstone, set in silver, suspended on a simple wire hook, the stone dull, a pathetic little piece without a partner. She closed her hand around it and felt the wire against her palm.

The time was always ten to three, according to the clockface outside. Time for tea and speculation. She opened her palm and the pale moonstone lay lustreless against her skin. She held her hand away from the table and let the thing drop.

"My sister liked moonstones once upon a time," she said. "My father hated them. He said they symbolized virginity. Innocence preserved. I thought that was amber, with the bugs stuck inside. And then came the meteorite, froze them in life. Or something."

She sipped the wine; spoke as if she was continuing a conversation with herself. She had not liked the loneliness of the last two days: her voice had echoed.

"My father always gave flowers, every Saturday, as if mother hadn't enough in the garden. They must have driven one another mad." She seemed drunk on the single glass of wine, or was it two? He could hear the glug, glug of the bottle, but he kept his eyes on the window, the floor where the moonstone lay, anywhere but her face in case he made her stop. Nobody could be drunk on so little. He noticed the bottle still half full, one large glass each.

"There might have been a label with the first lot," he said. "You'll have to ask Flynn. He lost it."

Her glass was empty. He registered the movement as she threw it against the wall above the sink, his head ducking automatically at the sound of the crash. Only a single goblet, most of the pieces landing on the draining board. They both sat and looked at it for a moment. Then she got up, wearily, fetched a dustpan and brush, removed the fragments from the floor, mopped up the rest carefully with a cloth and put both cloth and dustpan contents inside a paper bag and then into the bin. He watched in silence.

"Do you do that often?" he asked.

"Yes."

She fetched another glass, filled it and refilled his. The small act of destruction seemed to calm her.

"The reverend seems to think the flowers were a superstitious gift of appeasement to the church. You know, to compensate the old girl for the lack of a congregation."

"Then why take them away?"

"Look, *someone* takes them away. Not necessarily the person who brings them. Just someone who hates waste."

"But he's dead," Elisabeth was saying to herself. "He's dead."

"Who's dead?"

She looked at him. The twist to her neck made her look sometimes sad and sometimes sly, but nothing could quell the impact of those enormous blue eyes. The windows of the soul, he remembered. Well, well. All he could see in this soul was trouble.

"The man who used to send the flowers is dead," she explained patiently. "To all intents and purposes, I mean. Dead. I may as well have killed him. Do you still want to stay?"

Trouble, dreadful trouble, as if he did not have enough of that working out what kind of man he was with which kind of future. Rootless, lonely sometimes, a soft enemy, a good friend, drifting from one thing to another with the sole motivation of curiosity. Examining everything objectively, this creature included, generally avoiding trouble: He had no real obligation. Only his own bit of guilt and the half-promise to Jenkins. This was the point when he should leave with his plastic sacks and broken camera, forget about the mortally ill clock and this fractured spirit, and he did not want to do it.

"Yes, please," he said. "I won't be around much, but I want to mend that clock." He was referring to something else. Maybe he was an enemy, but she did not care. All this time, craving to be alone, and now, when it happened, she was letting someone else in, on the basis of a whim and her own, utterly flawed judgement. Because Matt said he sounded nice and because she was a coward who could not face solitude after all.

"There's a condition, of course," she stated, businesslike in one of those sudden changes of mood, "which is perfectly simple. I know you have a studio, some little room somewhere, and I know you aren't a journalist, because I've been through all your things, including your wallet and I would have found a clue. Even I would have found a clue. So I don't need to know who you are. But I do need to know what you want."

Joe was not sure he could answer that. People had been asking him the same question since the age of three and it always seemed to require a serious reply, such as how he would like to save the world, or at least the whale.

"From me, I mean," she prompted. "No, I don't mean from *me*, I mean from this place." She waved her hand airily, encompassing the whole tower. There were strange sounds coming through the wall from the main body of the church below. Only sounds of a certain resonance could penetrate the walls; telephones, the noise of a tuneless trumpet, followed by a few notes from a clarinet. Elisabeth looked at her watch for guidance.

"British Legion band practice," she said, sighing. "Can you answer the question, please? Almost anything will do."

I want to look after people and things which are damaged, he almost said. I want to know why Emma was killed and you, almost killed. I want to know about Jack and who showed the photograph. I want the whole story and for some, unaccountable reason, I want to look after you, ever since I saw you on that hospital gurney and watched you make them laugh. He pretended to deliberate.

"I want some exquisite photographs," he said. "Of broken bells and other things which can be mended, if only anyone would bother."

"I want to be content," she said fiercely, not listening. "Not happy; that's asking too much." She stopped, puzzled by her own outburst, then went on in a murmur, "That's why I left home. I might have stopped Matthew being content. I should never have gone back. One day he'll have a new mother. I'm not brave enough to take that. Not brave at all."

The music beyond the walls grew louder. Laughter penetrated the brickwork far more easily than speech.

"But it's all so ugly," she finished, apologetically. "So very ugly."

"No," he said, thinking slowly of corpses and jewels and paintings, and all the inanimate things of which the lens was witness. "It isn't. Very few things are ugly, you know. You've been ill. You just can't see."

Diana Kennedy had not quite liked to go into her elder daughter's room after she had left with those two frightful girls, nor had she asked Mary to do so, and for all these days, it had fretted her. But with the evening light still strong and the house quiet while her guests were all out to eat, the time seemed right and she had little else to do. They had passed the longest day of summer weeks before, and the prospect of darkening evenings was a relief, because it would be easier to sit in front of a fire, read, sew and do all those contemplative things; whereas the light demanded that she should be more active. She could remember being scolded for reading in the afternoon. Sitting still in daylight seemed almost immoral.

Diana had given Elisabeth the nicest room on this side, of course, so that she could have space and light and a view of the sea. Speaking for herself, she did not want to look at the water every minute and preferred her own room on the corner, which looked over the side road and received less of the gusty winter wind. Elisabeth had shared this room with her sister when they were children: they had liked frightening themselves with the sound of the gales, huddled together, shrieking, before they remembered who they were and began to quarrel again. When they went away, it became a grand spare room, ready, by tacit consent, if either of them came back, in particular Emma and her husband. It was time to clean it now, not because there was any urgency, or a prospective new occupant, but because Matthew, whose little room was next door, had begun to appropriate the space, and that was not to be encouraged. Matthew colonized spare space like an invading army, sending forth a battalion by stealth. He was like roots, going underground. At the moment he was in the bathroom. Diana was grateful she did not have to share it, shuddered to think what he was doing in there to the tune of running water.

To give her her due, Elisabeth had not left a mess of any kind: Diana had checked, but it was fairly messy now. The twin beds were rumpled from bouncing, the window ledges littered with shells and pebbles, the cat which seemed to shadow him curled into a chair. There was a cushion in the middle of Elisabeth's bed depressed by an object in the middle, half covered with a once-clean pillow case. Diana approached; the object moved. She bent closer. The cat stretched, mewed a warning.

A tiny pink snout emerged from the cover tucked around it. There was an earthy smell. Removal of the pillow case, done with a shaky hand, revealed the hedgehog, reacting to this sudden exposure by retreating the snout and ruffling its spines. Fascinated, she could see the presence of small red fleas among them. Then she screamed, ran out of the room and banged on the bathroom door.

"Matthew! Matthew! Get rid of it!"

He was prompt to answer, sticking a tousled head around the door, suspiciously fully dressed. What was he doing with all that water? Didn't he know they had a meter?

"Get rid of it!" she shrieked. He knew exactly what she meant.

"Why?" he asked with an air of injured innocence.

"It's got fleas! I'll have to fumigate the room! It's ugly!"

He marched past her, picked up the hedgehog cusion, pillow case and all, cradled it and tried to kiss it on the nose. He looked at her defiantly.

"It isn't ugly," he said. "It's lovely. Promise."

They regarded one another with mutual defiance. Hostilities, hidden for the last few days, were naked, for once. Then the blaze in his eyes faded.

"Lizzie would have given it milk," he said.

"I am not your Aunt Elisabeth," Diana screamed. "And I'm not your mummy. I will not have this . . . INTIMIDATION!"

He thrust the hedgehog towards her, level with her face, so that the twitching nose, briefly, touched her own.

"I know that," he said. "I hate you. Hate you. HATE YOU!"

Chapter

TEN

Now there was a word. In timid *ashun*. There were no timid ashuns around here, Matthew thought, although there had been at home. London. My friends; my place. The place where I grew crystals in the boiler cupboard, and had to leave them.

You are only as good as the people who love you. Teacher said that. You gotta earn respect. Stoopid. How do you make people love you? What do you have to do? Be good, I'spose, but Lizzie says it wasn't just that. The gooder they are the more boring, sometimes, she said. "Just keep your eyes peeled," she said. "Try not to hurt anyone, and if you get into trouble, try and see why and say sorry even if you don't mean it. Keeps 'em quiet."

"By the way, Matt, I think you're fucking ace. Who gives a shit you aren't good at football? All that overarm stone throwing, you'll be wicked at tennis."

No-one but Lizzie wondered if this was *my* home, and now that she's gone, I don't feel right. She was the only one who played with me and said it was OK to laugh: she was the only one who kept wanting me to hug her and even when it hurt, she hugged me.

I don't like my dad, much, because I don't think he likes me. He is afraid of me. They are all afraid of me. They are all timid ashuns. They want to send me away, just like they sent Lizzie away, even though she says it wasn't like that . . . I don't feel right. They are waiting for something and then they will send me away.

"What she doesn't realize," Audrey said to Donald as they heaved the usual lumber out of the shop and onto the pavement, pausing to wave in regal acknowledgement at a mid-morning acquaintance, "is that you can't live in a place like this and have secrets. You can't be self-contained."

"Who are you talking about, dearest?"

"Diana Kennedy, of course."

"You've got the woman on the brain. Shall we sit outside?"

"Oh, go on then." She always responded to an invitation to sit in the sun as if it was a forbidden treat. He dusted a wooden chair with a flourish and bowed to her as she sat with a thump. The chair wobbled. Audrey balanced herself with one hand against the door frame and felt, with the other, for the trinkets around her neck. Freshwater pearls and three rings on a chain, one of them rather sharp.

"You can't live in any place and be self-contained," he said, joining her on the next-door seat, which wobbled also. "Look at us, exposing ourselves." Audrey was hitching her skirt above her knees, to get the sun. "People will talk."

"People always talk. That's what she doesn't seem to comprehend. Especially if you keep a guest house like a lady of the manor, however upmarket it is. What else do guests do but gossip about the owner? She fascinates them. You wonder what anyone as tight-lipped as that has got to hide."

"A woman of impeccable reputation, and mixed fortunes," Donald observed. "Not above financial need; not quite as rich as she looks like a few people round here. Or at least, she wasn't remember. She sold you something, coupla years ago . . ."

"Oh dear, I thought you'd forgotten. I do so rely on your bad memory. Diamonds, dear. I thought it might have been to pay for her daughter's funeral, but surely Emma's husband would have done that? No, listen, you and I are the only ones around here who exercise discretion—"

"You gossip like mad," he said indignantly.

"I do not! Well, only about peripherals. Things of strictly common interest and common knowledge, like bus timetables, who's moving house, that thieving butcher, Mrs. Jones ridiculous hair colour and her old man's toupee, that sort of thing; nothing personal. Not like that woman yesterday, telling us that Diana Kennedy was having a screaming row with Matthew. She said you could hear it all over the house. And the other guest who was in here saying how she heard her later, scuttling round in the attics, like a demented squirrel. Now that doesn't sound like Diana Kennedy to me. I worry about Matthew."

She shuffled, let go of the door frame. The chair groaned.

"What had he done? And where was he yesterday? And why is his dad so not like a dad, no punching and teasing. They all the time like uncle and nephew, the one taking the other out on a treat. They don't fight, or anything."

He watched, with amusement, the way she settled herself.

"Matt's acting up on account of his aunty buggering off back to London," he suggested. "And, perhaps because it's coming to the end of the season, Diana was searching in the attics for something else to sell. Perhaps he'll tell us. We must find him something *to do*." Donald looked up, waved to someone else, and then stood, with a decisive sigh.

"I know exactly what. Where are you going, dearest? We've only just sat down." Audrey disliked getting in and out of seats; so much effort.

"I'm going inside, aren't I? The little lad won't come and talk if we're sitting out here for everyone to see, will he now? It's like gossip, ain't it? Everyone knows what you're doing, but you feel that much better if you can act as if they don't. See?"

He bent and kissed her powdered cheek. It was always such a pleasure; a whole range of pleasures, from the comfortably erotic to the childhood memory of fresh, soft baked, warm rolls. Every boy should have a girl like this. Make him feel like a lion.

—

Matthew slunk in around two in the afternoon. He bypassed the chandelier in the armchair, without pausing. We could have sat outside for longer and stayed warm, Donald thought, uncharitably. It could get cool in here, even in the height of summer, cool enough for him to wear a sweater at all times, and there was some compensation for the lack of decision in that. The boy looked furtive, but jubilant, so Audrey went straight for the jugular.

"Where have you been then?" She asked, calmly enough, keeping her eyes firmly on the sharp ring which she had removed from round her neck. Horrible, spiky thing, fit to tear flesh; a pink stone held in a platinum claw; she could only think of one woman who might like it.

"What d'you think of this, fatface? And why were you rowing with your granny the night before last? Shame on you, if it was your fault. Mind, I love a good row myself. Don't we, Donald, darling? Ice cream would be nice."

Donald took his cue and shambled off. Matthew held the ring between his fingers, feeling the points of the metal which rose like a miniaure battlement of swords. He looked at it, looked away; felt it again with his eyes closed.

"Nasty," he said. "Horrid."

"Do you think so? D'you know, you could be right. Clever fella, you damn well are right. What the fuck did they do wrong with such a nice stone?"

He felt it again with his eyes still closed, thought about it. He was always flattered when an adult swore in his presence: it made him feel accepted.

"They fenced it in," he said, finally. "With ugly stuff. Don't know what it is. A nice stone should have something to make it look nicer, instead of something to poke an eye out. I think, anyway."

Audrey thumped the table in delight, just hard enough to make the cups, the pens and the tissue paper littering the solid surface vibrate slightly.

"You are absolutely right," she yelled. "You clever little fucker!" Then she lowered her voice, pretending not to see him blush.

"So why was Gran romping round the attics, then? Oh gawd, look at Donald; hovering. He likes semaphore. What he means is what kind of disgusting, bad for us food, do we want? If you give him two fingers it means, get whatever you like. Go on, give him two fingers, he loves it."

Matt gestured, obscenely and violently: Donald, tapped his own head and departed.

"She threw out the hedgehog," Matt said after a pause. "Out the window. Straight out. Yjumph. Plump, out you go. Plump. Fucker."

"Was he hurt?"

Matt shuffled in Donald's chair. He replied with diffidence.

"No. I don't think so. It walked off, anyway. But I thought he might be."

"Which was why you were shouting, I suppose. Here, hold these."

He opened his eyes and found himself with a handful of garnets. A small handful: six carob seeds of something. He made them warm in his palm, although they were warm already. He threw them from one palm to another; three or four fell to the floor, rolled on the dusty carpet. Matt was testing her and she did not move: she wasn't going to scold him for clumsiness. He heard her next question as he bent to pick up his own litter.

"So why was Gran going batty in the attic, then?"

"Oh, she does it from time to time. Looking at Mummy's things. Father used to do it, too."

"Are they mad, or what?"

"Nope. She just thinks that whenever I've been naughty, I've gone up and looked at Mummy's things. Her toys and stuff."

"And do you?" Audrey asked, swallowing a lump in her throat.

"Not any more," he said simply.

They were silent for a minute. He played with the stones recovered from the floor, sorry for having let them fall.

"They've been through those things, so many times," he complained. "Ever since we moved. And Granny found a letter. To Mummy, from Grandpa, in Mummy's writing case. She kept it in her handbag for ages."

"And you read it, I suppose," Audrey suggested carelessly. He shook his head.

"Couldn't read the writing, could I? I pinched it one day, showed it to Aunty Lizzie. She read it to me and told me to put it back. Slushy stuff. To my darling girl, I leave everything I have and all my love, something like that."

"You remember it well."

He was becoming restless. Audrey watched Donald's slow progress towards the front door of the shop with a mixture of exasperation and relief.

"Well, I do, remember it, 'cos Lizzie said it just showed how everyone loved Mummy. Everyone." He emphasized the last word, as if challenging her to deny it. Audrey patted his hand.

"Yes they did, darling. Everyone. But did Grandpa have anything to leave?"

He shook his head. "Nope. But granny thinks he did. Something hidden."

He had a momentary suspicion of her, thinking she might be joining the ranks of all these others who were always asking questions of him. And suddenly he felt claustrophobic, blood rushing to the head. He wanted to be out of here and onto the beach, cool his feet in the water, throw stones, find crabs. He was never lonely by the sea, even though he was slightly afraid of it. But he had sulked through lunch and no-one had forced him to eat it, because Granny was sorry for shouting at him: he was hungry and Donald was bringing greasy sausage rolls and ice cream shaped like a rocket, the kind of food banned at home.

"We missed you, boy," Donald said, "We've got a bit job for you. Has she been swearing at you? Tell her to fuck off," and everything was all right again.

Not all right later though. Sated from this impromptu teatime, the sea had lost its allure but he still did not want to go home. He was supposed to sleep at Dad's house tonight and Matt did not like Dad's house. It was neat and tidy, like a classroom at the beginning of the day, so that any trace he left of himself was startling obvious. Living between two houses, he was often confused, forgot where he was supposed to be, sometimes deliberately. The more self-sufficient he was, the happier they were, and also the more concerned. He made up the existence of friends, but when *they,* meaning Granny and Dad, questioned him closely as to who these friends were and from which families, the edifice of their pretended existence crumbled. Before Lizzie had come home, they had tried to find him friends. There was a lout of a boy, who had been dumped on him one afternoon in spring, a boy who never wished to leave either the television or computer screen. They had argued, mildly, punched one another once, Matthew inflicting the greater damage, to his own surprise, and parted with indifference. Matthew saw him now, around the town, with his own gang, avoiding him as a person not even worth bullying. Then there was the girl they had found for him. "Play with Cathy, Matthew, there's a good boy." He hadn't minded Cathy, but he had managed to make her cry.

He had brought her to play in the steep-sided graveyard with its view of the sea. Matthew knew every inch of these streets: he had either hidden or searched in every corner and he was fond of the graveyard because it was the most untidy place he could find. The environs of the church were beautifully groomed, but the sloping graveyard was difficult to keep and the grass grew long around the older graves. Matthew had made Cathy struggle to read out the legible descriptions and guess how the people had died, especially the children. He had showed her his mother's grave, which clearly unnerved her as much as his suggestion of a game of hide and seek in such a place. He had shut his eyes and counted to one hundred, slowly, obeying the rules with rigid fairness. She had run away.

He had told Lizzie about that, and she had laughed, but by that time Lizzie was his companion so he did not need friends and they had stopped trying to find them for him. It was when Lizzie went out in the evening, he worried. He had waited for the sound of her car coming back, followed her once or twice.

He had waited for her on the night of her birthday, when she went to the pub. Saw the man standing on the other side of the road, not quite hiding, but sort of avoiding the lamp light. Matt had felt foolish all of a sudden, realizing Lizzie would not be pleased to see him; then realizing that he knew this man, although at first he couldn't quite remember from where, until he got home and thought about it. He had seen this man standing by the fire in their London house, ages ago.

And now, there was the same man strolling through the churchyard, looking like any old tourist lost in admiration of the mellow stone walls of the tower. Matthew did not know why his instinct was to run. Ordinarily, the presence of another person would not have prevented him from lying down in the graveyard and letting the long grass tickle his nose, because after a while, anyone who might have noticed went away. He was not afraid of people, merely indifferent: it was they who avoided him. And although no-one had ever asked him and he had not volunteered, even to Lizzie, his sight of this dimly remembered man, he knew in his bones that there was a connection between the man's presence on Lizzie's birthday and Lizzie's absence for so many weeks afterwards. "She got run over," he had been told, and the sheer terror induced by her absence, made him ever more silent. "she got burned by a nutter," he had been told more tersely at school, and then, once she came back from hospital, curiosity had turned quickly into relief, 'cos having her captive where he wanted, stuck in one room, from which she could not move for a long, long time was best of all. He had overheard enough, despite their elaborate precautions, to know that she had not been hit by a car; everything in Budley went too slow, for a start, but everyone said it was all over: the person to blame was far away and everything was going to get better. He had let himself believe that, too.

The man saw him. He looked different in this setting: smaller. He was very clean with thick hair and sunglasses and he reminded Matthew of someone off the telly. Like all the other people who used to visit mum, he was never mentioned because Daddy would not like it. Thick hair, a lot of the stuff, even though it was short: He remembered that: a lot of hair for a smallish man.

"Can you tell me how I get into this church?" the man was shouting as he moved closer. The tone was pleasant, even though they were too far distant for conversation.

Matthew wanted to run, but he was suddenly, horribly unsure of the direction he should take. Uphill, downhill, which house? So he stood still, politely, and let the man catch up, which he did by breaking into a jog so elegant it did not seem to disturb his clothes; soft polo shirt of blinding white, khaki cotton slacks held with a brown leather belt, partly hidden by the sweatshirt tied loosely round his waist, his feet noiseless in canvas shoes. Taking off his sunglasses as he ran those few steps, halting without effort, addressing Matt as loudly as if he were deaf, but grinning nicely.

"So sorry, to shout like that . . . Do you know this church?"

The man gestured to the church towering above them, as if he might possibly be referring to something else. There was no glimmer of recognition in his smile. Matthew nodded. He stood with his arms akimbo, legs wide apart, trying to look streetwise. The violence of his nod made his hair flop into his eyes: that was intentional, too.

"Well, how does one get in? It's locked. Only I want to look at the tower."

"Why's that, then?" Matt ducked his head and scuffed the loose pebbles of the path with his toe. One of the stones glinted: it distracted him for a portion of a second, no longer.

"Because I *do*," Mr. Handsome said impatiently, his eyes moving to the ground and back in the direction of the church. "I suppose all these church towers are the same, aren't they? All the same, but I still want to know."

Load a crap, whatever he was saying.

"You best ask vicar. He live naaxt door," Matt mumbled, adopting a Devon slur which was not his own, pointing vaguely and with less emphasis than the man had pointed. He had no idea where the vicar lived. And then he skipped away, out of reach, but it was really a flight. Humming as he skipped, to make it look careless and rude, dumpy dump dum, he skittered down the path, hoping he looked like someone with something on his mind. Out of sight, he paused, looked back, sauntered, plucked at a daisy from the bank in case he was still, somehow, visible; felt a berk until he started to run. Proper heart-in-throat running, without direction.

Michael Jacobi looked after him. All boys looked the same, but he watched this graceless specimen with regret. He had once been a boy, like that. Released, like a coiled spring, into air like this and encouraged to get dirty. Get covered in soil, that meant, not quite the same as actually being dirty. He had found his first, real friend: run a little wild with a local lad, got into trouble, or what passed for trouble, then. Stealing might still spell trouble now, he supposed, although no-one thought to punish a magpie and his own awareness at the time had been roughly similar.

It had been no more than a conviction that he had a right to pretty things.

He remembered that house: No children, no dogs. As if they were all the same. A newly invented rule for Mother and he, bundled out, as if they were rabid.

He looked back at the tower with impatience. Of course they were all the same and his desire to understand the architecture of the church died as soon as the attempt to see inside was thwarted. It had been a secondary ambition in any event. He had come to look at a grave, and he had done that, noticing with some satisfaction that it was now being tended with pragmatic, rather than daily attention. No more fresh flowers, but a gravel-filled plinth, planted top and bottom with two miniature rose bushes in full bloom. So, Emma did not require much weeding: she was memory now, rather than tragedy.

Michael strode downhill into the town. Work had brought him to Exeter: compulsion the rest of the way. But it was a long way for such a small errand. The high street was full of traffic, marking the five-o'clock exodus of bodies from the beach, cars moving slowly, full of complaining children. Outside the antiques shop, the old couple were about the purposeless business of carrying indoors all the junk they had put outside. They moved with the languidness of age and patience, rather than exhaustion. There was never any hurry or suddenness about anything they did: he remembered that. Except when he walked into the bowels of the shop, and touched the old lady on the shoulder as she stooped by her desk.

"Excuse me," he said. She jumped, turned with her arm extended, ready to slap, almost hitting him, glaring at him with her bright green eyes, suddenly a cat rather than an apple-cheeked senior citizen. He retreated a step: he had been too close and it was only when there was three feet between them that she allowed a smile to reassert itself. The old man came lumbering up from behind, coughing warningly. He seemed to be in possession of a large, weighty pan.

"I'm so sorry," Michael said, the apology, as always, automatic, whipping off the glasses with a practised gesture. "I didn't mean to startle you. I thought I might have missed you and I've got an urgent errand. You wouldn't happen to have anything with a ruby in it, would you? For my mother?"

Donald went outside, putting down the pan gently as he went to water the window boxes. This was not his part of the business. He admired it, but it was not his.

Tomorrow, they would do something about the chandelier. First thing in the morning.

They had begun rather well in the morning. It felt like a beginning. Elisabeth did not quite see it like that, but Joe did. She did not know she was being carefully handled, but Joe was half aware of what he was doing. Or thought he was. Trying to distract her.

He was looking up at the bare bulb, far above his head, and they were talking in desultory fashion about how the room in which they sat could be improved. The morning was dark and thundery, showing signs of promise. He decided talking about common ground was safe. It was all they shared. A respect for the place they were in: an accidental affection. The more his interest showed, the more she would accept him.

"That light," he referred to the huge bulb meagrely dressed in a large, tin shade, "makes it all look a bit spartan after dark, even with the lamps. Needs something different."

"Could be very contemporary," she said, suddenly animated. "Paint the walls blinding white. Have a dozen or so tiny little halogen lamps recessed into the ceiling. Paint the ropes black. It would look like a film set for something. Is that what you mean?"

"Black geometric chairs," Joe said. "Italian, of course. A black and white rug, like a chessboard. The chairs could be the pieces."

She was smiling and shaking her head.

"Nope. Definitely not. It would alienate the ghosts."

"You could start with a book on *feng shui.*"

She too, looked at the light. Crossed her thin arms and leaned back. Absorbed.

"Something to fill the space. A sort of upside-down Christmas tree, with fairy lights. Could I get something to grow upside down? My nephew would like that."

"Something magnificient and silly and decorative," he agreed. "To make it look more like a folly."

She seemed to lose interest, as if the prospect of change was all too much.

"It is a folly. And probably a folly to live here. Why make it look more like one? Why make an effort at all?"

That was the way she was at the moment, he surmised. Full of the diffidence of the depressed, trying to rally, but finding everything difficult, not sure she had the will or the energy for it. His father had told him it was ever thus with convalescents, with all of Dad's robust common sense. You should have been a doctor, Joe: you're good with patients.

He had heard her talk in her sleep this morning as he crept to the bathroom. "It's over, get on with it," she was muttering, which sounded like a contradiction in terms. Joe decided he would call her Elisabeth. Other people might call her Lizzie, even her nephew, but he would not. He struggled to keep the conversation afloat. It was no good finding something to talk about and then letting it go.

"This place is at its best in the morning," Joe said. "But it lacks a certain something after dark. You'll have to do something about it. One of these days it'll be winter. It's already getting darker sooner, have you noticed?"

She had: she noticed everything. He suspected she might look forward to winter, it would give her an excuse to hide, behave like a tortoise. He was polishing a piece of undistinguished metal from the clock, holding it over yesterday's newspaper, letting gunge from an old piece of rusty steel wool drip on an open page. There was a photograph and an article there he did not want her to see. They could have been an old couple, he thought, rather than an odd couple, oddly at ease after so short an acquaintance. Perhaps that was her mental state. Now that was a really flattering conclusion. He was allowed to stay and watch her because it made no bloody difference, one way or another.

"Something silly," he repeated. "And gorgeous and old, and grand and superfluous. A centrepiece. How about a chandelier?"

She looked at him with more than a glimmer of interest, lit another cigarette and continued the contemplation of the ceiling. The clouds were clearing: in one, bright second, she could imagine light, striking on crystal. Matt would approve of that. So would she. She found herself nodding enthusiastically, seeing it, hanging in splendour, a daft contrast to the rest.

"Oh yes. Definitely. Just a large one. Yes."

"Right," he said, springing to his feet. "We'll go and find it, shall we?"

"How?"

"Looking in shop windows, 'course."

"Why?"

"Because they're there."

He was putting things into the pockets of his jacket as if the decision was made. His left hand was scrunching the newspaper, absent-mindedly, but deliberately. He did not want her to read about murder.

"I've got nothing to do until this evening, no work to go to, that kind of thing. Oh I am out this evening, by the way, not late—"

"I don't need, or want, your bloody timetable," she said flatly. "The more often you're out the better."

"Only I want to be out *now*," Joe said. "This minute. Right now. Out. Come on, come with me."

She was touching her hair, a feature of her life and appearance she had forgotten until she had come home. It had once been her pride and joy. Emma and she had once joked about the fact that they had spent three hours in a row, discussing the state of their oh-so similar hair. Should I cut it short? Should I let it grow this time? It does this, it does that, why won't it do this? "A copper and a paid-up mother," Emma said, "such serious, dedicated people we are: we've spent longer discussing hair than others spend on the law of relativity." Now Elisabeth's hair hung limp. She had not washed it in months without assistance and it felt a shameful thing to admit. After a few days in dirtier London, it felt like an unfamiliar, greasy wig simply because it was impossible to use both arms and all fingers in coordination with each other; she was getting better, rapidly, but she still could not wash her own hair unaided. To think, she had despised her mother's help, without realizing how much she needed it. Then she looked at Joe, yawning and stretching, scratching his great big chest, obviously dressed for the great outdoors, in more or less the same uniform in which he slept. Same kind of scrubby shirt, clean but unpressed trousers, and even in this sultry weather, boots. Why worry? They were all ugly out there. Who would notice her?

"Yeah. Let's go."

And the fact was, the world outside was different with Joe. He insisted on the bus, rather than the efficient Underground. "You haven't been on a London bus in *how* long?" he asked. "You haven't lived. Top deck, front row. Now what do you want to see and where do you want to go?"

Elisabeth failed to say she did not mind where the hell they went. Puzzled as she was by this willingness to be led, it felt ungrateful to resent his energy.

"Look," he kept saying, pointing all the time to punctuate his running commentary on all they passed, "look. Look at the sun catching that roof, knocks your eyes out. Quick, look at that woman, that one over there, on the zebra crossing, with that amazing dog; she's dyed her hair red to match."

"She hasn't . . ."

"OK, then, she dyed the dog. Look!" As the bus lurched and swayed, she looked. She saw the gracious lines of buildings on Euston Road, not the traffic; saw the groups of youths, loud and nonchalant, calling to a group of girls, all of them delighted with and wary of each other, but lovely in their preening. She saw people who were purposeful, listened to the grumbling jokes of the passengers. Look! There's the Lloyds building: don't you love to hate it, great monster, covered in intestine. Now here's Westminster Palace, looking like an old wedding cake. And the Abbey, full of statues. You could pinch one, to put outside the door. See if anyone would miss it.

They changed on to another bus, amid a crowd of tourist, cackling with questions, glorious in their colours, said Joe. If that one keeps his camera to the end of the day, it'll be a miracle; bet he doesn't know how it works, anyway, he points it like a gun. There'll be tears before bedtime with that child, but isn't she pretty? It was a nudging, whispering commentary which made Elisabeth feel like an ally, and made her laugh. It made her watch the world go by, to the tune of his pointing.

Matthew might love this, she was thinking. When I'm better, I'll bring Matthew. We'll go on the river.

"Pimlico, this is where it's at," said Joe.

"What is?"

Chandeliers of course. And other things. I like people best, he told her, but there is an enormous compensation in things. If you ever happen to be out of love with the human race, try loving objects instead: it works.

She found herself looking at a row of shops in a corner of central London she had never known before. "You go round with your eyes shut, you," he teased her. "I thought you said you were a policewoman." "Officer, not woman," she said without rancour, "and not a very good one at that. It perverted my view of the streets, you know, like this neck alters it now. You were never looking ahead, always sideways. You were never relaxed and you were always looking out for malice and for thieves, not for ordinary, everyday kindness. When you looked at a shop window, you were looking to see how easy it would be to rob, not what was in it." "I see," he said. There was a shop, as vaguely promised, with chandeliers.

"We've come to look at your stock: we can't afford to buy it, but we are really theatrical impressarios in deep disguise, imagining a stage set and a limitless fortune," Joe announced.

"Go ahead and welcome," the woman said.

Crystal dripped into a small room, pear-shaped and diamond cut, a slight tinkling to the touch. Small chandeliers and elaborately large. One with seventy-five lights, once seventy-five candles. Can you imagine lighting that, and then putting out the lights? No wonder so many old houses burned down. The thing had curved, tapering branches, like so many antlers, with linked chains of cut crystal droplets, each the size of a tiny fist, suspended in between, small glass saucers supporting the little lights which stood slightly crooked, like tired soldiers at ease. The woman flicked a switch. The whole shop blazed with light: Elisabeth could imagine a thousand different rooms and with her neck extended, her eyes unblinking, she said, "Oh!"

"These would be hellish difficult to photograph," Joe was saying. For her, it was enough that they existed. She was entranced. Joe pointed to the mammoth with the seventy-five lights.

"We'll have two of those," he said. "Can you wrap them?" and she laughed in total delight.

"Just the two?"

They lunched, late, and talked about nothing. They fantasized about the position of the chandelier in the belltower, whether Reverend Flynn would approve and how you would hang the ton of a thing from the ceiling, let alone get it up the stairs. They had wandered, seen elegant ladies buying beautiful things.

"You don't have to own a chandelier," Joe said. "You just have to know it exists."

"Yes," she said. "I know that. I have always known that. My father," she told him, in a rush of information, "was a jeweller and it was not enough for him to know that things existed: he had to possess them. He thought gemstones were the most fascinating things in the universe; people always came second or third. He could bore for Europe on the properties of stones. I loved stones, too, any form of crystal, but I liked them for their impurities, not their perfection. He couldn't understand that: nor could he understand my mother's less than total fascination."

Once she started, she could not stop. Talking was a glorious luxury.

"She liked what a gem could buy, saw it as a piece of trading stock, quite pretty really, but not as good as money. My sister loved jewellery with a passion. Rather a nice kind of passion, the same she had for many things, but my father never seemed to notice that her interest was only the same kind she might have had for a doll or a dress."

"Highly feminine . . . frills?"

All Joe had to do was prompt, express the interest.

"Oh yes, a perfect little lady, with tremendous airs and graces, loved dressing up, and the dolls, too. She looked after things, though, that was what he liked. I was never forgiven for losing things. Not many children play with diamonds. I lost a couple, Emma, never. She looked after people and pets in the same way, though. He didn't notice that. She was always more likely to cry over a sick dog than she was over a stone with a scratch, sort of thing would break his heart."

"I may as well tell you," he said, casually, stirring the third coffee, "that I know of your sister Emma. Oh, and I once did some work for the police. For someone called Jenkins. He kept in touch. So, I know that Emma's dead and how she died. Besides newspaper reports stick in my mind, especially pictures. You look so like her and anyway, Flynn told me."

She paused, looked suspicious, decided it was too late to stop. She put these revelations into limbo, and went on. She knew she was talking way too much. But the combined effect of this single day and this large, easy stranger, made her want to explain.

"Flynn thinks that I'm secretly a rich eccentric. I think, when I see that chandelier, that I can understand my father's passion. He wanted to shower Emma with gems, probably gave her many, but I never knew, because I never cared. Emma married about the time he died. He may have given her something then . . . he had quite a collection, but no-one knows what happened to it because by that time, she didn't care either. She only cared for living things. People and animals. Objects bored her." There was another pause.

"Why am I telling you this?" she demanded.

"Because of the chandelier. I wouldn't know the difference between paste and diamond. Is there any? Go on."

"I often wondered if Emma was killed because of the gems, if there were any gems. If only there had been a motive as clean as that, but there wasn't. There was no motive at all."

"A stranger?"

"We may never know." She was guarded again. Ashamed, by now, of talking too much, ready for him to change the subject. "Look!" she said, pointing out of the window. "Look!"

On the far side of the junction where they waited for a bus. A boy, on roller skates with a spotlight on his hat.

Elisabeth shivered. It was suddenly a boon to be alive. It was not an ugly world at all.

Chapter
ELEVEN

"You should be careful about the effect you have on people, Joe," the
Owl said in a hectoring tone.

"My devastating charm, you mean."

"I was thinking more of your size. It makes it all the more insulting when you aren't listening."

"Sorry," Joe said, sincerely. "I've had a nice day. I wasn't paying
attention." He liked the Owl, even though he wished he was elsewhere
himself. Of all his old-time friends, (were they really friends or merely habits?) he rated Owl highest, for his sheer, bewildered integrity. An
old mate. A remnant of a tribe which grew and then diminished.

"Well, I thought you might want to know the latest," Owl said.
Even to Joe's distracted mind, Owl was hedging slightly around some
preoccupations of his own. "Rob's been to that introduction agency.
Shaken, but not stirred, old Rob. Says it was like being put through

the mill, whatever that means. Michael's been too. Says he thinks the woman in charge is very thorough, smooth bastard. Your turn next. We agreed, remember? You're a mate, remember? We all promised."

Yup, an old mate. There were old mates agreements' to climb the Matterhorn and get killed; drink sixteen pints of ale; take E; race to the North Pole; risk death, disfigurement and disease and run over cliffs like lemmings. Old mates agreements were bad for the health. They were crap.

"I haven't got the money," Joe said. "But I'm on my way."

"Even though you've got a girl? The one who wouldn't let you in?"

"Oh, her? Come off it. I'm a sort of uncle to her. She's not a prospect, more of a liability, but she might have nice friends. I do her garden. Got to make ends meet when the photography work's slow."

"I'm sure they'd have you back in the firm, you know. Michael always says so." Owl was always sweetly anxious about other peoples' income, or lack of it.

"Thanks but no thanks."

Owl did not know if he was on the brink of confiding in Joe because Joe was so damn feckless, so insecure and so open about it— not a man to gossip, either—or because, even though Joe teased, he never scorned: he was the one who called off the dogs, rather than set them on. He could not confide in Michael, because Mike was so suave, nor in Rob, because Rob would laugh.

"You gotta go to that introduction agency, Joe. Check it out."

"Course. I've said. C'mon, fella, what's up?"

Owl's face crumpled. Joe wondered why it was always thus: a man going all the way round the houses and two thirds of the way down his second pint before he got to the point with a massive clearing of the throat, as if the words were hidden in there, waiting to be forced out.

"I did. As it happens. Dated a dead woman, didn't I?"

Owl took off his new tinted glasses with less than a flourish, not sure after all if he managed the gesture with Michael's kind of panache.

"And now I've got another one, to compensate." He brayed his nervous laugh. "Who knows? I shan't dare phone her. Maybe this one'll stay alive until I meet her."

Somewhere inside of me, lurking like a virus, there is the person I once was. A fatter person, Elisabeth concluded. The kind who would buy a chandelier.

There were no flowers outside the door, no more of these practical jokes from her lodger when she came home alone, imagining that when she arrived, her house might be full of people. There had been parties here, once, and also in her mother's house; father resisting them, except for the chance they gave him to show off his daughters. Yes, both his daughters: he had loved her too, in his own way. She was alive: she was lucky, and she had been ungrateful.

Elisabeth phoned her mother. The twist in her neck and the crevice of wasted muscle made a convenient hook for the phone: would it ever get better? Dammit to hell: she still had eyes: she wanted a fuller life, not this depressed shadow of existence shrouded in regrets. Something had opened her eyes. What was done was done, and if her revised life was not going to be the same, she could at least refashion herself into something amiable. Get back that eye for beauty and colour which was returning now as forcefully as the pain of circulation returning to frozen fingers. Wear crazy colours and crystals round her neck, go along clanking, learn a different kind of vanity. Because she did like that huge world out there, and she did love so many of the people in it.

"Hullo, mum? How are you? Yes, yes, I'm fine. Hot, is it? Have you been in the sea? No? Don't go, Mum, don't go, wait a minute."

Wait a minute, please: don't be so damned efficient and let me tell you something clear and simple. Such as, I'm sorry I was such a lousy patient: you were marvellous to put up with me and it's only now I'm realizing quite how much you did, because I can still scarcely shop and I'm trying to work out a way to wash my own hair. Let me say it, please. But Diana was calling for Matthew.

Elisabeth could see her mother now, standing in the hallway of the house where telephone extensions into rooms were regarded as frivolous, where no expense was spared on polish, calling for her grandson in that imperious voice of hers which always managed to carry without her ever raising it. Diana, looking critical, thinking all the time what she could do to the place if she had money.

I am no compensation, Elisabeth thought. I accept that there is nothing I can ever do about that. You can't make people love you.

"He isn't here!" Diana barked. "In fact he keeps on disappearing. That child! If we had the money, he'd be off to boarding school next term. Tomorrow . . . oh, here you are. Matthew! Here he is . . ."

"Mummy, wait . . ."

"Matthew! It's your aunt." The dog, barking.

Not *my* daughter; your aunt. Elisabeth was suddenly furious with her mother all over again. Not for the stiff upper lip, but for talking about sending Matthew away when he was able to listen. How could she be so crass? Then, Matt, blythe spirit who, if he had heard, seemed not to mind, although there was a note of hysteria in his voice.

"Allo, skinny Lizzie aunty!" he was saying. "When can I come and see you?"

"Soon," she said. "Soon." Feeling tears at the back of her eyes. Soon: when he had learned that she did not, could not ever replace his mother. Not in his father's eyes, as she had once, fleetingly hoped, and not in his own. The phone receiver, held long after the call ended, felt heavy in her hand.

Think, Lizzie, think. Stop hiding and resenting. Pen, paper: you can't do much, but you can write. She wrote, but she could not write fast. Her mother would not like that chandelier. Too fussy and too ornate. She would say it was pretentious.

Dear Mum,

If I write this quickly, I may get it right . . . I *know* you are not as distant as you seem; but I got my warmth from somewhere and I can't believe it was my real father. (I wish you could tell me about my real father, but that's another matter.)

Listen; you have been a good mother; a very good mother indeed and none of my behaviour in the last few months reflects that. You should have shoved me out. And I know that my going last week was insulting, too, even if it was a relief, but I had to go, even if I can scarcely cope now . . . Because Matthew will never find his feet, (or will grow three of them) unless I am absent. How can I be so arrogant when I can't even wash my hair!

We've been very angry with one another. I never explained to you why I was there so much when Emma was killed and then suddenly absented myself into silence, and it wouldn't do to explain now. I know you wanted more from me: I wasn't entirely truthful, saying I was ignorant of the whole, police thing. Enough to say, I couldn't explain, but one day I might, and you were very diplomatic not to persist.

It might explain, I suppose, the fact you were cold as ice when I came home jobless and I can quite see why. Matt was easy with me, not with you. I mocked your house and your life, and although I can't even *pretend* to say that that swine of a mugger, (*Why* did he do it?), did me a favour with his caustic, he did at least make me sit back and think. And stop drinking, of course.

Why the hell did you never drink, Mumsy? The only time I remember was just after Dad died and I came back to find you getting plastered with Mrs. Smythe. Mother mine, why did we never talk? Why can't we talk now?

She chewed on the pen.

"Is it because you think that Dad bypassed both you and I in favour of the one we both loved best? Look, Mum, be fair: if that's what he planned, you can see his point. The reward of virtue: Emma loved him best. She was the sweetest and kindest, especially to all the people *we* rejected, much nicer than us, so why shouldn't he favour her? He just couldn't stand the fact that you loved the house better than its owner: he wanted you to pay for that. As for his cache of jewels . . . yes, I do know about that . . . everyone did. But he was a *dreamer*, Mum, and I doubt if this cache ever existed. Let's face, it, he didn't believe in pension plans, couldn't tolerate that stuff; he only believed in tangible things he could pick up and examine, like stones, but he was also a lousy businessman, a failure in trade, and he didn't expect to die, so why the hell would there be anything? Stop looking for it. (I've heard you: we've all heard you.) We wouldn't know it if we found it, would we? So what's the fucking point? Life's not going to get better. This is what there is . . ."

■

She put the letter away. To be continued later. There was no way to do this briefly or quickly. Writing was too slow: communication agonizingly difficult; no wonder they had avoided it.

But she still had an urge to go on talking, an urge to mend fences and make resolutions. Make contact. Patsy: yes, Patsy. Suggest going out, as a thank-you for the lift and the patience in the face of lethargy. Let her know about being back in the land of the living, definitely. Talk about nothing, suggest a meal, a drink. Listen for once instead of being afraid of being heard.

She had a fleeting memory of all the phone calls she had made and recorded on tape. How subversive that was; the same sensation of treachery had infected even the most normal conversation, so that, for a while, she could scarcely talk on the phone at all, unable to forget an imaginary audience, listening, breathing hard . . .

"Oh, it's you . . . Gotta rush . . . you all right? Speak to you tomorrow?" That was Patsy, surprised and evasive.

"Where're you going?" Elisabeth found herself demanding. "Somewhere nice?" scolding herself for a cliché.

A nervous chuckle.

"Mind your own business. A blind date. Wish me luck. I need it."

"No, you don't. He'll fall at your feet. You're drop-dead gorgeous, Pats. Just act like it. Remember not to be nice."

Another nervous giggle, followed by a hesitant sigh.

"Might be a total washout."

"So? Something better round the corner, in that case. Down to experience."

"I've had too much experience," Patsy said. "But thanks." There was a long pause. "I love you, Lizzie. I'm stupid and I'm shallow, but I love you. Always have."

Elisabeth swallowed, surprised and embarrassed.

"Good God, stop talking nonsense," she laughed. "Have a good time. Tell me about it tomorrow. I owe you, Patsy."

"Lizzie?"

"What?"

"Nothing. Can wait."

"Take care."

Elisabeth prowled. Her eyes went back to the wooden ceiling. A chandelier would be glorious. There was comfort in things. For the moment, the bleak past was over. And there was something wrong with Patsy. It worried her. Slowly, Elisabeth began to rewrite the letter to her mother, starting from the top. Remembering to include some words of affection and not to swear. The process was like climbing steep stairs.

Those steps again, this time in daylight, and again Joe forgot to count because this time he took them quicker than before, three at a time, the way Joe took the belfry stairs. As if he was weighted, but inspired, by the scrunched up, stained piece of newspaper report in his pocket, and what dear Owl had said. Joe was like a racehorse carrying extra kilos and frisky with the challenge. It felt like the seventy-fifth floor, let alone the fifth, and the door was locked and barred. "Call any time after nine to five," Jenkins had said, "I'm always in, if not always welcoming." Joe knocked. You could knock the skin off your knuckles on this metal-lined door and still it only made a minor rat tap tap of sound, falling into semi-silence. Then a shuffling of movement.

"Who's that?"

"Me."

"Go away."

Joe waited. It seemed as if the story of his life was waiting on the wrong side of a closed door for someone to ask him in. Jenkins was a pale man this evening, ashen, wanting a drink as if there was no tomorrow, and Joe, not really understanding the extent of the craving, worried about him for the first time. He seemed even smaller than he had previously appeared, a little facsimile of his larger self. There was a rancid smell of beer on his breath, and he looked with a glance of intense hunger to see if Joe might have bought supplies, like the last time, hope fading as he turned away.

"Had to come home, boy, lock myself in, before it got worse. Wish I hadn't now. Why did I do it? Why, after all this time?"

"You tell me," Joe invited, filling the kettle, finding the impedimenta of coffee and filling in the gap of the man's self-recrimination with the noises of the cure.

"Thought you were going to bring your camera?"

"Must have guessed you wouldn't be at your best," Joe said

mildly. Cigarette smoke curled up towards the yellow patch on the ceiling.

"It's all a matter of deceit," Jenkins announced, with the coffee beside him. "Deceit compounding deceit. No-one being able to tell anyone the total truth. So that everyone's version of the truth, however honestly held, is ever so slightly wrong, if you see what I mean."

"I don't, really."

Hell. If the only advantage of finding Jenkins half-cut was to have him speak in riddles, there was less purpose than ever in his being here. Joe waited. Jenkins glared at him.

"Look," Joe said. "Cut it out, will you? It's me doing you the favour. You aren't doing me any. Elisabeth's getting better. I'm doing a reasonable caretaker job, but I can't do it any more. Not as long as you won't tell me the whole story. Unedited. I can't go on pretending. Not when there's been another murder. Just like Emma. Are you listening?"

Jenkins had attempted to light the filter end of the cigarette. The smell was disgusting. He threw it away.

"Oh, all right. I'll give you the whole report then. The one into the complaints against me. That's what you wanted, isn't it? Give it to you, like I'm not supposed to do, and see if you can make more sense of what we did, and why, than those fuckers. Then you'll see what she was told and not told. Why she was such a bad choice for the job, because she couldn't be told everything."

It was the partially sighted leading the blind. Jenkins presumed too much. He assumed that everyone else spent as long thinking about Lizzie as he did. It had been a kind of love, Joe guessed, which lingered into wistful, haunting regret. How would someone like Jenkins ever make someone love him? He was so oblique in whatever he said. If he loved, the subject of his affections would have to guess.

Joe felt in his pocket for the newspaper report, and then stopped. A longer report, same subject and same photograph, an awful photo, he thought, lay on the coffee table. Three differing versions of the same murder; one he had from the day before yesterday, then Owl's, then Jenkins, from a national paper. Is that what Jenks meant by deceit? Each report would give a different slant on Angela Collier's life, omit, out of ignorance or misinformation, some detail of her death.

"Are you working on this murder?" Joe asked, pointing. Jenkins snorted.

"Naa. I'll never be let near a murder again. Or any serious crime for that matter. I put in my two penn'orth and was told to fuck off. Not before I found out more than this newspaper would ever tell me. It's him: I know in my waters, it's him. Or his brother, or his twin, raised from the same gene pool, with the same fucking fantasies. It's him, all right. Mr. Hygiene Conscious, putting the boot in."

"Emma's murderer? But Jack's dead. As in doornail."

Jenkins raised his head, with his most cunning smile. "*Dead?* Did I ever say so? The *suspect's* dead. Not the fucking culprit." He paused. "Naa, that's wrong. He doesn't fuck. Seems to get excited and forget about that side of it. Gets his rocks off by kicking. Varies it a bit with a knife."

Joe shook his head. "I don't believe you. He's dead. Only prophets rise from the dead. The suspect, Jack, was seduced, exposed and even when there was no case against him, utterly humiliated. Kills himself . . . He dies of shame."

Jenkins wagged a finger in front of bloodshot eyes.

"Jack might be dead, but ah no, not this one. The real culprit toughs it out because he doesn't have a conscience. What would humiliation mean to a character like him? This one may not have stopped. Whoever said he stopped? Who'd connect him to this new killing, since we were all so convinced that our suicide was the man? The culprit isn't a fool; he can change his method; he can control himself. He can read in newspapers, just like anyone else, about the debacle of the case. He can have a sudden fit of pique that no-one's taking any notice and repeat the old sport with the old hallmarks. Even if he's varied them in the meantime."

"Hallmarks?"

Jenkins was getting drowsy, despite the coffee. He had retreated from the chronic need for a drink: Joe could see him slump with relief as the worm inside him resigned itself to abstinence, and slept.

"Covering the head, that's one hallmark," he murmured. "A fascination with the neck. Probably the neck crushed with a foot, while covered, just like the face. Black plastic sack with Emma, big green towel with Angela, so that he couldn't see what he was doing and keep his feet and hands clean. Fastidious in brutality; the woman an object of hate, to be reduced to nothing. Kicked and stamped to death.

Melted down. We never told Elisabeth about the bleach. We just weren't sure about the bleach."

He got up and roused himself by walking in a circle. Small, precise steps which he counted under his breath, one, two, three, four as he paced round the furniture on an obviously familiar route. Three times round, leaving Joe looking for worn marks on the cheap carpet.

"Emma'd been spring cleaning, you see, on account of them planning to move house. Scraping together savings for something better. Her husband, Steven, wanted it more than she did. There'd been arguments about his determination to get a big house. Their friends said she'd have been happier with what she'd got and another baby, but he wanted her to go out to work. Not her style. Where was I? Cleaning fluid, bleach all over her clothes. Could have been thrown. Could have been an accident. Had to be dismissed."

"You've lost me," Joe said. Jenkins gave him a look of contemptuous scorn, lighting another cigarette although the first still burned in a heaped, foul-smelling ashtray. He seemed to notice, got up again and transferred the debris to a wastepaper basket. There was a slight smell of scorching hair.

"Angela Collier. Bleach stains on her carpet. Could have been an accident, spilling something and using the wrong stuff to mop it up. Sort of thing a man would do, though, rather than a houseproud woman. Maybe a man trying to get blood out of his trousers."

The beer Joe had drunk with Owl regurgitated into heartburn.

"Elisabeth was attacked by a man who threw caustic fluid all over her," he murmured.

"So she was," said Jenkins. "Amazing. Why did you think I asked you to look out for in the first place? Didn't I say there was a connection? But no young-blood DI is going to listen to me. I made too much of a cock up the first time. Here, I'll get you the report."

He shambled to an array of shelves made of bricks and builder's boards, where books and papers were arranged in pristine order. Like the rest of the flat, the equipment was makeshift, the sense of control complete.

"You can have the judgement in the case, too," Jenkins said.

"No thanks," said Joe. "I've already seen that."

"You think," Jenkins said, sneering, "that you can see whatever you want to see through the wrong end of a fucking lens."

Suddenly, Joe was furious. So utterly furious, he could have stran-
gled the man and shouted for joy. Smashed him to a pulp, to wipe
away that half-smile on that sick face. Obliterate it.

"You knew all along that the suspect wasn't the one, didn't you?
You knew poor Elisabeth was chasing a harmless hare whose only
crimes were a few, puerile fantasies learned from videos and a puppy
love for a dead woman? Violent? Jack might have hit a woman who
was pulling his plonker, that's all. Anyone might do that. You knew.
You let the murderer get away. Put that poor bastard up for sacrifice.
Not much of a man, but he was still a friend, once. And you knew
exactly what you were doing."

Jenkins shrank, aware of danger, visualizing what Joe could do.
Hands like hammers, face white with anger, blood pulsing. He was
wide awake now.

"No," he said softly. "No, I didn't know in the beginning. But I
knew at some stage. When it was too late to stop. When it didn't matter who we got, as long as we got someone."

Joe's face was level, like a man aiming to spit.

"Someone? Anyone? Did Elisabeth ever know she was forcing con-
fessions out of the wrong man?"

Jenkins was shrinking like a pricked balloon. If Joe hit him once,
he would hit a dozen times. Good men were dangerous.

"No. At least, I don't think so." He was trembling, bracing his arms
against the chair, the knuckles white and his face livid. "I couldn't bear
to tell her. I thought she might work it out for herself. Oh SHIT!" He
paused, kneading his knuckles into his eyes. The danger passed. "Instead, she pitied him. Suffered for his suicide not just because she was
in disgrace, but because she pitied him. Almost had a nervous breakdown. 'A life for a life is no answer,' she said, 'it only punishes me.'
How could I tell her it wasn't even that? That it was all for nothing and
the murderer was still alive? She was in pieces. How could I tell her?"

The hands scrabbled like crabs towards the cigarettes.

"Go on, boy, hit me."

Oh, God, if only they would bury her. Take those people out of the
office with their incessant, repetitive questions about Angela. Take
away the voice of Mrs. Collier, breaking with tears, leaden with guilt,

saying why, why, WHY? The police seemed so large, even the women: their questions a series of accusations. What was Angela like? I don't know. Tidy.

The red shirt was too aggressive, the cobalt blue calmer. Should she wear large earrings or small, the whole box tipped out on the bed to find the two which matched, a daily, time-wasting exercise which Patsy repeated and resented. She loathed the fact that they were never tidy, symptomatic of a wasted life. Why the fuss? Why come all the way home to change to meet a man for a drink, when the clothes she had worn for a shaky day at work would have been adequate? Why go anyway, when her mind was unhinged? One quick look out of the upstairs window, to see if the weather was still welcoming, suddenly reluctant to leave.

She felt a total bitch, doing this, when she should have been out on the streets with what seemed like dozens of others, hunting a murderer. She hoped he would understand, because she might have to talk about it.

Patsy, in front of the mirror by the door, positioned for the last minute check, examined her own face for signs of grief and could see none. Cobalt-blue shirt and white skirt, when she should be in mourning. Look, she told her reflection, if this was a business meeting you would go, Angela or no Angela, funeral or no funeral, police or no police. You'd go if you were half-dead, so why not a date? Tapping along the street to her car, (safe enough, she was not going to drink much, might only stay for one) she tried to grind the feeling of guilt under her heel. Fumbling for the key, she realized her hands were shaking. Stupid cow. Then she thought of how she would need more than one drink to steady her nerves, and still put the key in the lock and drove away with all the uncertainty of a learner to the tune of jumbled thoughts. A real bag of shredded paper. "Do not make any commitment on your first date . . . Always meet in a public place . . . early evening or lunch, so that both of you can go separate ways, without offence, after an hour . . ."

Mrs. Smythe's sterling advice rang inside the ears which were, after all, wearing the wrong earrings; they should have been small and understated rather than large and far too white. Drop-dead gorgeous, Patsy, that's what you are; Lizzie's words echoed with less strength. She had so wanted to tell Lizzie about Angela: ask her advice on what to say; get her to intervene and tell them to *stop;* it had been an act of bravery to keep quiet in the days after, when she wanted to tell everyone, felt that she must have had a notice stamped on her forehead saying "My friend has been murdered, because I did not care for her enough." But the one thing Lizzie did not need was bad news, even about a person she had never known, and the thing she had always done to Lizzie was dump on her, and let's face it, that was why she missed her. Yes, she had been restrained, for once.

So these are the choices, Patsy, old girl. Life over death.

The nights were darkening sooner and the long, hot summer taking a toll. Sticky air, low-lying fumes; a certain sense of the jaded, as if the city had run out of flimsy clothes and everything had been washed once too often. A frayed feeling to the awnings: café chairs in need of repair, a sense of nostalgia for a winter coat. Tired blooms going browner in baskets, beyond the redemption of mere water.

How many times? Patsy thought. How many times does one have to do this?

Outside Café Bleue in the Convent Garden piazza, the crowds seemed thickest, and for a moment, Patsy panicked. However would she find him, or he her, but as the indeterminate, hunting tourists drifted and parted, bound for the market stalls and shops, they revealed only a scattering of custom under the dusty parasols. For a moment, she felt a total fool: a child on the edge of a crowd, searching for mother; a teenager, pretending nonchalance on the way to meet a new gang. She wanted to dive underground and find a place to brush the hair, retouch the eyes and remove the earrings.

"Excuse me . . . are you . . . ?"

The same height as herself, or maybe an inch taller, a discreet card with the Select Friends' logo peeking out of the top pocket of his shirt. Hair which managed to look windswept and controlled at the same time; a wide smile. The shirt was blue, the trousers pristine white.

"You have to be," he laughed. "Look, even the colours match."

"Not quite the same blue," she stammered.

"Maybe not quite," the lines crinkling round his eyes, scutinizing her, dipping his head in acknowledgement of approval. Nothing forced about the laugh, or hers.

Drop-dead gorgeous. Remember not to be nice. Stop it, Patsy, stop it; but stepping out of doors would be worth it for this disingenuous, almost childlike smile alone. She knew, in a moment, that the beast was civilized; that the evening was not going to be a disaster because he would not let it be so. He was allowing his hand to hover, not presuming to touch, a shade of shyness. He was clean and courteous, but then so was she, dismissing from her mind the fleeting thought, why does he do this, but, then, why do I? That fine head of hair dipped again in a nice, ironic bow and he passed the back of his hand across his forehead.

"What a ritual," he said. "I'm not used to it; it makes me *so* nervous."

"Me, too."

"Good," he said, touching her then, guiding her elbow. "It should, shouldn't it? We should be nervous. It isn't a game."

She nodded. He laughed, confidingly, her arm, effortlessly inside his own.

"Don't worry. I'm quite safe. I learned my manners from my mother."

This son's mother had done a good job.

Wait till she told Hazel. But she would not tell Hazel. She had lied, ashamed of herself for going out at all. Said she had not heard from the agency.

A long evening. Some people, Hazel was thinking, have the knack of making an hour last a lifetime. The policemen did that, too. She shuddered. (Always be polite to your date even if you do not like the look of him . . . he may be as apprehensive as you are . . . wait and see what he has to say for himself . . . give him a chance! copyright Mrs. C. Smythe.) All those rules and whatsits, could have been straight out of a magazine, Hazel thought without irony: Mrs. Smythe was probably brought up on *Woman's Realm*, circa 1950. First find your man. Ignore the fact that he is not even a noble savage and quite unsuitable for life indoors: tame him. Step one, listen, as if the words tumbling from his mouth were pearls of fascinating wisdom. Instead of all this boring rubbish from a man with white sock and shiny shoes.

"Ever been skiing, Haze? It's great, honest. Me and my mates go most years. Great. Do you drive a car, Haze? No? Shame. Turning mine in this autumn, don't like to keep the same one long. Still, the old company's good like that. Don't your lot run to cars, then? Enjoying that, are you?" Pointing in the direction of her empty, froth-lined cocktail glass, his voice grating. The steeliness of the decor did not absorb the babble of the Soho crowd or the deafening vibration of music. She put her lips close to his ear.

"I thought you were self-employed. Own business."

"Naa. Gave that up. Didn't work."

She leant even closer and said what she knew he wanted her to say, "I'll get these, shall I? Same again?" A fool with a hole in his credit card, that was it. Hazel was all too familiar with the type: all mouth and trousers, but shocked by the price of her drinks, as if he didn't expect a girl to go for the fanciest combination on the menu. God, she hated cocktails: but they served to test the mettle of the bloke buying. Happy hour over, this bloke was losing his. Two pints, two of her brandy sours and he started to panic. He looked like a star athlete squashed by a truck, head like a bullet, ultra-stylish hair but cheap shoes. Tie loosened at the neck to make him look like a city stockbroker, he probably ran with a crowd like that, without earning a fraction of it. A male groupie: an old mate: he never stopped talking about his mates, wore them like a shield. Hazel put her gimlet eye on the barman, got a swift shot of bourbon at the bar, and carried back to the table a double each and two bottles of some fancy Belgian beer which was about the same proof as wine. That should loosen his tongue, as if it had ever stopped wagging. *In vino veritas* was too slow. Spirit and hops were quicker.

"Thought I'd have a change," she said.

He looked at her with new appreciation.

"Gottit," he announced, thumb in air, as if about to nail a drawing pin to the wall. "I mean, basically, you're a girl who likes pints. Good on yer! Cheers." A long gulp and a short sip. "Good this, innit?"

She nodded. So it should be, at that price.

"My wife hated drink," he announced. "I mean, hated the stuff. She was about as much fun as a wet blanket in a snowstorm. Hated booze, sex, a good time, everything. She was a bit like that."

Hazel nodded, pulled out her ciggies, lit one.

"I disapprove of smoking," he said, suddenly pompous. "Hate it, you know."

"Sorry," she said as mildly as she could, but continued, resting the hand with the cigarette on the edge of the table, so the smoke went into the eyes of them next door, not his. They at the next table were smoking like converts; arguing, too. Something to do with money, his, hers or someone else's, far more interesting. Rob was back in his narrative.

"I was too young to marry, you know? Should never have done it. She changed as soon as she was a missus. Turned into her mum. Wallpaper everywhere. No more going down the boozer with the team . . . always busy. Cow."

"Did she earn more than you?" Hazel asked, innocently, letting the ash fall between the two tables.

"Well, yeah. S'pose she did?"

"So she left you the house, then, did she? I mean, she wasn't such a meanie in the end."

"She was a cow. A proper cow. Made me buy her out." He sounded wistful.

"Cheers." She tipped her glass towards his, leant towards him. Not exactly leering, simply trying to find a common interest over the noise, the arms crossed modestly under her breasts acting as a soft shelf, supporting the cleavage which seemed to sprout from the lycra.

"Tell us about the house, Rob. What kind of house?"

His foot began to tap with the music. He wanted to get up and strut. It wasn't a bad body under all that, she noticed. Shame about the rhythm. She'd seen a dozen middle managers just like him, but he was a suit. She had to try.

"Tell me about your house, Rob, where is it?"

"House? *My* house? Not exactly mine, more the building society's. Actually, it's a flat in a block. Out in the sticks. Gotta garden. Everybody else has got a baby. I suppose she was thinking of babies. Fat chance!" He roared as if he had been witty and let his eyes wander, clocking the fillies at the bar, before resting his gaze on her cleavage. He was a man with a fixed blueprint of the kind of woman he liked, eyes bigger than his prick.

Hazel finished the drink. He was welcome: no he wasn't. This one had a grotty flat as full of debts as he was full of shit. There was a jug of water on the table, some little compensation for the price of the drinks. Olives and crisps were free, too. She took the jug and poured some of it into his half-done beer, ruining it. OK, another day she might have persisted, but it was all to do with Angela and life being short and that, so she could not even try to be nice. Even his face wasn't worth it, nor his bum covered in that nice bit of suit. Mortgage sounded nasty.

"You're a complete pillock," she said, enjoying the clean-shaven feel of his skin as she stroked his cheery chappy, stupid face. "A wally. Got that?"

"What?"

It wasn't even as though she left the room, he mumbled, later. She only got as far as the bar. Sat there, ordering up another, as if he had never existed. Sat up there, crying.

"Well you see, I don't know what to do. About my life and career in general. The same things aren't important any more," Patsy finished. Michael held her gaze. Perhaps she had bored him, but he did not seem bored.

"Look, you don't have to do anything. No, what I mean is yes, you do, but you don't have to do anything immediately. What my mother says is, you have to do what you can. Don't expect the impossible."

If there was anything about him which stirred irritation, it was this constant reference to a mother, the way a film star might have referred to a spiritual leader, a kind of guru; but it was the most passing of irritations. The food was his choice, maybe his mother had told him how to eat, and yes, a long, lovely evening with nothing to mar it. Patsy felt ridiculously high, only she could not remember where she had parked her car. It was late enough: taxis thin on the ground, people spilling out of theatres like a stream of lava, the area covered with slow-moving pedestrians; she simply could not remember which car park and it was so humilating not to remember. Accepting a lift looked like a come on, but she did not care, he was fantastic.

Do not, do not, do not.

And then they were outside the block and she did not want it to end, because she was proud of her flat and wanted him to see it, wanted to see him again. Not bed, not now: not this first time, but sometime: he was, after all, lovely and listening, and she did not even think, did not think at all, when she said, come up for a coffee. Nor did he grab her at the door, nothing like that.

It was when she was busy, about the business of making coffee, hunting out the booze, although it was the last thing she needed, while he went to the loo and came back, that she had a premonition. Consumption of wine had been heavy in the last few days: who could blame her, but in her mind's eye, she could see a written set of rules, all broken, and in that one moment, she could see how silly, excitable Angela might have died.

A different man had come back from the bathroom: a predator. He tried to kiss her, and she giggled a bit, "No, no, wait . . ." twisted her head away, presenting her neck, rather than her face, felt the first real sensation of fear. He was enormously strong.

So she did what seemed wise, kissed him full on the mouth, but he knew, by then, that she was afraid, that she had, however minutely, rejected him, and that whatever else she did was artifice, a mere pretence of love.

He hit her, hard. She screamed, bastard, bastard, that old insult, nearest to mind, without meaning: he hit her again, punches to the abdomen, leaving her winded and coughing, clutching her stomach, choking.

Then he took the shawl from the back of the chair. Black and orange, worn on winter days, a favourite thing.

"Look," she said, "do whatever you want: just do whatever you want. *Don't hurt me.* I love you."

That stopped him, confused him into a smile.

"No you don't, no you don't, no you don't. No-one does."

Then there was the second, chameleon-like change, as she cowered at his feet. He was standing still, holding the shawl, looking down at it as if wondering how it had got into his hands. She scrabbled to her feet, looking around wildly for any kind of weapon, backing away, towards the window. In a minute, she would hear it, the diesel sound of the ambulance coming to take her away. He came towards her again. She did not scream, simply put out her hands before her, pleading. He drew her into an embrace which she did not resist. Michael put the shawl round her shoulders, patted it into place. While she stood with hands by her side, he folded it beneath her chin, saying, "Tut, tut, tut." She stared at him.

"I'm sorry," he said, with a dreadful, formal politeness, "but you're the wrong one."

The door closed quietly behind him. She moved on spongy feet to the bathroom, where she was sick.

Chapter

TWELVE

The keys on her lap top felt sticky. The screen had assumed the colour of brown blood. Caroline Smythe suppressed the second wave of panic. It felt as if the pumping of her heart was trying to force that spiky little ruby through her veins. Michael would not . . . he could not . . . And then there was the apalling revelation that yes, he would; he had got the habit and the days when she could control him were long gone.

She looked at the sharp-cornered ring, wanted to gnaw the real, but tiny ruby, held in a claw. This time, he had acquired the jewellery in advance, instead of bringing it back as a trophy. He was confusing absolution with permission.

"Michael," she called, rapping on his door, desperate that he should be in, knowing he was not, but still going on, knocking and calling like a demented salesman. She was afraid for him and of him;

furious with him, terrified for herself and yet this was not the terror of conscience: it was purer than that.

He copied her, that was all. He emulated her gleeful messing up of other lives, but *he* took it to extremes. She had taught him to copy: it was his only chance.

Gin. Tea. *Think.*

He had once taken to heart any insult issued against herself and let it become his own, festering wound. He had done that as a little boy, her self-styled protector and she—so proud of him, so touched by it— talked to him all the time. Told him everything, promised him every- thing; rocked him to sleep explaining her own injured feelings as if he understood, with his little heart resting against her own, hammering a tattoo in syncopation with hers; indignant when she was; furious when she was, revengeful when she was. And all because he had hurt her so badly.

She always ran out of tonic far sooner than she ran out of gin. What a pity.

Because he had not understood, not entirely; his understanding was out of sequence: he did not comprehend that her statement that she hated that man/woman/bus conductor was not a cue to hit them with a stick. Nor was the rudeness of a sales assistant a cue to kick. His re- sponses were all exaggerated, took no account of youth, age or degree of insult offered. No-one was ever going to hurt her again. He wanted to make up for it, all the time. There was a series of pictures in her mind, such as, when he broke the arm of a much smaller boy who canoned into her, or when the hamster she had bought him languished, despite her blandishments and, after howling with grief, he smashed it to pieces for refusing to mend. There was no finesse about the boy.

She sipped, listening to the venom of memory . . .

"Take him away, your nasty little thief." That was what Diana Kennedy had said, but it was long before that when Caroline had sat him down and began to teach him manners by rote, as she had con- tinued to do for all the years since. Diana would never see that: *her* darling daughters charmed without effort. Caroline referred to them all the time and used them as models while she was making Michael learn a set of responses as another child might have learned his cate- chism by heart. She had finally taught him not to steal, although he only stole for her. She had rewarded him when he was word and action perfect, reminded him of what he had done when he was not, weeping as she did so, so that he feared recrimination as the catechism child feared the devil. All she had to do was to scrape back her hair and say, remember what *you* did? All by yourself? Her marionette son became a charming young man who was also entirely artificial.

She shook her head. Three, multicoloured hairs emerged on the desk. She examined them minutely.

No. That was not true. There was the one side of his brain with perfect memory, incapable of forgetfulness, superb at acquiring knowledge and simulating response. The perfect mimic, who remained silent when in doubt. Then the other side, which could not gauge any feeling but anger and up until now, the dreadful fear of her tears and the sight of her peculiar hair.

Caroline knelt at the door of his flat, clutching the handle and staring at the lock. "Sweetheart, are you there? I need you, darling." She went back upstairs, to the accusation of the screen in the little box room.

She *knew* how her son had gone to meet Angela Collier, because he had told her in that little boy voice reserved for her alone: she could hear it, now.

"Well, Caro Caro Mummy, I knew John Jones was going to meet someone, 'cos he was like a cat on hot bricks and I knew he'd enrolled with you. I get them to come to you, don't I, Mummy?"

She had agreed: praised him. Because some of the clients came through him and she was proud of his ability to have male friends. Men were so absurd: they loved the strong, silent, type. She never asked him to recruit unless her enterprise needed new blood as an antidote to the disappointed old men and divorcees of a certain age who were, quite frankly, the bulk of a fragile business.

"And he left the letter on the desk, Mummy. I was angry with Owl: he didn't tell me, so I phoned him just as he was leaving, made him hang on and made him late. And I went instead of him, Mummy. But she didn't like me. And," this was cunningly added, "she said she didn't like you, either."

Ah, he was still her warrior. Even though he hated those little blonde role-models she had mentioned night after night. Caroline moaned aloud. Not out of pity, out of dread. Pulled herself together.

She looked at the screen, trying to piece together what he might have done. There were letters she had never written. She tried to think *when* had he done this? The day after she had seen the one called Patsy and the one called Hazel, yes, that was it: she had been out the whole day after. So, he had sent Robert Bircham's profile to Hazel, and he had sent his own to Patsy. Christ, those two women must have thought she was efficient; it usually took more than a week for the first, suggested contact, and there they were on the screen now, just as she was about to look them up, ready to enjoy herself and engineer some splendid mismatch for them both. Evidence on the screen said she had already done it, wishing them luck by return of post.

In the absence of interference, she would first have paired them with someone nice, then with some piece of shit. Then, sat back with acute enjoyment to imagine the miserable fireworks to follow.

Jean, Jenny, Janice, Jane: John, James, Jarett, *Jack,* (oh yes, she remembered Jack: the only one she had liked on sight) the names melded and rhymed and tumbled round in her head like washing in a dryer. Michael's meeting with that girl Patsy might not occur at all, might not be tonight, but Caroline felt in her bones that it was. Patsy was tough on the outside, but she would need to do more than take care with a Michael Jacobi in the mood he was in.

At least Patsy was not blonde. Fine. Made her safe, didn't it? Caroline looked at her glass. There were messy fingerprints round the rim.

Patsy had friends: she and the girl Hazel *knew* one another: they said so. And if one was hurt, the other would come asking, for sure. Naa they wouldn't, women hated one another, but all the same she was teetering on the brink, all as a result of Michael thinking he no longer needed her to engineer his life, resenting the fact they were no longer allies and he had the nerve to suggest *she* took away his friends. "You wouldn't HAVE friends without me," she had screamed.

You took away Jack. You liked him better than me.

She was calmer now. The full recognition of crisis always made her calm: it was the moments before made her ravenous with shock. Go round to Miss Patsy's upmarket address. If he was there, grab him by the scruff of the neck and haul him off . . . if he had already done harm, try to scuffle round the evidence . . . Oh God; it was too late for all that. Too late for God, for that matter.

She imagined the slamming of the door downstairs and the door to his half of the house, closing more gently. She raced to her own, stared down into darkness, shrieked, "Michael, Michael, Michael." No response. The house vibrated with silence.

All he had ever done was copy her, like a shadow on the wall copying a figure of substance, learning to hate what she hated, but Angela and Patsy, they were purposeless frolics of his own. She should never have befriended Jack, but Jack was a lovely son without a mother; someone who talked her own language. Surely she was allowed to love other people apart from her own flesh and blood? Find them easier to like? She looked at the rings on her hands. Then she took them off, carefully.

Oh, it would hurt. Denying Michael's existence. Denying that she even had a son who used his father's name.

Joe sat in the half-light of a street lamp and read what he could. All these officials talked in code. There were more recriminations in this report than there was praise: the whole thing ended in a witch hunt, the word "disgraceful" repeated often. A dreadful reflection on supervision that a man of Jenkins' rank could be allowed to do what he did, so secretively; something must be done, etc, etc. Damnation on his head, and the only, remote blessing of the murder of Emma Davey was the fact that neither her family nor the disowning family of the suspect had any instincts towards litigation while the Press had given it second place. Whenever poor, bungling, unprepossessing Jack had made his brief appearances, he coincided with a serial-killing paedophile or a piece of Royal scandal and was relegated to page five, every time. The story of his life, one could say. Thus had Jenkins kept some kind of a job. And the world forgot the fates of Emma, Jack, Elisabeth.

Joe could not stay angry for long. It was that tolerance of his which others deplored as lethargy. As soon as he saw the reason, he saw the excuse. He could see why they did as they did and why they were wrong. Only cruelty made him angry.

He shivered as he unlocked the door and went up the stairs. She had been a hoyden, a temptress: a vicious angel of revenge; she had driven a man to death, for nothing, not much of a man, but then who was? Elisabeth Kennedy was a nasty piece of work, all skin, two-inches thick, the soul inside shrunk and rattling round against those skinny ribs. Thus she was portrayed. Thus she must be.

The living room, straight ahead, was full of light and radio music. He stopped, imagining the chandelier in place. There was a letter exposed on the table, which he read, beginning with "Dear Mother," noting how she could not write straight, yet, and crossed out every other word. He stored away the fragments of history revealed there; more messages in code. Joe regarded himself as having a right to read any piece of paper which the owner had forgotten to hide. He remembered the boy, Matthew, he had talked to on the phone. The voice saying, "Shall I go and dig her up?"

There was a sound of running water and muffled swearing from the bathroom, next to the kitchen.

"This right arm gets tired, see?" Elisabeth had told him. "There aren't any muscles in it. It's nothing but a bunch of string, all of uneven lengths, beginning to knit. Trying to control this thing is like learning to work a puppet."

He followed the sounds. The bathroom was rudimentary, namely a bath, a basin and a lavatory. No shower and little space for manouevre, clinical white fixtures. It was chilly, even now: it would be an ice-box in winter. The hot water came from the kind of wall heater of indeterminate age which a public health inspector would have condemned for delivering, in gulps, water which varied between boiling and freezing. Elisabeth was stripped to a bra and a towel round her middle. With the right hand, she was attempting to control the tap, while the left made a clumsy business of pouring water from a mug over the foam on her head.

Like open letters, Joe regarded unlocked bathroom doors as far from private. The slippy lino floor was awash.

"Hello," he said loudly.

She half-turned, revealing a mess of damp hair, dropping the mug. I am not only clumsy myself, Joe thought, I inspire it.

"Get out of here!"

But he could not, not quite, eyes rivetted to the puckered back, the scar an insult to the gentle curve of her spine, each wrinkle in it representing pain, pain and more pain. No-one deserved that. The skin had the pink rawness of the newborn. Joe backed out and found another mug.

"Stay still, will you?"

"Get out!"

"Oh, shut up."

His hands were so large they were able to encompass her whole head. He filled the basin, testing the water, then pouring it, working out the foam, pouring, massaging gently, tussling the thick hair which looked like sticky honey. He repeated the process, deftly. He could sense that her arms, braced against the edge of the basin, trembled slightly: he knew there was a moment when she truly feared he was going to push her head into the water, and hold it under. She was always, always waiting for punishment.

"All done."

The fear was still there in her face when she lifted her head and let him wrap the towel, turban style around her hair. Fear dissipating with the steam in the mirror, replaced with embarassment. She shrugged into the dressing gown hung on the back of the door, and pushed past him.

"Thanks."

"No problem." He began clearing the bathroom, whistling. Soaking up the slop on the floor with the cleaning cloth, wringing it out.

By the time he came back, the cigarette was lit, the smoke curling up towards the tin hat of a light. Thank God I've no aversion to cigarettes, Joe thought: it is my lot to be a passive smoker. The letter was now in a stamped envelope.

"There's something I want you to do for me."

"Anything you want." He knew exactly what he wanted to do. Which was cradle her to his chest and rub her hair dry, rubbing away those scars at the same time until her skin was all the same, unblemished white of her face.

"I want you to take me to see a friend."

"It's midnight and you've just washed your hair, and that's what you want?" he asked, mildly. The strings in her arms appeared to have become rigid.

"It's just a feeling. Been growing on me all evening. I just want to know she's all right. Home safe, that kind of thing."

"What for?"

She hesitated. "I don't really know. Because I'm getting back my sensations. Normal sensations, that is. It seems to include premonitions and nonsense ideas and the desire to talk to people. Even write to them."

"She might not welcome you at this hour."

She looked at him and shrugged. "No, she might not. Anyway, I meant 'see' as in drive by and see. Not necessarily meet. If her lights are on and her windows open, I'll know she's OK."

He was not a man to question eccentric requests. He nodded.

"I'll get my van. Where does she live?"

"Not far. Thanks."

"Post that letter on the way, I would," he suggested. "You know how it is."

They met at the foot of the belfry and he felt this ridiculous concern because her hair was still wet as he ushered her into the old van with the sticking door and the rust almost obscuring the white paint. She directed, he drove; companionably silent and yet with a sense of tension. Perhaps she just wanted to get out of the house; more like, she just wanted *him* out of the house.

"If you just wanted me out of the house," he ventured, "you could have sent me on my own. Told me drive round, steal that chandelier, check on your friend on the way back."

"I want that chandelier, some day. And this is where she lives. Stop here . . . No, on the right."

The handbrake made a sound like a ratchet chain, Yeeeeerp. Elisabeth was looking out of the open window on her side. She turned her whole body to compensate for the twist in the neck, then opened the door and stood in the street which was stuffed with cars but empty of people, and examined whatever it was she wanted to see, standing with her arms crossed, checking, nodding. Joe craned to see what she saw: the top floor windows, all lit, one open, in the only apartment with any sign of life.

This was all irritating. If she was worried about her friend, why didn't she ring the bell and say she was passing, at least? Even if the friend said bugger off, come back next week, I've got better things to do? Joe had plenty of friends like that. The sort who said, "I'm in pain, look after me," until he arrived to find some female in residence and himself an embarrassment. Old mates always talked in code.

Then he noticed a man, standing in the basement area to the right of his despicable van. The area was lit with a bright light and the man stood, half-baked in it, half-hidden by the basement steps, so that the sharpness of the contrast and the light made him look like a bisected, cardboard cut-out, one half black, the other half brightly pale. Joe looked back towards Elisabeth, glanced again to the man.

The shadow disappeared. Into the shadow or into the light, Joe never knew. His van shook as Elisabeth got back inside. He saw a flash of blue moving busily down the road, a measured walk breaking into a run, illuminated and darkened in turn by the lights he passed, the ghost of a perfect figure. Elisabeth was breathing deeply.

"I think it's all right," she was saying. "Patsy's in. She has to be all right. Why am I worried?"

They stared at one another in mutual incomprehension, the gaze faltering. Her hair was still half wet, hanging in corkscrew curls over her shoulders. She was a shrunken little wretch, and she was wrong. It was not all right whatever all right was. Cigarette lit, she breathed on it, as if it was a source of inspiration.

"Ring the bell," he said. "What harm? A flea in the ear?"

She was out of the vehicle, stamping on the cigarette, crossing the street, before he finished. Joe hesitated about whether to leave the engine running, decided he would on account of the poor old diesel's reluctance to restart and the lack of risk anyway, since a joyride in this old brute was no joy at all. By the time he joined her, Elisabeth had finished speaking into the entryphone. The door buzzed: he shut it carefully behind them.

Stairs and more stairs. Joe thought it must be a feature of any of Elisabeth's acquaintance, and his own, that they should love the existence of stairs and revel in living at height. Plush, carpeted stairs in patterned red which he did not like. If ever he had a house, there would always be stairs, without carpet, so that he could hear who came up or went down. He had no business here.

A woman was standing at the door. Without the puffy eyes and smeared make-up, he would have said she was a trifle tarty with her brilliant blue blouse awry, as if she had just got out of bed. She smelt of a mixture of booze, perfume, vomit, and on seeing them, made a valiant effort to change her stance, leaning nonchalantly against the door-jamb, rather than clutching it for support, struggling to find defiance.

"Lizzie, you must be psychic. No! Don't touch me!" She shrank as Elisabeth moved towards her. Looked over Elisabeth's head towards Joe.

"Is that your sodding van out there? The diesel?"

"Yup."

She sighed. "thank Christ for that. I thought it was an ambulance." She was winning through, making angry noises, leading them in. There were no signs of disturbance in her expensive, minimalist sitting room. Whatever the argument, it must have been brief. Elisabeth was calm.

"Do you need a doctor, a social worker or another drink?" she asked, so crisp it was callous. Colour flooded Patsy's cheeks. She sank into her own sofa, spoke almost normally.

"I haven't been raped, Lizzie. I'm not good enough for that. I've just been reminded that I'm a one hundred per cent, gold carat, bloody fool."

This time it was not her imagination. She *did* hear the door slam and she abandoned all pretense of sleep. Caroline had left her own door open: she was up and across the room, screaming, before he had time to put his own key in his own lock.

"Come up here at once! Where have you been, Michael? Where *have* you been?"

He obeyed, and the sight of him, clean tidy, even assuming an expression of injured innocence, was so reassuring, she almost wept. She was careful to be obvious in brushing away the tears pricking her eyelids.

"Don't think I can't *guess* where you've been. I just need you to tell me about it, that's all. Sit down, good boy. Would you like a little drinkie winkie?"

Her head was bare and bent towards him. He had already had a little drinkie winkie, she decided, but nothing excessive. He did not really like it, but sociable drinking was something she had taught him as part of his repertoire. She had also taught him how to loathe that loosening of control. He seemed both distant and receptive, like someone digesting bad news. No scratches on his hands, no smell about his person other than his own smell. She could feel the relief explode inside her skull, making her face flushed. Her hair stood out in ugly tufts.

"Tell me about it, sweetie pie." He paused, not for long, looked at the brandy glass placed in his hand with curiosity, as if he could not think what it was for. His voice was a whine.

"I don't know what to do when they like me, Mummy. I know what I want to do to them when they don't like me, but I don't know what to do when they do."

"So what did you do, petal?" she coaxed.

"Hit her, Mummy, but I didn't hurt her, honest. Then I went away."

The relief again, ebbing and flowing. He could dissemble well enough: he did it all the time, but he could not lie. He could not handle the ambivalence about desire which she had instilled in him, and for a moment, she felt immense regret. God, you could teach a boy a number of things about sex, but not how to do it. Although she had never wanted him to do it, not with anyone.

"And what *do* we do, honeybunch, when we think we've hurt someone's feelings? Especially a girl?"

"We send them flowers, Mummy. First thing. Lots of flowers. With a note saying we're sorry."

"That's right, darling." Oh Lord, their progress through life had been littered with flowers. She had paid over a fortune in flowers before he even stopped being a child. Now he could pay for his own. Her mind was working rapidly. Was Patsy the sort of girl who would make trouble? Expose herself and her needs and, doubtless, her own stupidity, to the police? She thought not. And if overprivileged Patsy should complain to her, she would express wonderment and ask her if she had complied with the rules. Which the silly bitch would have ignored.

He rose from his seat and came over to hers. She thought he was going to kiss her, but instead, he drew back his hand, balled it into a fist and punched her, below the ribs. Once, before he resumed his seat. Her glass shot out of her hand. It was so sudden, she could not believe it and yet she had expected it, all this time. She struggled for control, kept down the scream. Then she uncurled herself without saying a word. She would behave as if they had simply bumped into one another. Picked up the glass, nursed it. She had always known that one of these years, she would finally lose him. The sight of the results of childish rage no longer worked.

"Like that, Mummy," he was saying dreamily. "But I like it when they scream. But she wasn't the right one, was she, Mummy?"

She leant towards him, bile in her throat, trying to keep her breathing steady. She reached for his hand and touched it gently. His fingers were colder than hers.

"I know where the right one lives, Mummy. The one who killed my friend Jack. The nice girl you wanted me to like. But she didn't like us, just like Emma didn't really like me. We gotta pay back when someone is unkind to us, haven't we, Mummy? You told me."

He had his face turned away from her. The light seemed to hurt his eyes.

"And she's got the jewels, Mummy. Emma didn't have them. I'll get them and I'll get her. And then you'll be happy."

She pretended to ignore most of that, as if it were not important.

"I'm sure she's got them, Caro, Caro. I asked her when she was down on the ground. I said, just tell me and I'll stop. I gave her a chance, and she said yes, and then she was out like a light Caro, and she couldn't speak."

Caro shuddered. Distaste, delight, fear. They were two of a kind. Selective magpies for things which glittered, inspired by old hatreds. She wanted to tell him she had liked Jack, because he was one of the same kind when it came to hatred and acting on it.

"Do you like the ring, Mummy? I paid good money for it. Went a long way to get it."

"Yes, darling," she said softly. "I love it."

"This one tonight wore cheap stuff in her ears, Mummy. She wasn't worth it, was she?"

"No, darling one, she wasn't."

He let her hug him, briefly. She knew she should try to stop him. She also knew she would do no such thing.

"It'll make us both happy, Mummy, won't it?"

"Yes, darling. Yes."

They drove back, later, as Patsy insisted. She did not want to know where they slept and she did not want a man in the house.

"Why did you want to go in the first place?"

"I told you, I don't know why."

"Was it the blind date?"

"Probably."

"Are you going to talk to me, Elisabeth?"

"Why should I?" She was rigid and cool. The way she had been with her rat-a-tat questions of Patsy. Did you? Why? What next, you fool? What kind of imbecile lets in a man on a blind date? What did he do? If you won't call the police, Pats, and you won't even give us his name, why should any one of us care?

"Talk to me. Because there's no-one else."

"You flatter yourself."

"I mean no-one else here and now."

She did not answer, her feet trailing on the stone steps inside the tower. The same irritation assailed him. What was it with all these people, so slow to talk, the self-appointed keepers of so many secrets which were not even theirs to keep? And, ye gods, if the mother to whom she wrote her letter was cold, this bitch had certainly inherited something. He slammed the keys of the van on the table, let out a "phew" of disgust. Stumbled up the next set of steps . . . stairs, all these stairs . . . ready to kick off his shoes and fall into bloody bed. Let them all rot, and all their victims. Save him from people who were broken, but would not bend, articulate, who failed to express emotion, and any woman too sassy to cry.

The door to the back of the clock was open. Joe had tinkered with it this morning, same as other mornings, with no real purpose other than his own curiosity about its amazing components. He lay down: a floorboard creaked as the edifice did its breathing routine with a *crick* and *crack* of brick and stone. Then, in defiance of any logic, the clock itself issued an enormous TICK. Another. TICK, TICK, TICK, TUTT, tutt, tutt, and stopped. He looked at the immovable pendulum. No clock could tick without a pendulum. The sound echoed in his ears, a portent of the impossible, something telling him yes, it could be, would be mended. Like the bells, *wanted* to be mended. Joe put his feet back into his boots and went downstairs again.

Elisabeth was by the kitchen sink, her hair a bright orb of brilliant friz. She was rattling away at something and he saw she was making an attempt to sharpen a carving knife. Every knife, large or small was out of the drawer and onto the table. Her dedication to the task was chilling and ludicrous, as were the knives themselves. She could not sharpen knives with any degree of precision on something like a device for sharpening pencils, and besides all that, she was crying.

A silent sobbing, a private exercise, an exorcism of demons, turning them into gobs of tears so that she could wipe them away, breathe deep, get on with it. Joe was more than a little afraid of her. She was extraordinarily beautiful with all her damage, the spine beneath the scars one of tempered steel, if only she knew. He had never wanted anyone half as much, not a fraction of this. It had been the same, from the first, terrifying moment.

Jenkins' voice. "You've got your wrong eye on the lens, boy. Be like Nelson, give it the blind eye. Stick to the camera, boy. Ignore your prick."

He put his arms around her and she did not resist. Around and around: he felt he could have spanned her twice, his arms could cross around that spine and meet themselves like a pair of tentacles at the top of the waistband of her skirt. He was cradling the bird body, feeling the bones, with nothing to say but "Shh, shh, shush," like the chorus of a song or the ticking of the clock, tut, tut, tut, and wondering with his ever-conscious mind if this were not peculiar, and then coming back down to earth again, because she had not stopped crying, and although it had subsided, she was holding a knife, clenched in her fist.

So he kept on holding her, one arm cradling her head, the other her waist, until, finally, she dropped the knife and the crying stopped. In that order.

The tower gave another, predawn creak. It was only in his imagination that he heard the clock tick again.

"He is going to kill me," she said into his collar. "Which would be all right if only I were the last."

"Shush," he said. "Shhhhhhhhhh."

Again, in his imagination, the clock: one, two, three. When the bells sound thrice, you will deny me. He hefted her, arms still around his neck where they had crept, until they both lay on the futon, arranged like one large and one miniature spoon, and he drew the covers over them both.

"Will you talk, Elisabeth? Do you trust me?"

"I don't fucking know what you mean." There was a sigh. "As much as I can."

"That'll do."

He remembered to kick off his boots, before they slept.

Chapter

THIRTEEN

Thundery today, and about time, too. The weather was the sole topic of conversation. Steven Davey came out of his estate agent's office in Budley, carrying a smart umbrella, his son Matthew following at his heels. The boy was wearing baggy shorts with enough room inside for three of him, a T-shirt, socks and trainers. Each piece of clothing seemed to be quarrelling with the other. The T-shirt was half tucked in, flapped like a tail at the back and looked as if it had been crushed in a fist. The socks were irregular; one reaching halfway up one calf, the other corrugated around the ankle. His hair was unbrushed: he looked like a boy who needed ironing. From the far side of the road, as the shops opened, he could be heard, complaining unpleasantly. Don't want, don't want . . . Don't WANT.

They stopped on the street corner opposite the bakers, next to the burbling stream which might have sweetened the mood. Father could be seen confronting son, wagging a finger at him while Matthew stood with his hands deep in the pockets of his shorts and his toes turned inward, looking sulky and stupid. Then he responded to a command and continued to walk downhill to his grandmother's house. Steven Davey watched him for a second, then followed.

His mother-in-law was in the hall of the house and kissed Steven's cheek. She had the same invariable smell of Yardley's lavender, the upswept, white hair resembling a veil.

"Hallo, my dear, I wasn't expecting you. Coffee? The herd have gone."

The herd had been too large this summer.

"Only a minute." He was following her into the living room. "I'm busy. That wretched American's back. He's been up and down the coast, looking at anything and everything for sale, and now he's back. I only came in to make sure Matt actually got here without skipping off. He's in the mood, I warn you."

"Take him with you, then. Spice up the day. Tell the American all houses in Budley come equipped with a Matthew. Condition of sale." Steven was not so much impatient with his son, she decided, as simply flummoxed, like she was herself. The boy seemed to have given up any attempt to seek approval from either of them. As if he knew there was something about himself which neither of them could forgive, such as still being alive when his mother was dead.

"The American wants to see this house," Steven said, "For 'points of comparison' he says. I've told him a dozen times it isn't for sale."

He was noticing, not for the first time, the slight shabbiness of the room. There was a carpet, well past best, faded curtains, the uphol-stery good, but worn. It was a splendid advertisement for a policy of buying only the best in order that the life of it could be prolonged into a tired elegance by care and patching, but all the same the years had taken a toll. Nothing lasted forever. There was a stain on the ceiling which had the patina of age and expense.

"Let him look, if he wants," Diana murmured with a trace of bit-terness. "Let him look and dream of what he would make of this place with money."

"He would make a mess with his money."

"Yes, but I wouldn't. Tell him the entry fee runs to thousands. When does he want to come?"

"Whenever suits. I'll tell him. He wants a house with ghosts."

She looked through the window towards the sight of Matthew tormenting the dog. They had a love-hate relationship, those two, with Matt constantly expecting the animal to behave like a human being.

"We certainly have ghosts. Ghosts, but no treasure."

"Matt wants to spend the day inside that grubby shop. They said yesterday they'd be happy to feed him."

Dianna shrugged. She was quietly and profoundly hurt.

"Fine by me."

"It was your idea to do an inventory, as well as his to get round to the chandeliers. So you do it," Audrey said. In general, Audrey did not approve of any disturbance to the status quo on the basis that mess was good for the soul. Pick things up, remove them from where they are and mice come out and bite you. They had only been in this site for twenty-five years. Nothing much in the annals of time. "What about those chenille curtains we kept forever?" he demanded. "Eaten to death?"

"They were always dead, darling. Didn't suffer at all. Frightful things."

"Yes, but we'd paid fifteen pounds for them—in 1978. Fifteen pounds, I ask you! A fortune!"

"So we wouldn't have made a profit even if we'd got the damn things cleaned."

"And we paid too much for that chandelier . . ."

"Yes, because we bought it unseen and we thought it was complete. Oh, we were fools. Mind, she never actually said it was a heap of jumble, I just assumed, knowing her, it wouldn't be. Come on, darling, it can wait another ten years. It'll be like one of those bloody awful jigsaw puzzles, only with spiders at the bottom of the box."

"Matthew won't mind. He likes spiders."

There were actually three chandeliers about the premises. One, a miniature, hung crooked from the central light, two rings, one smaller than the other, attached by gilt chains to each other and the ceiling, each ring decorated with droplets of crystal and the whole effect somewhat marred by the two, oversized bulbs in the middle. Donald said it reminded him of an Australian bush hat, with corks round the brim, and it did not even give adequate light. The second was hidden under rubbish, and the third, the big one, sat in the box, on the armchair. It and its box were occasionally moved from the chair, but since this took the combined efforts of three people, it did not happen often. There was a hook in one of the ceiling beams which had been placed there expressly to hang it near the door, before enthusiasm faded and an old bird cage had taken pride of place.

Donald wandered to the front of the shop. Exiting from the estate agents was a large man, dressed in tartan, seersucker trousers, which in Donald's estimation, should not have been worn out of doors, accompanied by that dull egg, Steven Davey, who was, as usual, impeccably dressed.

"Give us a hand, chaps," Donald yelled. Steven hesitated. Donald's invitations to give a hand usually meant get dirty for nothing, buy you a drink later, which he never did, but this was Budley: when someone asked a favour, one did as one was bid on account of courtesy and never knowing when you would need the favour returned. The seersucker man trotted over the road after him, looking like a willing caddy.

"Only take a minute," Donald said, smiling. Age made him perfectly shameless in his lies. It took twenty minutes of heaving and swearing to thread the nylon rope which Donald swore would keep a frigate moored in a storm, "A *what?*" the American asked, before confessing to engineering qualifications which enabled him to suggest a better way. Another hook—one of those would never be enough—a sort of cantilever motion and the thing crawled out of its box with ominous rattling and unmusical tinkling, leaving most of itself behind. "Stop there," the American shouted. "Is this a frigging antique, or what? Jeeze."

"No, it's half a greenhouse," Donald muttered.

"I kinda like it," the American said. The half-complete object was filthy, yellowed and greasy, like an object once hung in a room heated with the poisonous calor gas and paraffin stoves of another era.

"I'm so sorry," Audrey said sweetly. "It's not for sale. Something else for your wife?"

"Yeah, give me anything which *is* for sale," the man said, laughing and showing his white teeth, giving Steven a light punch in the ribs.

"I cannot imagine who on earth would want it," Steven said, gesturing at the chandelier hanging about three feet from the floor, looking like a half-plucked peacock. At the same time, he was noting with disgust the state of his suit while satisfying himself that the client was dirtier by far, and trying hard to remember that he did already owe these two kind people an awful lot of favours, for keeping Matthew out of mischief, which was more than he was able to do himself.

"I know," Audrey sighed, fixing her bright gaze on the American. "And so should you, Steven, dear. Your mother-in-law thought the same about this monster, oh, thirteen, fourteen years ago. Why don't you ask her if she wants it back?"

Rumble rumble, crunch. That was the sound his feet made on the pebbles of the beach. They want to send me away, if they had *money*, they would send me away at once. I am not nice.

This time, Matt skimmed the stones so close to the bodies, the few who sat out so early, fully clothed as yet, waiting for the fugitive sun, that he positively frightened them. Aiming low, he skimmed the stones. One, two, three . . . The sun came out on the sea with a sudden intensity, then withdrew. There was a swell on the ocean without any froth in the greasy waves which munched at the gravel before spitting it out. He did not fancy swimming alone. He had enjoyed intimidating the people who seemed more upset by one, small, loose canon of a boy than they might have been by a gang.

He was ruminating with each stone, as far as his concentration allowed. Send me away—send me away—yes, yes and knowing he did not really want to go, not even if he had some choice in the destination. If there was no money, he might stay. Another stone shot into the water, missing the wave, shit. Another thought was dragging at him like the waves dragged the shingle. It took money to send people away: it even took money to keep them in prison, so his Aunt Lizzie told him, so unless there was treasure, somewhere, like his mother had said, he would not be going anywhere, because money was something they did not have. His father and Granny told him that all the time. Don't give that meat to the dog; food costs money, you know. Don't, don't, don't. They were not poor: they simply did not have money, or as much as they thought they should have. He was beginning to see the distinction. Which mattered to them, not him. Money sent people packing. There was no money and nothing worth money. Relieved by his own conclusions, Matthew scrunched up the beach, kicking the pebbles so hard he made his own feet hurt. He remembered to be exceedingly humble in asking Granny's permission to go to the shop, and was astounded to find it given without questions or fuss. Take Mrs. Compton these flowers, was all she said.

Maybe Lizzie was right, and being nice was the best route to getting what you wanted; but once the permission was granted without a fight, the odd thing was that he wasn't so sure he wanted to go. He went slowly up the street, muttering replies to the more robust of the greetings. "Hallo, young man! How are *we* today?" as if there was more than one of him. Granny wasn't so bad really. Outside the sweet shop, there was a man with funny trousers and muck all over his shirt. See? Matthew wanted to shout. I'm not the only one.

"I'm not having anything to do with that fucking chandelier," Audrey bellowed at him, without preamble. "It's all fucking yours."

He smiled for the first time that morning.

Noon, announced by the bells, waning into afternoon, and still the sun flirted with the tourists. Diana Kennedy read the post, and without expectation of reply, wrote to her daughter about the things which were on her mind. She had walked around her house, mourned for her own life. Write now, while she had the chance.

Maybe she thinks of me.

"There is an American who might want to buy the house. I just thought I'd mention it, to see how you feel, although I expect the prospect would not alarm you at all. The house is in trust, as you know. Each generation of Kennedys can only leave it to the next generation, which they always have. So it was Emma's, and will be Matthew's. You didn't come into this equation, apparently, nor did I. All very complicated, but I gather there's no such thing as a legal arrangement which can't be broken and refixed, these days.

"You always wanted to know about your real father, but I can't tell you much. I met him in the days when I was a bit of a hippy and you always slept with the man whether you wanted to or not. Sort of seduction, (not quite rape) by peer pressure. Since I can't tell you any more, I'll tell you about your adoptive father instead.

"He bribed me with this house . . . the greatest love affair of my life, although there's been precious few from which to choose. Love at first sight, certainly. When he fell for me, (and you) he fell for objects of beauty and I for this house by the sea. He was socially and sexually inadequate: it took me a while to work that out: we were disgracefully ignorant in the Sixties, you know, despite all that so called freedom. If your conception was the result of that, Emma's was the result of endurance in the face of revulsion, although I can hardly blame her and never did, quite the reverse. I knew it would be the end of everything if we did not have a child. She was the cement between two people who had no interest in one another at all. He gave me the house: I gave him the child. It was enough, for a long time.

"But he wanted to be the provider and the master and I could see he wasn't. His jewellery business did badly, despite his knowledge, because he was such a hoarder (a miser, I would say) who loved to buy and hated to sell. Me taking in paying guests humiliated him hugely. The house was all he had to offer, and there was I undermining it, stripping it, changing it, confining him to corners of it. Even with Emma to dote upon, she was growing up and away and he stayed out more and more, hence the ridiculous sailing. By the time he got pneumonia, he loathed me, and Emma was away somewhere. With Steven. If only Steven had chosen you.

"He couldn't bear me to touch him. Not that I wanted to, but I would have tended to him of course, if he'd let me. The house was full: I couldn't get help. Caroline Smythe was back, (even after I'd banished her terrible boy for stealing my rings) and she helped. Your father didn't seem to mind her: they had similar interests, talked together a lot: I really didn't know how serious his illness was until he died. I wouldn't let Smythe stay for the funeral, I resented her help, but of course I've never been able to refuse to have her back. Emma always said I was brutal to Smythe.

"It is *awful* to have someone die, knowing they hate you. I do not want that to happen to you and me, although I don't plan on dying for quite some time. As for what your father (and he was a good enough father, you must grant him that) did with any gems he managed to keep, God alone knows. If it weren't for the house falling down, I wouldn't have cared. I just wanted to explain to you that I'm subject to your opinion about what I should do. I don't own the house. I've kept it in trust for Emma and then for Matthew, who does not want anything from me. You don't own things just because you happen to love them. That isn't the way it works . . ."

She sighed and flinched as she penned the word "love." It was almost obscene: she wanted to cross it out, thrust the paper out of sight. Post it. Let words do their evil work. She had always been afraid of words.

Elisabeth was shy of words. Words out of the mouth committed the soul. There were too many words flying around like missiles.

"He was seduced by words," she said, hesitatingly. "It required very little else, I promise you. A touch, a gesture, a kiss."

"Did you ever bring him here? Jenkins thinks you did."

She frowned. It was Joe's reiteration of what he called slight acquaintance with Jenkins which had set in motion all these words. As if she needed a trigger. The words were waiting.

"No. He sent flowers here. That was as close as he got. I would come back here and sit in the cold and work out what to do next."

They were sitting with their coffee at the very top of the bell tower. The bells rested on wooden beams, seven treble one tenor, God bless you Robert Cross. Tapped with a fist, the bells made a sad and hollow sound, echoes of a previous life. The ropes tied to the wall in what was now the living room, connected to the head of each bell, but if the ropes were hauled, in order to turn the bell into the position where it could let out its clarion call, the bell itself would move in creaking silence. The clappers to the bells had been removed; there was another church, somewhere, which had found some use for them. All of them rendered impotent, except the bell for the clock, which was never turned by a rope. That remained fixed, like the leader of a pack who could not quarrel with their captain because someone had taken their tongues. These bells had no words to speak. The beams on which they rested, covered with a deceptive layer of dust, looked solid enough. There was space for Joe to lie on the dusty floor and peer beneath, and read the inscription inside the bell which served the clock. She watched him, carefully. "God made me as an instrument," it announced, "that I might serve his will." Joe found himself angry on behalf of the bells and their humility. Also the humility of anyone else. They were so immobilized by touch, gesture, kiss, it rendered them stupid enough to let someone take their clappers off. That was what Jack had been like. Biddable.

"What was he like? Our suspect called Jack?" He hated to deceive, but knew it was necessary.

"Revolting, but somehow, he could be sympathetic, if you got beyond the filth. Kind, in his way. He needed a ruling passion, although any would have done. Destined for sterile pursuits, should have been an academic, a boffin, the kind who remained in some small society, free of worldly pressures. He reminded me of my father, in a way."

She tapped out the ash among the dust, a delicate smoker.

Joe found himself nodding, one-enthusiastically, surprised by her accuracy.

"A little toad of a man. Fat, short of hair, sweating and smelling most of the time. Ignorant of social niceties, arrogant too. Short of the kind of benign, female influences which teach a boy to wash, at least, as well as change his shirt. They exist, these little moles, with pink snouts and thick skins. My father was a better version, I hasten to add, much better, but he was on that side of the line. Jack was further down the scale. He was pretty disgusting. And rendered incoherent by rejection, even though he wouldn't do anything to improve his chances. His fantasies about covering the face and brutalizing the body came from that. The fact he was plain and desperate for any kind of affection, was the sort of thing which would have appealed to Emma. Not for the fantasies, of course: he didn't tell her those. Only for the pathos and the untouchability. I don't know how she met him. He lived near. She wouldn't have minded his oddity."

Joe stood up, ducked beneath a beam, rapped his knuckles against the second tenor bell, smelt the rot of the supporting wood. The breeze, undetectable at street level, made a whistling sound up here.

The bell made a dismal, tinny sound, like a cheap, unenthusiastic doorbell, unlike the bell for the clock, which gave off a sonorous, low key, DONG! when kicked, hard.

"When I hit this," Joe said pointing vaguely to the nearest bell, "it means I'm asking why?"

She looked up towards the windows, sniffing with a kind of pleasure. Whatever had been engendered by yesterday's expedition and the memory of the chandelier was not lost. She drank a slug of coffee, tried to shrug her shoulders in a circular way, looser in the limbs than she had been, rejoicing in it. There were racing clouds and a blue sky.

"Because she was so hopelessly nice."

"Tell me again. I'm sick of hearing it."

Joe was on the prowl, ducking the beams, his boots crunching on the grit of the floor: strange bits of gravel, bird droppings which seemed to exist even without birds, dust which seemed to have formed a cloak for his feet. He knew why she wanted to live here. *He* wanted to live here. He felt a dizzying sensation of conviction. It was not the same as happiness merely certainty. He looked out of the slats into a workaday world: strangely scaled down people, and his own vehicle, looking like a dinky toy, badly parked. He knew he would see something different from the east side, or the west. Who else could see a whole one hundred and eighty degrees? Way down there, a miniature woman tripped and stumbled on the pavement, clutched at a railing, looked at her shoe, cursed without voice, walked on. That was reality; not this.

"You know, whenever I hear about Emma, I get bored. I want to put her in a book. What was she? The siren on the rocks with virtue? Such a sweetie. Like one of those statues. The model virgin with tears. Her death enough to reduce a nation to mourning and raise a monument, but that task left to her family, who made a plastic effigy of her memory. C'mon, twistneck. She can't have been such a paragon."

"Cynic."

"Me? Never."

"Oh Lord, Joe, don't you believe in innocence? She was preserved like a precious stone. With the difference that she wasn't particularly bright. Fire without brightness. Kindness without discrimination." More tapping of the ash and a long pause. Dead smoke descending on her hair, suiting her, like a form of angel dust.

"She couldn't judge, Joe. She didn't know the sick from the healthy, the weak from the strong, the good from the bad for that matter."

It was her turn to get up, feel, touch, tap each bell in turn. The tracksuit she wore suited her fine. It hid the thinness and the pockets accommodated the cigarette packet and the good lighter, which he had noticed, creating a bulge against her hips.

"Which is why she was so vulnerable and we were so angry. Because she never noticed how rude or gauche anyone was; she liked them that way. She was truly tolerant. The perfect victim, who always loved people far more than they were worth."

"Might have been loved far more than she was worth," Joe ventured, thinking to himself that this woman whose death had wrecked so many lives sounded to him beautifully deficient, not someone he would have liked. She sounded as boring as a badly researched saint, canonized for being mysterious, and her very existence made him angry enough to risk causing offence.

"She sounds to me like an over-privileged, over-endowed flirt."

Elisabeth shook her head. "There are women who will drive men mad. Beautiful, impossible women. Men want them, women want them. Model beauty, torrential sexuality, all that. The stuff of famous courtesans and the mistresses of kings. Women who start wars and foster deadly rivalries. The kind of woman with an incandescant quality difficult to comprehend until you stand in the same room. Emma was not like that. Not the kind of woman whose murder you could understand. Emma didn't generate that response. Patsy might have done, once . . . It required not only beauty of a special type, but ego."

"Ego," she muttered, nudging the clock bell with her foot. "You have ego. Obdurate faith in self.

"Emma was spectacularly pretty," she went on. "In a ballerina kind of way. Childishly exquisite, extremely self-willed, rather than powerfully sexy. She wanted to make amends."

"For what? What had she ever done wrong?"

"Oh, you miss the point. Some people want to make amends not for their own deficiencies, but for everyone else's. They take a personal responsibility for righting wrongs, real or imagined. They listen with horror but without an ounce of scepticism to hard luck stories: they are drawn to misery in the belief they can put it right. Emma didn't believe there was anything which couldn't be changed; any person who couldn't be altered. She took on board the silliest of crusades,

the most unlikely of people. She would've learned, but she hadn't yet."
Elisabeth laughed, a short bark of remembrance.

"If I had hit a girl at school . . . which I did, temper never very certain, I would come home bawling and swearing that it was her fault, the cow, and I was never going to apologise, not I. Emma would find out and go and do the apologising on my behalf. Unbidden, I hasten to add. She did it when Mother was rude to people. She befriended the lonely guest in Mother's house: she would descend on the party wallflower, drag them in."

"I'm sorry," Joe interrupted, "she sounds insufferable. I'll just get some more coffee. So I can digest her."

There was an art to these stone steps, so narrow at this level and so steep, there was a temptation to manage them on all fours. Or to creep up and down sideways, crab fashion, hands extended against the wall. Joe simply walked, bent double. Emma would have worried about his ability to manage two mugs without falling: Elisabeth did not. She leant by the window and thought what a privilege it was to watch the world without being watched. And she agreed with him, yes, Emma could be insufferable, with all that high-tuned sensitivity towards others which Emma could afford, because after all, she had never had to work. No, no, no, that wasn't the division. It was just that Emma's constant solicitude could irk and offend. Elisabeth had a vision of Emma, standing downstairs, looking round the place with the interested inspection of one who would not dream of saying anything negative, but thought it, all the same. You *must* do whatever you want, Liz, of *course* you must. And then, repeated invitations to *their* house for unwanted meals designed to guard against the cold and show, ever so gently, the benefits of a civilized life.

Enough: he was back. Seeing him emerge through the undersized door was another revelation. First the head, ducked like an expert, then the long torso, then the longer legs. She had the sudden, happy thought, that the ideal candidate for these premises would have Joe's torso and arms, the better to pull the bells, together with tiny wee legs, in order to scale the steps without fuss.

He handed a thick mug of dark-brown brew. Doctors had told her to avoid caffeine. Doctors had told her to avoid everything. Joe kicked the central bell.

"Not a why," he muttered, "but a *when*. When did you know that
Jack was not the man who had killed her?"

Joe could not have told her how much he dreaded the reply. It mattered, desperately, just as any hesitation would count against her.
There was none.

"I never knew while he was alive. I couldn't have gone through
with it if I'd had the slightest doubt. Not the very slightest, even when
he was being nice, and he could be nice, I was utterly convinced.
Couldn't have let him paw me, tell me his filthy fantasies, plan what
we would do when we were through this self-imposed probation. If I
felt pity for him then, it was a gleeful sort of pity, just you wait, buster,
just you wait . . . and even when it was all over, the judge threw it out,
branded me as a whore and Jack killed himself, I tried to make myself
think, good riddance. But I knew later, when I had all the time in the
world to think. Then I knew that I'd driven a man to his own death
and all for nothing. How ironic. My last love affair. The greatest effort
I had ever made to impress another living soul. For that. For his
destruction and for mine. Oh yes, he deserved his revenge."

"When?" Joe insisted. Then she hesitated. Dragged on the cigarette, sipped the coffee, wincing as it burned her mouth.

"You want the specifics? As if all realizations have a single, cata-
clysmic moment? Instead of something which burns a hole before
causing pain?" She stared at the cigarette in her long, thin fingers.

"When I was in the gutter. Drunk and burned. I felt that man press
his knuckles into my eyes. I imagined this was the man who killed my
sister. He took my rings and pressed them into my eyes. That was
when I thought I knew. But I probably knew before that. After Emma's
death, and before the acid."

She smiled her crooked smile. "that's when things fell apart. Flesh
from the bone, fuel from the spirit. There was nothing of me left. I
have never, in the whole of my life, done a single, wise or courageous
thing."

"And another man was accused of attacking you," Joe said flatly.
She looked at him with the pity of the schooled for the ignorant.

"He was not accused. He confessed. He had a pre-existence before
me, a nuisance, easily believed. He probably saw something which
made the confession stick, I don't know. I wasn't exactly in a position
to intervene, and who would believe me if I had? I never saw him. All

that happened was that it gave an excuse for them to put away a man who had begged to be put away. I am part of his repertoire now, he's proud of me. I said nothing, because even though I imagined I knew, that isn't the same thing as being sure. And . . . something else."

Joe kicked the bell. Blood out of a stone, this was. He was confused with the whys and the whens and the wherefores.

"What else?"

She had her hands loosely clasped in her lap, sitting in the dust as demure as a lady at a tea party.

"Well, I thought it might be Matthew. Which shows how mad I was."

The hands fluttered, at a loss without the cigarette which gave them purpose. "Trying to stop me going away. I was wrong again, of course. But that's what I thought. For about three days, that's what I thought. Among other things."

He stared at her. So cold, so contained, so controlled. So fucking twisted. Looking at him, and the bells, as if they were all under the same microscope. If only he did not like her.

"Patsy's man," he croaked. "Could he be the man?"

"Possibly. He was going to cover her face. She said he asked her about her rings. She told us about her friend Angela wearing rings. That wasn't in the paper."

"Angela Collier?" So much for him hiding the newspaper. She had known, long before Patsy had blurted it out. Elisabeth shook her head. "I don't know. Patsy said Angela wouldn't go to the agency. I think it's possible she did. Met the same man."

"Warn them."

She leant forward, retrieving the coffee cup from the floor. They were practically nose to nose.

"Of what, oh wise one? Of what? My fantasy?"

"A man," he said weakly. "Just another man."

He nudged the nearest bell not aggressively but affectionately, one last time. The wooden support creaked ominously and he stepped away. She stood in front of it, stroking the surface, as if out of all of the bells, it was her own.

"Better tart myself up," he said. "Make an appointment. Find a wife."

"Tart us both up, then. If you're going to that agency, so am I."

He looked at her, and looked away. Shifty.

Her feeling of trust, as if she had known him forever, was such a relief, she could not quite bring herself to ask *why*, Joe. Why should you? She could not spoil the relief, even though whatever he had told *her* was so incomplete. She had to trust him and reason why, later. There was no-one else.

"What are you going to tell me, Joe?" she said, sadly. "That no-one would believe that a girl who looks like me could dare to be a lonely heart?"

Chapter

FOURTEEN

The day after her Select Friend debacle, Hazel had another envelope, in her hand, when Patsy phoned, first thing, talking about not coming into work. Hazel had muttered about how there was no need to give any more reminders about how no-one was indispensable and what about the bloody police, who were still there? The thought that she, Hazel Turner, could do Patsy's job, with her hands tied behind her back, had become recurrent, and although Hazel did not entirely approve of herself for thinking thus, it was a school of thought encouraged by their management who found senior personnel expensive. Perhaps this might be a point in her life when she should forget about men for a year or three and concentrate on ambition. Men were not nice. They were not suitable for more than one purpose; they were a drag on the rations. All the same, the buttermilk envelope was tantalizing. It contained not one profile, but two.

"I have given your profile and work phone number to these *delight-ful* men," Mrs. Smythe's accompanying letter gushed. "So you should be hearing from both of them! (Unless you phone first!)"

Hazel was not in the mood on this particular morning. It all seemed like so much effort; she could not shift her own depression, but all the same, she saved the envelope until she was halfway over the bridge and, feeling like a spy sent into a dark corner to decipher clandestine instructions, she read carefully.

"John Jones works for a multinational company as an executive and has his own (small) house in North London. He describes himself as shy and loyal . . ."

Probably keeps a cat and a budgerigar. Which might make for better conversation than the car and the mates. The second profile was intriguing.

"Derek Taylor is in his middle years, divorced with grown-up children. He finds he rattles round in his own, large house and seeks companionship. Interests include music and interior design."

That was more like it. A sugar daddy with walls. She immediately envisioned someone tall, slim, well-preserved, grey-haired and grey-suited, plays squash once a week. Maybe a dog and a nice, old-fashioned motor, with leather on the inside.

Phone him, but first savour the thought, while Pats was out. So she wouldn't have to tell.

There was something about the shared horror of Angela which was making them wary of each other, as if it contaminated them with shame. Perhaps they had never really been that close.

Autumn was near, sniffing round the corner. She could smell it, drifting off the water.

The early smell of change.

OK, Joe thought, I'm under control. I'm sitting in a pub, waiting for Owl like I promised I would and now I need to be. What worries me is what *she* might be doing. I read that number on the man's profile, Owl. I read everything. Patsy put the profile in the bin, but I got it out. I recognized that number. I never forget numbers, or faces, and I read everything which is not locked away. Even pieces of paper already torn up.

This is what we know, Owl, he would say, without specifying who *we* meant, rehearsing the emphasis in his own mind to make it sound like a team, while really meaning this is what I know, which is not a lot. Make himself sound like a private detective with a glamorous, dirty raincoat. Joe had never met one, couldn't imagine what they were like. Not in lovely London, with a nip of cold in the air.

Look, Owl *we* need an ally. This is what *we* know. (*we* equals one injured woman whose sister was killed two years ago, plus a not so reformed alcoholic police officer of amoral tendencies and completely powerless any way, and myself. Not an impressive team: between us, we command not an ounce of credibility and we do not pull together.
We know these facts.

1. A man accused of killing the sister went to an introduction agency . . . our agency, Select Friends. He showed signs of a nasty disposition, according to the woman who ran the agency, and that helped cast suspicion upon him. He did not meet Emma Davey through the agency: he knew her already no-one quite knows how and it doesn't matter. This man did not kill Emma, although he knew a lot about how it was done . . . Because someone, in the later stages of the whole business, showed him a photograph.

2. The murderer stabbed once, then covered Emma's head with a black plastic sack and beat her to death. No sexual assault. He may have used some sort of bleach to cover traces.

3. After the failure of a case mounted against the subject, the deceased's sister, (Elisabeth, to you) who had entrapped him into suspicious admissions only, was attacked by a man who burned her with caustic soda. No known connection. This was not in London, but in the place where the sisters had grown up. (You might say what has this to do with anything . . . well, it might.)

4. Two years after the murder of Emma Davey, Angela Collier is killed (in own home, again) by a man who covers her face. Again, brutal and frenzied. Traces of bleach. Only you and I know, Owl, no-one else, (a lie: Joe saw all lies and evasions in brackets, since Elisabeth knew, and probably Jenkins too) that Angela was a client of Select Friends and the woman in charge of said agency asked *you* to say nothing about it.

5. Last night another client of this agency was attacked by a man with whom she had been on a blind date. He seemed to wish to cover her head with a shawl, but he relented and backed off. This morning he sent flowers, Interflora. She is adamant about not complaining . . . feels it was her own fault. It is the regime of Select Friends that profiles are sent out by the agency which do not give addresses . . . only contact numbers for the punters place of business. (Everyone who goes to Select Friends must be employed: it costs too much for the unemployed, who would not be eligible candidates anyway.) The number given by this violent man relates to a mobile phone.

It just so happens that this is *your* phone, John Jones, old chap. (Could Rob or someone have borrowed it?) Don't worry. We know the blind date wasn't you: the man in question was handsome with thick, dark hair. Which is why, Owl, you have to go to the police. Not *we, you.*

"He won't go," Elisabeth predicted, after they had descended from the bells. "He'll say it's all nonsense and he won't go."

"Why on earth would he react like that?"

"Because, from all you've said about him, he'll be afraid of looking a fool."

The Owl would not go. He stood his ground, small, obdurate, frightened. Or at least, he would not go immediately. Where should he go? Who should he contact? Where would they start? What was Joe doing to him? *Please,* Joe, what are you doing to me? There is nothing to connect me to any of this. I know about Emma Davey. I read about that case eighteen months ago, Joe. I know we never talk about Jack, but do you want me to be like bloody Jack? I'm NOT LIKE JACK! Jack was a pervert, a fucking loser. Everyone knows they got the right man and a stupid judge and the bugger killed himself, as he should. And you want me to go to the police? GET LOST, JOE.

It's your mobile phone number, Owl: I recognized it. Rubbish. And so what? It certainly wasn't my call. There are fifteen men in our office, Joe. The phone lies around. Anyone could have used it: Rob's always pinching it. No, I'm not going near a sodding policeman, Joe, I'm not. And if you fucking send them round to me, I'll tell them you're an unemployable bum and a liar.

But he would go, Joe thought, eventually. Once he had thought about it. Strange how they both thought of Rob, with his volatility and aggression. They could both see Rob hitting a woman, even though that was unthinkable in an old mate.

Joe was surprised by Owl's resistance, but on reflection, he decided he should not have been. Owl would want to think about it. Owl always did. Owl had known Jack, peripherally, as they all had. Apart from Michael Jack had been Michael's special friend. But it felt like stalemate, the little dribs of knowledge burning holes in his pockets. And the shadow of the man he had seen, outside Patsy's, flitting round his head, like a moth.

I have never done a wise or courageous thing in my life, have I? Who would deny that?

The tower was silent. Jack's words, replayed in this still holy place, reverberated. I want to fuck a woman from behind when I can't see her face; I want to see her shudder, but I want her masked, mysterious; I don't want to see her eyes.

Oh yes, she had breathed, deceit following deceit like chasing shadows. Oh yes, tell me what you would like, and why: I need to understand you. How can I love you if I don't understand? She had listened to it later on the tape, wanting to gag. His hot face, always glistening with sweat, even in December, the hair, always greasy. The time he had terrified her, while the tape had recorded nothing of the rustling of her coat as he put her hands beneath, round her waist, squeezing her buttocks until, even beneath the thick jeans she wore to each assignation, he hurt. She had always confined provocative clothing to the half-undone shirt, with a touch of Wonderbra cleavage: he liked that, but could not look at it, or her, kept his head buried in her shoulder during an embrace. In retrospect, he was more like a frightened child seeking reassurance.

The tape had not recorded what she wore. It recorded words. "Don't get close," Jenkins always said. "We don't want the bugger coming in his pants, we want him talking." Tell me, she would croon, tell me. Hiding a gasp of pain. Keeping control, because it was easy to keep control when the man who fumbled with his lardy hands was a man she found disgusting. He did not like their eyes. The windows of the soul. Deceit upon deceit. She had known then that Jack had been to an introduction agency, but that was simply a part of his whole pathetic history she never had to investigate in person.

She was the foot soldier, those behind her were the intelligence, and he, the casualty of war. He had never done more than pummel and squeeze. And apologise.

Elisabeth was trying to make herself look beautiful. Presentable, desirable, but it was like trying to make something out of a dishcloth. A silk purse out of a sow's ear, her mother would have said. No-one could make this body beautiful.

She shivered. The memory of Joe's warmth against her back made her flush. Both of them curled against the dark the night before, his softness against the bones protruding from her own skin, all restless angles as she slept those few hours before dawn. It was generous of him to blot out other memories with the warmth of his big body. Kind, that was all: he would cuddle a sick dog and she could not reconcile herself to this quixotic trust of him: it seemed unreal; it was far from complete.

Where was the make-up? A bag full of sticky equipment, in the bathroom; a tan-coloured foundation leaking slightly, crusted round the screw top. Mascara. Cracked eyeshadow, the wrong colour for a sunny day, use sparingly. She could not see her own face without adopting an awkward pose, as if she was sitting on a love seat, twisted so that she could see not the other face, but her own eyes. The friz of hair held back with slides and allowed to expand as if it was a statement rather than an accident. Then the clothes, the armour. A pale-yellow linen blouse, a skirt with matching yellow dots on blue, held up round her waist by a belt of soft stuff which could be knotted tight, the wrong blue. Almost human, a little mismatched perhaps, creased in places where a person once proud of grooming would not be, but passable, without being impressive.

Enough to present herself as a viable specimen at an introduction agency? Somehow, she doubted it. She had the shell-shocked look of a certain kind of neurotic, but the purpose was only to get inside the door. Without an appointment. On the kitchen table, pasted together with selloptape was the profile of Michael. Patsy had torn it up, she said, in between the time of his departure and Joe and Elisabeth's arrival, thrown it in the kitchen bin and refused to give his name.

Elisabeth had retrieved it, and carried it away in her pocket. She studied it again. In one corner there was the clear impression of a set of teeth, sign of Patsy's anger, above a single paragraph on a piece of heavy paper, the name of the agency on the top. No proprietor's name.

This was what she was going to do: She would go to the agency, fling down the reconstructed piece of paper and say, I want to meet *this* man. Not another man, this one: I'll pay you.

Floating down the steps, careful of the dust. Out into the sunlight. How different was the world from this angle. Picking up the post from out of the letterbox on the door. Two letters for Joe, the cheek of him! Anyone would think he lived here! One for her. From her mother, the writing as recognizable as her own hand, stopping her in her tracks. She put them all back in the box. She could not afford distractions.

There was still that same, almost sneaky, feeling of joy as she got on the bus. She was purposeful, while still conscious of her own reservations about her own judgement: she was afraid and she was hungry and tired, but never more aware of the colours of life outside the window and the energy in her limbs. She refused to think about Joe, but she could not stop thinking about Joe, with all his questions and all his suspect motives and what the hell did he want; big, warm, nonchalant, bell-kicking Joe? Something. And that was enough of that: this was her stop. Everyone's stop, the bus emptying at Piccadilly with all the noise of a flight of geese, yelling, where is it, where is it, this place, what time, where shall we go.

It was not a place where the bare necessities of life were acknowledged, except, maybe, by a fruit stall. You could eat cake rather than bread, buy lycra at Lillywhites, purchase gear for the trend of your life, tweed and evening dress, suits in Jermyn Street, popcorn and chocolate and a-pound-a-slice pizza. You could gamble and gawk, see film after film, eat if you had the price of a modest Chinese meal and knew where to go, eat McDonald's, eat fashion and, at this time of day, drink downmarket or upmarket tea, with solid, leftover scones or delicate cakes, again depending on knowledge. You could not buy groceries: you could only acquire ephemera. You came here to be ripped off and entertained, to fight and get drunk, to queue and to watch from narrow pavements with too many cars fighting for space. It was not a place to come without a gang; a place meant for those who liked going out after dark, when the tawdry scenery mattered less and the neon signs looked pretty.

Elisabeth had always found it difficult to be entertained. She was a spoilsport, a nonbeliever, immune to the spells.

She walked away from the crowds and into the hollows of Jermyn Street. Fantastic shirts with high necks: she craved the one in pink and white stripes, made for a man. Also the same model in green. She felt scruffy, startled to see herself even further distorted in the same shop window and even more surprised to find she had arrived. She was panicked by the stairs.

These were not her own, solid stone steps, which made a gritty sound underfoot, unlike the linoed, police-station steps which had made a slapping sound, as if being punished by feet; these creaked. This was one, vertical tunnel, with landings leading onto half-glassed doors with names inscribed: it had the same effect as if it had been underground, but warm and busy, like the world outside.

How would Patsy react now? Not the Patsy of last night, who had substituted brittle anxiety for the confidence she had once possessed, but the person she had been. She would want to feel contemptuous. Patsy had been good at staying cool: it had been Patsy Elisabeth had emulated when the man squeezed. All of a sudden, Elisabeth wanted to change her mind about how she should approach this: Joe was right. She changed tack at the top of the stairs and almost capsized.

She stopped, took out her little lipstick mirror and checked it. Too loud. She dabbed at her mouth with a tissue. The sellotaped profile crackled in her bag: she pushed it down and opened the door.

There was a woman arranging flowers, fussing over them, plucking at a leaf which had dropped. Such magnificent flowers reminded Elisabeth of a wedding, perhaps that was the idea, suggesting the hope of the big day.

The light was uncertain, diminished by the flowers, as was the woman. The flowers were a clever arrangement, Elisabeth observed, the sort of thing her mother would have done, combining economy with style. Plenty of inexpensive foliage of the kind a florist might give away and her mother might gather from the garden, to offset a very few, expensive blooms.

"How lovely," she said politely.

The woman on the far side of the flowers was wearing a wig, another instant impression. The hair on a wig stood still, like hair stiffened with laquer: it was arranged to show no hint of a hairline and it did not respond to surprise. Although the woman was merely pretending surprise: footsteps on the creaky stairs would surely have the same effect as a herald, unless she had been entirely absorbed and not, as she appeared, waiting.

"Sorry?" the woman said, imperiously. "Have you made an appointment? Only I don't recall it. Appointments only, I'm afraid."

She moved into the light. The recognition was slow at first and not entirely mutual. Elisabeth would not have recognized Caroline Smythe at once, except for the voice. She had heard the voice, so recently, out in the garden at Budley, distinctive above the sound of the sea, as shrill as a seagull when she had raised it to emphasize some platitude about a bloom. "Oh how *sweet* these dear little pinks are! How *clever* you are Diana!" said Elisabeth, lying in bed, faintly enjoyed the thought of her mother's irritation, hidden beneath some smooth reply. She had not actually seen Caroline Smythe in years: their visits had not coincided and Elisabeth had always endorsed that huge division between family and guests in a way her sister never did. Caroline Smythe was squinting at her, removing her glasses, conscious of familiarity, but uncertain of it as yet. Elisabeth knew that recognition would dawn any second. Mrs. Smythe was not a woman who forgot a face and, in particular, she would not forget hers. Even if it was fifteen years before, she was still the girl who had slapped her son and told him to give back the rings he had removed from her own mother's bedroom.

"Well, do sit down anyway, now you're here."

"Mrs. Smythe?" Elisabeth said, extending her hand, putting warmth into her voice, like sugar into tea.

"Emma," Caroline said, faintly. "Is it really?"

"No, I'm Elisabeth."

"Oh, my dear . . . Of course!" She was rallying, the colour in her face turning from ghastly white to pink. "How *are* you? Did your mother send you? I thought I'd seen a ghost . . . Oh what a surprise. I thought you were still at home, dear."

"I'm fine." Not quite. There was a bubble of hysteria rising which might yet break into nervous laughter. Caroline Smythe with an introduction agency; how they might have added that fact into the melting pot of their contempt for her, if only they had known. Not an employment agency, as she had told them, a scrubby little introduction agency, a joke. Even Emma, who was so nice to Mrs. Smythe, scolding Steven and she for their snobbish mimicry of her, might have found that funny. Elisabeth felt she was playing a game of charades.

"No, my mother didn't send me. Although I'm sure she might have done, if she'd known. No, I'm under my own steam, Mrs. Smythe. Saw the agency advertised, what a clever name, I thought. I didn't know it was yours, of course. Is it yours?" She looked as uncertain as she felt. "And I was only thinking, what with my convalescence and my non-existent social life, it might be a good idea. I've been feeling so hopeless and I was passing and . . ."

She was talking too fast. Caroline nodded, the smile a travesty of puzzled compassion. She had not advertised recently.

A wig, in the warmth of these closed rooms? Elisabeth was thinking. Did the woman reinvent herself and her flowers every day, in the same way she had seemed to reinvent herself each year in Budley? Sometimes attempting to copy Diana Kennedy's elegant simplicity, but always with the wrong colours and buttons?

"Let me look at you, dear. Such a long time."

Despite herself, Elisabeth flinched under the scrutiny. It was a long, searching stare, during which she waited for Caroline to touch her, steeling herself against the stroke of a finger against her averted cheek, a kiss, even. The feeling of endurance was almost unbearably familiar, but Caroline had her hands firmly in her pockets, as if ashamed of bitten nails, grinning girlishly, then looking concerned.

"Naughty girl. I can't understand why you came back to London, dear. Such a lonely place. Me, I'd never leave darling Budley and that lovely house, if I had the choice."

"I don't have the choice. My mother's house isn't my home. This is my home."

"Your tower? It sounds wonderfully quaint, I must say. Do call me Caroline. Do you live there alone?"

"Yes, of course, how else would I live?"

"Are you looking for a particular kind of man? Is that why you came here?"

It sounded like an accusation, so uncannily near the truth, Elisabeth was horribly aware of the letter in the bag. The plan to flourish it became wildly inappropriate. She fiddled with the buttons at the neck of her blouse, checking if she was quite as naked as she felt, and then she nodded, looking genuinely foolish, exposed and reluctant. A deep breath before a confession.

"Yes, to be honest, I suppose I am. You see, one way and another, I've lost contact with all my friends. I feel marooned, I couldn't think what else to do. You know I was in the police, before Emma, well you know about that. You meet men, of course, not the right kind, and then, this accident, you see . . ." She let the voice trail away petulantly.

"Yes I do see, dear, I really do," Caroline said patiently. "But I'm not sure. You aren't exactly love's young dream at the moment, are you?"

Elisabeth was surprised to find this hurt, albeit slightly.

"Fact of life, my dear. Men go for looks, always did, always will. They like women to look like healthy adverts for something or other, but . . ." She gave a big, reassuring smile. "I'm sure there's something we can do. Hang on a minute, will you?"

She left Elisabeth standing by the waxen flowers, disappeared into the room behind. There was the sound of drawers being opened, the clink of something dropped, a rustling and then she was back with a set of forms.

"Such nice men come here, dear. I'm sure your mother would approve. Fill in the address and the phone number. No need to do the background stuff, I know all that, don't I? Sorry to hurry you, it'd be so lovely to chat, but I've got an appointment you see, in a minute or two. I'll write it for you, shall I?"

"I'm a bit slow at it," Elisabeth apologized. Caroline scribbled at her dictation. "No fee of course. Not for a family friend."

"I couldn't possibly," Elisabeth said.

"Well . . . we can discuss that some other time. I'll ring you dear, or write. Give me a day or two. You don't mind about age, do you? No, I didn't think so. One of our older gentlemen, I think."

"You're very kind."

"Not at all. Byeee. Love to your mother."

This dusting her off and practically throwing her down the stairs was elegantly done, and it left Elisabeth troubled and outmanoevred. She wanted to go back and kick her, to ask one question which may have hurt. How's your son, Mrs. Smythe? Is he still a thief?

She burst headlong into the sunlight, boiling with rage, frustration and indignation. She wanted to shout, scream, tell someone. Boiling mad, clenching her fists. Instead, smiling a smile as false as Caroline Smythe's, sauntering, lighting a cigarette as she faced the shop window with the green and white shirt which would look nice on Joe. She waited and watched, saw him striding down the street, checking numbers as she did in the doorway.

There was that absurd feeling, watching him go in. She wanted to protect him from Mrs. Smythe.

He groaned. Stairs and more stairs, taken in furious leaps and bounds and a muttered, "Sorry" when he almost flattened a small woman with a large screen moving from one door into another. He knocked at the top door with the glass panel, Select Friends in Gothic script and the name underlined by a depiction of a long-stemmed rosebud. Colour that red, and it could look like an outpost for the Labour party. The door stuck: he remembered to dip his head. Attic levels and Joe did not go together. Maybe that was why he liked the belfry rooms, because of the height. Small rooms like this made him feel aggressive.

He was supposed to be on a voyage of discovery, but women like this also made him feel aggressive. Especially those designed to calm the fevered brows of giants and convince them into domesticity. The man in question would be particularly amenable if he loved the dulcid smell of pot-pourri and thought it a sign of civilization. Joe was not sure about that. The smell only reminded him of the smells it might mask. Bleach, polish, rot. The abundance of flowers reminded him of hospital wards.

He seemed to have surprised her, sitting at her desk, apparently in the act of putting rings onto her fingers, two already on the left, one, slightly tight, being persuaded over the fat knuckle of her left little finger. She was nicely dressed, nothing pretentious, a homely, verging-on-elderly businesswoman with the rings her only ornament. She looked competent and friendly. He could see why the Owl had liked her, why she would have kept Rob in his place and why even Michael had been impressed. There was a quiet competence: a facade which made him rebel.

"Here's the hot seat," she said, gaily. "Joe, isn't it?"

"S'right," he said. For today he was not accentless English, but vaguely Australian. Joe had the knack of copying voices. It amused the old mates. There were a few escapades, years ago, when they had put him forward as the foreigner, confused by *l'addition*.

"And who recommended you, Joe?"

"Bloke called Michael. Said he had a woman friend who come here. Nice woman, too. So I thought, if you have nice women on the books that I might like to meet, this was the place for me. Right?" He winked, lewdly.

She laughed with a gentle shake of the head, like a kind teacher anxious to make an essential point without actually wagging her finger.

"Are you looking to settle down, Joe? Or are you looking for a crowd? Can't help you in the latter case," her voice assumed the receptionist style, posher and more deliberate. "This is a place with serious intentions, you know. Didn't your friend tell you? Who did you say?"

"Michael. Never can remember his name, and yes he did, mam." That was slightly over the top. He was looking at her intently, flirtatiously even, examining her familiarity. She had such distinctive eyebrows, unplucked, but sweetly shaped with a little quirk at the narrow end, and a thick thatch of stiff, artificial-looking hair.

"Matter-of-fact man, he resembles you, Aunty. Our Michael, I meant. Could be a son of yours. Or maybe lots of people have that kind of hair."

She laughed, immoderately, while pulling forms out of the drawer in her desk. "Oh, no, no, nooo. My clients are my children, Joe, I've none of my own, only those who get adopted by me. And I *never* discuss other clients. You work with this Michael, do you?"

"Did. Gave it up. I like to travel, see?"

"And how do you earn your living, dear?" Obviously an important consideration, when her fees, discreetly apparent from the top form turned towards him, revealed themselves as a thousand a year. De luxe service, that was.

"Oh I'm a rolling stone. Freelance photography, never forget a face. I do bits and pieces, you know how it is."

She did not know: she was frowning.

"Actually, you can earn quite a lot that way," he added helpfully. Frowning, she looked even more like an older, female version of Michael, with rings on her fingers and, possibly, her toes.

"I've done bits of works for the Fuzz, even, would you believe. Some for medical journals, but it's mostly insurance, crashed cars, burglaries. Also floral displays, shop signs, body scars, you name it I snap it. I'm hoping to get into food, though. A lot of dough in photographing food. Geddit? So I could do with a bird who cooks."

She was disliking this, finding him distasteful, eyeing the drab jacket, the tieless neck, the clean scruffiness and the awful pony-tail. He could see she could not envisage him as fit companion for some executive Miss, but then neither could he. In a way, he was enjoying himself, forgetting what it was all about and trying to push down the acute temptation to provoke her. He smiled, gave her another roguish wink. Again, as he did it, he realized it was a mite over the top. The receptionist voice had become glacial and the sarcasm was scarcely veiled.

"I see. Is there anything else you would want from a partner that I should know about?"

He put his feet up on her desk, leant back so far on his spindly little chair, it creaked on the verge of self-destruction. Scratched the crotch of his jeans: thought about it.

"Well, as long as she comes across, big tits and blonde hair would be nice."

She rose, unfazed, but outraged.

"There's the door, Joe. I'm not a service to vulgar predators. Get out."

"I've got cash, honest. Don't you want the story of my life, mam?"

"No."

Get out. That was the story of his life. He could not remember if he had ever heard it said with greater conviction.

Owl was wandering round the office in the late afternoon, chewing indigestion sweeties after three hours of chewing almost anything else which was sweet and sticky as an antidote to beer without food in the middle of the day. He was looking for Michael. What a fucking mistake to explain what was not, after all, his problem to fucking Joe, even if Joe had bought the beer. *Not his problem.* Michael was a non-participating listener, brilliant in meetings, for keeping quiet and only giving a reserved opinion, later. Like some kind of mathematician who needs time to do his sums. Owl was also looking for his mobile phone. Open-plan office, monitored phone calls, people kept pinching his phone and standing in the corridor. *I didn't lie about that, Joe.* Perhaps he had, because it was there, on his desk, making a bleep, bleep, bleep like someone in pain. He picked it up, listened.

"Michael, is that you?" The woman's voice was distorted. Reception varied. Everyone sounded like a goldfish.

"Yes," he said, furious. "Can't you tell?"

"Go and get her, Michael. Don't wait."

He dropped it. Bastard. Off. The sound stopped. It bleeped again. He snatched it.

"Lo."

"Rob?"

"No!" he yelled. The sound of his voice was unnaturally loud over the hum of other, telephonic activity. Owl looked at his state-of-the-art machine as if it were a snake. Then he put it on the floor and stamped on its head.

There was nothing he wanted which he could call his own.

Chapter

FIFTEEN

Matthew now understood the importance of light and why people talked about it. Dark nights drawing in, they'd say, and he could never see why it was worth mentioning, because there was always something to do, dark or light, and food appeared at the same times. Now, he could see how the quality of light mattered so much and how it changed between noon and three, and how by five in the afternoon it was perceptibly duller because of the longer shadows. And also how he was a little duller himself, tired by the fiddly bits of soft wire, and the reflection and the interruptions in the shop. Customers saying "What is he doing?" as if it were not perfectly obvious and Audrey saying, "Enough, enough," but he was mesmerized. As well as proud.

"If you use your eyes for different purposes," Donald told him, "it gives them a break. They come back into focus, good as new, but they like a change." His eyes had been fine the night before, when Matthew was looking in the book Audrey had given him. A new book, nice to the touch, with little enough to read and plenty of pictures of *Some Famous Gems*. The Ko-i-Noor diamond, just a hunk of sparkling rock; the Timur ruby, big and red; the Dresden green diamond which was lost in its setting and, his favourite, a dagger from the Topkapi palace, which made him smile. The hilt was set with three enormous, very, very green emeralds the colour of a sticky liquer, and on the top of the hilt there was an emerald lid which flipped back on a hinge to reveal a small, jewelled watch. Well, he didn't know much, but he knew that no-one but a sultan was going to rush about getting blood or mud on this, and what did it have the watch *for*? Was the sultan going to take the knife out of its sheath, flip up the lid and check the time before he stabbed someone with it? Oh yes, quick draw. Matt had stood in his bedroom at granny's, swinging his right arm and plunging an imaginary dagger into his pillow, remembering to check the time first, and then putting the dagger back into its gold sheath. Feeling the thing in his hand, guessing the weight of it with the emeralds cold and uncomfortable and the diamonds sharp.

Piecing together the chandelier gave him enormous pleasure, although after so many slow hours of it over two days, there were times when he wanted to smash it and scream. Parts of it were intact, so you could see the way it should be and none of the branches were broken. Each branch was designed to hold a little glass dish, with a holder for a candle and beneath each dish was a large crystal pear drop, attached by twisted wire. Connecting each branch was a rope of multifaceted crystals, the size of small marbles, with one bigger droplet in the middle of each row. Dozens of rows, six branches at the top, twelve on the next tier, twenty-four on the third. It was a repetitive, jigsaw-puzzle kind of game to find the right kind of piece and connect it to the piece before, and his fingers ached. But what puzzled him, when he thought about it, was the fact that some of the drops, only a few of the small and a couple of the large, were colder to the touch than the others, and they were not all the same colour.

He could not explain it to himself or to Audrey, because he needed to work it out. All the stones were white, but once some of the filth had come off on his hands, he could see different varieties of white and different kinds of light. He was not to clean the thing until it was as finished as it could be. There was no point Audrey said, 'cos you muck it up as you go along, but, clean or dirty, he could still see the differences. Mostly they were the same: not uniform, but the same. There was other stuff in the book he had been reading, too. About what all these kings and queens and tsars and merchants did with their jewels to hide them. Sewed them into clothes. Scratched the surfaces to make them look cheaper. Made marks with a laundry pen on the lower facets to create the appearance of flaws. Jewellers boiled them with laundry blue, heated them to disguise and change colour, put wax on the bottom of a ruby to make it look "sleepy." Anything to hide the fire inside. He was sleepy. He loved the thought of sleepy stones.

Topaz is yellow, but it need not be yellow: it can be colourless, pale blue, golden-brown and pink. There are five thousand different categories of diamonds. A rock crystal can be found in a stone which looks like a potato. Beryl, the stuff of emerald and aquamarine, need have no colour. Tourmaline shows the greatest colour range . . . Matthew liked the idea of it best, because it could come in stripes.

There was a stone in the chandelier he handled now which looked as if it were tinged with pink. He blinked: he was tired and when he looked again, the pink had gone. Not all these larger droplets were cut the same: some had so many more facets than others. Why? He felt a great fear gripping his heart. That and a sense of wonder.

"Enough," said Audrey again. "You know what? You are a grade A smashing lad and I fucking love you. Am I right or am I right?"

"Right," he said, faintly.

"When it's all together, it has to be washed. Or there might be a spray. Are you game?"

"Right."

"And after that, petal, it's all fucking yours."

"Oh no," he said. "No, no, no. Where would I put it?"

"Can we talk about something else?"

"Nope. Impossible."

"Can we talk at all?"

"Oh yes. You get used to the noise."

Band practice, again: British Legion junior brigade, going on in the body of the church. The walls hid the shrill sound of young voices and the more sonorous sounds of those who aspired to control them, without disguising the tuneless blast of a tribe of trombones. The cat did not like it, Joe had noticed it spitting and retreating from Father Flynn, who was herding the troops inside, like a benign warder, wearing his jeans and trainers and Mickey Mouse T-shirt which he thought was cool and they thought ridiculous, his jacket pockets clanking with keys. He took the British Legion children to heart as a future congregation. Joe had waved, Flynn had waved; you could get a lot of promise into a wave. The noise was like a series of distant car crashes. Phrumph, prumph, prumph and then in with the cymbals, kids going bumm, bumm bumm on the drums, silence and then a lonely wail of despair from the one with the horn.

"I'm already used to it."

"The hell you are. How long have you been squatting here, Joe? You even get post."

He coughed. The sound beyond the wall slackened into a series of tuneless moans.

"Only a couple of weeks before you came back," he admitted.

"Ruining my reputation, no doubt."

"What reputation? Besides, I wasn't here all the time. I do work you know. I've got regular commitments all over the place. I was away for half the time and even when I was here, I was quiet as a mouse. I didn't want to draw Flynn's attention. He likes me, you see."

There was wine on the table, food in the fridge and a very temporary sensation of all being well with the world. The nights were drawing in, a man in the corner shop had observed with the wisdom of a sage; it was cooler, but Joe was willing to bet it was hot and stuffy in the church, like Mrs. Smythe's rooms. Elisabeth lit the cigarette which was the preliminary to anything.

"We were discussing the lovely Mrs. Smythe."

"You shouldn't have gone there. Do you know that?"

She ignored him. "It might just have put a different complexion on the whole thing if I had known what Mrs. Smythe did, from the very beginning," Elisabeth said. "I knew that Jack had gone to an agency, something I didn't quite see a man like that doing. Jack was arrogant after a fashion: even going through a lonely hearts column wounded his pride. He still thought women should come to *him*–that was part of his bitter disappointment–although he was a sucker for those who did. I got the impression, somewhere along the line, that for Jack to write a letter, or to go to an agency and spend the money, well, that would have been someone else's idea. Jack always had to be led. Someone talked him into it, said, why don't you try? The sort of thing my sister would advise. She was a great matchmaker."

Emma simply sounded secure and well kept, liked flirting from a position of safety, Joe thought, sourly. She would have had a coterie of people who adored her and she liked to arrange their lives.

"Emma was nice to Caroline Smythe, because, in her understated way, which can be devastating, even without a hint of bad manners, my mother was nasty, so was I. If not to her face, certainly nasty about her. She stayed for two weeks a year and she always seemed to coincide with a crisis and make herself indispensable. I don't know why she kept coming back. I think she was, how can I put it? Slightly in love with us. Whatever my mother says, about my father, that was a private issue." Elisabeth sipped the wine and let the end of her cigarette ash drop on her mother's letter before brushing it away impatiently. "On the face of it, we were an enviably happy family unit. Buffeted against the world by that beautiful house."

"I must see that house."

"You must. It's entirely photogenic. Unlike me."

"Oh, I don't know about that. Mrs. Smythe didn't dismiss you entirely. She did me. As she should have done. Very right and proper of her."

Elisabeth chuckled, a lovely sound. Joe wanted to become accustomed to hearing it.

"I think I can thank her son Michael for my misguided ambition to join the police. I took a perverse pleasure in exposing him."

Joe's heart was doing a funny pitter-patter.

"For what?"

"For being a thief. He stole jewellery from Mother, jewellery from a shop; they forgave him, I didn't. He was destructive. He was awful and he always smiled. He pinched children and he pinched things. A pincher."

Joe got up slowly, as if his bones ached. One turn of the big room. Must not get compulsive, like Jenkins. He wanted to see Jenkins, not wanted to, needed.

"Dear Mrs. Smythe told me she didn't have children," he said. "But she did sport a nice wedding ring. If the wedding ring was a wedding ring. She had so many."

Elisabeth shook her head. "She wasn't wearing rings," she said definitely. "I would have noticed. I always notice jewellery." She held the cigarette aloft, examining otherwise unadorned fingers. "Hardly surprising with my background. You men always get details wrong."

"She was wearing rings," Joe roared, banging the table. "Two on each bloody hand. Plus a chain round her neck."

He regretted shouting. Pale as she was, she had gone the colour of chalk and her blue eyes blazed, brighter than a jewel.

"Yes, of course, she was," she muttered. "Only this time she kept her hands in her pockets. Until she had time to take them off."

She had let him read her mother's letter. Or had it been lying there when he arrived? The contents of it gave him the impression of two like minds, running in parallel lines. It was a shocking letter, showing such bloody-minded unhappiness, and all the more appalling for its rigid self-control.

"Could it be," he ventured slowly, "that someone told Mrs. Smythe about your father's mythical treasure trove? The good old family legend?"

"Now who would do that?"

"Your father, showing off to a woman who liked him and talked to him, shared his interests where no-one else did. Your mother, when he was dead or dying. Wasn't there a time when both of them trusted her?"

"Emma," Elisabeth murmured. "Emma, you big-mouthed fool."

"Emma, the saint who befriended everybody."

"Ah," said Elisabeth, knocking back the wine, a pink flush appearing in her cheeks beneath the unfamiliar make-up, "drink is a terrible thing. Give me more."

Phrumph, phrumph, phrumph, crash, bellow, crash: Flynn loved it. He told himself that the terrible racket was all to the greater glory of God, and yes, the talent was minimal, but the sound would become wonderfully orchestral when combined with the effects of their uniforms, next Remembrance day. The urban existence of a boys' band–albeit a unisex band, of which he did not entirely approve, although the girls kept the boys in order–created in his mind some sort of continuity with the noisy religion of his youth. Those were the days of folksy guitars; this was better.

A man was leaning against the wall by the open door. Flynn had caught sight of him earlier, gave him the big welcoming smile which was returned in full measure. Maybe he was a proud parent who liked to look in without being observed, moving round to get a better view of the offspring. Bit young for a dad of one of these, but you never knew. Maybe not a parent: maybe a talent spotter. Maybe someone with a nice commercial interest in church space and the cheque book to match. Flynn was sure he had seen him before.

"Can I help?"

"Oh, no. I just heard. Came in for a look. Is that all right?"

"Course."

"May I watch a bit longer?"

"Be our guest."

Later, when the band dispersed with raucous relief, Reverend Flynn found to his annoyance that he had mislaid his jacket. Some little pig . . . Miss Jones had to use her key to lock up the church and there was nothing he could do about it now. His wallet was in his back pocket, there was someone at home and an urgent appointment to keep. Somehow the joy of the early evening had gone.

Then he saw it, draped over the bonnet of his car, hurried towards it, making the sign of the Cross out of sheer relief. God was good, after all. He looked up towards the windows of the tower, with a slight envy of the occupants, waved vaguely in their direction in case they were looking out at him. There was a light in there: it looked both remote and cosy, and the chill breeze made him shiver as he shrugged on the jacket, checking the sleeves first in case it was booby-trapped. There was something irritating his memory like an itch, about Joe, how it was he had come to be there in the first place. Was he the residue of the exhibition, or had he somehow just arrived with a message from Elisabeth? For the life of him, Flynn could not remember anything, except a guilty sensation about how vulnerable he was to the wide smiles of young men. He crossed himself again. God would forgive him and his fear. God had no choice.

"I know why envy is a sin," Elisabeth said. "It corrodes, like the rust on the bells. It makes the envier swell and then contract and then crack, one big crack or a million pieces. A sort of poisonous heat."

"Are these philosophical observations on the real world's example to man, or do you have something to say?"

"Caroline Smythe, of course. Oh I know envy is as common as mud in a farmyard, it's a question of degree. Do you see what I mean?"

He considered. "I don't know anything about envy. Never felt it, at least, not so much that it hurt. Passing envy, maybe. Jealousy, for a minute. What's the difference?"

"Envy is jealousy entering the bones, I think. Jealousy becomes envy when it begins to eat, when you can't shrug it off and it makes you hate the person you now envy. Makes you wish them harm. Is there any more of that? Oh, what a shame."

"What a demanding little cat you are," he remarked, pleasantly. "It could have been vintage and you drink it like water. Then ask for more."

The music below had stopped. It was a long time since he had last eaten. She looked as if she never ate at all, but he knew better. She could eat like a trooper.

"Flynn waved at me," he said. "Maybe we should have asked him up for a drink."

"And have him think us a nice, cosy couple? Or have me say you're a trespasser, no use except for pulling corks and opening tins."

"You don't mind what people think. What Flynn thinks."

"I do," she said. "I do mind what people think. I mind a lot."

Joe's mobile phone bleeped. Elisabeth looked at it with distaste, as if he had brought some unpleasant, scab-covered pet indoors.

"And you can get rid of that, too," she said, handing it to him.

It was the Owl, slurring his words a bit, the phone distorting them even more. "Come on down, Joe, wherever you are. Me and Rob, having a drink."

God save him from old mates. There was chatter in the background. Joe looked across at Elisabeth, about to suggest, come with me, but bugger it, he did not want that. She was studying the contents of the fridge, and he could count her vertebrae through her blouse. Rob would stare, Owl would be Owlish and he would be ashamed. Joe did a mental review of the tower. One way in, one way out. Three keys: Flynn swore there were only three, exhorting him to be careful.

"Where are you?"

"Where are we, Rob?" The music behind the chatter sounded as bad as the kids' band.

"Got something to tell yeeeou, Joe."

"OK, OK, stay put."

Elisabeth spoke from the fridge. "Friends of yours?" she asked.

"Old mates. The owl. I told you. Will you come with me?"

She shook her head adamantly. "You don't want me to come. I'd be in the way. And I don't particularly want to go anywhere with you. Besides, girls don't go with old mates. They'd clam up."

"Please."

"Oh bugger off, Joe. What is this? Do you think I'm not safe on my own here, after a few days with you. What gives you this fantastic right to bully me?"

"I don't think you're safe anywhere. Look what you damn well do. Get mugged. Do exactly the opposite of what you say will—"

"Sod OFF."

There was a regime for the keys, hers and the one Flynn had so willingly given him, both lay on the table. Big, old, difficult to replace, almost items of apparel rather than instruments. Joe could not look at the key to the sole entrance to the tower without thinking of a belted cassock, hung with similar keys. He simply did not want her going out, alone. Gut instinct ruled on that one, so he took both the keys and took to the steps. He could forestall any adventure of hers simply by locking the door behind him. Hurry. In a while, Owl might fall off his perch.

She was shouting at him as he thumped down the stairs, the shout becoming inaudible as he closed the door behind him. That was the advantage of stone-built insulation: it prevented one from hearing a woman yelling, "Bastard! Bastard!" and other language of pure invective. All the same, Joe did feel he might have overplayed the charm.

Elisabeth was speechless with rage. Then she opened the second bottle of wine. The effort and sense of achievement absorbed the fury: there was a knack and she had found it. She forced herself into calmness. Talked out loud.

This was, after all, what she had wanted. Isolation in a safe place. She would have preferred a choice, but it was nice, in one sense, to be marooned without a choice. If that great, interfering, suspicious fool did not come back, she would simply phone Flynn in the morning and get herself let out. The situation was so ridiculous it was tempting to laugh and cry in turns. This is what someone should have done with you eighteen months ago, girl. Locked you up.

The phone rang again. Hers this time, the only penetrating sound, shriller than that poxy, intrusive little mobile he had left behind. Revenge: dial the speaking clock in Australia on his mobile and leave it . . . She picked up her own phone, held it to her ear, barking into it.

Silence. Two more hallo hallos. More silence. A click, a tone. She dialled 1471, heard that familiar, metallic voice. You were called at . . . The caller has withheld their number. Her fingers, punching keys.

"Patsy? Was that you?"

" 'Lo. Me what? I am *not* me."

Patsy was drunk. Cheerfully drunk. The kind of state which was suddenly devoutly to be wished.

"So I phoned this bird at her office, got no reply, first time. Then I got a sodding answermachine. Then I got some other bird, who said, sorry, the other one was in a meeting. So I said, you sound nice, can I talk to you instead? Got a date with *her* didn't I? Who needs a fucking agency? Stopped the cheque. Actually it bounced. You just haven't got the knack, have you, Owl?" Rob roared with laughter.

Just the two of them having an extended drink after work, Owl inveigled into it because he did not want to go home, Michael not to be found. Rob had decided that they needed Joe, and Owl was not willing to admit that he did not quite want to see Joe at the moment either, any more than he wanted to sit here with acid boiling away in his stomach and Rob sitting opposite with his ghastly, dated vernacular and his terrible traveller's tales, but there he was. Life might have been so very different if the women in the office had been anything other than those two old bats. He was wondering, vaguely, how Rob actually lived, but it was difficult to concentrate. What Rob described as his bachelor pad was somewhere in the arse-end of somewhere else: the Owl could see it fully equipped with dirty pans and other signs of Rob's incipient laziness as well as his expectation that some other bugger did the mopping up. They never met at one another's houses. Houses and flats revealed too much.

Owl decided, wearily and blearily, that he did not like Rob and never really had. The same sort of realization had happened at school with contemporaries once revered and adored, the very stars in his firmament, until they took their feet of clay out of their football boots. It occurred to him that the only one of them who seemed capable of making independent decisions was fucking Joe. But he was not that keen on Joe either. Condescending git. Always bought his round. As he did now. Looming up out of nowhere, like trouble. Rob was talking about the agency, again. Had a cracker last night, Joe; worth every penny. Owl listened in disbelief. Trouble was, Rob never knew when he was lying. Relied on him not to point out the contradictions in every second breath.

"What's yours?"

"Pint."

"Sure about that?"

"Ssh sure I'm sure."

Fucking condescending git.

Owl wanted to say something about Michael. Along the lines of Michael, whom they all revered and adored like some fucking glamour-puss Hugh Grant, head boy pin-up *wanker,* was a bit of a fraud. Smooth bastard and so fucking mean he would pinch a mobile phone. Rob did it, too; Owl knew he did, but Rob had method. He would ask, can I make a personal call, John, old chap? (personal, know what I mean, nudge, nudge, wink, wink) and then make three, but whatever fucking liberties he took, he did ask. Not long calls, either.

"No sign of Mike, then?"

"Got a date," Rob said. "Smooth bastard. Secret life of Michael Jacobi, the boss. Now there's a story. Soon to sell in seventeen languages. Mostly Urdu."

"Wanker," said Owl. He felt rather than saw them turn on him in surprise.

"That's a rude word, Owly boy," Rob said. "Tut, tut."

"Why a wanker, Owl?" That was Joe. All fucking Joe ever did was ask fucking questions. His voice was like one long question mark. Owl shook his head, stirred his thoughts into one last burst of articulation. The last for a long time.

" 'Cos he uses people. 'Cos he can't think. Haven't you noticed? He's a cyph cyph . . . psycophant. Tha's it. Psychopath . . . sycophant, wa's the difference. Never says a single original thing. Never. Funny, isn't it, how that stupid Jack used to hang on every word? That's what Mike makes," and here Owl described with one hand the circle of the moon, shaped like a fractured saucer. "Never. Automatic Mick. Dick. Th'as why management love 'im. Fucking echo. Rule-book genius. An' he uses my fucking phone to call his bloody mother! Mother? Did we know about a fucking mother? I bin going through the bills. This afternoon, I did, I did. First time she ever called me back. And he called me on *my* fucking phone, not the fucking office phone, when I was going to meet that bird. He was the one kept me late." He nodded, significantly, towards Joe. According to his own arm, his pint glass had moved, so far over to the right he could scarcely detect it. There was a hand, which may have been Joe's, retrieving it. A voice which was surely Rob's, laughing, and then Joe again, propping him upright. Speaking in his ear. "Go on, Owl, go on."

He could not go on. That was it.

If she were to instal a chandelier, the bell ropes would have to go. The two would look bizarre together. As it was, the ropes made shadows. And it was no use pretending that wine was a route to oblivion. Perhaps nothing worked on a person in captivity, even though captivity, Jenkins said, was a relative concept. A release from strain: the captive no longer responsible for his, or her, own fate. The only way to benefit from captivity was to be resigned to it. Use it. I have been captive for months and months. I have been captive ever since Emma died. I may be a captive for the rest of my life. Drink meant nonsense and truth, in unequal proportions: she had no head for it any more.

Is it me he wants, the man who killed Emma? The ghost of Jack, does he want me? Did the man who killed Emma and a girl called Angela want something else entirely? Gem quality stones. Those stones her father had prized so much, he might have prayed towards their shrine, would surely have died for, and might, in another age have killed for. Might it be that, this illusion, that the man wants?

Joe. What does Joe want? He wants pictures. He has no means of sustenance. Maybe he has taken pictures of jewels. Craves them, too. Maybe just another thief.

She prowled. She nibbled cheese and thought irrelevantly of mice and their supposed love of cheese. Untrue, as far as she knew: they liked sticky toffee stuff with sugar uppermost and they loved warfarin, poor sods. Her initial fury with Joe filled her with the antidote of lassitude, plus wine, though not much of the wine. She yawned and stretched and waited and went on prowling like the downstairs cat, up into the tower. It was cooler, up there.

I'll show you Joe. Get off my back. I'll show you how I would defend myself here. I know my terrain: know where to hide, and how. I know better than anyone how to hide and avoid the blows. I know the dangerous bits which a big man would bypass; I know the different heights of each stair, the ones which slip and dip in the centre; I know the height of each door. I know the bells.

She paused in the room level with the clock. The room Joe had sequestered and now made his own by his tidiness. What a domesticated beast he was, to render it so free of dust and, glory of glories, he had attached the pendulum to the mechanism of the clock. In a moment, he would turn back time. If only.

Joe and gems, an odd combination. Jenkins would not have said so. Jenkins knew that everyone was a thief at heart and men who denied materialism might be the worst. She was scrabbling, like a mouse, inside her handbag for Jenkins' number. In here, somewhere, on a piece of paper tucked inside an address book, unless she had destroyed it, wanting to forget him. The sellotaped profile of the man called Michael got in the way; she retrieved it, smoothed it and put it to one side. She dialled the Michael number. It rang and rang. She prowled some more. Mice and birds had been the initial problem here. Birds getting into the bell chamber and beating themselves against the slats with heartbreaking noise, unable to get out, impossible to capture. She had wept to watch them die and then helped a grumbling, unwilling man with no head for heights to put fine net over the windows. Whatever one did, one never owned the place in which one lived, or ever fully controlled its independent life. She thought of her mother's house, never free from the encroachment of sea and salt and decay . . . Poor mother, guarding it as she might a child, knowing she would have to let it go. Listening for the sounds of decay.

There were sounds now. Tapping at the big window, a rattling as if someone had thrown gravel. *Slish.* Another shower of sound, like hail. Children had tried to break the windows before she had come to live here–that was how she had met Flynn–they had tried since. *Slish*. Like sharp branches brushing glass, but there were no trees. She looked at the window through the plume of her freshly lit cigarette, inhaled. No rain, no hail, one of the panes cracked. Bastards.

Elisabeth was at the bottom of the steps before she remembered she could not get out. She stood by the door, snarling. In the light from the tiny vestibule window, set high in the wall, she could see the large, wrought iron handle on the door turn a fraction. Then stop, turn back, resettle itself, quietly and carefully.

She kicked the door with both feet in turn, pounded it with one fist, willing it to give way. The sound of her onslaught was puny, without an echo. There was a shuffling outside the door. She took a drag of the cigarette, bent down and blew smoke through the keyhole, stupid, futile gesture. The shuffling stopped: she could hear footsteps, going away. She scampered back up the stairs, pulled a chair and tried to look through the window. Peering in vain through wavy glass, she could see nothing but street lights in an empty street.

For the first time in a long time, she was not afraid. The anger was so intense, it pained her. She paced, smoking without stopping, hearing the time pass. Then the sound of Joe returning. Without his van: in a taxi.

He came in, whistling. Big grin, his arms held aloft in submission as if he had just been threatened with a gun, anxious to please. One key in each hand.

"Sorry, sorry, sorry. Shouldn't have done that." He was slightly drunk.

She threw the empty wine bottle at him with as much force as she could muster. It hit his shoulder, bounced, fell to the floor without smashing and rolled away. Not as satisfying as she might have hoped, but the shock on his face mollified her.

"You should see me with a knife."

"No thanks."

"Put the keys down. Both of them."

He did.

"If I were you," she said. "I would be a very good boy and go straight to my room."

Chapter

SIXTEEN

There was some splendid stuff you could use to clean a chandelier, Audrey said. She had read all about it in a magazine. You sprayed it like spraying flies, and all the bits of dirt dropped off as you waited. Which saved you standing up a ladder and washing it piece by piece, like some poor parlourmaid. She was not sure where you could get it. She would ask them in the posh shop down the road, if she could bear to speak to them.

"No," Matthew said. "Please."

"Why, petal? Don't you want everyone to see what a fucking brilliant job you've done? Because I do."

"No. Not yet."

And yet, he was immensely pround of it, they knew he was. Maybe he had simply acquired their own preference for procrastination, as well as for things more than a little jaded and dirty. Or perhaps, Donald suggested, *sotto voce,* in case the walls could pick up his own version of classified information, Matthew wanted his granny to see the thing. Wanted to rub her nose in it for throwing it out, like she did the hedgehog, all in the interests of her clear, cool taste. Her taste required the rooms to speak for themselves; all streamlined, no fuss. She used the features of the house and added the minimum of fine furnishings and in the nineteen-seventies she had been ahead of her time in Budley. Or perhaps Matthew was simply being a right little sod, lying to everybody, like he had the day before, and might do again today. Donald could see him doing it. Telling them he was going to be with his father, telling his father he was bidden to them, while telling his grandmother something entirely different and making himself scarce. Having everyone running round, looking for him. Dizzying everyone with lies.

"Not lies, dear," Audrey said. "Fibs."

"What's the difference?"

"Been alive all this time and not know the difference? When were you born?"

She was not laughing today.

The chandelier was almost complete, but Matthew seemed unable to fix the last few bits and it was dirtier than it had ever been. He seemed to make it dirtier as he went on; some of the small crystals were grey with grime. Ah, well, let him. It was his. Bless him, it was also rather lopsided, even if it was only a couple of feet from the ground. It was a big, cumbersome, ballroom beast. It would never have looked right in that house. Audrey could see why Diana Kennedy had wanted rid of it, also why they had left it alone so long. It made her feel both sentimental and sick.

"Shall we go somewhere Matthew?" Diana Kennedy said. "What would you like to do?"

"Nothing."

"Whatever you like."

"Don't like anything."

"We can bring your friends."

"FUCK OFF!"

"DON'T SPEAK TO ME LIKE THAT!"

It was only another game he had been playing. Going up the cliff path, further away than any eye from the village could see, scrambling down to a new cove only accessed by boats and serious walkers, looking for a cave. That was what he was doing: looking for a fucking cave, so that he could live in it, until Lizzie came back, because then she would have to come back. There were loads of caves along the coast, but Lizzie had shown him this one in the weeks when they had played all day, even after dark and even when it was cold. She would know where to look. That was what happened in stories and he had read lots of stories. Videos were unheard of in either of his houses: telly was rationed.

Breathless and dirty and scratched and slightly frightened, Matthew found *the* cave. Not as he had seen it the winter before, swept clean by high tides, but as it was now. A shallow room, a picnic and trysting spot for the brave. There were beer cans which he kicked aside, cartons and polythene bags, a damp old sweater and a lingering smell. Something glittered in the gloom, but it was only broken glass. Oh, he could dream, but even he knew that he could not stay here, not ever, not alone. So he had scrambled back uphill, slowly, refusing to look back. Going home in the grey afternoon.

Go to your room, Matthew. There's a good boy. Go to your room and play with Mummy's rings. If we had the money if we had treasure, we would send you away. Because we think that would be for your own good, the way it would always be for his own good, to make him a bit more like other boys and girls.

Home, before four, ravenous. Missing for hours, such a fuss. But nobody would ever hit him, although he almost wished they would. He could tell they wanted to, especially Dad, but they were never going to do that. He looked at all the polished stones in his Grannyhouse bedroom; did not like them very much any more. Besides, he had given the best of them to Lizzie, and he was getting angrier and angrier with her, too. For being somewhere else when he needed her.

Elisabeth examined her face in the bathroom mirror, along with millions of other people doing the same thing at the same time: checking they were fit to be seen before going out in the workaday world. She was almost sure the twist to her neck was less pronounced. She simply looked quizzical rather than distorted. She nodded at herself, not allowing hope or vanity to intervene. There were going to be no more mornings of evading the bloody mirror: there was too much else to do, but what? What did one do, when dread lurked like a dental appointment, when life seemed full of threat and recrimination? And yet she was so fed up of being fed up, that the urge to forget it all and go out and play tickled and itched worse than the scar on her back had done. There was only one, real imperative for the day, and that would have to wait until after office hours. She patted her face dry, made the ponytail. Easy.

Joe was lounging against a wall, waiting. He shot into the bathroom as soon as she came out, desperate. Serve him right.

"Someone tried to get in last night," she yelled through the door. The phone was ringing. Elisabeth regarded it with deep suspicion, snatched at it. There was Flynn, burbling. Would she let in the district surveyor, again?

"Again? For what?"

"The bells, my dear. They're rotten."

"Father, they've always been rotten. Tell him another day. Tomorrow. Day after."

Get off the line. Let her sort out what to do with her energy. Light a cigarette. Let the caffeine tell her there was nothing important to do, the anger with Joe still boiling, the suspicion worse. He emerged, the sound of running water half-drowning his words. Plumbing in the tower was noisy.

"What did you say, about someone wanting to get in?"

"It's all right. Could have been the fairies. All these men of mine, trying to get in. Could have been anyone. Not the first time. Flynn's got the only other key."

Daylight made everything so innocent. It could have been anyone. Could have been Flynn, looking for big, burly Joe. And since this was the last day she was going to take Joe at face value, she may as well enjoy it.

"You're going shopping? You?" He looked half-asleep, badly tired and a tad hungover, his hair in tangles, and his movements clumsy. It was endearing in a kind of way, if one liked that kind of thing.

"Yup. What the hell are you doing?"

She was angry with him and still wanted him there, where she could watch him. She wanted to look at him while he did not notice.

"Well, I do work, you know," he said defensively, lumbering back into the bathroom, slamming the door. "I've got a job."

"What kind of job, Joe?"

"Taking pictures of someone's broken leg. So they can sue the boss."

"Oh, nice."

He was back out again, trundling upstairs, banging around and coming down again in miraculously tidy clothes. Entirely separate clothes in dry cleaning bags, to be worn for single occasions, stripped off and reincased as soon as he came home. Where is home, Joe? No-one travels as light as you. What do you want?

"I'd cancel it," he said. "But you don't want me to do that."

She shrugged, irritated by her own disappointment; feeling like a poor, spoiled little girl, who did not want to be alone while everyone else goes to work and so, takes refuge in sarcasm.

"Presumably you aren't going to fight for the keys and lock me up?"

"Nope. That was a mistake. I'm very, very sorry. Just go shopping will you? Stay with the crowds and come home in daylight. If I work, I get paid. Champagne at five, promise. Lots to talk about. Can I have a key?"

"No. Yes. I suppose so."

He looked a different animal in professional mode, until he turned round and she could see where the back seam of his nice canvas slacks had been sewn up in darker thread. She was not the only person who needed to go shopping.

"Why the hell do you photograph injuries?"

"It pays," he said. "Working for lawyers and doctors pays. Something has to."

After he had gone she remembered the man behind a camera, the first bringer of hope, leaving a pink rose. Where *was* Jenkins? At work. She had found the number; now she could not find the man, only the message on his machine. Available after six. The tower had a certain stillness. She was suddenly homesick for the sea, and for crowds. She took off the sweat suit and put on yesterday's clothes, checked the door on the way out and found it reassuring.

What did he want?
She had forgotten to phone Matthew. Or her mother.

Mrs. Smythe banged on the door of her son's apartment to wake him up. This was such a regular ritual, she was no longer sure if he resented it or not, but she did it anyway. Punctuality was so important and she recalled that he had hated getting up for both school and college and she presumed it was the same now. No words were exchanged: she simply knocked until she heard movement. Then, as like as not, she went back to bed for an hour. Life did not begin at Select Friends much before eleven. This morning the ritual was the same, only she slid one of her buttermilk envelopes under his door. It went against the grain to put on paper anything pertinent to their own lives, so she had written in code.

"Profile: E is a little older than you and very concerned about her appearance. You know about that, don't you? By the look of her, she has not forgotten you and is longing to see you! As soon as you can! Don't forget to take flowers!"

Please, she murmured to herself, *please.* She will let you in with flowers: she is lonely. Do not tell me, as you did last night, that you have had enough, that you do not want to see any more girls. Do as I tell you. Have I ever let you down? Will you please realize that she hates me and wants to destroy us both?

Caroline washed. Cold water on hot skin, which fell in folds round her neck.

Those lovely Kennedy girls, a disappointment to their father. Of whom Caroline herself had entertained such hopes, so fleeting they were more in the nature of daydreams. About how she could drive out the divine Diana, because she, Caroline, really did know what poor Dorian liked and what he wanted, apart from his diamonds. She had wanted a daughter, but a son was what *he* needed; a boy with eyes and tastes to match his own. It was Caroline's boy who deserved whatever Dorian Kennedy raved about leaving for his daughters. Why could he not see that?

Perhaps his death was the point when her admiration for them all and her desire to be like them them, changed into envy. It was then she had realized that he, and they, rejected her as they always had. Found her dispensable and laughable. Caroline could no longer define why it was she hated them so much; she who had been so enchanted with them all and wanted them to love her; or why she inflicted on herself the delicious torture of her visits, still giving them a chance to make amends.

She scrubbed at her face; selected the hairpiece and the earrings. They would never love her, but she could taunt them, silently. Dear Diana had no idea of what she had done to *her* family, and what she had power to do. She could smash them and seize the inheritance. By God, if she could not have respect, she would settle for revenge and a small fortune. She would be content to leave them in ruins.

The make-up was all wrong. There was no time to change. Who would notice? Whoever noticed *her?*

There had always been a choice. *They* had made it, not her. But there was no choice about Elisabeth. Not now. Elisabeth was clever: she would work it out. She was the one her father would have trusted.

Caroline heard Michael leave with his usual, carefully controlled speed. Michael, neat and clean and beautifully dressed, as she had taught him, making his well-mannered way to work. He had been neat even when he had played with Emma Kennedy as a child. He still remembered to look as if he was thinking when he was doubting, smiling when it was expected, keeping his face in order, as she had taught him. Caroline could only think of Emma, patting him on the head and making him follow her round like a puppy: they could have been twinned in their beauty. Then she remembered Emma's adult voice on the phone. "Hallo! Thought you might be lonely. Would you like to come to tea and meet my baby?" The condescending bitch. Opening the door to let her in and then closing it again, just like her hypocrite mother. Bitch.

There was a knack, Caroline decided as she exited the house and walked to the bus stop, a skill some people had of living as if they had all the money and status in the world. Emma was like that, a spendthrift in a dozen ways. Oh, it'll be all right: our ship'll come in. Which had meant to Caroline that there was a ship to come in and dock alongside this creature already over-endowed with blithe-spirited happiness, but it was only her knack of living; an illusion. Caroline had wanted a little of that knack, and then wanted whatever else the silly bitch had got. As for Michael, mooning over his tea cup, he had simply wanted Emma.

So kind of you to invite us in. How perfectly *sweet* of you to notice *us*.

Sitting opposite lumpy Mrs. Smythe on the bus was a girl of peculiar beauty. A tiny little thing, she reminded Caroline of a blackbird, smiling disarmingly as she gave up her seat, continuing to smile as she stood, close. Stud earrings which glittered quality, the rest of her ensemble consisting of cheap clothes chosen and worn with the coordinated flair which made her chic.

She would do for him, Caroline thought. When all this was over, she would do nicely.

"Some people have the knack with clothes", the sales assistant was saying to Elisabeth. "I'm sure you have too. That frock looks nothing on the hanger, but it will look wonderful on you. You've got the eye." The evil eye. Elisabeth did not want help, or at least, not that softening up kind. She was killing time. She had once had a knack with clothes. To make cheap look class, so Patsy put it—you can thank your mother for that, I suppose. Or your dad. Give a girl a string of pearls, limit her dress sense for life. C'mon, Lizzie, be daring, and she never had been, except for Jack.

All that was left for the last two weeks of summer were hangdog rails, with the long-lost remnants of sales; and nobody said madam any more. She would not have minded being called madam, for once, as long as it meant that this bored person in Dickens and Jones kept out of the way. She did not want gasps of astonishment when some harridan peeked through changing-room curtains. She was only here because there were individual cubicles, rather than a communal room full of unblemished flesh, although she had liked that, once, too. Enjoyed the expressions on faces, the hope, the scorn, the laughter and sometimes, the delight in a new garment, greeted with intense pleasure, like a best friend.

Sod the frock, drooping and sagging, sick to its own heart for someone with a bosom to wear it and make it fall right. Bugger the blouse with the padded shoulders slipping and itching and the buttons in the wrong place, and God help anyone who could wear the cool wool trousers which felt like thermal pants and covered her feet. Sod all that. There was nothing of her to dress, so she left it all behind, gazed at winter woolies and wandered through the vaulted halls, unable to resist looking. It was so long since she had looked, the prices maddened her. Sod that too: she had money to spend, for a while.

Menswear. She had bought a couple of presents for Jack. A tie, a mixed fabric shirt, not recorded on tape. The last time she was in a shop like this she was buying stuff she hated, for Jack.

Joe would look good in that knockout yellow sweater. He would loom up out of the mist in that, frightening the horses. Or the red; he was sallow-skinned, he could take it. Or stripes, rather than lumber-jack checks. Plain bottoms and colourful tops, that would suit Joe. Nothing which required a tie because a tie could not go with a pony-tail. Get out of here, Lizzie. What, for the last time of asking, are you doing? You cannot abide pony-tails on men. Even if he does have hair which looks like rough silk, and the kindest of eyes.

Children's department. Her own eyes screwed up, suddenly looking shrewd, the way Emma's did when she went shopping. Plenty of results here for Matthew. Clothes for kids were so nice, she could have gobbled up what she bought, let alone touch and pay for it. Jacket, trews, the respectable end of clothing. Outside, in junky stalls at the back of Carnaby Street, she found T-shirts with slogans. I AM NOT ALONE, said one. FUCK OFF SOONEST, said another, BRIGHTEST TRIBE, the third. Matthew might not wear this trash, but he would think he would. Dear Matt: I want you smoking and drinking and putting your back into rebellion as soon as ever. Got that? Get rid of all the shit in your teens and then go in for learning. I wish I was your mother, but I am not. Your father is a nice man, but even your mother found out that he was well on the way to becoming a solid, worthy bore.

She savoured this new realization over cigarettes and coffee. The whole process took hours of stopping, starting, remembering. Going home with all she could dump in a taxi, kid's stuff, prepacked food and a carton of cigarettes for Jenkins.

Home to a frantic message from Flynn: more about the surveyor. Oh, go away. She knew that it was not the bells which were rotten, but the wood which held up one, two and three. She had been up there in the moonlight, night after night. She took out the wine and put it in the fridge after three trips upstairs with her burdens. She was in love with the black taxi cab. After that it was easy to wait because she was so tired, it felt like injury time.

Joe loved to see the injured en route to rehabilitation. It pleased him, doctor's son that he was. There was quite a trade in house-to-house photography of people and objects, stolen things and damaged lives. One day, he supposed, he might go back to a proper job, but not yet. When he was forty, maybe, he would cut his hair and settle down. The pictures were taken, the pleasantries exchanged. Joe congratulating himself on the brevity and bedside manner which ensured a supply of this kind of work. All done and dusted, he went to look for Michael, asking at the desk on the modern-block floor where he had once worked himself. He was still recognized, so they let him past all the unnecessary security, created to make it look as if there was something to hide. People were always less suspicious of the man with the camera, although it should have been the opposite. No Michael Jacobi this afternoon: in a meeting, elsewhere. Joe trailed across town to the other place, missed him there, went back to see if he could find the Owl and by this time, the desk was fed up with him and the day faded. Joe had quite liked all of this once: orders, sales, targets, the discovery of a new widget which did a different job. Looking at the sanitized set up now, he could not imagine why: he would have been bored to death if it had not been for the old mates. He still hated himself for thinking ill of an old mate. It never came naturally.

He checked his alternative abode, a tiny studio with sleeping space in Clerkenwell, and then went back to the greater spaces of the tower, wishing there was more cause for celebration, loaded with food and a cold bottle of Moët, and hoping that she would not throw it at him. He needed to see Jenkins.

There was no sound from the church. Joe admired the weedless territory he had created round the side and thought about how an able-bodied man could landscape that and turn it into a shady haven. Yet another project. He looked up at the clock face with affection, admiring the gold letters on the blue face which were so visible even at night. Each time he came down the road, the clock deceived him for a second into believing its own version of the time, making him check his own watch. It was never ten to three: the clock was always wrong and he would always want it to be right.

Elisabeth was as settled indoors as a housewife, reading a paper and eating crisps. Joe's relief was profound and he did not know why, only that if he had to lock her in again after dark, that was what he would do. He waved the bottle by way of greeting.

"Now?"

"Cool it."

You were supposed to wait for the sun to go over the yardarm, he told her. That was one of the advantages of winter days for anyone who obeyed the rule. You could tip the first one down the hatch in the mid-afternoon, excused by darkness. "Good Lord," she said, "I never let that worry me."

Joe knew he should not drink anything except water. There was still the residue of alcohol swimming round his system from yesterday and he might need to drive. Still, a little never hurt: it was a catalyst. He got out of the better clothes and into the second best; shed the shoes and put on the favourite boots, just like a regular working man coming home. The first glass she handed him tasted foul. So did the olives she pressed on him, the salt and garlic making his mouth pucker. Perhaps he was sickening for something, or still affected by the taste of all that beer. Then he plucked up the courage to speak about what he could not quite believe. It embarrassed him, as if he was responsible.

"Listen, I know something, or I think I do. I think I know the someone who might have picked up Angela Collier. It's very likely the same man who met Patsy. I said, I *think* I know, but I find it incredible."

"Tell me. Why didn't you tell me?"

"I was trying to work it out. It takes some working out, I can tell you. I don't want to be sure."

He imagined he could still hear the band playing on the other side of the wall and found himself braced for the yell of the trombone.

Elisabeth was moving about, unable to settle in one place and he was watching her, wondering how to say what he needed to tell. Wondering what time it really was, and how long it was since he had eaten more than a disgusting little nibble. Watching her; thinking, do I fancy her? Yes, yes, oh, yes.

She was standing over him, arms either side of his shoulders, pushing him back. Her neck was slightly awry; it merely gave her a distracted look as if her mind was elsewhere, like a cocktail-party socialite, looking sideways all the time, in case there was a better prospect. He was used to that kind of treatment. It went with the territory of resembling a gardener.

She was back from wherever she had gone, changing the angle of her intent gaze. A silhouette with the sun behind her, giving a general impression of concern. He felt enormously tired. There was a soft hand, arranging his hair.

"Joe? Are you OK? It was only a couple of mashed up Mogadon, Joe. You'll be absolutely fine in an hour or two, big man like you. Useless stuff, but the docs gave me a ton of it, silly fools. Joe?"

He was lying on the futon where he had first sat, snoring. The glass was by the side of him where he had placed it, his arms were folded over his chest and his legs crossed at the ankle.

"Joe?" This was all wrong; all terribly wrong and as such, in tune with all the other things she had ever done, neither courageous nor wise. Crossed ankles were bad for circulation. She uncrossed the feet in their boots, noticed that the laces were undone. Why, oh why, oh why? Sorry about this, Joe, but I like you too much and I've got to know what you're up to and you aren't going to tell me. I can't take the protection of a stranger: I need to know the motive, because I know it can't be me.

She looked at the label on the bottle with regret. What a waste. She had once thought she could drown in that stuff, and recognized the fact it could happen again. You are a pretender, Joe, and I don't know what you are. She took a bottle of red from the table, along with the carton of cigs, and tucked them inside her elbow as she left. He looked sweet and safe and she felt guilty. The yellow light of a taxi beckoned outside: she had the vague address of where Jenkins had come to live. The man with the yellow light would be able to decode it. She had taken both the keys, locking up as she went, but there was no sweetness in revenge.

—

Jenkins would be in at the time he regarded as appropriate for a meal. He was a man used to accommodating his food long before night fell and the eight o'clock shift began. He was such a dark soul, she had always imagined that he preferred the black hours, so that he could merge. The steps up to his flat were broad and deserted, everyone else indoors, eating. I had a basement once, Jenkins had told her. Hated it: never live underground and never be afraid to open your door, even if your time is up.

He would always open the door for her and for anyone. That was the advantage of size. He did not seem surprised to see her and, for a brief moment, looked positively pleased, as if he had been waiting with pleasurable anticipation. "Skinny Lizzie," he murmured, shaking his head. "Skinny little Lizzie. Well, well, well."

His home smelt of cooking—something fried—and the dishes had been washed and put away before he had finished eating it; a man following the alcoholics rule of never get hungry, but unable to find any interest in what he ate because it had the sole purpose of spoiling the thirst. He observed the wine under her arm. Shook his head.

"Ah, Lizzie. Do you hate me so much?"

"Yes. So much."

Uncle. Mentor. Father, friend, rogue. He had played all those roles. Son of Machiavelli, spoiled priest. She had thought of him with such venom: she had conversed with him in her head, written letters to him in her mind, all filled with hate and accusation. You wicked bastard: why did you string me along like a puppet, watching and listening like the voyeur you became? Come on, you old cesspit, tell me why. What was it made you hate the suspect so much? Or did you want me to succeed to cover yourself in glory? Or was it me you hated? Now all the questions were abandoned because they were irrelevant. She no longer needed to know why and she did not hate him, either. Hatred was a fleeting taste on the tongue when it was mixed into a cocktail of so many other reactions. Elisabeth could define hate, but no longer knew what it was. She put her arms around him, briefly. It was both the most and the least she could do to acknowledge him and to recognize the fact that although he had lied to her, she had also lied to him. They had both exaggerated the evidence: they had both believed in it.

"Drink the wine, Lizzie. I'll watch. Will that be torture enough for me?"

"Give me some coffee."

"Sit down. You make me nervous."

They lit their cigarettes in unison, smoked at the same pace. She sipped the coffee, as bitter as she remembered, although it was the whisky and the wine she remembered more. In those days he may as well have given her an intravenous drip of the stuff and she had needed it. Peppermints before meeting Jack. Looking at Jenkins now, she wanted to weep and knew that would run the risk of making him despise her.

"Go on," he said, reading her mind. "Cry if you want to cry. That's what women do best. You deserve to cry, Lizzie. I wish I bloody could."

She was furious with him again. This was no sentimental reunion, this was business.

"Who the fuck is Joe? Why the hell did you talk to him?"

Jenkins shrugged. "I thought he was a nice man. He was the link in the first place, I felt I owed it to him. You knew there was a link: the man who took photos of the similar victim, led us to Jack. You knew about that, although you never saw the man. Joseph Maxell wouldn't have meant anything to you then. I still think he's a nice man. So I sent him down to Devon to look you up. Bring me back a photo. Look out for you. He was willing enough."

She was breathing deeply, as if she had run up the stairs. There was scarcely the breath to scream her sense of outrage.

"I think he could be a thief," she said. "I think he could be looking for exactly the same thing Emma's killer could have wanted. With the difference that I doubt he'd kill for it. Wrong temperament. Like Jack."

Jenkins shook his head. "What would he want to steal from you? Your father's mythical gems? But you said they never existed."

She averted her eyes, did not answer, went on. "All right, you set him up. You're amazingly clever at that. Joe, Jack . . . me, what's the difference? But why the hell else has he made himself an ally? What's the trick? What does he want?"

He sighed, got up and paced the room. He had done that in his office, making her disorientated. His eyes strayed to the wine bottle.

"No," she said. She threw the carton of cigarettes towards him. He caught them neatly, tore of the cellophane with the eagerness of a toddler with a gift.

"I asked him to find you," he said, slowly, "because he was curious. And a truly curious man has a gift. He watches. He sees things. He wants to know purely for his own satisfaction. There's something complete about him. I like him. That's why I asked him. I was worried about you."

"Bit late for that, wasn't it? Who asked you to worry? I didn't. How much did you tell him after he turned up the first time with the link that led to the suspect? He flattered you, I suppose, so you kept him posted. Long after you showed him photos of my dead sister."

"I had to do that. To verify the similarity. Besides, he was interesting and he was knowledgable, so I also showed him pictures of your sister when she was alive. God knows, I was so excited by what he gave us, I needed an unbiased mind. He was helpful. Yes, I showed him too much."

Elisabeth was tugging at her hair in frustration. The slide which held it on top of her head came loose.

"And then, of course it all went undercover until the judge chucked it. That was when Joe came back. Upset. Told me that although he certainly hadn't realized it at the time he put the finger on him, our suspect, now dead, was someone he had known. He felt guilty."

She leapt to her feet in agitation, knocking the ashtray to the floor. "He knew Jack? Oh, Jesus Christ, you're kidding me. Don't tell me. He *knew* Jack? That's enough to make him hate me. He *knew* Jack? What were they? Best friends? Blood brothers?"

Jenkins shook his head. "Nope. Nothing like that. An old mate. The fallen-into-disuse kind of mate, but still, an old mate. Some work-based band of brothers. You've been in the Fuzz; you know the kind of thing. Blokes, working and playing together. Not often as close as it looks."

She was silent. Lies and more lies.

"I didn't tell him anything much when I first got in touch," Jenkins continued. "I wouldn't. But I did tell him how to find you, and said why don't you ask her? He keeps coming back with questions."

"And you believe in him," she spat. "You believe that he puts an old mate in the frame without knowing he did so, then agrees to do whatever you ask, and then gets curious all over again? That's some gift, isn't it?"

There was an eloquent shrug of the shoulders.

"Yes. I believe him. So should you. Stick with him, I should. He's your best chance. A good man. Who else will listen to us, Lizzie? Who else? We're tainted, Lizzie. Failures."

"But why? Why does he seem to want to stick with *me*? What is it? Am I a freak show for some kind of pervert?"

She was tearing at her hair, twisting it into ringlets. He sighed.

"Don't do that, Lizzie. It makes you look demented. And stop saying why, why, why, you silly little fool. Can't you get it under your thick skull that someone could simply like you? Love you on sight, even? I hoped he would. God knows, I did. We all did. You just never knew." There were angry tears standing in his eyes: he brushed them away, lit another cigarette and coughed, long and loud. Elisabeth squatted by his chair, took one large hand in both her own and chafed it until it was warmer, using the action to distract herself from the renewed urge to weep herself silly. Then she rose, paced the room as he had done, shivering, as if the cold of his hands was infectious.

"No. I can't have that, Jenks, really I can't. I can't accept that he has a gift of curiosity and nothing else. I can see guilt and curiosity mixed. Layers of guilt. Guilt for a friend and,"—she puffed furiously, excited—"and you know what else I can see? I can see it now, clear as daylight, can't you?" She stabbed her finger towards his chest. "*He* was the one who sent the photograph of poor, dead Emma to Jack, wasn't he? *He* found out his old mate was in trouble which *he'd* caused. *He* knows enough about the law to know what would sabotage the whole damn thing." She paused. "Maybe he sent the photo to Jack for fun. He had the access: you let him look at the things. I can see him now, putting an album in his pocket. He doesn't regard anything as confidential. For an old mate. For a memento. For shame. Anything to stop what he'd started."

"No."

"What do you mean, *no*?"

"No. Joe doesn't volunteer the truth, but he isn't devious. God knows, angel, he's far more of an innocent than you are, far more. You think he might think like you would think: he can't. Can't do sabotage. Couldn't steal. Isn't prurient. He didn't send it."

"Well who did?" she howled. "Who made it finish like that? Finish without even a trial to establish the truth and let us all go free, you, me, Jack? *Who* sent it?"

Jenkins got up. Held onto her shoulders, bracing himself. There was pleading in his eyes. For hope, forgiveness, recognition, understanding: she did not know for what.

"I did!" He was shouting. "I fucking sent it! It was the only fucking way to end it."

His voice dropped, wearily. "Oh come on, Lizzie. Grow up. I couldn't rely on a jury to acquit him. Who could ever rely on a jury? And I couldn't tell you."

The silence sang. Finally, she nodded. Pushed him back into his chair. Then she uncorked the wine by his kitchen sink: let him listen as she poured it away.

The flats in which Jenkins lived seemed to have come alive with the onset of darkness. Doors stood open: televisions blared. Elisabeth wanted to run, but she could only walk and go on walking. Down the stairs, into the stret, into the warm light of the Underground, with dangerous, shouted words, echoing along with the train. He fell in love with a photo of your sister. An old mate. He's a nice, generous man, that Joe.

There were lights in windows as she walked up her own street. Someone was having a party. The quality of the cars was improving over the years, the place on the cusp of change into something more genteel. The owners might want her home back, soon. There was scaffold on half the houses, heralding a better-moneyed congregation moving in. Regeneration was beginning: it was their turn.

She looked up at the tower, grateful for its substance and its remoteness, as she always was. Stopped.

The clock said ten to four.

Chapter

SEVENTEEN

Drugs of any kind had never accorded with the mixture of blood, muscle and confusion which was Joseph Maxell. Pharmaceuticals worked all too well. So much for trying to be Joe the juvenile lad with a poly bag full of dope, the effect was giggles and sleep; likewise the first tranquilliser advised by a dentist who feared being bitten. It was absurd for a large boy to be so sensitive to these exaggerated, short-lived effects; he had always been ashamed of it. Mix a benign dose with a smidgeon of booze plus an ounce of fatigue and then, he was anybody's. Joe could hear Elisabeth saying what she had done with the Mogadon and he wanted to kick her, but it was too late for that, so he listened instead to her stepping around him with a bit of hand-wringing and did not even care any more. Sleep, proper sleep, without evocative dreams and the sound of the dead clock, had been rare lately and he needed it. He was born with a shortage, slept on his couch now with a variety of visions as the sun faded and the slant of fading light in his eyes made him twitch and the dark finally woke him to a groggy hunger. And a boy's voice, wailing a message into the answer-machine. "Where are you, skinny Lizzie . . . where are you?"

No old mate would do this to him, only a woman. He was cold and disorientated; cross without the energy to be angry. A couple of hours, she said, but for all he knew, he had slept for twelve and the time could have been dusk or dawn. Joe stared up at the ceiling and worked out where he was and what hour of the day he was in. Still the evening. The growling of his stomach seemed inordinately loud: it was the only incentive to move. Until he heard the other sounds.

Someone there. Coming up the steps. Joe listened intently. He was not going to call her names: he was going to remind her what a poor, mean creature she was, and when Elisabeth reached the foot of his couch, he would kick her as she passed, not hard, but hard enough to make a point. He closed his eyes, finding it all too easy to feign sleep, because he felt as if he was made of lead.

Lead in the roof of this church . . . amazing it was still there. He thought of Elisabeth with her pathetic sharpening of the knives and the question rose in his fuddled mind as to whether she had gone out with one of these weapons, such as the vegetable knife, and what kind of mission had it been, anyway? Listening, he opened his eyes to the slow realization that they might not be her footsteps coming towards him. These sounds were so uncertain, made by someone who scuffled and lost the way, paused at each step, feeling the wall for support. All too slow for Elisabeth, although she could not move fast; oh Lord, how he wanted to see her run. Slow as she was, she was never that deliberate, never so uncertainly precise.

So, she was drunk then; arseholed and serve her right; he would not mind seeing that, either, but he knew it was not her. It could be Flynn with his precious third key, doing a speculative survey of the inhabitants. Joe shot off the futon, then sat down again with such abruptness, the shock made him dizzy and he obeyed a perverse instinct to lie back and close his eyes again.

The half-open door to the room creaked. Joe could smell the uncertainty and alien aftershave of a man coming forwards. Standing over him, staring at him, breathing heavily. Joe had a desperate desire to keep his eyes squeezed shut, but that was impossible. There was the crinkly noise of stiff cellophane and the cutting edge of sweet scent, perfume, natural and unnatural, unequally mixed.

Christ almighty. Michael Jacobi with a bouquet of flowers in hand. An old mate. Joe studied that face in the pale light from the window, his own eyes still glazed with sleep. Cleft chin, a hook on the end of each eyebrow . . . why had he ever doubted? A face he had so often wanted to photograph for all its intelligent vacancy. The clock face which covered a mechanical mind with no judgement of its own. Emminently loyal, highly employable.

Joe continued to look at the face as if they had all the time in the world. Never quite been able to make you out, Mike, old mate. Such an utterly consistent fellow with the manners of a gentleman and the imagination of a sparrow. You never seem to do anything rash and you never said anything remotely original. In the early days at the same firm, Jack adored you: you listened to him, while someone like me avoided him and his constant whinging, and he was sacked, and you rose, and I left and stood still. Jack always made a man feel guilty, didn't he, Mike? You didn't seem to mind that he needed too much, he never really listened. You listen without contributing; take it all in like a sponge and then make a pronouncement. I would never have thought I would be afraid of you, but I am, now. Joe could scarcely blink, licked his dry lips.

Michael was strong, Joe remembered with the clarity of fear. He had that muscular strength which came from mindless hours in a gym, kickboxing and hefting weights. He was slightly awkward in movement, hated dancing, preferred to watch. They had joked, Rob and he, that Mike would be more at home with the prescribed steps of a Viennese waltz. There was no spontaneity in the man, apart from the smile, which might not have been spontaneous at all. A slow, uncertain grin, more like a grimace, split Michael's features now, as if he was suddenly uncertain of what else to do. It put the other, amiable smile, into context.

"Wasn't expecting you, friend," Joe murmured, unable to smile himself. His heart was galloping, fit to burst out of his chest and assume a life of its own.

"Where is she?" Michael's voice was polite and insistent, like someone trained to answer a telephone complaint line.

"Search me, mate."

The smile had vanished. Michael was looking at the champagne bottle and the overturned glass on the rug. It seemed to explain something and make him nod, disapprovingly. He picked up the bottle, turned it upside down and let the contents dribble out onto the floor, then he continued to hold it by the neck. If that connects with my head, Joe was thinking, I do not know which will break first.

"Where is she?"

"Told you, mate, I don't know."

What the hell were they doing? Joe had an overpowering sense of the ridiculous, but he was mortally afraid, more than he had ever been in his life. Bottle: weapon. No-one had ever found the weapon used on Emma and the girl, Angela. The something used to make the preliminary cracks before he used his feet to kick and crunch, and a knife to stab. He must enjoy the sound he made. A bottle could be washed, taken away, left innocuously where it was found. Bleached, to sear it clean. Did he have a preference? Would the bottle have to be green-coloured glass? Could it be blue?

He felt it connect against the side of his head with a flash of pain, rolled away over the futon and dropped to the floor on the other side, startled by his own speed. He was bigger by far than Michael, stronger, but he was clumsy, less agile. Smaller men make better fighters, the silly cliché ran through his mind, reminding him of weakness. He could not replicate the strength born of fury, glimpsed in Michael's sapphire eyes. Nor could he avoid the second and third blows, deflected but crunching against his collar bone. Crack, rolling away, crack. A foot connected with his ribs before he got to his feet, panting, and they faced each other, circling like gladiators. The sweat beneath his armpits felt like grit: he could not breathe.

"Mike, stop it. What's up? What for?"

"Where is she?"

Joe's feet connected with the cellophane wrapping of the flowers: he felt them underfoot, smelt a wave of appalling, sickly scent as he skidded. He felt utterly helpless: he had never initiated violence or trained in combat—it was anathema to him—he could hug a man to death, that was all. He knew a momentary relief as, with eyes locked into his own, he watched Michael put down the bottle, gently and deliberately, as if he was going to need it again. It was shortlived relief.

The other hand held the knife. Joe backed towards the door, kicking aside the bouquet. He felt for the doorjamb, sidled through and began to scramble up the stone steps. It was utterly dark on the inside of the tower; as dark as a well. Get up one level; get up and find the advantage of height. Find another door to close against him. But he knew as he moved that he was a fool all over again: he should have gone down and out into the night, instead of going on and up into a trap, like some stupid, thriller-movie fool. He knew these steps: he was faster, but one arm seemed useless and his blundering feet acted as a guide for his pursuer. He stumbled through the next door into the clock room, turned to face Michael, tripped on the laces of his boots, heard his knee hit the ground with another sickening crack and felt breath on the back of his neck, the arm round his throat. For one appalling moment, he thought Michael was going to kiss him, so close was the embrace. Say, "There, there, where does it hurt?" in a motherly voice: say it was all a joke in the same way he had tried to tell himself it was since Owl had spoken. No-one listened to Owl, either. He did not feel the sensation of the blade through his flannel shirt, only the force of it, like an almighty punch which knocked him forwards from his half-kneeling stance, onto his face, over the threshold. Then nothing but the thunderous rattle of breath.

There was barely space left in which to raise a foot and kick; Michael tried, once. Then the phone rang one level below and made him hesitate. He waited until the imperious echo of the ringing ceased. Please speak after the tone . . . then, as if compelled, he followed the sound of it, hurriedly. With one backward glance at the big body, felled like an ox, groaning without screaming, he was satisfied it was safe. Going down as if he knew who it was. Getting to the door of the room with the huge window, hearing the tail end of a familiar voice. His mother.

". . . so do phone back, tomorrow, Elisabeth, dear. I've the perfect man for you. Just wait. *Just wait.*"

Click. Burr.

Michael forgot where he was. Messages from Mother were always for him. He waited. Amused himself. Looked at the flowers on the floor, touched them with his foot, looked for a vase to put them in. He found a blue-speckled one and then decided, no, wrong colour, and put it away carefully. He checked her cupboards for cleansers and such, shook his head. He found the lavatory. Prowled; looking at books and hiding places. Always ask first. Waited.

Upstairs, Joe lay on the floor, clutching his side. He wondered about the pain and tried to pretend it did not exist. He opened his mouth to shout and found he could produce no sound. He tried to remember all over again what time it was. Found the saturation of his shirt, as he pressed it into the wound, terrifying, and more terrifying still, the thought of what would happen when Elisabeth came home and it was all his fault. His fault, his fault, his fault. The ticking of the clock came again into his imagination, in tune with his pulse. He was on fire, the wound corroding the whole of him, burning him with its own shame. Sorry Lizzie, what a fool, sorry. Then he began to crawl, like an uncertain child with a lolling head, across the wide desert of the floor.

People did not always polish diamonds, even though they treasured them, they did not know how, nor cared. Matthew had learned this from Audrey. Five centuries ago, they would put a rough-cut diamond in a wedding ring, prizing it as an emblem purely because it was so marvellously hard. Not beautiful, simply harder than anything else, and it would sit in a precious metal setting looking like a frosted rock. So hard, it took a day, even now, to saw through a one-carat diamond and it was a series of skills, used in descending order, which made it brilliant. The cleaver would cleave it; the crossworker create the first eight facets determining the final shape; the brillianteur the rest. Even the half-cut diamond did not look like a rock, but it did not look as precious, either. It looked . . . ordinary.

Matthew knew he was far, far too old to wet his bed. That had been a brief rite of passage of a different age, about the time when his memory began, treated at the time with bribery and reassurance. Now it would be regarded as a crime. He shuffled away from the dampness he had created, but there was too much, the discomfort was too extensive and the shame of lying near it was too great. But it was also a comfort, because it had woken him from the half-dream, and he could see, as he lay in the silence, broken only by the background whisper of the sea through the open window, that there were no footsteps, no immediate questions, nobody. The lovely, inhuman music of the sea lulled him, reminded him he was home and he began to breathe normally, to tell himself there would be no opening of the door and no face peering round as he pretended to be asleep.

He shifted away from the damp, to the very edge of the mattress, swung his feet onto the floor, felt under the pillow and felt for the light. The stones were sharp and cool and refused to be warmed. Eight of them, irregular, half-cut lumps. Maybe they were so cool because he refused to hold them for long enough to make them warmer: they seemed to sting the hot palms of his hands, stick to them and refuse to be dropped. A diamond will stick to grease, he remembered, although he could not see why on earth it should. Such little pieces of stuff, with metal glued on one end, each in the rough shape of a drop. On closer examination, three of them consisted of two smaller stones glued together, to give the same, rough shape as the rest. A couple were frosted. He was sure that some of them were pure glass: he was equally sure that most of them were something else. He dropped them back into the packet and put it under the pillow. There were other pieces of glass and crystal from his own collection which might look equally harmonious on the chandelier, making up the gaps no-one had yet noticed, but he wished, he wished, oh how he wished, he had never taken these off. These precious stones were too much of a responsibility. Better, he supposed, than doing what he had wanted to do. Smash the whole thing. Cut the rope which held it to the ceiling, let it fall, but that would not have damaged it enough. He could have dragged it outside, got a bulldozer and run over it again and again. Now that was childish. Tomorrow, they were supposed to clean it.

Matthew did not know what had happened to his mother's rings. She had so many, mostly small and delicate. Someone had prized open his fist and taken them from him, gently, but brooking no argument when he had refused to part with them. It was not the same person who had looked round the door, shut it and gone away while the radio had blared downstairs, on that last day with Mummy in their house. It was another person, large and male, who wrapped him in a blanket and carried him away downstairs and out into a car, while he sobbed and clung and fought and yelled for his mother. Daddy's face, looming, puffy with shock and tears. The end of life as they knew it. Matthew's brow cleared. Daddy must have the rings, which Mummy had folded into his hands before sending his upstairs to bed. Yes. No. Maybe.

There was an infinitesimal noise from the far corner of the room. It chilled him for a minute until he remembered. It was a tiny, scratchy, itch of a sound, less than the distant buzzing of a fly, but enough to dispel the last of the nightmare and his own, dull ache of fury at Lizzie for not being there. He rushed across to the cardboard box, lined with newspaper and padded with tissue. Harry the Hedgehog had also wet the bed and that made Matthew feel a whole lot better. Harry was snuffling around, trying to find a way out, but he was half asleep and less than enthusiastic. Milk and yoghurt and excreta were trodden into his bedding, poor pet. Matthew removed Harry with infinite care, crooning, "Helooo, Harreee," and set him down on the stack of newspapers next to his home. He told himself that yes of course Harry mark two was the same as Harry mark one, thrown out of the window, but like so many other things, he also knew it was a lie. Not one which mattered and certainly one worth preserving. This Harry, found in the early hours of the morning and carried into the house as guests congregated for breakfast, had been observed by Granny without comment. There had been no challenge.

"We can do what we like, can't we, Harry?" he whispered, putting the creature back onto clean newspaper. It crapped again, it leaked all the time, he ignored the little red fleas. No-one would dare touch Harry. Matthew took the polythene envelope from beneath the pillow of his own bed and put it under Harry's. Let him crap on it. He did. Harry was not always easy to love. Matthew could see that. Nor was a boy who wet his bed.

They would both be sent away, then. If there was money. If, if, if there was money and they knew it.

Stay in your room, Matt. Do *not* come out.

He looked at his clock with the funny faces on it. Ten to twelve. Hours before daylight.

If it really had been ten to four in the afternoon, all her responses would realign themselves. There would be the common sense generated by daylight, the logic invited by sunshine and the bravery she had always felt at dawn. But now, on the verge of midnight, after her long dawdle home all that deserted her. So he had managed to change the clock. Brute strength could turn the hands from the back. Strength was something he had along with the ability to tease. *"I think I know . . ."* was what he was saying, last time she heard him speak, and her response, I'm out of here. Gone on an errand to find someone else who reckons you might be a thief and support my strange, distorted view of men. Getting it wrong, again.

He's a nice man, Lizzie: deceitful without subterfuge. Compared to you, an absolute innocent. We are tainted, Lizzie, you and I; tarnished beyond rot and belief. What will happen if you go down the road and call 999 because the clock does not read the same time as when you last glanced? Fool. She was a powerless fool, fumbling with the key, realizing as it turned what a grand old, creaking noise it made, what a nuisance it was, how powerless this key which turned to no effect when all the time, the door was open. Shut but unlocked. Sshh, she told herself, shhhh: it is all hysteria. This is home, you have to go in; there is no choice and no option to run away. But she delayed, lit a cigarette, waited a minute, watched the red tip glow, walked around and saw there was no light from any of the windows, and then set off up the stairs, humming. Never had much of a voice, teacher said: never had much of anything except that blood-minded obstinacy. Quite unable to abdicate from a problem which was her own, because the curing of it had also to be hers, even if it killed or hurt. She did not feel brave, treading up the steps: merely fatalistic, doomed to do as she did. She was making an offering to the gods.

For the hundredth time she admired the way the bellringing chamber never quite achieved darkness. There was gloom rather than black, sepia rather than colour. She felt for the light, let her hand drop. She could see perfectly well. There were flowers trampled into the floor and a man sitting at the table, staring at her and smiling.

"Hallo," he said quietly, "I'm your date."

Then she did turn on the light from the switch which was placed high on the wall. No stranger would ever be able to follow the mind of the amateur who had wired this place.

"How nice," she said.

She crossed the floor briskly, treading over the flowers, as if it were normal to have the floor of her living room strewn with broken blooms. She was extending her hand, challenging him to take it as if, this was an everyday encounter with all the standard pleasantries. It was crucial for her to be able to touch him, feel his skin, lessen the fear and the revulsion which went with it. Perhaps achieve some advantage. He was surprised into the automatic response, extended his hand, too, and let it be shaken. The hand was cooler than the last she had touched: his palm was soft and dry. He was not a man who had ever used a spade. The contact confused him: he withdrew from it, quickly.

"I've been waiting for you," he said, petulantly, "a long time."

"Have we met before?" she asked conversationally. "Only I think we may have done. Have we?"

He smiled. She had seen similar smiles on dead bodies. It melted away into a frown.

"Oh yes. Of course."

"Let me guess," she said playfully. "You're my date, but not quite a blind date. Where did we meet? In a club? In a pub? By the seaside?"

He was shaking his head, disliking questions. If they were his to ask, he was in control, but in response, he could not quite find his way to a lie. He had to be literal.

"Where was it?" she prompted.

"Seaside," he replied grudgingly, and then added, "You look like your sister. But not as pretty."

He was handsome, she noticed. Sculptured hair. She did not recognize him, but thought she might have found a clue in Patsy's evasive description. She was not as pretty as Emma, not as vibrant as Patsy, never, ever would be, now. He wore dark-coloured trousers and heavy boots and his mind was clearing. She could see him now as one of Emma's consorts. The sort of man Emma encouraged before she became a wife.

"If you're my date, who sent you?"

He was remembering instructions. Bring her flowers. Be nice. Kill her.

"Mummy sent me."

There was a rising note of panic in his voice. She looked like Emma, but she would not look at him. She had a twist to her neck and seemed to look at a spot beyond his shoulder, tempting him to turn.

There was no sign of fear in her and he was used to fear. Fear was the trigger, the eyes, staring straight into his own, the final catalyst which created the frenzy. Fear and pleading and lies. Not questions.

"And what does Mummy want?"

"You. Rubies and diamonds and you." The voice was rising.

"For God's sake, why?" Her voice was shriller in return, breaking the fragile, artificial peace, losing it. This was the man, she knew it, sensed it with utter conviction, who had whispered to her as she lay on the ground in the alley in Budley. "Diamonds," he had whispered, "where are they? I want them for the friend of mine you killed, and even if she takes away my friends, I want them for my *mummy*." She knew who he was.

"JOE!" she screamed. "JOE, JOE, JOE!"

"He's dead," Michael shouted. "Dead. SHUT UP!"

But she went on screaming until he hit her once across the face. It was a loud sound in the silence. Her head snapped sideways: she did not feel pain, only damage and the abrupt end of her scream. Then he was rocking her in his arms, holding her in a tight bear-hug which was clumsy and strong, his body pinioning her arms to her side and squeezing until she thought her ribs would crack. She could smell the scent of soured perfume, feel his teeth against her neck and the bulge of his erection against her groin. She stood still. His excitement had a strange and calming effect. Thus she had stood with Jack by the river, feeling his crude, confused desire, thinking in self-defence how ludicrously powerful and cruel this beast of a tool was, what a lousy trick it was of nature to play on man that it should turn them into self-deceiving fools. Thinking of it too, as a rotten piece of fruit. Scorn made her objective then and worked that way now, clasped in the embrace of a virgin.

"Emma," he was saying. "Emma."

Had Emma fought with him? Pleaded with him? Shrieked at him with the full array of normal responses to such a threat? Instead of this paralysis, of which she, Elisabeth, was so capable because she had schooled herself out of any normal responses except that overriding fear of pain. He released his grip. They were much of a height. She could sense, as he raised his head, the impression of his teeth in the wasted muscles of her neck and she wanted to vomit all over him. His teeth were bared, shiny white, carefully tended, polished teeth, and what happened to him and to her did not, in that moment matter much. It was Joe who mattered. The Innocent.

"Listen to me," she said, clearly, despite the tremulous, sing-song note she could not control. "I've some pretty jewellery. My father's treasures. That's what Mummy would like, isn't it?"

He shook his head. He had retreated from her warily. Ready to burst, waiting for the trigger, and now, armed with the switchblade. Elisabeth had not seen it appear, only heard the click of the blade. Jesus, poor Joe . . . she was choking back the fatal scream. He's a nice man, Joe. Keep calm: think of a rotten banana. You cannot fight this man: you always knew it would not be possible, because he will tear you into shreds, like the flowers. Cannot fight, cannot run.

"Look," she said, businesslike, "I didn't have them before, but I do have them now. They've been hidden here, all this time. Mummy should have thought of that, shouldn't she? Tcch, tcch, all this fuss for nothing. C'mon, I'll show you. You can bring the knife."

Unhurriedly, she went to the door and began up the steps. He followed, close enough to grab, cautious enough to stay back in case she should turn and kick. He must know, she thought, that if I kicked, it would scarcely effect him. He has on his kicking boots. He might not know that I can scarcely carry a bag of shopping further than a taxi and a flight of stairs. Or how my legs are the consistency of jelly and my flesh so very weak.

They drew level with the door to the clock room. She paused and looked inside, felt the point of the knife pierce her hip.

"Not in here," he grunted. "No. Don't look in there."

She managed a desperate glance, seeing more than he would see in the gloom, knowing the highlights of the room. She could see enough to see nothing: no Joe supine on the bed, or anywhere, and she felt a huge sense of relief, followed by sorrow. He had gone, fled, safe; but he had abandoned her. Would Joe do that? No. There was still only the two of them, hunting each other up the steps. Joe was not free: he was dead. This man had not yet told her a lie. But she did not have to believe him.

Up steps, on and up. She made herself chatter like a tour guide.

"Watch out for cobwebs. Mind your feet. Dark, isn't it? Not as old as it looks in here. What's Mummy's favourite, then? Does she think emeralds are unlucky? My father did. Said it was rare to find one perfect. So often flawed."

She paused again, panting, short of breath, nudged on by another vicious jab from the point of the knife. He was not breathless: he seemed to be gaining strength.

They stood on the threshold of the bells. The moonlight was half as bright as day through the wooden slats. The chicken wire over the wood made the room resemble a prison, while the bells themselves with their dulled gleam, made it look like an engine room.

"Here?"

"Yes, here. But I'm not quite sure where."

Again the pinprick of the knife. She could feel blood seeping down her trouser leg.

"We need more light," he announced.

"There is no light," she lied.

"Hold out your arm."

She did as she was told. White flesh in the moonlight. He flicked at it casually with the knife. Blood welled and she almost screamed. Rebuilt muscle, damaged again. She had nothing more to lose. He pulled the door behind them. It was stiff and unwieldy, the least used door in a place whose architect had a passion for medieval doors. There were planks of wood by the side, left over from previous restorations. He flung one across the door. The ease with which he lifted it filled her with momentary envy: she had once been stong, almost like that. The plank and the door and the wound would delay escape. Yes, he was mad, but not foolish. Elisabeth stood, one arm cradling the other.

"Where are they?" There was panicky greed in his voice as he came closer again.

"Under this one. Taped inside at the top. Only a few."

"Rubies," he murmured. "She loves those best."

"Two. At least."

"Get them out!" He was hissing: she could see the knife blade tremble.

"I can't," she whimpered. "I can't. I can't. I hurt."

There was no lie in that. The bell, suspended on a cross beam, hung eighteen inches from the floor. Room for a small and agile man, even better, a boy to put his head and arm beneath, and reach. He looked at the space in the semi-dark, looked back at her.

"Lie down."

She sat and then lay. The fresh woodshavings on the ground tickled her spine. Obedience was all he required: there was a greater need, even than that, a need which he could not control. Michael touched the bell, feeling a half-ton of smooth metal. Then lay beside it and pushed himself beneath like a man examining the underside of his own car. He shifted further, reaching blindly into the dark of the cavern, first the rim. Robert Cross made me.

She was on her feet, grabbing the axe beneath the rag which lay by the planks in the place which he could not see in this dim light. She had memorized the spot. She could not, even then, have brought it into contact with soft flesh, but she swung it high above her head and down. Once onto the bell, making it shriek and boom, then onto the cross beam which held it. The beam shuddered and cracked. Once more, the muscles in her back and arm groaning and tearing, the beam splintering, the bell thumping down and the whole bell chamber shuddering in protest. There was the kind of silence which followed the blast of a bomb. Until he began to scream.

She did not want to see what she had done. She was hauling the plank from the door, making her hands bleed, fumbling with the latch, scramling back down into the pit, hugging the wall. Joe, Joe, where is Joe? She knew where; she knew each inch of this place. Into the clock room, turning on the light set high in the wall, over to the mechanism he so liked. There he was, hunched into the narrow space reserved for the pendulum, clutching it, and as she reached for him, he tumbled into her arms like a monstrous, bloody puppet. She fell beneath his weight, cushioned his fall, pulled herself out from under him and looked for what she could see. Only blood and more blood. Blood in his beautiful hair and upstairs, endless screams.

Dawn on the southwest coast. It was fair today, rain expected later. Matthew Davey slipped out of his grandmother's house, went through the garden and out of the gate which led to the sea. It was brilliant, the light so intense it pricked his tired eyes. The sky was whiter than chalk, filled with the mist which cloaked and weighted the sea and made it unnaturally calm. Matthew shivered. One of these days it would be cold again and people would talk about the light.

He took off his trainers, took the packet from his pocket and tipped the stones into one shoe. Then he changed his mind, scraped them back into his fist and into his pocket, and put the trainer back on his foot. Then he picked them out, one by one. First he tried to skim them across the flat surface of the water, but that was never going to work: they were not flat: they were too light, so he played a different game. He threw them individually as far as ever he could, running towards the edge of the water, flinging overhand, each one further than the last, a tiny plop, into the swell of a wave.

Chapter
EIGHTEEN

Patsy walked across the bridge on her way to work, holding flowers for her secretary, part of the ritual of apology for being away. In comparison to others she had known, the hangover was manageable. Gone were the days when she could phone her friends and compare notes. Nobody else drank alone. Not as far as she knew.

Time for a forward look on life, never really had time to do it before. Surely the policemen, with their unanswered questions about Angela's life, would have gone by now. A nip in the air, taste of wine at the back of the tongue, nothing terminal. She felt slightly cheerful and almost ashamed of it. This was it, this was life and this was all there was and maybe when life reached an all time low, there was nowhere to go but up. She bought ten copies of the *Big Issue* from the seller on the far side of the bridge. He had told her once there were two ways to go. Down into the river, or up.

Up, into the lift and out into a room which looked over nothing but other rooms. Hazel trailed in after her. There were flowers for her, waiting at reception. She looked at the card, pulled a face and bore them aloft into Patsy's office, kicking open the door.

"About bloody time, too. Where do you think you've been?

"Sulking."

"Three days" worth? You give up answering your phone . . . Tell me why. Apart from the obvious."

"There is only the obvious. Do they still think Angela had a secret lover?" Hazel sprawled in a chair. There was plenty to be done, moguls to be pleased, contributors placated, stuff to be produced, working arrangements for flexi-time mothers, meetings, office politics to be diffused. Stuff: all that, diminished into nothing by a common, if temporary boredom. Because none of it really mattered and there was nothing which could not wait.

"Shall I tell you what I did yesterday evening?" Hazel said, assuming, rightly, that Patsy would want to know. "Well, I went out with one of Mrs. Smythe's à la carte; where else would I have found him? A very select friend. Drinks at the Savoy, my dear. Dinner at the Ivy, and not a thing to wear! Oh, he was so sweet, and not even terribly fat, and so lonely and *so* boring. More than twice my age, darling, and then add some. Lonely, like I said. Flowers this morning."

"Bugger flowers. Cheap currency. Debased."

"Look, if I'd wanted champagne and roses for breakfast, they'd have been there."

"You didn't . . ."

"No I fucking didn't. He told me about his house. His grown-up kids. He was . . . nice. Don't think I've ever met anyone more ready for the taking. I could see it, you know. A bloke like that, he was any-body's. If I played it right, if any woman played it right, I bet they could reel him in like a fish. Get herself into the house and behind the wheel of his Daimler before the end of the week."

"So? Get on with it. That's what you wanted, isn't it? The house?"

"Is it? I couldn't, Pats, I couldn't. It'd be like taking an ice cream from a baby, only easier. I looked at me and I looked at him, and I thought, you cow, you even considered it. Or, you might have done if he was thinner and younger, know what I mean? Couldn't ever speak the same language. So what do I want, anyway. Nothing at that price."

"Spare me the virtue, just spare me. You couldn't fleece a man you don't fancy. Didn't you know that?"

Hazel examined her nails, blushed.

"I'm not sure about this introduction agency stuff," Patsy said.

"Nor me. Phone up that old cow. Go on."

"She scares me."

"Go on."

There was an answermachine. Closed today. Please speak after the tone.

"I want my money back," Hazel raged. "I paid for a year."

"You want instant results."

"Dead right I do. I'm going to buy a caravan and call it Mon Repos."

"It is *not* like you to give up easy."

"It is *not* giving up! It's adjusting the sights. Looking for someone sweet and truthful, like Angela wanted. A little boy in long trousers waiting to be remodelled. Along with his house."

She was knitting together the pile of paperclips, forming them into a chain. Her eyes held tears. Her right leg, crossed across the left, kicked at nothing. She held the paperclip chain aloft, gazing at it as if it was a work of art, or a talisman.

"Oh, by the way, Pats. Watch your back, will you? As soon as you're away for the day, three of the lean and hungries are after your job, OK?"

"We'll see about that."

For the first time in the encounter, they smiled at each other.

Mrs. Diana Kennedy, together with an American gentleman of indeterminate years, sat in her drawing room over tea. The house seemed extraordinarily peaceful today. It looked at its best: light fell gently through large, sparkling clean windows onto a gracefully faded carpet, once a darker green, but she had the clear impression that it was the garden which fascinated him most. "The achievement of growing so many disparate plants so close to the sea," he said. "Now that's a challenge, mam. Not only a challenge, but a triumph."

"Triumph?" she said, indignant at the mere suggestion of luck. "Oh I don't know about triumph. Constant effort, perhaps. You've got to know what's friend and enemy; what flourishes against all the rules, what won't. I suppose," she added, surprising herself, "that in many ways I love the garden more than the house."

"Is that so?" he asked shrewdly. "So, if you move to an even better garden, it would be some kind of compensation?"

She shook her head. The fine white hair stayed in place.

"No."

He dipped his grey head. Diana found him peculiarly restful, not at all as Steven had described him. He was nodding, gravely, twinkling at her with a smile which merely raised the corners of his mouth.

"No, I didn't really think so."

He remained restful, about her own age, looking younger than he was until one looked again and disregarded the foreign nature of his clothes. Check and stripes never did go together. He was polite, with none of the evasiveness she had perfected and she found herself copying him.

"I adore this house, mam. You may as well know that."

A man, making such a statement with such fervour, was bound to be appealing. He accepted more tea, looked around himself, a big man comfortable in a big chair.

"Wouldn't change a thing," he muttered. "Love the drapes."

"The what?"

"Excuse me?"

They laughed, politely enough, but it was still laughter.

"Was there ever a chandelier of kinds in this room?"

"Yes. We took it down. It's the wrong kind of house for a chandelier. My husband's mother had pretensions to grandeur, no, I lie, she simply entertained a lot, wanted to make it look like a little ballroom. You can open these doors to the garden, extend the place indefinitely, in summer. I've often yearned to have a party here, but I can't. Even so, it was always the wrong kind of house."

He carried his tea cup and saucer halfway round the room, examined the ceiling, took his time.

"You are quite right. Wrong kind of house for any extra glass. Can we take another look at the garden?"

They walked the paths. There was a little, late-summer litter lying underfoot and intruding on to the lawn: she noted it with such a slight frisson of disapproval, it was nearly indifference. Dead leaves, the breeze spreading them, and the Michaelmas daisies which always looked shaggy from the moment they appeared, and the dog at heel, yapping at the wasps.

"Will you just sshh, you," he ordered. In the following, bewildered silence, Diana wished the animal would do the same for her.

Matthew came from the gate by the sea, stopped at the sight of them, skinny little runt, ready to scowl. Then recognized the man who had been so good at shifting the chandelier, the one who did not even notice about getting dirty. He grinned, broke into a trot and made for the house. His house.

"I guess that one rules the roost," the man said.

"I guess he does. Doesn't know it, though."

"Mrs. Kennedy, let me tell you something. I am not going to push to buy your house. What for? That kid and your daughters would be hanging around like a tribe of ghosts forever and ever, Amen. So I'll just take a room for a while, if that's OK. Look for something else, again. Do you think I could have a cutting of that?" He pointed to a clump of daisies. He was a liar, pretending he knew nothing about plants.

"No. You can't cut, it doesn't like it. You can have the whole thing, with pleasure. For your wife. If we can dig it up and you can get it home."

"Wife? Who said anything about a wife?" He shook his head. "Not in a long time. You don't think my wife would ever have let me choose a house or a plant, do you?" His laughter was loud and genuine. "I'd be dead, Mrs. Kennedy, I tell you. Dead."

"Joe? Are you awake?"

"No."

"Joe?"

"Go away."

"All right. I'll go. I'm going now."

"No, don't. Stay."

"I'm sorry about this, Joe."

"Oh, Jesus, Lizzie."

"Don't call me Lizzie. Or take anyone's name in vain."

He opened his eyes. Opened them wider.

"Christ's sake, Elisabeth, what have they done to you?"

"Seen worse, have you? You're the same. I'm sorry, Joe: they had to cut your hair."

He felt his scalp, a mixture of tuft and stubble. Memory came back like a tidal wave, drowning him. He struggled for reality.

"What time is it?"

"Ten to three."

"Lizzie, why are you such a liar? It is never, ever, ten to three."

The man in the separate room, guarded against visitors, could not understand why his mother was not there, holding his hand, adjusting the discomfort of drip and tube. The impedimenta kept him chained: he had no voice. Where are you, Mummy? There was no-one else to call for. He wanted her like never before, even though he had begun to loathe her with a loathing so fierce, it choked him. He could not recall the precise moment when obedience had turned to resentment, he struggled to remember. When she would not let him touch Emma; when he introduced her to Jack, and she seemed to take Jack over, leaving him so lonely and confused. Jack was the closest he had ever had to a friend: she should not have done that. She had made Jack laugh, promised him things, took him far away. She took things away, just as she did with his independence. First, she let him have things, and then she took them back. And he let her, because of what he had done to her.

Michael was in a room by himself, pinioned and bound and dizzy with morphine. If he closed his eyes, he could feel the weight of the bell crushing his chest and shoulder, just as his fingers touched . . . Felt himself fainting away in that total darkness: waking again to scream for Mummy, Mummy, Mummy. With his eyes wide open now, he looked towards a sealed window and a patch of sky which was turning from brilliant blue to grey and black. He was terrified of the very thought of darkness. Once it was dark, he would be back beneath the bell, and he would have to scream again, this time in words, unless she came and told him what to do.

"I'd stop his fucking painkillers," Jenkins suggested, brutally. "Then he'll sing like a budgie."

"Get out of here: who asked you?"

"Listen, I know more about this man than anyone else." Someone, at least, had conceded that.

"He won't talk. And he's too sick to persuade, even nicely."

"Put a man outside the door, to listen. No, not me."

"No, Jenks, not you."

They paced down the long corridor to the room where he could smoke. Even without the cigs, Jenks might have managed to sit all night outside that door and listen to Michael, singing. He would hum the fucking chorus.

"What did the mother say?"

"Hysteria. Total shock. No idea about the proclivities of her boy. Says he's still a child at heart. They all say that, don't they?" There was a ventilator rattling like an old train in the window of the airless room.

"She says he cheats: he's a liar and a fantasist: she keeps him away from her business and anything to do with it, but he gets access to her computer and plays around. None of that's quite true. 'Cos his friends at work say he got them to go and see Mummy, sort out the love life. He even pushed one aside to get at Angela Collier. Funny, ain't it, the way that little chap with the big specs turned up last night, all on his own, to tell us that? Amazing. Mummy knows a thing or two, but I don't know how sonny boy got inside Elisabeth Kennedy's place. I really don't; nor does Mum. Maybe she asked him in."

"Naah, not even Lizzie," Jenks said.

"How can she live there? Is she mad or what? She must be. Will she mend, d'you think? Don't like to lose a witness."

Jenkins coughed, sounding like a rusty trumpet with spittle in the corners. Looking at this model for a mobile health warning, the other man pocketed his own cigarettes. Jenkins spoke between the hacking, prolonging it, without shame.

"Oh for sure she'll mend. She was already mended. Now she's got her culprit, she'll mend, all right."

"Why the hell had she carved away at that cross beam over the bell? There was only an inch left. Bloody thing may as well have been hanging on a piece of string. She's mad. Why the hell did she do that?"

Jenkins turned, found no space to pace up and down, walked, then half ran down the corridor, turned back. He thought he knew why. She was waiting for someone. It could have been Joe, under that bell.

Skinny Lizzie, better at subterfuge than fighting, making a virtue of weakness, always something to hide, just like before.

The other man hurried to keep up with him, afraid of what he might do; remembering his instructions to watch Jenks more than the prisoner.

"Can we get this woman, Patsy watsername, to identify him?"

"Yes."

"But what about Emma Davey? Can we get the boy?"

"No. Lizzie says don't involve the boy. It's too long ago. He didn't see anything."

He had a peculiar tick to his left eye when he knew he was lying. The other man did not know him well enough to notice.

"So, unless this Michael sings, we're a bit stuck on that one, aren't we?"

"She should have killed him," Jenkins muttered without irony. "Fucking Lizzie should have fucking killed him."

"Let me see my boy, please."

"No, madam. He is not a boy. He is over thirty years old."

"If I tell you something, will you let me see him?"

"Depends."

"My son, well, he knew Emma Davey. We both did. She took pity on us, used to ask us round. Well, not so much Michael, as me. To make up for the fact that her family had been so . . . unkind . . . and . . ."

"And what?"

"Nothing. Only I never let him go there without me. But he might have gone. All by himself. She didn't want him, you see: he didn't understand someone asking him in and not wanting him. I was always afraid he might find out, if he went by himself. Can I see him, please?"

"Can you tell us why your son might have attacked Joseph Maxell? Or Elisabeth Kennedy?"

"I've no idea. Who's Joseph Maxell? A friend? Friends fall out. I don't know about Elisabeth. She was always a naughty child. Not as pretty as her sister."

—

After dark, Michael Jacobi began to sing. A confused rant against fate and parenthood, until the nurse put him to sleep. She could not believe that a man with his eyes could be guilty of more than pride. "Look, I'll be good, like a little girl," he shouted. "Don't send me away. I should mean to burn her."

In the shop, Audrey and Donald sat and debated the merits of going away. Not immediately, of course: not until the weather really turned sour and the wind and rain, which had begun the afternoon before, began to show signs of serious cold instead of mere inconvenience. The change in weather was good for trade. Stragglers took shelter, abandoned the edge of the water to look for compensation, crowding in among the furniture removed from the pavement. The wooden board they placed outside each day had fallen over twice, with a resounding crack. When the door was shut, the ping of the bell each time it was opened grated on Donald's ears and made him feel like a bus conductor. Three people had inadvertently knocked bits off the chandelier, which they had tried, in vain, to hoick closer to the ceiling: three others had expressed interest in buying it, giving him the great pleasure of saying it was not for sale. A man could get sick of the human race for disturbing his afternoon snooze.

Every year on the brink of autumn, they talked about going away. Either for Christmas, for November or some other indefinable period when it was cold, to the Bahamas, the Caribbean, southern Spain or the Canaries, purely for the warmth. The subject and the planning occupied hours: the travel agent was denuded of brochures, and yet, somehow, they never quite went. At the end of it all, there was a distinct lack of interest in foreign parts for anything other than an alternative climate, as well as the strong, understated feeling that if they went away for any period long enough to be worthwhile, they might miss something. The chandelier had not yet been cleaned. It no longer seemed important. Young Matthew's interest in it seemed to have died once he had completed the reconstruction. Yesterday he had talked of nothing but the computer his father was going to buy, the imminence of the new school term (yughh!), and, with a glee which bordered on smugness, the prospect, not yet definite, that his aunt Elisabeth might be returning home for further convalescence. There had been another . . . accident, which served her right for going away.

Matt was sceptical about the convalescent bit: she sounded fine on the phone, only a little weary. There was a debate going on in Granny's house about whether he should have Lizzie's room, with his own, far smaller one, reserved for the guest. He was not totally averse to the idea. Everyone, suddenly, wanted to keep him close. They were hiding something, treating him like something precious and he did not mind.

Daddy came and fetched him, took him for a walk, which was a strange thing for Daddy to do. Daddy not only talked about the computer, but about the boat they might get in the spring. Spring was another lifetime away: it had no relevance. They walked on the cliff path, almost blown away, laughing about it. "We can't afford a boat, Daddy." Well, no perhaps not a big boat, but they could hire a little one. Matthew said he would rather have a proper dog. As big as he was. "Mummy had always wanted a proper, big dog, hadn't she?"

They sat in the lea of the wind, a place Matt had found and showed his father with diffident pride. "I know this place, all these places, much better than you, Daddy." "I know you do, Matt." "Mummy and Auntie Lizzie showed me some, but mainly I found out by myself." How strange he was, alien child, to seek solitude, when all the others sought the crowd. "Got something to tell you, Matt." Plucking at a daisy and putting it down. Picking a blade of grass, slitting it and blowing so that it sang.

"What?"

"They think they've found the bad man who killed Mummy."

"Oh." There was a long pause.

This was worse than pulling a plaster off a wound, worse than telling the child that the dentist was fun. It reminded Steven of all the tasks he had abdicated when Emma had died and he had been cocooned in his own grief. Blaming the boy.

"What's he like?"

Now what did that mean? Did he mean, is he big, tall, black, white, a member of the same species as us, or what? Would it make sense to say that the man might once have been a boy who ran this path like a sure-footed dog, with a mother, barking at his heels, "Come back, come back, don't fall,"? A boy with the same interest in pebbles and stones?

"Well, he's about the same age as me. Only he has a very sick mind and a lot of dark hair and he isn't very tall."

Matthew nodded, as if that information was adequate. "Yes. That one. He came to our house, sometimes. He came here, last week."

Steven had the sensation of being suspended over a snake pit, clutching nothing but a frayed rope. Angry and hurt at the same time. All those people, coming to his house when he was away from it, working to pay for the roof and the walls. Emma's coterie, the antidote to her boredom and the outlet for her energy. So many, Matt could only remember a few. Quite right he would be confused. All those deadbeats, moths to a flame. No, no, Emma was a saint. He had to remember that. "That last day, Matt . . . oh I know you've been asked a thousand times and it doesn't matter, not really."

"*You* never asked me, Daddy. It was never you who asked."

"Didn't I?"

Another body blow. "Oh well. I just wondered if you could remember if it was a man a bit like that when you opened the door. Blue eyes. Smiley sort of man."

Matthew considered for more than a minute while his father held his breath. Then he shook his head. He was trying to look for the right answer before he gave it, and then opting for whatever he could find.

"I didn't answer the door, Daddy. Remember it has that glass bit, quite high up? Mummy looked when I had my hand on the door. Then she told me I could watch my telly upstairs. I liked playing on my own, Daddy. I often went upstairs when people came. So I went. I didn't see who it was, Daddy, I didn't, I didn't."

"Course you didn't. Jolly good thing." Steven patted his son on the back, feeling he was being rather overhearty, then left his hand resting on the boy's shoulder for the sheer pleasure of it. Unusually, the touch was not resented, or shrugged away with the customary irritation. They were getting chilly. Steven stood up and hauled the boy to his feet.

"Did she say anything else?" he asked as they set off back down the path with the wind in their faces. Matthew wrinkled his nose, spread his hands, which were grubby from the ground and wiped them on his shorts. The shorts fitted him better when the pockets were not weighted down with pebbles.

"Yes. I think so."

"Now what was it? Did she say, fuck off?"

This attempt at levity raised the ghost of a smile. They were having chips and hamburgers and all the things which made Granny shudder, for tea.

"No, don't be silly! She wouldn't say that!" He stopped and concentrated, as if he could not remember it with such crystal clarity. He stuck his finger in his ear, to aid concentration.

"She said, 'Oh bother. Bother, bother, bother, it's that old cow again.' That's what she said."

"We shouldn't call people 'old cows,' Matt."

"Mummy did."

"Thank you, Mr. Jenkins, for your trouble. You may go now."

Yes, sir, you arsehole.

"What about similar fact evidence, sir? This man, Michael, cannot tell a lie, sir. He can hide things, but he cannot tell a lie. So, he admits to Angela Collier, although he can scarcely say why. It's the same modus operandi, her and Emma, exactly. On all fours with it. A stolen kiss, rejection, he goes ape-shit, stamping out the fear in their eyes. That's what he said. He couldn't bear it. 'Like being hated all over again,' he said. But he's still a well-trained boy, worries about the mess and even more, he doesn't want to see the eyes. He covers the face and the head, smash it, finish it with feet. Washes the bottle in bleach or some such, washes the shoes. Same. Charge him on both: he did both."

"But if he can't tell a lie in response to a question, why won't he say he killed her?"

"He won't lie: he simply refuses to say anything. Have you ever heard of shame, sir?"

"Look we've got him for Angela Collier. We go for that one first. Similar fact evidence is tricky stuff, and how do we explain the last episode? Not invited in, a knife, a man before a woman, what's similar about that? Or throwing acid at Kennedy, which he only half admits he did, too. Says it was her fault. Life inside is life inside,

Jenkins. At the end of the day, does it matter what the hell he goes down for?"

"Yessir, *with respect.* You don't put him on trial, you never know. Emma Davey's family never know. Lizzie never knows."

"Oh, she knows all right. What do you want, Jenkins? Another debacle in front of another judge? Another miscarriage?"

They were both exhausted. One man with history, one, far senior, with a future to consider and no real knowledge of this particular past. After forty-eight hours, things began to slip: there was a dangerous complacency after any kind of confession. No-one could concentrate. They all hated hospital corridors, especially after dark when they were full of mumbled nightmares.

"I wish he was dead."

"He sees no reason to die. He says his mother needs him. I thought it was time to let her in. She seems a nice woman. Cooperative, concerned. Made no fuss about us searching his flat or hers. Nothing of course. She keeps asking about the victims, quite touching really. She cried when I said Elisabeth was up and walking about, but then she weeps all the time."

"Has she seen him?"

"Like I said, didn't I? She's seeing him now."

"Alone?"

"Look, Jenkins, we serve the people. We have to be humane. Let her, in everyone's interests, let her. If he sees his mother in private, he tells us more, get it?"

"Arsehole."

There was a phone ringing as Jenkins ran from the room they had borrowed, somewhere in this modern rat run, access to different patients in different sanctuaries. This was London: victims and culprits went to the same place with nothing but floors between them. He ran for endless miles, his chest heaving, his heart on fire, stabbing the button on the lift, then the next, waiting for the minutes it took for the doors to open and close, the sweat on him and the high colour frightening the others, tidily dressed and relieved of their flowers after a visit. He burst out at the wrong floor and ran again, slurred to a halt, turned back, tried again. How long, oh Lord, how long. Slow down: count, but he could not slow, even though his speed, compared with the young who passed at walking pace, throwing a curious glance in his direction, seemed curiously akin to theirs. He pushed out of the second lift: by this time, the customers were shouting. It was not the same lift he had come out at before; he felt the same, momentary confusion he had known before, stalled and looked at the numbers on the wall. Lizzie, Lizzie, stay up your tower, don't come down.

Shuffling, now, not running, maybe it had never been what anyone else would call a sprint; he felt like death. There was a good man in uniform standing outside the door, not sitting, but not looking or listening, either. Being humane.

It was a heavy, swing door which seemed to take the final effort to push, more so because there was no handle and he found himself pushing at the hinge. He was alarming everyone: he was screaming. He heard the man under the bell, screaming, "Emma, Angela," screaming, and the words Lizzie said she had heard Michael say, "I COPIED HER, SHE TAUGHT ME EVERYTHING."

He burst through the door with the man in uniform behind, trying to grab him back.

A little old lady, with short, stubble grey hair, saying a rosary of shiny stones, dressed in worn tweed and frayed cardigan. Turning on him sluggishly, as if slow to recognize sound. A trifle deaf, maybe. Her son in the bed, turned from her with his arm hung like meat from a drip, his mouth open in terror; hers, smiling bewilderment, while she put the rosary back in her bag, all done with the minimum of movement. Patience shone from damp and powdered cheeks, through which the moisture from her eyes had worn tracks as deep as furrows. She was not alarmed but bewildered. Even in this soundless room, he could hear footsteps behind his own, also running. Arms beginning to clutch him as he fell with hands outstretched for her papery throat, wavering; screaming in his cracked voice "YOU MURDERING BITCH!" Stuttering, pleading, praying and sweating as they dragged him out and ignored the finger which pointed to the tiny wee knife in the bag they had not searched.

There was another room on another floor for him, for now.

"Can I stay with my son, please? Just another minute?"

"No, madam. No."

Chapter

NINETEEN

Joe's father was a nice man, too, surprisingly petit in comparison to his son. It was the mother, a terrifying specimen of spectacular proportions, who carried the genetic clues to the height and breadth of her son. The voice which emerged from her magnificent chest was sweet and light; she looked as if she could sing, even when she cast the full blast of nuclear disapproval on Elisabeth Kennedy.

"No," Joe said. "No, No, no. I was mending a clock."

It was impossible for them to approve of what they saw, apart from the haircut: tolerance was the best they could offer. With all the robustness of a medical family which discourages the offspring from taking any form of ill-health or accident seriously, they still wanted to bear him home to rest on clean, cotton sheets until scar tissue formed and well meant lectures began. He went, but would not stay for long. He told them he needed to look after his friend Elisabeth, who would take longer to cure. Which gave rise to brisk remarks about what a good job he had done so far, and who, pray, would be looking after whom? Self-pity was regarded in a worse light than sin.

Muscles mended: bones knit and wounds healed. Elisabeth was told, in a series of platitudes, how everything would cure itself in time, and for once, she began to believe it. She watched the waning of the year.

And, on an afternoon when the autumn began to slide into winter, after she came home from the coast, they met in the tower, and with one accord, climbed to the top. He noticed that she was scarcely fatter.

There were vast stanchions like pillars in the clock room, supporting the ceiling above. No-one had actually declared the place uninhabitable, because no-one had imagined that anyone would wish to persist. Even squatters quailed at the sight of blood, just as Flynn was appalled by the presence of suitcases, until he thought of rent and purchase and budget and how much better it was when a place is heated and dry, and loved, and how much effort he had made to lure them back. He was still guilty about letting someone steal the third key, from his own pocket. In the spring, when a committee had decided how best and cheaply to achieve it, the bells would be removed. All except the bell, so closely related to the face of the clock, which told the world, day and night, that it was only ten to four. By five, it was beginning to become dark. On this evening, a mild twilight.

"Joseph Maxell, how the hell did you move the hands on this clock? They weigh plenty."

"I haven't got the faintest idea how."

The floor had been scrubbed, leaving the faintest of marks. He looked at them and tried to cover it all with the heel of a training shoe.

"Never knew I had it in me."

"Have you been drinking?"

"Not yet. I hope to start, as soon as possible."

She had longed to see him; and that was the politician's understatement. He had been the lifeline. Thrown, after his careless fashion: she was pretending now that she had never clutched such a rope. She was brittle, still. Tainted. With his cropped hair and ironed clothes, he looked as conventional as a banker. She missed his mass of hair more than she missed her own.

"Everything at home all right then?" he asked, infected with her awkwardness. As if he did not know. "I'll go and dig her up,": that boy Matthew must have said it dozens of times. He knew that when she came to the phone, she had hurried and arrived out of breath, which was enough for a man to imagine she was pleased to hear him. He had sat by his own, imagining the curl of her cigarette sneaking towards the ceiling, as it did now.

"I've got this chandelier," she said. "Arriving tomorrow. Enormous. We'll have to bring it in pieces. I thought you might like to put it together. Your kind of task."

"Matthew told me," he said. "He talks a lot, doesn't he?"

"Oh yes."

Still that awkwardness. Too much to say. The bell chamber was sheltered, but becoming cold. Someone had swept it clean and clear. She hesitated, feeling as she had with Jenkins yesterday, the same old urge to weep.

"Will you forgive me, Joe? Will you forgive *us?*"

"For what?"

She waved a hand, as if the "we" included the bells and the bricks.

"Encouraging you into this morass. Introducing you to . . . evil. For want of a better word."

He shook his head. "I don't know what evil is. Only that it has a certain scarcity value. And you didn't encourage me in. I walked, I trespassed, I barged. I insisted. And even if this were an ending and not a beginning, I wouldn't have any regrets."

"You can't mean that."

He grinned, thought about it. "My hair," he said plaintively. "Took years to grow."

"Ah, poor Samson. You shouldn't have risked it."

Mocking him, while she touched his short crop, reaching up to do so. He touched the curls which nestled into her neck. The beating of her heart sounded louder than any bell.

"You were brave," she said. "Did I ever tell you that? Brave to give a fool a warning."

"Me? Brave? Don't get that idea. I'm only stubborn. And . . ." he choked on a vital word and amended it into something else, ". . . *I like* you. Ever since—"

"You saw a picture of my sister," she said flatly.

"Oh, no. Sooner than that."

She lit another cigarette. His liking of the smell, was, he supposed, simply another perversity, easily as odd as love.

"You don't know me, Joe." There was something bubbling below the surface of her voice. Joy, relief and an urge to shout, even if it throttled itself in doubt. He did not yet know how it was she threw things at walls when she was happy as well as enraged. There was a yearning to keep on touching, without ever again thinking of a witness to what she said, or did. "I am utterly corrupt. Secretive, jealous, a liar . . ."

"Oh, I know all that. I know it could have been me under that bell. I know you had this place booby-trapped. You could have killed me. You would have crushed me. *If* I had been a thief."

She stared at him, the joy fading. "You know."

He kissed her, lightly, on the hair. Her hands fluttered. Her fingernails had grown long. She did not know what to do with her hands. Pray with them. Pray that he meant what he said and this awful, breathless sensation would leave her throat.

"Elisabeth Kennedy, I know you that well."

He snapped his fingers. "Like *that*. You'd never set a trap without baiting it with something real. Such a thing would be a cheat. You might have done it once, but never twice. First time went against nature. You're such a capable liar, but you don't know how to be dishonest."

The bell lay on one side, abandoned, the inside of it dark as a cave; the metal cold to the touch. Joe knelt beside it, holding the rim, extended his long arm into the depths, felt with sensitive fingers. There was a small packet, waxed around the fitting for the poor, mutilated, clapper: the packet so small, it was almost undetectable against the size and roughness of the rest. She watched him retrieve it and pick at the wax, finding the little plastic pouch.

"Hold out your hand."

She did so and he saw how it trembled.

He shook into her palm half of the contents. Chips of nondescript stone, each the size of a baby's thumbnail, the colour of dull brass. A small shower of playthings, unbeautiful, uninteresting, undecorative, with no apparent purpose. Except perhaps, to fill the base of a fish tank, or act as ballast for the roots around an indoor plant. Pieces of nothing.

"What are they?"

She sighed. He flicked on the light from the high switch by the low door. He knew this place; everything in it.

"Industrial diamonds. I don't know the value, never did. My father said, 'Enough to buy a house.' He didn't say what kind of house. These are what he collected in his working life. Other bits and pieces, too, but these, the most reliable. A fitting gift for the plainer daughter, but of course, they aren't mine. They never were. He knew what I would do with them." She said this without rancour.

"He knew I'd keep them safe. Until it was the right time to use them to preserve my mother's house for the next generation. And that's what I'll do, what I was always going to do, when I can find some way of explaining to her. I may have to pretend to win the lottery. He wanted to torment her, poor soul. Now that's an aberration. I'm not his daughter, and yet I inherit all his deviousness. I might belong to Caroline Smythe."

He was shaking; his top teeth biting his lower lip. Her hand, back in his hair, wanting to touch, but uncertain.

"Put them down, Lizzie. Get shot of them as soon as ever. They worry me. I hate them."

"I suppose a few of these would mend the clock."

"No," he said, frowning at her. "That bloody clock is *mine.*"

She flicked the little, light fragments back into the packet with the ease of an expert, and let the packet drop.

"I don't suppose you want a small blonde lightweight thrown in? Only if you're going to live here, I've got nowhere else to go."

"Oh, you are a fool."

The shadows of two bodies fused. The light faded into dark, as if there had never been daylight. He was murmuring into her ear, tugging at the curls with a kind of urgency. Muttering that there was something important he had to say.

"What? Oh God, Joe . . . it's been so long. We're getting dusty . . . can we go downstairs?"

"You do know I don't have a pension plan?"

—

It was a nicely silent house, creaking to sleep. The unseen sea, murmuring.

". . . Oh, a little patching hither and thither, and we shall see out
another winter . . ." Mrs. Diana Kennedy wrote to her daughter. She
had never been comfortable with the telephone. She was of a generation which would always find it easier to write a letter, once she
regained practice. The idea of a fax machine was abhorrent. There
was something pleasant about the thought that a letter took time to
arrive, as if the thoughts inside the words might take it upon themselves to mature en route, and any silly sentiment would become wise.

"I suppose it gives one a purpose. Our American is returning to
Chicago, but he might be back for Christmas. Isn't that nice?
Tomorrow, I'm going to change my hairstyle. What do you think?"
Diana looked away from the page and frowned at the stain on the ceiling. "Well that's the best news. I worry about you, darling. Wish you'd
stayed longer. And, on a more serious note, I can't, of course, stop
thinking about things. I'd be a liar if I said I could. I *wish* there had
been a better resolution. I *wish* I knew which of them killed her; the
mother, or the son, but neither of them is ever going to tell us and neither will be tried for it. Perhaps, some day. I *wish* you could bring
yourself to tell me what you had to do with finding the first suspect,
poor man. I don't suppose you'll ever be able to tell me. Don't worry,
darling. It may be better I never know. You're quite right. It isn't
always wise to be open about everything. No-one deserves to know
everything about anyone else. I *wish*, above everything else, that I had
not unlocked that rage in Caroline Smythe: what did I have to envy? I
wish that I'd never given her house room, or failing that, never rejected her. What demons we foster, including our own. I feel it's all my
fault. You told me not to think like that, but I do. I do, and that's my
burden. I have to live with it, but I since I must, I shall. I get so *angry*
with the garden at this time of year. It's so dull and ragged. Do you
know, I do believe Matthew is taking an interest? Not for long. The
computer rules: I do wish it didn't. He can type, with two fingers. Un-
believable. Says it's easier than writing. He wrote something strange,
yesterday. It was a story for school . . . he has this crush on the English

teacher. It made my blood chill a bit, but it didn't seem to worry him. He was writing something about two people coming to a house where a little boy lived with his mummy and daddy. 'Oh, bother, it's her,' Mummy says, and sends him to bed. He doesn't see who comes in, but he hears them all saying hallo. 'Hallo, Caroline,' says Mummy, and then 'Hallo, Jack, how are you?' She's acting surprised to see them together. Puts her fist in her mouth, but she may be yawning. I don't know where 'Jack' came from. Do you? Have you ever heard him mention a Jack? All these strange companions of his, Sylvester, Joe, Sammy, Motar, Oza, but never a Jack. I don't know where this wretched Jack came from. He doesn't either.

"The saddest thing about the story, though, is what the mummy says next. She says, 'I'm sorry, but I'm busy, you can't come in.' So they give her a bunch of flowers. Then they leave. If only it had been like that. For darling Emma, and that other girl. I've written to her mother.

"Mustn't brood. Whatever is the point?

"Take care, darling. And don't be afraid of the dark. Or of him. That's all for the moment."

She paused. Thought of what else to say.

"There's a lovely high tide this evening. Do you know what I thought when you were born? I thought, if this is love, you can never get enough. Don't forget, will you?"